Jo Carnegie has worked as Deputy Editor for *heat* magazine, interviewing stars from George Clooney, Simon Cowell and Will Smith, to Posh and Becks and Cheryl Cole. As well as still writing for *heat*, she writes for many other publications and is also a regular contributor on radio. *Wild Things* follows her first two novels, *Country Pursuits* and *Naked Truths*. She lives in London and Cardiff.

For more information on Jo Carnegie visit her website at www.churchminster.co.uk

www.rbooks.co.uk

Also by Jo Carnegie

COUNTRY PURSUITS
NAKED TRUTHS

and published by Corgi Books

WILD THINGS

Jo Carnegie

CORGI BOOKS

TRANSWORLD PUBLISHERS
61–63 Uxbridge Road, London W5 5SA
A Random House Group Company
www.rbooks.co.uk

WILD THINGS
A CORGI BOOK: 9780552160865

First publication in Great Britain
Corgi edition published 2010

Addresses for Random House Group Ltd companies outside the UK
can be found at: www.randomhouse.co.uk
The Random House Group Ltd Reg. No. 954009

The Random House Group Limited supports The Forest Stewardship
Council (FSC), the leading international forest certification organisation.
All our titles that are printed on Greenpeace approved FSC certified
paper carry the FSC logo. Our paper procurement policy can
be found at www.rbooks.co.uk/environment

Mixed Sources
Product group from well-managed
forests and other controlled sources
www.fsc.org Cert no. TT-COC-2139
© 1996 Forest Stewardship Council

Typeset in 11/14½pt Palatino by
Kestrel Data, Exeter, Devon.
Printed in the UK by
CPI Cox & Wyman, Reading, RG1 8EX.

2 4 6 8 10 9 7 5 3 1

To Hels

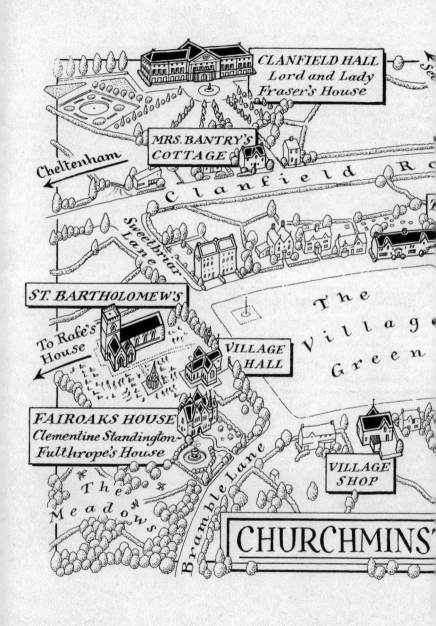

CLANFIELD HALL
Lord and Lady
Fraser's House

MRS. BANTRY'S
COTTAGE

Cheltenham

Clanfield R

Sweetbriar Lane

ST. BARTHOLOMEW'S

To Rafe's
House

VILLAGE
HALL

The
Village
Green

FAIROAKS HOUSE
Clementine Standington-
Fulthrope's House

The
Meadows

Bramble Lane

VILLAGE
SHOP

CHURCHMINST

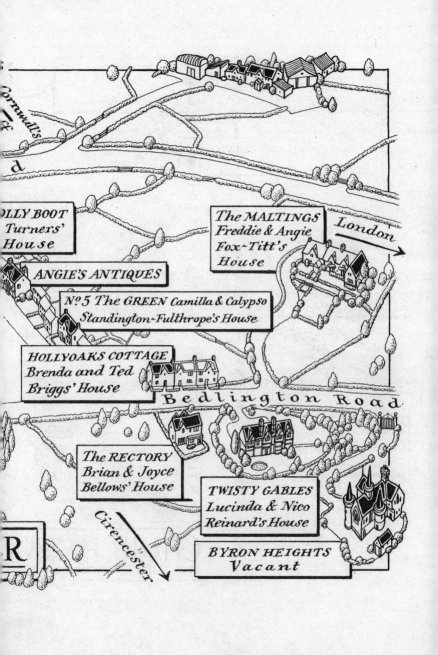

JOLLY BOOT
Turners'
House

ANGIE'S ANTIQUES

Nº 5 The GREEN Camilla & Calypso
Standington-Fulthrope's House

The MALTINGS
Freddie & Angie
Fox-Titt's
House

London

HOLLYOAKS COTTAGE
Brenda and Ted
Briggs' House

Bedlington Road

The RECTORY
Brian & Joyce
Bellows' House

TWISTY GABLES
Lucinda & Nico
Reinard's House

Cirencester

BYRON HEIGHTS
Vacant

R

PART ONE

Chapter 1

'Bugger, I bet this never happens to Jamie Oliver!'

In the kitchen of No. 5 The Green, Churchminster, Camilla Standington-Fulthrope stared down in dismay at a bowl of cake mixture. Somewhere in there was one of her prized pearl earrings, an extremely expensive present from her parents for her twenty-first birthday. She'd been meaning to get the clasp fixed for ages.

Cursing herself for not being more organized, Camilla tentatively poked at the gluey mess with her wooden spoon. It was a fruitless search, so she gave up and plunged both hands in, finally striking lucky. The pearl had stuck to the underside of a particularly plump raisin.

Camilla exhaled in relief and looked down at her hands, which now looked like they were covered in wet, dripping cement. Christ, it had gone everywhere! The cookbook pages were stuck together, and it looked as if someone had flour-bombed the front of her apron. Flustered, Camilla pushed a lock of hair off her

11

forehead, leaving a huge clump of mix stuck between the strands. This *definitely* didn't happen to Nigella.

The late afternoon sun streamed into the kitchen, lighting up the cosy, low-beamed room. Despite the surrounding chaos, Camilla's heart lifted. After a desolate January and February, spring had finally returned to the village of Churchminster. Swathes of yellow daffodils blanketed the village green, and through the window into the back garden Camilla could see the first fresh new leaves on her apple trees. She loved this time of year more than ever. Last year she'd travelled extensively round the glorious climes of South America, and returning to such a cold, dank winter – even somewhere as picturesque as Churchminster – had been a shock, to say the least.

An hour later, after tackling the mountain of washing-up she'd managed to accumulate, Camilla had just sunk down at the kitchen table with a cup of tea when the back door opened. She looked up, surprised. 'You're home early!'

The delicious form of Jed Bantry stood in the doorway, brandishing a bunch of wild flowers. He held them out, a slow smile spreading across his face. 'Maybe I was missing you.'

Even after nearly three years together, Camilla's heart still skipped when she looked at her boyfriend. With his tall, lean physique and angular face Jed could have just stepped off a catwalk in Milan or New York. Not that he cared about things like that: Jed wasn't interested in possessions and labels. He was still

12

wearing his work uniform of scruffy navy overalls, which had been pulled open to the waist. The white vest underneath gave a tantalizing flash of impressive pectorals. Above the overalls, Jed's jet-black hair was messy and tousled. It was longer than usual, flopping sexily into his extraordinary, pale green eyes.

He took in the cake, now cooling on a wire rack on the table. 'Something looks good.'

'It's a new recipe, I thought I'd give it a shot.'

He'd pulled her out of the chair before she knew it. 'I wasn't talking about the cake.'

All the manual work he'd been doing had made Jed's body harder than ever. Camilla felt herself quiver. She looked down at her Emma Bridgewater apron, the pattern completely obscured by crusty cake mix.

'I'm a bit . . .' she said apologetically.

Jed pulled her in even closer. 'A bit what?' he murmured. 'A bit so sexy my boyfriend would like to fuck me right here on the kitchen table?' With that he crushed his lips down on to hers, pulling the band out of her ponytail so her blond hair tumbled down over her shoulders.

Camilla had never known what sex could really be like until she'd gone to bed with Jed. There had been other boyfriends, of course, and even a fiancé, but none of them had been as wild and passionate as this. Jed knew every inch of her body and exactly what to do to turn it on. For Camilla, who had spent years being un-satisfactorily rogered by braying oiks, Jed Bantry had been a sexual revelation.

Still smiling, he carried her to the kitchen table,

pushing her down on the surface. Camilla's buttocks encountered something soft and warm.

'The cake!' she cried, but somehow Jed managed to lift her off it while undoing her bra strap. His other hand moved down to yank off her jeans and knickers.

'You should bake more often, my little housewife,' he said huskily, laying Camilla back on the table. 'It really is quite a turn-on.'

His overalls were off now, too; pulled down below his waist to show off a wide-shouldered, narrow-waisted torso that didn't have an inch of surplus fat. Jed's cock, which was as perfect as the rest of him, was so hard and swollen it seemed bigger than ever.

'I've been thinking about this all afternoon,' he murmured, looking down into her eyes.

Sighing happily, Camilla parted her legs. She could never exactly describe the joy she felt when she had Jed inside her. Slowly, they began to rock back and forth, marching to the beat of their own drum.

'Hold on,' said Jed, pulling Camilla's legs up around his neck. As she felt him go in even deeper she arched her hips up, wanting every millimetre of him. His hands moved under her T-shirt now, raking over her body. Grabbing her full breasts, running over her gently rounded stomach, trying to take hold of as much of her as he could.

'This is amazing,' she gasped. Above her, Jed's eyes had locked on to hers, in the intense, faraway state that showed he was close to orgasm.

Camilla could feel the beginnings of her own

orgasm. Her head was dizzy with lust, lights danced before her eyes. Somewhere, she even thought she heard a bell going off. That had never happened before! Oh God, it was going to be a good one . . .

'Hello? Is anyone there?' The voice was coming from the hallway.

Camilla and Jed froze, looking at each other. 'Shit! It's my grandmother!' she whispered in horror.

Clementine Standington-Fulthrope's commanding voice rang through the letter box again. 'Camilla! I can hear strange groaning. Are you in pain?'

Camilla gestured wildly to Jed. 'Quick, hide! She'll come round the back.'

With some difficulty they extricated themselves from each other and grabbed their clothes. 'Your grandmother has spectacular timing,' was all Jed could mutter, as a hyperventilating Camilla pulled them both into the pantry.

Sure enough, a moment later the back door opened.

'Darling?'

Frantically hitching her trousers up, Camilla called out. 'I'm just in the pantry, Granny Clem! Won't be a minute.'

The tall, upright figure of her grandmother appeared in the pantry doorway.

In contrast to Camilla, Jed was cool as a cucumber, his overalls buttoned right up to the top. 'Hello Mrs S-F.'

'Oh, hello, young Jed.'

'Jed was just helping me get a tin of er, er, apricots down,' said Camilla.

Clementine frowned, 'I thought you didn't like apricots.'

'I don't. I mean I do, really. Just trying to increase my five a day and all that.'

'Hmmm.' Her grandmother didn't sound too convinced as Errol Flynn, Clementine's elderly black Labrador, ran between Camilla's legs into the food cupboard, on his eternally hopeful quest for food. 'Errol! Snout out!' scolded Clementine.

Jed caught hold of the disgruntled dog by his collar and dragged him out, closely followed by Camilla.

Back in the kitchen, Clementine's steely gaze fixed on the table. Camilla saw with dread that she was looking at the carrot cake, one side of it now completely flattened by a buttock-shaped imprint.

The old woman shot Camilla a reproachful look. 'Oh darling! How could you?'

Beneath smears of flour, Camilla's face turned puce. 'What do you mean?' she stuttered. To make things worse, she had the distinct impression Jed was finding it all rather amusing. A wry smile was definitely playing at the corners of his mouth as he crouched down to scratch behind Errol Flynn's ears.

Clementine sighed in despair. 'Did your Prue Leith cookery course teach you *nothing*? One should never open one's oven door while one's cake is baking!'

Camilla's knees almost buckled with relief. 'Of course, Granny Clem, it makes it sink in the middle. I just couldn't resist checking. I won't do it again.'

'I should hope not,' said Clementine, but her voice lacked its normal scolding tone.

16

Camilla gazed forlornly at the cake, and it was a few moments before she clocked the sudden air of expectancy in the room. She looked up at her grandmother. In her tweed skirt and sensible walking shoes, her grey hair pulled back in its normal severe bun, Clementine looked the same as ever, but there was definitely something different. Her eyes were shining, and the normal rigid lines that governed her face had been replaced by something freer, more animated. It almost looked like excitement.

Camilla was suddenly alert. Her grandmother never got excited. Something huge had happened. 'Is everything all right?' she asked.

To their complete astonishment, Clementine threw her head back and roared with laughter. Across the other side of the kitchen, Jed raised an eyebrow, and Errol Flynn wandered off, one ear turned to his mistress and this uncharacteristic sound.

'Oh dear girl! Dear boy! Something *wonderful* has happened!'

Camilla was seriously confused. 'Have you won the Lottery?' she asked her grandmother. Clementine made a 'Pff' sound. 'It's *far* more important than that.' She snapped open her industrial-sized handbag and carefully extracted a letter, holding it aloft triumphantly.

'I've been in Stow-on-the-Wold at that talk on environmental gardening, but I came home to find *this* on the doormat. I had to come straight over.'

Clementine's stiff upper lip momentarily wobbled. 'It

really is the most marvellous thing. It's going to change all our lives for ever!'

Camilla couldn't bear the suspense as, with agonizing care, Clementine slowly took her reading glasses from her handbag, shook the letter out importantly, and started reading in her cut-glass tones.

Hortensia House
1, Blenheim Gardens
London

15 March

Dear Mrs Standington-Fulthrope,

I am delighted to inform you, on behalf of the judging panel, that Churchminster has been selected as one of the final four villages in this year's Britain's Best Village competition, in association with Greenacres Garden Centres.

'Oh my God!' squealed Camilla. Clementine looked like she might join her granddaughter in jumping up and down on the spot, but collected herself and carried on.

As I am sure you are aware, this is not just a competition about aesthetic qualities, and we were particularly impressed at how the residents of Churchminster rallied round after the dreadful flash floods of last summer.

The judging will be held on Friday, 18 July, and full details of each category (community spirit, local

18

investment, best-kept flowerbeds, etc.) will be sent to
you shortly.

The winner will be announced in a grand ceremony
at the Grosvenor House Hotel in London on Friday
1 August, hosted by world-renowned gardener Alan
Titchmarsh.

As well as receiving the distinct honour of being
crowned Britain's Best Village, the victorious village
will also receive £750,000 prize money to be spent on
community projects.

May I once again take this opportunity to congratu-
late you and wish your village the very best in the
competition?

Best Wishes,
Marjorie Majors
Head Judge
Britain's Best Village

Open-mouthed, Camilla looked at Jed. He seemed just
as stunned.

In the ten years since it had started, Britain's Best
Village (known in gardening circles as BBV) had become one of the UK's most prestigious competitions.
Sponsored by Greenacres, one of the biggest gardening centres chains in the country, the first prize not
only came with the accolade of being the best place
in Britain to live, but a life-changing amount of prize
money. After the last few years of recession doom and
gloom, the nation was desperate for a feel-good factor,
and the event was receiving more publicity than ever.

'That's amazing!' Camilla gasped, for the second time in ten minutes. Clementine drew herself up proudly, like a ship's figurehead going into battle. 'This is going to be Churchminster's finest hour! We're going to show the rest of this country *exactly* what we're made of.'

'Bravo!' Camilla shouted, bursting into spontaneous applause. Jed followed suit. 'Go Mrs S-F!'

With that, Errol Flynn trotted out of the pantry with Camilla's knickers in his mouth and promptly deposited them on his mistress's feet.

Chapter 2

It was the day after Clementine's announcement, and she was sitting at her desk in the sunny drawing room at Fairoaks House – a large, imposing building on the other side of the village green to Camilla's cottage.

Photographs of the family adorned a grand piano in the corner, while a portrait of a stern-faced man with huge white whiskers and a gun dog by his side hung over the fireplace. Clementine's beloved husband Bertie had passed away years earlier but she still took comfort in talking to him.

'This is a turn up for the books, Berts,' she said briskly, shuffling a pile of papers. 'If only your mother were alive! What delight she would take from knowing we've made it through to the final of such a prestigious competition.' Clementine's mouth twitched. 'Fortuna was always terribly vocal about the fact Churchminster was the only village in the Cotswolds worth a visit from London.'

'Oh God, you're not talking to yourself again are you, Granny Clem?'

Clementine looked up to see the leggy blonde figure of her youngest granddaughter Calypso. As usual she looked like she had just stepped out of an Aerosmith video, long wild mane tumbling down her back.

'I was just relaying the recent events to your grandfather,' said Clementine.

Calypso rolled her eyes affectionately and looked over at the portrait. 'How about helping me get these sent out, Pops? I could use an extra pair of hands.'

'I'm sure your grandfather would have much more pressing things to get on with,' Clementine retorted, but her mouth had softened. She adored twenty-six-year-old Calypso, who was the youngest of the family and quite a handful. Ever since their parents had emigrated to Barbados, Clementine had kept a close eye on her three granddaughters, including the eldest, Caro, who was living in London with her husband Benedict and their two children. Calypso was now living back at No. 5 The Green with Jed and Camilla, eating them out of house and home and using the back garden as a giant ashtray.

Calypso threw herself down in the chair opposite. 'I'm shagged!'

'Darling, we didn't bring you up to speak like a trucker,' reprimanded Clementine. She peered over her glasses. 'Are things not going well?'

'Everything's going *too* well, that's why I'm so knackered,' said Calypso, throwing her tanned legs

22

over the chair. 'Not that I'm complaining really, it's all been brilliant.'

After a successful stint working as an event organizer in New York, Calypso had come home to set up her own company, Scene Events, which she was presently running out of a spare bedroom at Fairoaks. Despite the fact she had always struggled to apply herself to anything, Calypso seemed to have finally found her calling in life. She had been working flat out and, fingers crossed, it seemed to be paying off. Of course, it helped to have a contacts book that put Tara Palmer-Tompkinson's to shame.

Calypso shot her grandmother a perceptive look.

'This competition's a turn up for the books, hey?'

The previous autumn, the nation had been ravaged by flash floods that had charged through homes, up-turned cars and devastated hundreds of thousands of lives. Churchminster had been no different and Clementine could only watch in despair from the safety of Fairoaks, which was built on a slight hill, as the merciless brown waters had swept through her beloved village. To their anguish, it was the first time Calypso and Camilla had seen their grandmother cry. But when villagers had gone to the council to ask for money to floodproof the village, they were regretfully informed there was no money left in the pot to help them. The wealthier ones had put their hands in their pockets, coming up with an impressive three hundred thousand pounds between them, but it still wasn't enough. They were sitting on a ticking time bomb – and winning Britain's Best Village would safeguard their futures for ever. Clementine wouldn't even entertain the idea that they wouldn't.

'Anyway, what are you up to grandmother dearest?'

Clementine held up a piece of A4 paper.

'I've drawn up a poster for the Britain's Best Village meeting in the village hall on Sunday. If we're going to win this thing then we need to start a proper committee, so I need people to volunteer.'

Calypso pulled a face. 'Why is there a lollipop in the corner?'

Clementine looked put out. 'It's meant to be a tree.'

'Riiight.' Calypso leant back in her chair and folded her arms. 'Not meaning to diss your art skills or anything, Granny Clem, but it's a bit, well, rubbish, isn't it? It's not going to get them flocking in their droves.'

Clementine frowned. 'What do you mean? It's got all the information, time, date and location. I thought my tree drawing rather jazzed things up.'

Calypso rolled her eyes again. 'Yeah, but people need more than that these days, don't they? Something eye-catching and inspirational, that'll get them off their bums and down to the village hall.'

Clementine looked uncertain. 'You think so?'

'Like, deffo! Look, let me go and post these, and I'll come back and do something on the computer for you.' Calypso sprang up, revitalized, and bursting with one of her frequent bouts of energy.

'Well, if you insist . . .' Clementine wasn't sure. She knew her granddaughter's outlandish taste. 'Just don't do anything too avant-garde, will you, darling?'

Calypso's hazelnut eyes, the exact same colour as her

grandmother's, twinkled mischievously over the desk. 'Granny Clem, as if I would!'

Jack Turner, landlord of the Jolly Boot, polished a beer glass reflectively.

'Interesting poster.'

Behind the bar his wife Beryl was sticking it up with Blu-Tack. As usual, every window in the bar was wide open, trying to get out the last lingering vestiges of the damp smell from the flooding.

'There! Pride of place.' Beryl smoothed down her tight pencil skirt. 'I think it's lovely, Clementine. Your Calypso is really talented.'

Clementine steeled herself to look at it again. 'Do you think so?'

'Oh yes!' said Beryl. 'It's very er . . .' She trailed off, searching for the right word. '*Colourful.*'

It certainly was. Printed on bright green shiny paper, the words 'Come join our garden party!' stood out in large, neon-pink letters. Taking up the whole of one side was a voluptuous woman, wearing some sort of sunflower headdress. Whichever way you looked at it, it was hard to ignore the fact she was completely naked, her comely charms barely covered by three strategically placed leaves.

'It's a photograph of a reveller from the Mardi Gras carnival, apparently,' said Clementine weakly. 'At least that's what Calypso told me.'

'Mardi Gras,' echoed Beryl. 'How nice!'

There was a brief silence.

'You don't think it matters that the words "Britain's

25

Best Village" are rather small?' Clementine asked anxiously.

Jack seemed transfixed. 'No, no,' he replied, eyes glazed over. 'They're not small at all.'

The door at the back of the pub burst open and a buxom young lady with a combative look in her eye bounced in. Despite it being mid-March she was dressed like a podium dancer from Ibiza, in a crotch-skimming minidress, shiny black bomber jacket and towering high heels. Several lurid-coloured hoops dangled from both ears.

Jack was overly protective of his only child, and he did not like what he saw. 'What the bleedin 'ell do you look like?'

Stacey Turner tossed her head, her shiny dark pony-tail swinging like a show pony's. She ignored her father. 'Ma, I'm off shopping with the girls. Can I use your car?'

Jack interrupted. 'Oi, young lady! Don't forget you're working tonight. We need you back at 6.30 p.m. sharp.'

Stacey rolled her eyes, no mean feat under four tonnes of black eyeliner. 'As if I could forget! I'll be stuck behind this stupid bar while everyone's out having fun. *And* Kyle's going's to be at the Royal Oak later!'

'You're lucky you've got a job in this climate,' Jack pointed out reasonably. His expression darkened. 'Hold on, who's this Kyle?'

Stacey sighed dramatically. 'Dad, don't start!' She caught sight of the poster behind the bar and her face lit up. 'Are we putting on a rave?'

'Certainly not!' interjected Clementine hurriedly. She knew the poster would send out the wrong message!

Stacey's shoulders slumped. 'Nothing ever happens round here,' she muttered. 'It's *well* boring!'

Beryl smiled at her daughter. 'Come on, Stace! Most people would give their eye teeth to live in Churchminster.' She winked at Clementine humorously. 'You never know, Orlando Bloom might pop in for a pint tonight!'

Stacey shot her mother a contemptuous look. 'Like that's ever gonna happen. Celebrities would never come to a dump like this.' Snatching her mum's car keys off the bar, she flounced out.

Chapter 3

On the outskirts of Churchminster stood Clanfield Hall, a magnificent stately home, with breathtaking gardens and a fountain that Queen Victoria herself was rumoured to have dipped her feet in during a summer party.

This particular afternoon the owners, Lord Ambrose and Lady Frances Fraser, were heading back towards the hall having just attended a charity lunch. As he floored the Range Rover round the winding country lanes, Ambrose was full of his usual bile about the 'bloody silly sods' who populated such functions.

'I don't know who the hell I was sitting next to, but she didn't even know her Belgian sheepdog from her bearded collie.'

Ambrose had been born and raised at Clanfield Hall, which had been in his family for generations, and he had a morbid dislike of what he called the 'town set'.

'That was the Marchioness of Glenvale, she was

hosting the lunch,' his wife pointed out. 'Ambrose, I really hope you weren't rude to her.'

At fifty-four, Frances Fraser was nearly twenty years younger than her husband. An elegant Joanna Lumley lookalike, her cool manner and unruffled appearance couldn't have been more at odds with her volatile husband. When Ambrose went off on one of his legendary rants Frances was the only one who could calm him down.

'Harrumph!' retorted Ambrose. 'A bloody waste of time if you ask me, sitting around drinking champagne and talking about flower shows.'

Frances didn't rise to this. She was actually rather surprised she'd got her husband along to the lunch in the first place. These days, Ambrose barely left the confines of Clanfield Hall, preferring to be out in the grounds walking his dogs, or shutting himself in his study with a tot of his beloved single-malt whisky.

By contrast, Frances missed their once-lively social life and, in spite of its size, she was beginning to find the whole house rather claustrophobic. Of course, she knew how privileged she was, and that many women would love to be in her position, but still. Frances couldn't help feeling that something was *missing*.

'It's wonderful news about Britain's Best Village,' she said, changing the subject. 'I saw Clementine when I was out riding yesterday. She's holding a meeting on Sunday, to form a committee to get the village in tip-top shape. In fact, I was thinking of attending.' She held her breath.

Her husband gave a derisive snort. 'That Standington-Fulthrope woman! She'll have you litter-picking on the green before you know it Frances. How old Bertie S-F put up with her, bossing everyone around . . . Must have been like sharing a bed with Mussolini.'

As they rounded a sharp bend his inflammatory comments were quickly forgotten. A large silver estate car was heading straight for them. Ambrose slammed on the brakes and the Range Rover came screeching to a halt just feet from the other vehicle.

Frances lurched forward, only just stopping herself from going into the dashboard. She could see a middle-aged man and woman and two young children in the car, with a boot full of suitcases. The man was shaking his fist out the window at them.

'You bloody lunatic!' he shouted. In the back, the little girl started crying.

'He's right, Ambrose! Why do you have to drive like a maniac?' Frances felt as though her heart was about to jump out of her chest.

Her husband muttered something about tourists clogging the place up, and Frances tried to regain her composure. The lane was so narrow, neither vehicle could get past. One of them was going to have to move.

'Ambrose, there's a lay-by back there. Just reverse and let them past.'

Her husband sat back and folded his arms. 'Why should I? I live here, not him. It's my right of way.'

'Don't be so ridiculous!' Frances cried. In the other car, the man had also crossed his arms and was trying to out-stare Ambrose. Frances and the woman exchanged fleeting sympathetic glances: why were men so childish? But before Frances could tell him to reverse again, Ambrose had unbuckled his seat belt and was climbing out from the car.

'Ambrose!' Surely he wasn't going to confront the other driver! But instead he disappeared round the back of their vehicle, and Frances heard the boot being opened. A few seconds later, Ambrose marched past her car window carrying a shooting stick and a copy of the *Daily Telegraph*. Frances's mouth dropped open: what on earth was he doing?

She didn't have to wait long to find out. To the astonishment of the onlookers Ambrose sat down on his shooting stick in the middle of the road, opened his paper and started to read. In the other car the man looked at his wife and made a 'he's crazy' hand gesture to his head.

'Ha!' Ambrose called triumphantly. 'I'm retired and I've got all the time in the world to sit here all day. I very much doubt *you* have, sir!'

Frances slid down her window. 'Ambrose, get back in the car this instant!' she hissed.

Her husband turned a page, making a point of sighing contentedly. The other couple were looking extremely cheesed off.

'I'm frightfully sorry!' Frances mouthed through the windscreen at them. The man shook his head in disgust and begrudgingly started to reverse back down the lane. It was a full minute later that Ambrose looked up from his newspaper, folded up his shooting stick and finally returned to the Range Rover.

Frances's throat was tight with mortification. Her husband's behaviour was becoming increasingly questionable, but this was taking it to a new level. She watched him turn on the ignition. 'Are you happy now?' she asked crossly.

Ambrose just shot her a smug look and pulled away with the air of a man who had won an important battle. As the green fields started to fly past again, Frances gazed out of the window in silent despair.

Dear Lord, she thought. *Is this what my life has come to?*

Chapter 4

The day before the meeting in the village hall Clementine received a letter from the Britain's Best Village judging panel. As well as the different categories, the letter also included the names of the other three villages that had made the final. Clementine groaned aloud when she read the name of the last one. Maplethorpe was an outstandingly pretty village in the Yorkshire Dales, and had won the competition the previous year. Its village committee was run by a fearsome old battleaxe called Veronica Stockard-Manning.

Veronica and Clementine had history, which Clementine had never even told her family about. The two had done the debutante season in 1950, and fallen out later in an event society had chattered about wildly for months. It had rocked Clementine's world to the core and, although she would never admit it to anyone, she hadn't been the same person since. Afterwards, the two women had run into each other occasionally, but somehow Clementine had kept her emotions in check and swiftly removed herself from the situation. Clementine hadn't seen her nemesis for over twenty years, not since Bertie had died, and had almost succeeded in forgetting about her. Until now. Clementine pursed her lips, this was one face from the past that definitely wasn't welcome.

By the time the meeting came round in the village hall, Clementine had managed to put all thoughts of Veronica to the back of her mind. It was another gorgeous spring evening as she made her way down Bramble Lane to the village green. Errol Flynn's nether regions had been particularly active recently, and fearing he might expel noxious vapours into the hall and disrupt proceedings, Clementine had shut him in the kitchen. Indignant at being left inside on such a nice evening, she could hear his mournful howls all the way down the lane.

The village hall was only six months old, but Clementine had been insistent it was built in the mellow Cotswold stone that was such a feature of Churchminster. The villagers had raised the extra money for the stone themselves – one of the reasons the village fund was so out of pocket now – but as Clementine looked across the green at the handsome, yellow-gold building that fitted in so perfectly with the other cottages and dwellings lining the green, she knew they had made the right decision.

It was more municipal inside, with the usual emergency exit signs and strip lighting. Clementine had arrived early to set up, but Churchminster's vicar, Brian Bellows, was already there, putting chairs out.

'Evening, Mrs S-s-s-standington-Fulthrope!'

Brian Bellows was a tall, lanky man with an unruly brown beard that made him look older than his forty-five years. He'd come from All Saints Church in Bedlington, a small market town a few miles down the road. The Reverend hadn't had the best start, having been drafted in to replace Churchminster's previous vicar, who had died in unfortunate circumstances. Despite having an unfortunate stammer and giving the impression of being in a perpetual flap, Brian was a kind, conscientious man who was devoted to his parishioners.

'Evening, Reverend Bellows,' replied Clementine crisply. 'I see you've started without me.'

Reverend Bellows winced as he dropped a chair on his foot. 'Er, yes! Joyce and I thought we'd come down and, well, you know, g-get the ball rolling.'

As if on cue, a small, mouse-like woman came out of the kitchen area at the back of the hall. She was wiping her hands on a red and white spotty dishtowel, but that was the only bit of colour about her. From her shapeless cardigan and thick tights to her sallow complexion, everything about Joyce Bellows was beige. Clementine took in the thick NHS glasses and make-up-free face and wondered what Joyce made of the vicar's wife at All Hallows in Bedlington, a stunning six-foot Dane who wore tight skirts and jeans that showed off every inch of her figure.

Joyce beamed at them. 'I've just been rinsing all the cups and saucers so we can all have a nice cup of tea afterwards.'

Clementine smiled gently. 'My dear, you really didn't have to do that. You only gave the kitchen a complete scrub-down last week.'

'Oh, I don't mind!' said Joyce. 'Cleaning is one of my favourite hobbies! The amount of dust mites that can build up over just one week is quite staggering. You know they can lay up to a hundred eggs in one . . .'

Clementine was saved from the subject of microscopic household creatures by the arrival of Calypso, Camilla and Jed.

'Hi, Granny Clem!' called Calypso. 'We thought we'd come down now to see if you need any help.'

Clementine caught Joyce's horrified stare at Calypso's outfit, which consisted of the shortest imaginable denim skirt, and a T-shirt with a drawing of what looked like a man and woman copulating on the front of it.

'Actually, we could do with a strong man.' Clementine looked at Jed, dressed as usual in his overalls and work boots. 'Would you mind bringing in another stack of chairs from the foyer?' she asked.

Jed smiled. 'No problem . . .'

He walked off, the Reverend Bellows trailing uncertainly in his wake.

Clementine went over to her granddaughters. She looked disapprovingly at Calypso's T-shirt. 'Darling, do you think that's entirely appropriate?'

'Chill, Winston!' Calypso retorted, in a Jamaican accent. 'It's about making love, not war. I'm sending out a positive message.'

Clementine looked at Camilla, who was in a simple

36

sweater and jeans, her long blonde hair pulled back in a neat ponytail. Why couldn't Calypso dress more like her sister?

'How many people are you expecting?' Calypso asked. She wondered if she could sneak out beforehand for a quick fag.

'I hope most of the village will attend, I've certainly put enough posters up.'

Camilla smiled reassuringly at her grandmother, 'Everyone I've spoken to is coming.' She looked over at the kitchen. 'I'll go and see if Joyce needs any help.'

People began to trickle in a short time later and by seven o'clock the hall was nearly full. It looked like almost the entire village had turned up: among them the Fox-Titts, Lucinda and Nico Reinard, Brenda Briggs – who worked in the village shop and also masqueraded as Clementine's housekeeper – and her husband Ted. Even Beryl Turner had put down her bar apron and come along, dragging along a reluctant-looking Stacey.

'Jack's sorry he can't come, he's got to open up!' she shouted across the room at Clementine. 'He says to pop over after this and it's drinks on the house!'

'Wicked,' said Calypso, who was standing by her grandmother.

'Yes, well, let's see how we get on, darling,' said Clementine. 'We don't want people rolling home drunk. I need everyone to be on tip-top form these coming few months.'

She looked down at her carefully prepared speech.

She had read it so many times she knew it off by heart. As she stepped in front of her audience, a silence fell. Clementine was the kind of woman who commanded attention. She observed the familiar faces. 'May I take this opportunity to welcome you all here tonight, and to thank you for giving up your evening. I am sure all of you are aware of the exciting news by now, but just in case any of you aren't, Churchminster has got through to the final of Britain's Best Village competition!'

The room broke into spontaneous applause.

'Bravo!' cheered Angie Fox-Titt.

Clementine briefly glanced down at her notes. 'I don't need to tell you this is a huge achievement in itself. Thousands of villages entered, and to get this far is remarkable. Especially after the challenging year we have just experienced.'

Several heads in the audience nodded vigorously, including the Fox-Titts and Brenda Briggs, who'd all been badly affected by the floods.

'Judging week is the third week in July. Which means we have roughly five months to get the village into the best shape it has ever been in! With this in mind, I would like to form a committee to make sure all the criteria of the competition are met.' Clementine looked over her reading glasses expectantly. 'Who would like to join?'

Hands shot up. Camilla and Calypso had already been told, before the meeting, by their grandmother, that it was obligatory to volunteer.

'We'll do it!' called out Freddie Fox-Titt. On the row behind, Ted and Brenda Briggs followed suit, and so did the Bellowses. After what looked like a momentary struggle, Beryl gave up trying to get Stacey's arm in the air, sighed and put her own up. Stacey slumped down in her seat and returned to looking out the window.

A toothy woman, with coarse blond hair pulled back in a headscarf, stood up. 'You can count on me, Clementine!' Lucinda Reinard was the District Commissioner of the Bedlington Valley Pony Club, and lived in a rambling house on the outskirts of the village with her husband Nico and three children. She might be a bit overbearing, but at least she could be relied on to get things done.

'Excellent,' said Clementine briskly. 'I propose to hold a fortnightly committee meeting here in the hall, and I will let members know what their duties are.' She surveyed the crowd sternly. 'Of course, that doesn't mean the rest of you can slack off! Every villager is responsible for keeping his or her own property shipshape. I shall be counting on each and every one of you. A huge amount is at stake.'

'Three-quarters of a million quid!' someone shouted.

Clementine nodded. 'I don't need to tell you how much this village needs that money.' Folding up her speech, she looked round keenly. 'So! Do you think you've got what it takes to make Churchminster the best village in Britain?'

'Yes!' they all shouted.

Clementine's face broke into a smile for the first time. 'Good. Now, are there any questions?'

Fifteen minutes later the meeting was over, and everyone started to file out. Over the other side of the green in the gathering dusk the Jolly Boot waited enticingly.

'I'm going to give it a miss,' Jed told Camilla.

Her face dropped. 'Really? But I've hardly seen you all week.'

Since returning from travelling, Jed had been promoted from handyman to estate manager at Clanfield Hall. Camilla had been thrilled for him, and still was, but he was working longer and longer hours. She couldn't remember the last time they'd had a night out together.

Jed kissed her softly on the lips. 'One of the fences in a back field is down, I've got to go and sort it out before morning.'

'Camilla, come on! Beryl's said all committee members can have a glass of bubbly!' Calypso waved at her impatiently.

Camilla glanced over, and looked back at Jed. 'OK, sweet boy. I'll see you later.'

Jed started to walk over to his truck. He turned back with a wink that chased away Camilla's gloom. 'Keep the bed warm for me.'

Chapter 5

At Clanfield Hall, Frances was going through her correspondence. She was in her study, a beautiful, tastefully decorated room with high ceilings and two floor-to-ceiling windows that looked out on to the rolling grounds of the estate. Frances got up from her desk and went to stand at one of them; the view always made her feel good. It was another fine March day, and the muddy browns of winter were gradually being replaced by the first spring flowers and crisp shades of green.

Frances thought about the Britain's Best Village meeting, which had been held a few days previously, and which she'd wanted to attend. Ambrose had pooh-poohed the idea so much – 'Clanfield isn't even in the competition, why on earth do you want to go along?' – that Frances had thought it better not to. Besides, she would have felt a bit awkward: no one expected to see Lady Fraser turning up to a meeting in the village hall and mucking in.

In the distance Frances could see Jed driving along one of the fields in the tractor. Frances smiled; she and Ambrose had taken a gamble giving Jed the estate manager's job after their last one had left them in the lurch, but it had paid off. It was a big responsibility, but no one had such love and innate understanding of the countryside as Jed. She was sure he'd learn quickly. Frances had always found Jed a man of few words, but he seemed a very together young man who was devoted to his girlfriend. Frances thought of her own daughter Harriet, who worked for a glossy magazine in London. Harriet and Camilla were best friends, and Frances wished her daughter could find a nice stable chap. Frances had had high hopes for an officer in the army that Harriet had been seeing, but then he'd been posted abroad and the relationship had fizzled out.

She turned away from the window. There was a huge pile of invites to stifling lunches, dinners and charity events that had to be replied to, but Frances's normal efficiency had deserted her. Distractedly she wandered over to the radio and turned it on. A familiar song was playing, which took a few seconds to register.

Heart catcher . . . You're a heart catcher
You've caught my heart and I don't want it back . . .

Frances gave a start. The song was by a rock star called Devon Cornwall, who owned a huge Gothic house on the edge of the village. Devon had moved into the village a few years back, when his career had been on the rocks, trying to start a new life. Then he'd met

Frances, and the two had started an unlikely friendship, which had eventually led to a passionate affair.

Not one other person in the world knew it, but Devon had written 'Heart Catcher' for her. She started singing along softly, every word seared into her for ever.

Heart catcher, you've stopped me in my tracks.

In that moment, it was like Devon was in the room with her. Frances felt a brief twinge of elation. She had never dreamed of being unfaithful to Ambrose, but the marriage had been in trouble for years and Frances had found her world turned upside down when Devon had come into her life. There had been a chemistry between them she'd never felt with anyone before not even her husband. It was like they were soulmates.

Their liaison had been short-lived. After much agonizing, Frances had felt she couldn't go on living a lie, and had broken it off. Shortly afterwards, Devon's career had picked up, and he'd been away touring pretty much ever since. They still kept in contact occasionally, with the odd text message or email, but Frances hadn't heard from him for a while. She had told herself it was for the best: she had made the choice between Ambrose and Devon and chosen her husband. After all, it was her duty.

A tremendous racket suddenly started outside. Frances ran back to the window and looked out. Ambrose had driven his quad bike into the new pergola. She pulled the window up and stuck her head out, Devon forgotten for the moment. 'Ambrose! What on earth are you doing?'

Her husband looked up, blue eyes sharper than ever against his red, wind-whipped cheeks. His black-and-white sheepdog Sailor was sitting on the back of the quad, his tongue hanging out of his mouth like a red ribbon. 'Who put that bloody thing here? I could have fallen off and killed myself!'

Frances tutted. 'You did! You told the gardener to do it last week. Don't you remember?'

Her husband looked puzzled and let out a loud guffaw. 'I must be going mad. Bloody stupid place to put it.' He revved up the engine and zoomed off, Sailor hanging on with his paws for dear life.

Despite herself, Frances shook her head, smiling. Sometimes, Ambrose was like a little boy! Only last month he'd driven into a ditch after swerving to avoid a pheasant, and Jed had had to go and get the tractor to pull him out.

She turned back to the radio. 'Heart Catcher' had ended and Devon was gone again, some nondescript pop song playing in his wake. Frances walked over and turned the radio off. The silence was almost deafening.

She sighed and looked at the uninviting pile of letters. There was no point putting it off any longer: she was known for her prompt replies, and people expected her to attend all these things. It was what she did. '*Duty first*,' she thought, and sat back down behind her desk.

Chapter 6

The committee decided to call themselves the 'Garden Party'. 'It does have a nice ring to it, doesn't it?' declared Angie Fox-Titt, who'd come up with the name herself. Clementine had been appointed chairperson, and she had wasted no time in assigning committee members their duties. Litter-picking, hedge-trimming and fly-tipping duty were just a few of the things that needed to be done, and Clementine organized the whole thing with her usual military precision.

That morning, she was at Hollyhocks Cottage, Brenda and Ted Briggs's house. It was the first of three little cottages that sat on the Bedlington Road. The floods had affected all the houses along that particular stretch especially badly. As Clementine pulled up outside, she could still see the aftermath of the devastation. Brenda's beloved garden – which probably housed the biggest gnome collection in the whole of South West England – was still a muddy brown patch, while a tidemark ran across the front of the cottage, a permanent reminder of that dreadful week last summer.

Clementine could still remember turning up in the early hours of the morning to find the stricken Briggses coping with three feet of raw sewage and their neighbours' used toilet paper swirling through their cottage. All Brenda's family heirlooms, furniture and her new three-piece suite had been destroyed. The couple had literally been left with nothing. Brenda, who was the village gossip and could normally talk the hind legs off a racehorse, hadn't been the same since.

As Clementine made her way down the path to the front door, she looked up at the roof of Hollyhocks Cottage and frowned. Brenda loved Christmas decorations as much as her garden ornaments, and the garish Santa and Rudolph were still up there from Christmas. Brenda had said it cheered her up and, 'Lord knows I need it,' and Clementine hadn't had the heart to disagree up until now. But a ten-foot flashing Santa whipping Rudolph while the words 'Ho ho ho!' came out of his mouth in a speech bubble was not going to win them Britain's Best Village.

Brenda took a few moments to answer the door. 'Sorry I didn't hear you, Mrs S-F!' she said. 'I've been giving the place a good Hoover. The insurance money finally came through, and we got the new carpets in last week.'

Clementine followed Brenda into the kitchen. The cottage still had a bare, desolate feel to it, and one room was piled up with odd bits of furniture.

'The place isn't how I want, but we're getting there,' said Brenda. She gave Clementine a weary smile.

'Any word from Pearl?' asked Clementine sympathetically. Pearl Potts was a sprightly pensioner who lived in the middle cottage. Her elderly terrier, Kenny, had died of a heart attack the day they were flooded. Pearl had moved out soon after, and not been back since.

Brenda's face dropped. 'Still at her son's in Gloucester. Says she can't face coming back yet, not without the four-legged little fella here. I went to see her a few weeks ago, she's aged something terrible, you know, Mrs S-F. Says the whole thing's put twenty years on her.'

Clementine was upset to hear that. Pearl was a long-standing member of the village, and her cleaning and gardening skills could match those of a person half her age.

'Anyway!' said Brenda trying to lighten the mood. 'Can I offer you a brew?'

Clementine declined. 'I'm just making my rounds, and I thought I'd pop in and see how you're getting on.'

Brenda already ran a weekly bingo evening for local pensioners in the village hall once a week, and now she was starting a coffee morning for mums and babies in the café area of the village shop. This last had been Clementine's idea: not only did it tick the 'community spirit' box in the BBV competition, she thought it might be an ideal way to get Brenda back on her feet again.

Her idea seemed to be paying off.

'It's going a treat!' Brenda exclaimed. 'I've put posters up in the shop and have been out seeing all my old mates, spreading the word. The first one is next week, should be a good turnout.'

Clementine smiled. It was so nice to see Brenda getting back to her normal self. But there was one subject that she still had to broach. 'I noticed you've still got your Santa and Rudolph decoration up on the roof.'

Brenda chortled. 'Great, isn't it? Who says Christmas decorations are just for Christmas? Warms my cockles every time I see it.' She gave a cackle of laughter. 'Well, something's got to warm me cockles since Ted put his back out!'

'Hmmm,' said Clementine. 'As, er, nice as it is, I can't help thinking it's rather a distraction. Really rather out of keeping with the village, especially with the competition coming up.'

Brenda looked at Clementine. 'You're asking me to take it down?'

'I suppose I am,' Clementine admitted.

Brenda frowned, thinking. 'You're right,' she said eventually. 'It has been up there for six months. OK, I'll get Ted up there when he gets back from work.'

Clementine had been expecting more resistance. 'Excellent,' she said, pulling her driving gloves back on. 'Well, I've got a mountain of things to do so, I must be off.'

'Talking of changing things,' Brenda said as she led Clementine back through the cottage. 'I'm thinking of renaming 'Hollyhocks Cottage' 'Hollyoaks Cottage'.

What do you think? I mean, fresh start and all that, and it is one of my favourite programmes. I got the idea when I was watching it the other night.'

Clementine had no idea what she was talking about. It sounded like a gardening programme. Why had she never come across it? It must be one of those dreadful satellite channels everyone seemed to have these days. At least Brenda could be applauded for keeping with the spirit of the competition. 'Whatever makes you happy.'

Brenda looked chuffed to bits. 'Hollyoaks Cottage it is, then! See you, Mrs S-F.'

'Goodbye, Brenda.'

Chapter 7

Camilla and Jed were taking a walk around the Meadows, a peaceful fifty-acre woodland site on the edge of the village. For once, Jed had got home from work early, and they had decided to make the most of the lighter evenings.

They walked in companionable silence for a while. Camilla never felt the need to fill the air with unnecessary chatter when she was with Jed; he had a depth and stillness she found very peaceful.

Camilla found it bizarre to think that she'd spent all her life growing up in the same village as Jed, and yet, until three years ago they'd barely exchanged two words. She couldn't imagine life without him now. For over two decades they'd existed in separate worlds: Camilla in a big happy family, her life full of boarding school and skiing trips, Jed more out on the land than in school or college. Mr Bantry had run off with another woman when Jed was little, and it had been just him and his mum for as long as Camilla could remember. From what she could gather, Jed had practically bought himself up, as Mrs Bantry had worked all hours at the Hall as a housekeeper to make ends meet. Jed had always been a loner, and Camilla had wondered if his upbringing was something to do with that, but he had brushed off her enquiries, only saying his dad was dead to him and a waste of space. Jed was so self-contained and self-reliant; she'd never seen him get upset about anything.

Camilla had worried that he would feel claustrophobic in a proper relationship. She was his first serious girlfriend; in fact, make that his only girlfriend. She'd never asked him, but Camilla had the feeling there had been enough brief flings. A few whispers of gossip had floated her way over the years: an attractive divorcée from Chipping Norton, the young Cirencester riding instructor with legs up to her armpits and of course a brief liaison with Stacey at the Jolly Boot. Camilla tried to not think about that one too much. Besides, as she told herself, Jed was one of the best looking men in the Cotswolds. It was hardly surprising women were going to be interested. But no one had tamed him, no matter how hard they'd tried, until he'd confessed to Camilla – on one of their rambling walks in the early days – that he'd been in love with her for years. It was a rare show of emotion, and after that their union had come together wonderfully. They were both nature-lovers, both practical-minded and hands-on. Camilla was a natural homemaker and loved making a nest for her and Jed. Despite his physical and mental strength, she felt protective towards him; he'd been so alone most of his life, although she reminded herself that that didn't always equate to loneliness. Still, Jed was a challenging one to figure out. Her grandmother often referred to him as the 'Bantry enigma'.

'This is nice, isn't it?' Camilla said eventually, as they wandered through a field of tall wild grass.

Jed put his arm round her and kissed the top of her head. 'Everything's perfect when I'm with you.'

'Smooth talker,' smiled Camilla. She nestled into him. 'Can you imagine us with a tangle-haired brood of kids? It's the most perfect place for children to grow up.'

'Is that a hint?' Jed asked, smiling.

Camilla blushed. They'd talked about kids before, but never in depth. Jed didn't discuss his feelings much, preferring to show his love through physical contact inside the bedroom. In the early days, Camilla had worried that his lack of communication might mean he was going off her, or that she'd upset him about something, but she'd learned over time to trust him. If she were truly honest, it would be reassuring to have a bit of feedback now and again. But, as Camilla had reminded herself, no one was perfect, and Jed pretty much ticked every other box. 'No. You know, it would just be nice . . .' she trailed off. At thirty-two, Camilla's maternal urges were getting stronger and stronger. She couldn't imagine a person who would give her more beautiful babies.

Jed squinted off into the distance, apparently looking at something. 'Maybe we should try it. You could come off the Pill.'

Camilla stopped and looked at him. 'Really?'

His eyes flashed cheekily. 'We've got to take notice of that biological clock of yours, Cam. Now I've got this promotion at the Hall, I'm bringing in more money.'

Their finances had been a bit of a sore point between them before. Inspired by their travels, Camilla was working part-time in a travel agency in Cheltenham, but her family were rich enough to have bought her the cottage outright and provided an allowance that enabled her to live life comfortably. She knew Jed didn't like the feeling of being 'kept', even though she didn't think of it like that at all.

They grinned at each other goofily.

'So does this mean it's official?' Camilla asked. 'We're really going to start trying?'

He touched her face. 'It doesn't have to be a big announcement. Come off the Pill and see what happens.'

Given Jed's sex drive, Camilla didn't think it would be long before she would fall pregnant. An indescribably happy feeling surged through her and she flung her arms round him. 'Oh, Jed!'

He held her tight. 'I don't know what your grandmother would say about having children out of wedlock, though.'

Given his family background, perhaps it was inevitable that he didn't have much belief in the sanctity of the marriage vows. Even though she would have loved a big white wedding, Camilla had reconciled herself to doing without it. She had Jed, and that was enough.

'She'll get over it. Granny Clem's a lot more open-minded than you think.' As they embraced, Camilla felt him harden.

'Why don't we start trying now?' he said.

Camilla glanced round nervously. She was still reeling from her grandmother walking in on them, and had insisted on having sex with the bedroom door locked ever since. 'What if someone sees us? Granny Clem takes Errol Flynn for a walk around this time.'

'I don't care.' Jed was already unbuttoning his overalls.

'Isn't this going against the public decency act? We might get arrested!' Camilla was only half-joking. Jed's eyes glinted as he pulled her behind a huge oak.

'It'll be a great story to tell the grandkids.'

April came, and with it the first official Garden Party committee meeting. They had a full turnout and Clementine was surprised to see even Stacey Turner, glowering under a baseball cap and a tight *Fame* T-shirt, walk in with her mother.

'I hope you don't mind,' Beryl said in an undertone. 'She and Jack had a blinding row earlier, and he's banned her from using the car. I thought I'd better get her out of the pub before they killed each other.'

'Of course not,' said Clementine, thinking by the look on Stacey's face that she could well kill someone in the village hall instead.

Clementine waited until the scraping of chairs had stopped and everyone had settled down. 'Good evening, everyone. Welcome to the Garden Party's first official committee meeting. I'd like to get straight down to business, please, so let's have a catch up on what everyone has been up to in the last two weeks.'

Freddie Fox-Titt was the first to speak. He was a short, jolly man who lived in the Maltings, a large house on the Bedlington Road, with his fun-loving wife, Angie. Along with Jack Turner, Clementine had put him in charge of removing any graffiti in the village. 'I've finally cleaned the phone box up. Took a bit of elbow grease, but I got there in the end! Now we just have to hope they don't come back again.'

Beside him, his wife laughed. 'We were thinking of leaving Avon and Barksdale in there to scare any wannabe Banksys off.' Avon and Barksdale were the Fox-Titts' extremely bouncy border collies.

'Errol Flynn would be a safer bet,' remarked Calypso. 'He could blast them away with one fart.'

Several titters sounded. Clementine shot a mildly disapproving look at her granddaughter, and turned to the landlady of the Jolly Boot. Her hanging baskets were some of the best in the county. 'Now, Beryl. Have you managed to go round to the houses we talked about, to make sure they've done their planting properly?'

Half an hour later, the meeting was nearly over. Camilla and Calypso were to do alternate litter-picking duty on the green and Lucinda Reinard was making it her mission to hunt down any fly-tippers. The district had recently been plagued with people dumping rubbish in lay-bys and fields.

Lucinda gave a grim smile. 'Those litter-louts will

think twice about dumping their old mattresses here! I've commandeered my daughter Hero's old hockey stick to give them a whack across the knees if they try anything.'

Reverend Bellows was sporting a large scratch across his forehead from the unruly rhododendron bush in St Bartholomew's graveyard.

'My dear man!' exclaimed Clementine. 'Are you all right?'

Reverend Bellows blushed. 'Q-quite. I didn't realize quite what a f-formidable opponent I was up against! I've trimmed most of it back now, though.'

Joyce Bellows, a vision in sludge brown, looked up devotedly at her husband. 'Oh, Brian, you are brave!'

Reverend Bellows blushed deeper, looking rather pleased with himself.

Clementine put her clipboard down. 'If there's nothing else . . .'

Fifteen minutes later they were all in the pub. The Jolly Boot was the oldest building in the village; a slice of history with worn flagstone floors, tankards hanging above the bar and a huge fireplace that blazed merrily through the winter months, warming the frozen hands and feet of the customers who sat round it. The committee members stood in a circle, chatting away about the competition.

'Another sherry Granny Clem?' asked Calypso. It was a rare occasion to get her grandmother in the pub.

'No, thank you darling,' Clementine replied,

watching as Calypso ordered herself another large glass of rosé.

'Really darling, there's hald a bottle in there!'

Jack Turner was clearing up glasses when a small, spiky-haired young man approached him. Jack hadn't seen him walk in but he smiled welcomingly.

'Yes, my lad?'

The young man smiled back. 'I don't know if you can help. I was wondering if you'd have a village committee, someone I could speak to from it.'

Jack didn't ask strangers too many questions; from his experience it got you into trouble. Best keep your eye on them from a distance instead. He cocked his head at Clementine.

'Mrs Standington-Fulthrope's your best bet. You want me to introduce you?'

'Yes please,' said the man gratefully. 'I'm Dan, by the way.'

Jack nodded and putting down the glasses, took Dan over to Clementine.

'Mrs S-F, there's someone here who wants to speak to you.'

Dan stuck his hand out and rather bemused, Clementine took it.

'Hello, I'm Dan Blake.'

Clementine looked at the young man more closely. She was sure she'd seen him around the village recently a few times.

'How do you do, I'm Clementine Standington-Fulthrope.'

Everyone looked at Dan expectantly. He produced a

card from his pocket and gave it to Clementine.

'I'm a locations manager for a film company called Seraphina Inc.'

'I've heard of them,' Camilla whispered to Calypso. 'They did *Love On The Line*, do you remember?' *Love On The Line* was a British film, about an aristocratic girl falling in love with a London Underground worker. It had been a worldwide smash.

'Oh?' said Clementine politely.

Stacey Turner had been working her way through a packet of peanuts behind the bar. Her ears pricked up.

'We've been left in a bit of a spot because the village we were meant to have been filming in has fallen through,' Dan explained.

He looked round.

'Collapsed bridge, the place has been left completely cut off.'

Some of the group murmured their sympathies.

Dan looked back at Clementine.

'I've been checking out a few places round here instead and you see, your village is perfect!'

Clementine was lost. 'Perfect for what?'

Dan smiled winningly. 'To use as the location instead! I've been looking at loads of villages across the country, and this is by far the best.'

Everyone's mouths dropped open. Clementine regained her composure first. She had heard horror stories about villages being ruined by huge film crews and ghastly hordes of paparazzi. 'Certainly not!' She looked around for backup, but it became apparent she was in a minority.

'Oh come on, Granny Clem!' cried Calypso. 'It'll be, like, totally amazing!' Several other people nodded their heads enthusiastically.

'No!' Clementine protested. 'We haven't got time for tomfoolery, we've got to get ready for the competition.'

'Churchminster has got through to the final four for Britain's Best Village,' Calypso told Dan. He looked seriously impressed.

'Wow! It would be doubly fantastic to film here, then!'

Clementine didn't like how presumptuous this young man was. 'No, it would not!' she said.

To her surprise, Angie Fox-Titt spoke up. 'It sounds like tremendous fun! Freds and I have always fancied a walk-on part in a film. Remember that production of *A Midsummer's Dream* Bourton-on-the-Water's am-dram club did, Freddie? You made the most wonderful Bottom.'

Dan smiled gratefully at her. 'We'll definitely need extras, and you'll get paid a daily rate.'

'Ooh!' exclaimed Brenda Briggs. 'I'll be a proper actress, like What-ser-chops Winslet.'

'What is the film?' asked Camilla, hoping for a romcom.

'It's a costume drama called *A Regency Playboy*,' Dan announced. 'It's a big, lavish production and we've got a great cast and director.'

Stacey Turner spoke up for the first time. 'Who's in it?'

Dan looked a bit furtive. 'Well, if you can keep it

under your hats for now. Sophia Highforth is playing the female lead and Rafe Wolfe is the male . . .'

Stacey stopped him. 'Did you say Rafe Wolfe?'

'Well, we're just waiting for him to confirm, but it looks pretty defin . . .'

Stacey started jumping up and down. 'Oh my GOD! Rafe Wolfe! He is sooooo fit! Wait until I tell Lindsay and Chloe about this! Oh my God!'

Rafe Wolfe was a handsome young British actor who'd made his name playing the lead in Hollywood blockbusters. Even though he was Cambridge-educated, the 30-year-old looked like an all-American blue-eyed golden boy. He was often plastered across the celebrity magazines, linked with some beautiful woman or another.

Beryl put a placating hand on her daughter's arm. 'All right, Stace, calm down! You're gonna give yourself a heart attack!'

Stacey wasn't listening. 'The girls are gonna freak! I've gotta ring them.' As she ran towards the door to the living quarters, Stacey paused. 'I'll get a part, won't I?'

'Er, we can definitely put you forward,' said Dan, rather bamboozled by her jiggling chest.

Stacey squealed. 'Oh my God! I'm gonna be famous! That'll shut that bitch Chantelle Brown up.' Then she was off, excited gabbles fading down the corridor. 'Linds! Oh my God! You'll never guess what's just happened!'

'I think we can safely say Stacey's in favour of the film crew,' chuckled Freddie.

'I've never seen her so excited!' Beryl exclaimed. She looked rather proud. 'Stacey's a right good little actress, you know. Used to dress up and do a song and dance every Christmas.'

Calypso turned to her grandmother. 'What do you think, Granny Clem? It's like, a *really* good thing for the village.'

'I don't agree,' said Clementine. 'I know what these film crews are like: there'll be huge great lorries churning up the green before one knows it. They'll take over the village!'

'That won't happen,' assured Dan. 'I'll be the point of contact between the village and Seraphina Inc. Any problems or worries, you can come to me. We want to make sure you're all happy.'

'Hmmm,' said Clementine. She still wasn't convinced.

Dan held his trump card until last. 'Of course, there will be a location fee.'

Clementine eyed him suspiciously. 'Location fee?'

'Absolutely. We'd pay to use your village, recompense any small disruptions that might happen, et cetera. It would be a proper business arrangement.'

'And how much would this location fee be?'

Dan swallowed. The old woman was a bit of a dragon. 'Well, it would be a good whack, and we'd also pay extra for the short notice. I'd have to talk to my boss, but we're talking tens of thousands.'

'Oh, Clementine, we've got to do it!' cried Angie. 'Think of all that money.'

Clementine could feel a dozen sets of imploring eyes

on her. She wasn't ready to give in yet. 'I need to speak to the parish council,' she told Dan. 'We would need to get the go-ahead from them as well.' The parish council were an overly cautious lot. She was confident there was no way they would allow such a disruption, especially if it could jeopardize the competition.

'What do you think they'll say?' Dan's face was hopeful.

Clementine soon extinguished that. 'I wouldn't hold your breath, young man.'

Chapter 8

To Clementine's dismay, the parish council thought it was a wonderful idea.

'Just what we need to inject a bit of glamour back into the area!' said the chairperson, David Askew.

Clementine sighed down the phone. This was her last-ditch attempt to try and make him see sense. 'David, aren't you worried about the disruption? Wootton-under-Barley's High Street was closed off for a whole week a few years back for some television production. We just can't afford to take the risk, not with Britain's Best Village coming up.'

'I understand your concerns, Clementine,' he assured her. 'But I've spoken to the rest of the council and we think it's a manageable situation. Besides, you can't really afford to turn down that location fee, can you?'

Seraphina Inc. had come back and offered a whopping thirty thousand pounds for permission to film in the village. It was to be a ten-week shoot, starting in the middle of April. They wouldn't be out until the first week of July, which, in Clementine's opinion, left it far too late. The BBV judges were coming two weeks later!

Clementine sighed again. She knew she was fighting a losing battle. 'All right, you win. But I can't say I'm happy about it.'

Clementine put the phone down and rubbed her forehead. They badly needed the money, but she couldn't help feeling that they were dancing with the devil. No matter what anyone said, the village was going to be taken over, right at a time when everyone's focus should be on the competition. *People's heads are turned by glitz and glamour nowadays,* she thought. *What happened to community spirit and principles?*

Distractedly she picked up her fountain pen, twirling it through her gnarled fingers. It was all happening so *fast*; in a few weeks an entire film crew would be descending on Churchminster, bringing God knows what with them. The terms had been thrashed out and they were to film at various locations in and around the village, starting with a manor house called Braithwaite Hall on the outskirts, before moving on to Clanfield Hall. Clementine was rather surprised Frances Fraser had agreed to open her gates, but then Frances hadn't seemed herself lately. On the few occasions they'd met round the village, Clementine had thought she'd been rather preoccupied.

There was a thundering down the stairs and Calypso materialized in the doorway. 'So you've said yes? Old Davey-boy sounded as keen as mustard.'

'Were you listening on the upstairs extension?'

asked Clementine indignantly. Calypso rolled her eyes.

'Course I was! I was dying to know what you'd say. I knew you'd come round. It's a great thing for Churchminster to get involved with. I know you don't think it, Granny Clem, but it might even *help* us in the BBV competition. Add a string to our bow and all that.'

'I don't think there's a "how many actresses can you spot on the village green" category,' said Clementine wearily.

Calypso gave a snort of laughter. 'That's quite good, for you.'

Clementine resisted a smile as Calypso started to move round the room restlessly, picking up things and putting them down again. 'You look like you need to get out of the house,' Clementine told her.

'If only,' replied Calypso, as she moved on to rearranging ornaments on the top of the fireplace. 'I've got to wait for a call from a client on the office line, my mobile reception is crap here.'

Clementine eyed her granddaughter. There was some sort of stain from lunch on the front of her string vest, and her hair looked like it hadn't come into contact with a brush for a while. 'Darling, are you sure you're not working yourself too hard? You look a bit rundown.'

'I'm cool, I just didn't realize running your own business was such hard work. Though hopefully, if things keep going like this, I can take someone on next year.'

Calypso was normally the most sociable of her three

granddaughters, but Clementine couldn't remember the last time she'd had a night out.

'Why don't you go out? See some friends.'

Calypso shook her head. 'I'm about business, not pleasure, these days. That extends to my love life as well. I might as well be a nun.'

'I'd rather not know, thank you,' said Clementine.

A phone started ringing upstairs.

'Shit, that'll be them!' said Calypso, flying out the door. Clementine could hear pounding up the stairs again and the door to Calypso's office slamming shut. Clementine winced as the house shuddered, but she didn't really mind. She was awfully proud of what Calypso was achieving.

A few seconds later Clementine's own phone started ringing. She reached over the desk and picked up the receiver. 'Churchminster 498.'

The voice at the other end needed no introduction.

'My dear Clementine,' exclaimed Veronica Stockard-Manning. 'How wonderful to hear you! After all these years.'

Clementine sat up straight in her chair. Veronica's over-modulated tones seeped into her ear like treacle.

'Family keeping well? I had to ring up and offer my congratulations, you're in esteemed company, you know, getting through to the final of Britain's Best Village!'

'Quite,' replied Clementine acidly.

'I was rather surprised, I must admit. I hear the place has been left looking like Armageddon after the flooding. But still, it was nice of them. You know, the head judge Marjorie Majors is a close friend of mine. Typical of old Marjorie to bestow charity where it's needed.'

Clementine was in no mood to listen. 'Was there anything in particular you wanted, Veronica?'

Veronica laughed. 'Just a few friendly words of support! We're all in this together.'

Clementine was about to end the conversation when Veronica stopped her dead in her tracks.

'Of course, you'll be really up against it with this film crew arriving. I would never have agreed to such a thing for Maplethorpe, although I suppose we aren't as *desperate* as you for the money.'

Clementine couldn't hide her astonishment. 'How do you know about the film crew? It's only just been agreed.'

Veronica laughed. 'Oh, don't expect me to reveal my sources. Let's just say I heard it through the grapevine.'

If Veronica had expected Clementine to start begging to find out, she was wrong. 'Goodbye, Veronica,' she said.

'Goodbye, my dear!' said Veronica. 'And good luck.' She couldn't resist a final put down. 'You're certainly going to need it.'

Chapter 9

Camilla flopped down in the Laura Ashley chair by the fireplace. Around her the little cottage sparkled and gleamed like a shiny new ten pence piece. She had spent the last three hours doing a thorough spring clean. All the cupboards in the kitchen had been scrubbed. Every window had been cleaned. Carpets had been Hoovered, wooden floors mopped and beams dusted. A scent of fresh pine and lemon wafted though the building like a blast of spring. With the help of Jed's toolkit, Camilla had even mended the broken lock on the downstairs loo. She had always been the most practical of the three sisters.

Looking round, it was hard to believe that the room had ever been under six inches of water. The walls had dried out, and the tidemarks had been painted over. Camilla counted herself one of the lucky ones that only the living room, which was slightly lower than the rest of the downstairs, had been affected. Her mother, always an alarmist, had offered to stump up tens of thousands to have the whole cottage flood-proofed, but to her surprise, Camilla had said no. Even Clementine had urged Camilla to take up her parents' generous offer, but Camilla had explained she would feel uncomfortable, when everyone around her was struggling to cope. Especially as she was one of the least affected; it would be like rubbing people's noses in it. Until a solution had been found for the whole village, Camilla was prepared to rely on sandbags and goodwill like the rest of them. Significantly, Clementine had backed down.

Normally a good bout of cleaning left her with a feeling of satisfaction, but Camilla was still fidgety. She reached over for her mobile and called her sister. Maybe Calypso fancied lunch in the Jolly Boot.

The phone went straight to voicemail. She was probably in a meeting with clients. Calypso had barely been at home since she'd started Scene Events, and so her famously messy ways had not unleashed themselves on the cottage much. Camilla wouldn't have believed it, but she missed the ashtrays of overflowing fag butts, dirty plates, and fishnet tights hanging off the radiators.

She decided to call Jed instead, and was pleasantly surprised when he answered. Jed hated having a mobile and rarely took it out with him.

There was a lot of engine noise in the background and she could hear the 'beep beep' of a lorry reversing.

He had to shout to be heard. 'Camilla? Are you all right?'

'Yes, I'm fine!' Camilla said. 'How are you?'

'Fine. Was there anything?'

'I just wondered what you wanted for dinner to-night.'

'I'm easy. You know I'll eat anything you give me.'

'How about some kind of chicken dish? I'll use some of the herbs from the garden.'

'Great! Look, I've to go . . .'

'See you tonight. I love you.'

'Love you too, Cam. See you later.'

Camilla put the receiver down happily. Jed was working so much at the moment, it was a treat to have him back for dinner at a reasonable time. She loved having a busy house, looking after people and feeding them with hearty home-cooked dinners. For a moment she envisaged their children sitting expectantly round the kitchen table, filling the room with their laughter and chatter while she stirred a big pot on the stove. They'd have little girls with blonde hair and a little boy with dark hair and green eyes, just like Jed. Maybe he'd take after his dad and go to work at Clanfield Hall. Camilla had a vision of father and son returning after a fulfilling day at work, dirty but happy . . .

She shook herself. *You're getting carried away.* She'd only just come off the Pill, and things might not happen for a while. Her older sister Caro had taken ages to get pregnant with her first child, Milo. Camilla could already feel herself getting swept away with it, though, wondering, waiting . . .

Giving herself another shake, Camilla went to start on dinner.

*   *   *

The next day, as she drove back from another frustrating morning at Top Drawer Travels, Camilla's good mood was somewhat dimmed. She had been doing some research of her own on South America, and had found what she thought would make a great new tour, but when she'd broached it to her boss, Mr Fitzgerald, he'd looked at her as if she was mad.

'You stick to what you know, and I'll do the same,' he'd told her. 'Be a good girl and stick the kettle on, will you?'

Camilla had gritted her teeth. She was beginning to feel more like a glorified dogsbody than a trainee travel agent. Hopefully things would start to pick up.

Her stomach rumbled. Camilla decided to stop at the shop and pick up something nice for lunch, maybe a piece of one of the home-made quiches Brenda had started selling recently. A local farmer's wife made them; Camilla would never risk her teeth on Brenda's famously rock-hard cuisine.

The upcoming film had made the front page of the *Bedlington Bugle* two days running.

'RAFE TO RUN RIFE IN THE COTSWOLDS!' said today's headline on the board outside the shop.

The bell on the door tinkled as Camilla entered. Brenda popped up from behind the counter. 'Afternoon!'

'Hi, Brenda, how are you?'

Brenda slid a copy of the *Bedlington Bugle* across the counter. ''Ere, what do you think about this! Rafe Wolfe, in Churchminster! I never thought I'd live to see such a thing.'

Camilla looked at the front page, which had a picture of Rafe in a dinner jacket on a red carpet somewhere, looking extremely dashing. 'Yes, it is exciting, isn't it? I saw his last film at the cinema, it was awfully good.'

Brenda cackled. 'I'll say. Cor, if I was twenty years younger! I'm driving my Ted up the wall going on about it.'

The quiche was still warm in the brown paper bag as Camilla left the shop and made her way round the green to No. 5. It was a rather blustery day and Camilla saw an empty crisp packet flutter across the road. She went to pick it up.

A blacked-out Mercedes pulled up beside her. Camilla's heart stopped. The passenger window slid down and Camilla leaned eagerly in the window. To her disappointment the glorious vision of Rafe Wolfe was not sitting there, but a rather bloated, raddled man with an outsized diamond stud in his left ear. He reminded Camilla of a downmarket Simon Le Bon.

'Howdy. I'm Wes Prince.' He had a strong transatlantic twang. 'Director on *A Regency Playboy*.'

'Oh, hello!' exclaimed Camilla. Wait until she told Calypso about this!

Wes flashed Colgate-white teeth. Even in the gloom of the car, Camilla could see he had rather orange-coloured skin. 'Yeah, just got back from LA, and thought I'd come and do a recce. Nice little place you've got here. Can you recommend any good sushi joints or wheatgerm bars for lunch?'

Camilla pointed out the pub. 'The Jolly Boot does delicious food. I'm sure they can find you a table.'

Wes flashed the teeth again. 'We'll give it a whirl. Ciao.' The window slid up again and the car glided off down the road.

As Camilla let herself in through the front door of No. 5, she was surprised to see her sister's handbag lying in the hall, its contents spilling everywhere. She called out. 'Calypso, are you here?'

A voice sounded from the kitchen. 'In here, Bills.' 'Bills' was a nickname for Camilla her family and close friends used. The kitchen Camilla had left sparkling now had milk and sugar all over the surfaces, while breadcrumbs were scattered all over the table. Calypso looked up from her chair. 'Came home for some tea and toast.'

Camilla's maternal instinct kicked in. 'You can't just have that for lunch. I've got some home-made quiche here, would you like a piece?'

Calypso's eyes lit up. 'Wicked!' Even though she was as slim as a rake, her appetite was legendary.

'I'll dig out some baked potatoes as well, and pop them in the microwave.' Camilla put the quiche down on the side. 'You'll never guess who I've just seen!'

Calypso took a slurp of tea. 'Bin Laden.'

'Only the director of *A Regency Playboy*! Wes Prince. He's here doing a recce,' Camilla added knowledge-ably.

Calypso didn't look as impressed as Camilla'd hoped, but then it took a lot to impress her. 'Well, I've got a bit of news for you as well,' Calypso said. 'Someone from Seraphina Inc. called me this morning, they've asked me to put on a welcome party at the Jolly Boot.'

'Wow,' gasped Camilla. 'That's amazing!'

'It is pretty cool,' Calypso grinned. 'Apparently I was recommended to them, which shows people are already talking about Scene Events. Seraphina want to put on a party to "integrate the crew and locals". Show we're all one big happy family.' She giggled. 'I reckon Granny Clem's really got to them.'

'Ooh, do you think Rafe Wolfe will turn up?' Camilla asked excitedly.

Calypso pulled a face. 'Hardly. It's for the crew mainly, I can't see a big star like him hobnobbing with the hoi polloi.'

Camilla sighed. 'Shame. He's utterly gorgeous.'

'If you like that clean-cut look. He's a bit "frat-boy" for me. I prefer someone with an edge.' Sexually curious, Calypso's last serious relationship had been with a rather gruff girl called Sam. Apart from the odd fling, she hadn't been with anyone, male or female, since.

'I was reading about his latest dalliance in OK! Some LA heiress called Daphne. He always has gorgeous girlfriends.' Camilla sighed. 'I loved his last film, I cried my eyes out at the end.'

Calypso rolled her eyes. 'I can't believe you buy into all that crap. Are you going to put those potatoes on – or just look at them all day?'

Chapter 10

Life went on for the Churchminster residents, but there was a new frisson of excitement that not even getting through to the final of Britain's Best Village had produced. On a grey April morning, after weeks of anticipation, the film crew finally rumbled into town. Stacey Turner, who had never got up early in her life, was out at dawn posing by the phone box in full make-up and push-up bra. Beryl, worried her daughter would catch her death in the early morning air, went out with a coat for her, only to be told in no uncertain terms to go away.

'Leave it, mum!' she said crossly. 'How am I gonna get noticed with a full-length duffle coat on?'

Beryl gave up and went back in to make Jack his morning fry-up.

From 8 a.m. the first vehicles had appeared on the horizon. The village had never seen so many: huge articulated lorries, white trucks, what looked like a thirty-foot-long mobile home. Clementine watched from her attic-room window as they manoeuvred through the village like a procession of metallic ants, towards Braithwaite Hall. *At least they're out of sight for the moment*, she thought, dreading the day they would take over the whole village.

She eventually dragged herself away and went downstairs to make her morning cup of Earl Grey. She switched on the old-fashioned radio in the kitchen. The local newsreader was full of excitement about the goings on.

'Usually, A-list celebrities like Tom Cruise or Angelina are only seen on the red carpet of Hollywood, but today the world of showbiz has come to the Cotswolds! Our intrepid reporter Abby Jarvis is in the picturesque village of Churchminster, which has been chosen as the location for costume drama film A Regency Playboy. *Over to you, Abby, can you hear me?'*

'Loud and clear, Ray!'

'Abby, can you describe the scene around you?'

'I certainly can, Ray. Churchminster hit the headlines recently after it was revealed the village had made it through to the final of Britain's Best Village competition, but today it's more about glamour than garden gnomes. For the past few hours the cast and crew have been arriving in the village to start their ten-week shoot. We've certainly never seen the like of it before, Ray. I've just seen two Winnebagos go past, which I presume are for the two leading stars, Rafe Wolfe and Sophia Highforth. There goes a truck full of

camera equipment and, wait! Look at that! A lorry has just gone past with a life-sized pig strapped into the passenger seat! It's wearing a baseball cap and seems to have some kind of frill round its neck!'

'Abby, I noticed you mentioned the cast are expected to arrive today as well. Any sightings of the lead actors, Sophia Highforth or Rafe Wolfe?'

'Indeed, Ray. A blacked-out Range Rover, reported to be carrying 30-year-old Hollywood star Rafe Wolfe, drove through the village earlier. It's understood that while many of the cast and crew are staying at the Travelodge outside Bedlington, Rafe and his co-star Sophia are being put up in private accommodation during their stay here in the Cotswolds.'

'Sophia can come and stay at my house if she wants, heh heh! What do the local residents make of these extraordinary happenings?'

'Well Ray, standing with me is 22-year-old Stacey Turner, whose parents run the Jolly Boot public house. Stacey, I understand you're a rather big fan of Rafe . . .'

As Stacey's excited gabbling took over the airwaves, Clementine turned on to the more soothing tones of Radio 4. At least they'd mentioned the competition. It didn't stop the trepidation that was mounting in her by the minute, though. Shaking her head, Clementine switched on the kettle.

Luckily the village green seemed to have escaped unscathed as Clementine took Errol Flynn for a walk later. The film crew had finally passed through, and the village was back to its relative quietness.

Suddenly, the Reverend came rushing out of the rectory. It was a square, rather gloomy building which stood a few hundred yards up the Bedlington Road. 'G-good day to you, Mrs S-s-standington-Fulthrope!'

'Ah, hello, Reverend,' said Clementine. Much to the clergyman's horror, Errol Flynn bounded up and shoved his nose in the Reverend's crotch. 'Errol! Get down,' Clementine reprimanded, pulling him away. 'I am sorry about that.'

Reverend Bellows backed away. He was scared of animals, which didn't help his cause in a parish where every second person had dogs and horses. 'I just saw you through the window. Did you see the p-procession earlier?' he asked eagerly.

'I did indeed.'

'Joyce and I have watched all of S-S-Sophia and Rafe's films, you know, we're quite a p-pair of film buffs. Although Joyce did find Rafe's last one a little violent for her tastes.' His eyes twinkled. 'B-between you and me, I quite enjoyed it!'

Dear Lord, thought Clementine, *even the vicar's had his head turned.* She had expected more from a man of the cloth.

'Joyce and I are going to put our names down to be extras,' said Reverend Bellows.

Clementine arched an eyebrow. 'My dear fellow, are you sure that's entirely appropriate?'

Reverend Bellows's face fell. 'Oh. D-do you think it's a bad idea?'

'I'm sure I can rely on your good judgement to make the right decision.'

'What do you think?' he asked anxiously. 'I don't want to offend my p-p-arishioners.'

'My good man, it really isn't my place to tell you what to do,' she solemnly informed him.

'I s-s-suppose you're right,' he said glumly. 'How will people take me s-s-seriously in the pulpit if they've seen me as a toothless vagrant? It's not the right message to send out.'

'I think you've made the right choice, Reverend,' Clementine told him. Saying her goodbyes, she started to pull Errol Flynn back towards the village green. At the phone box by the crossroads, she noticed a funny little man standing smoking a cigarette. As she approached, he flashed an over-friendly smile and flicked the butt on the ground. Clementine took an immediate dislike to him.

'Lovely day!' he said. 'I bet there's lots of excitement, what with all these big stars arriving, and whatnot.'

'I really wouldn't know,' Clementine said.

The man flashed stained teeth into what Clementine supposed was meant to be an ingratiating smile. 'So where do you live, then?'

'Not that it's any of your business, but I live at Fairoaks. Just off the village green.'

The man's smile had faltered momentarily, but came back on again. 'So you're a local!' He walked over to her. Clementine caught a whiff of stale smoke. 'I think you and me could come to some sort of business arrangement. I'm after any stories of Rafe and Sophia I can get. You could tip me off with any gossip you get, sightings, that sort of thing. I'd pay you well, of course. What do you think?'

'What I think,' said Clementine, 'is that you should bugger off.' And with that, she marched off towards the village shop. Tying up Errol outside, Clementine pushed open the door and went in.

Brenda was perched atop a rather precarious stepladder, replenishing the top shelf.

'Are you sure that's safe?' Clementine called up in alarm. 'We can't have you tumbling off and breaking your neck.'

Brenda climbed down. 'Don't you worry about me Mrs S-F, this thing's as steady as a rock. If I landed on me head, I'd probably bounce, anyway!' She dusted off her hands. 'What can I get you?'

'Is the new *Cotswold Life* in yet?'

Brenda winked. 'Got your copy saved behind the counter.'

As Clementine went over to pay, Brenda started talking about that morning's events. 'Ooh, I was ever so excited, I can tell you! Got up early and put my Sunday best on to watch it all. Ted thought I was mad. "What you doing that for, woman?" he kept asking. And *I* said, "Well, that's what you do, isn't it?"'

'I just bumped into an oily little reporter outside,' Clementine said. 'Asking all sorts of questions and trying to nose around.'

Brenda tried to look resigned. 'Suppose we'll have to get used to that now, what with us being a celebrity hot spot and everything.'

'Oh dear, I think you've got us to blame for that,' said a voice behind them. 'Although once the initial excitement wears off, the press to tend to lose interest.'

Clementine looked round. A short, cheery faced woman was standing behind them. She was dressed in a fleece body warmer and sensible clothes, and had the ruddy complexion of someone who liked the outdoor life.

The woman smiled, rosy red cheeks creasing up. 'Pam Viner. Assistant director on *A Regency Playboy*.'

'Ooh!' breathed Brenda.

Pam twinkled at Clementine. 'Is that your black Lab outside? We just met, what a friendly chap.' Her face dropped slightly. 'Lost mine a few months ago. Dudley had been with the family years, we were all devastated.'

'I'm sorry to hear that,' said Clementine, meaning it. Maybe some of these film people weren't so bad after all.

Pam seemed to read her thoughts. 'We do all appreciate you letting us film here, especially with this competition coming up. Somebody told me your good news, congratulations!' She looked at her watch, which was a child's one with a picture of Scooby Doo on the face. 'I must be on my way, only came in for a packet of Revels.' She smiled conspiratorially. 'Helps while away the hours. It's not as glamorous as everyone thinks!'

'You should try telling that to the rest of the village!' Clementine laughed. Pam chuckled.

'Well, it's been very nice to meet you . . .' She looked questioningly at Clementine.

'Clementine,' she answered. 'Clementine Standington-Fulthrope.'

'And I'm Brenda Briggs,' Brenda added. She glanced at the packet of sweets in Pam's hand. 'Have those on the house.'

Pam looked delighted. 'That really is very kind of you.' She dug around in her handbag for something and produced a slightly bent business card. She gave it to Clementine. *Pam Viner, freelance*, said the swirly writing across it. 'Take that, it's got my number on it. Do give me a call if you have any worries or concerns about anything, and I'll make sure they're sorted out. I do know how film crews can seem like an imposition sometimes, but I want to assure you that we'll do all we can to make sure there'll be no disruption.'

'That's very kind of you,' said Clementine, pleasantly surprised.

Pam's eyes twinkled again. 'A happy village makes for a happy film set! Anyway. I'm sure I'll see you both around. Goodbye for now.'

The shop bell tinkled as the door open and closed again. Brenda let out a disappointed huff as a car engine started up and drove away.

'Bit plain, wasn't she? I thought she'd be in some kind of swanky power suit, her hair and make-up all done. She looked well, rather *ordinary*.'

'Ordinary is good,' Clementine replied briskly. Someone like Pam Viner could be a trump card to keep relations between the film crew and village as problem-free as possible. Pam seemed like one of them, and was just what they needed.

Chapter 11

Friday was the day of the eagerly anticipated welcome party at the Jolly Boot. All week Calypso had been haring round like a mad thing, making sure all was going to plan. Seraphina Inc. had provided a generous budget, and between her, Jack and Beryl they had made sure every penny was well spent.

There was a great feeling of expectant excitement in the village. Bar the odd lorry or people carrier, they hadn't heard a peep out of the film crew since they'd been holed up at Braithwaite Hall. Everyone was looking forward to a knees-up, and meeting the cast and crew. The one question on everyone's lips was, would Rafe Wolfe turn up?

At Clanfield Hall, Frances knocked on her husband's study door. As well as spending many hours a day in their respective studies, the couple also had separate bedrooms. Ambrose had developed prostate problems some years back, and told Frances he didn't want to disturb her in the night. Frances had suspected it was more of a pride thing and that he didn't want to admit to growing old, but Ambrose had been so insistent, she hadn't pushed it. Of course, it had been difficult for her. She still had her needs. Despite Ambrose's growing crabbiness, Frances still found her noble-looking husband attractive. By contrast she felt Ambrose hadn't looked at her that way in years. Sometimes Frances wondered why she bothered making the effort.

She knocked again.

'Enter!'

Frances pushed the door open and went in. Old *Racing Posts* and *Daily Telegraphs* littered the floor, while the dark green walls were filled with watercolours of the Fraser family's favourite hunting horses and gun dogs from over the centuries. Ambrose looked up from his chair by the fireplace. Sailor was at his feet dozing happily. 'Yes, Frances, what is it?'

She went and sat in the other chair, but not before having to move a pile of spent cartridges from Ambrose's recent shooting trip. 'Why do you keep these stupid things?' she complained. Ambrose shot her a look over his Lester Piggott autobiography but didn't say anything.

'The Jolly Boot are holding a welcome party tonight for the film people.' Frances told him. 'Do you fancy going? It would be good to introduce ourselves, especially as they're going to be coming here.'

'Do I have to stand by the bar making bloody silly conversation all night?'

'It's a welcome party, Ambrose. That's the whole point.'

'Harrumph!' he said and disappeared behind his book again.

Frances stared in frustration at her husband. 'I take it that's a no?'

He growled in response. Frances stood up and left the room silently, before she said anything she'd regret. They never went out any more! Privately, she'd been astounded Ambrose had agreed to let them film at Clanfield in the first place, but she knew beneath the bluster the plight of Churchminster had affected him.

Back in her own study, she walked over to one of the sash windows. The great expanse of the Clanfield estate stretched out before her. Frances cast her mind back to the day she'd moved in, as a young impressionable 20-year old. Her parents had been delighted at the match, even though Ambrose was twenty years her senior, and Frances had shared their enthusiasm. Ambrose had been romantic back then; Frances smiled as she remembered how he'd proposed to her. On one of their many walks round the estate when they'd first started courting, Ambrose had called his favourite gun dog, Trigger, to heel, got a ring out of a box he'd put on Trigger's collar, and gone down on one knee to ask her to become his wife.

'I'll make you the happiest woman in Gloucestershire!' he'd declared.

Frances had laughed. 'Aren't you meant to say, "the happiest woman in the world?"'

Ambrose had chuckled, 'Clanfield is the world,

Frances. You've got everything here you need.'

At the time she'd believed him. She'd had such aspirations for them, for the house, the future. Yet life had slipped her by.

Where had it all started to go wrong? she wondered.

The Jolly Boot looked fantastic. In keeping with the Regency theme, it had been decked out like a seventeenth-century tavern. All the furniture had been moved out and replaced with long wooden tables, on which stone jugs of ale stood. Straw littered the floor, while Jack, Beryl and the bar staff were dressed in period dress, the men in smock shirts and breeches, the women in low-cut long dresses festooned with ribbons and other fripperies. In one corner stood a huge, succulent hog roast, slowly turning, while in another a band dressed as travelling players were setting up. A flamboyant jester complete with black-and-white face paint was busy tuning his lute strings.

The place was already filling up with villagers and film people. A glamorous gaggle of girls stood in one corner chatting to the Fox-Titts, while several burly looking men stalked in wearing bomber jackets with 'security' emblazoned across the backs. Two urban-looking young men in skinny jeans and trilby hats stood by the bar eyeing up Stacey Turner, who was making the very most of her cleavage-enhancing outfit. The ale and Dom Perignon were flowing freely.

'Calypso, you look stunning!'

Camilla couldn't keep the admiration out of her voice. Her younger sister was wearing skin-tight black leather trousers, which showed off every inch of her long legs, and a pair of gravity defying heels. Camilla looked down at her own plain black dress from Whistles. It was nice, but nothing spectacular. Maybe she should start taking a leaf out of Calypso's wardrobe.

Calypso grinned. 'They're bloody hot, though. I had to shoehorn myself into them, Christ knows how I'm going to get them off later.' She looked uncharacteristically anxious for a moment. 'It's going all right, isn't it?'

'It's fantastic!' Camilla assured her. 'I thought people might be well, a bit snotty, but I've already met the wardrobe mistress for Sophia Highforth in the queue for the loo. She was very friendly, and has offered to dress me if I'm an extra! And I've chatted to the assistant director. Pam, I think her name was. She was super nice, too.'

Freddie Fox-Titt came up, two flutes of champagne in each hand. 'Great bash, Calypso! Here, I thought you might be in need of some refreshment.'

To their surprise, Calypso turned it down. 'Thanks Freddie, but I need to keep a clear head.' Over the other side of the room, Jack Turner was trying to get her attention. 'Excuse me, chaps,' she said.

'Good lord, did I just see that?' asked Freddie. 'Your sister turning down a glass of bubbly?'

Camilla giggled. 'Calypso's taking this all very seriously. She's doing a fantastic job.'

'I'll recommend her to Tam Butler-Spinkworth for his sixtieth, he wants something with a bit of pizzazz.'

'Calypso's your woman,' said Camilla. 'I wouldn't know where to start with something like that.'

Freddie scanned the crowd. 'No Jed tonight?'

'He's coming later,' Camilla said. 'Had to work late.'

'There's another one who's putting in the hours,' said Freddie. 'Angie ran into Frances the other day and said they're super-pleased with his progress. Thrown a lot at him, but he seems to be coping well.'

'He's doing a fabulous job,' Camilla agreed. 'What with Calypso working so much as well, it does make for an empty house, though. Sometimes I feel like I'm living on my own!'

'Next time you're on your own come to the Maltings for dinner with us,' Freddie said kindly. 'You know you're welcome any time. Gives me a good opportunity to get out the fizz!'

Camilla smiled at him. 'Thanks, Freddie.'

He put his glass up to clink against hers. 'Here's to a good night.' Freddie took a sip. 'I must say, I'm worried Angie might keel over if Rafe Wolfe does turn up. She thinks he's the best thing since sliced bread!'

Jed turned up not long after, freshly showered and looking gorgeous. He attracted a few looks from the film crew, and not just the girls.

'Someone's got the hots for you!' laughed Camilla, as a short man with bleached blond hair and some kind of dog chain round his neck eyed Jed up for the umpteenth time.

Jed looked quizzical. 'What are you on about?' He turned to see the man in full ogle. A playful look crossed Jed's face and he gave his admirer a big wink. The little man looked pleased as punch.

Camilla giggled. 'Don't lead him on! You'll probably get accosted in the loos, now.'

Jed drained his pint of cider. 'Actually, I thought I might head off. I'm knackered. Will you be all right by yourself?' He'd been there an hour, which was a miracle as Jed wasn't much of a socializer. Camilla knew he'd only come down because she'd asked him.

'I'll be fine, everyone's here. Go and get your beauty sleep.' *Not that you need it*, she thought as Jed kissed her and walked off, oblivious to the admiring looks in his wake.

By 11 p.m. the party was in full swing. The cover band was fantastic, and the little dance floor was packed with villagers and film crew enjoying a boogie. Several of the minor cast members had turned up, causing great excitement amongst the female population of Churchminster. Angie Fox-Titt, buoyed up by several glasses of champagne, dragged them all up to dance when her favourite Rolling Stones song, 'Paint It Black', came on.

'What about Rafe?' Freddie asked wrily, when Angie returned bright-eyed and with a flushed face afterwards.

She flung her arms round his neck. 'Who needs Rafe when I've got you?'

Freddie looked at his wife, her maturely curvy body spilling out of an old cocktail dress she'd had for years. Her wavy chestnut hair shone in the overhead lights, mascara starting to run, accentuating her big brown eyes. Christ, he fancied her! He whispered something in her ear.

Angie threw back her head and laughed. 'I'll hold you to that when we get home, Frederick Fox-Titt!'

Meanwhile, Calypso was outside on her mobile dealing with a work call. A shipment of champagne being delivered to a house first thing tomorrow had been held up. 'When will it be there? My client is going to freak out, she's holding a brunch for sixty!' Calypso listened to the person on the other end. 'No, that *won't* do. The brunch will be halfway through by then!'

'Excuse me,' a voice said. 'Is the film party being held here?'

Calypso looked up, cross at the interruption. In the half-light she could see a tall blond man standing there. 'Yep, it's inside,' she said brusquely.

'Thank you,' the man said. He had a rich, deep voice.

Calypso nodded and turned her back on him, her mind whirring with angry clients and errant delivery drivers. She didn't need this shit tonight! 'Are you still there? Now, what the hell are we going to do?'

When Calypso re-entered the pub several minutes later, she was aware of a different atmosphere. Everything seemed much more charged, the level of conversation hushed and excited. She'd barely taken two steps before Brenda Briggs gripped her arm.

'Oh my Gawd! Have you seen? He's here!'

'Who?' asked Calypso confusedly. After much

cajoling, the problem had been sorted. Her stress levels were still soaring through the roof.

Brenda's eyes were popping out of her head so far, Calypso thought she must be suffering from an overactive thyroid. Brenda jerked her head violently in the direction of the bar. 'Him!' she whispered dramatically. 'Rafe Wolfe!'

Calypso saw a gaggle of girls, all jostling and flicking their hair. In the middle of it all stood Rafe Wolfe, as though he'd just been beamed down from a Sunset Boulevard billboard. He was at least a foot taller than his admirers, light-blond hair bleached by the sun, complexion tanned and apple-fresh. The baby-pink polo shirt and dark jeans he was wearing couldn't hide the hardness of a killer body.

Calypso was probably the only female in the pub who wasn't swooning. Even Freddie Fox-Titt was thinking what a jolly handsome fellow Rafe was. *'How predictable,'* she thought scornfully, watching the women's desperate straining faces as they tried to talk to him. Rafe Wolfe towered over them, his arms crossed. Occasionally he would lean down to listen to what someone was saying to him and nod vaguely. He might be sending every female around him crazy, but Calypso thought he looked insufferably smug.

Suddenly Rafe looked over and their eyes met. His were piercing, the colour of a summer sky on a cloudless day. The film star raised his eyebrows and smiled at Calypso, showing off a set of perfect, milk-white teeth. Calypso had an urge to laugh. He was like a walking, talking catalogue model! Across the room, Rafe looked slightly puzzled at her smirk.

'Oh my God, he's staring at you!' Camilla had appeared at her side.

'He probably smiles at all the girls like that,' said Calypso dismissively. 'Look at him lapping up the attention.'

They watched as Rafe turned back to the girls and started giving the prettiest one his undivided attention.

'Angie just got his autograph! She says he's absolutely charming,' said Camilla.

'I bet he is,' retorted Calypso. '"Absolutely charming" means sleazy and full of it. Come on, Bills, he's just like the millions of pretty boys you see in Hollywood. Bland, vain and shagging anything that moves. Remember that up-and-coming Irish actor my friend Jasmine was seeing? She caught him in her bed doing it doggie with some 17-year-old model.' Calypso had gone to an extremely cool girls' school in London and was used to running with the beautiful, in-crowd. She'd met enough famous people in her time to not share Churchminster's fever at having celebrities in their midst. Talking of which . . . 'I see Sophia Highforth's graced us with her presence.'

Camilla looked over to where a tall, slender woman was standing. She had white-blonde hair teased into waves, and a dainty, doll-like face, her beautiful features creased into concentration as she tapped away on a BlackBerry. The actress was wearing cream silk trousers and a soft pink top that simply oozed class.

A short man wearing a suit and glancing around with keen brown eyes, stood beside her proprietorially. 'You can tell she's a film star,' Camilla said in admiration. 'I wonder who that man is she's with, though? Looks very short to be a minder.'

Calypso snorted with laughter. 'As if you'd need a minder in Churchminster!'

A young man came up to them. It was Dan, Seraphina Inc.'s locations manager. 'Great party, Calypso! You've stuck to the brief brilliantly.'

Calypso looked pleased. 'Glad to be of service.'

Dan smiled widely at them, beer in hand. His cheeks were rather pink and he looked well on the way to being merry. 'I'm having a top time! Nice to let off some steam.'

'We were just wondering who that chap is with Sophia Highforth,' said Camilla.

Dan looked over and groaned. 'Gordon Goldsmith, her manager.'

'Of Goldsmith Management?' Calypso asked.

'Yup, until Gordon fell out with his brother Stevie and kicked him out of the company. They had a huge bust-up over who should look after Sophia; each one reckoned he was the first to discover her. Gordon guards her like a pit bull now, causes some right old problems on set.'

'You must have an awfully busy job, keeping everyone onside,' Camilla said sympathetically.

'Tell me about it! Though in general the locals are the pain, issuing orders about this and that. I often feel like throwing the whole bloody lot in their precious village pond.' Dan's face suddenly flushed even redder. 'Shit, I didn't mean anyone here! You've all been great to deal with.'

Camilla laughed. 'No offence taken.' Her eyes twinkled. 'Granny Clem can be a bit much, but her bark's worse than her bite. She's just super-protective about the village. Anyway, you don't have to worry about anything tonight; she's at her bridge evening.'

Dan gave a relieved smile. Just then there was a shout and the door behind the bar flew open. 'Out you!' One of the trilby-wearing men from earlier shuffled out shamefaced, while Jack followed, Stacey firmly gripped in one arm. Everyone turned to stare. 'I just caught this pair in the cellar!' he shouted furiously at Beryl.

Stacey wriggled under her dad's arm. 'We were only kissing, you saddo. For God's sake, I'm not a teenager any more. I can do what I like!'

But Jack's grip held fast. 'Not on my watch you can't.'

Depositing Stacey in the arms of her mother, he marched Trilby-Man through the pub. Everyone scattered out the way, as Jack ripped open the front door and threw the unfortunate man out. 'Don't come back until you can keep your grubby little paws off my daughter!' He shut the door and turned round, a charming landlord once more. 'Sorry about that, folks! You just all carry on having a good time.'

The room started to fill up with chatter again. In the melee, Rafe Wolfe had disappeared, much to the evident disappointment of his hangers-on. All eyes were now on a drunken Lucinda Reinard, who was chasing the jester round with his own lute, and trying to spank his bottom with it.

'Are you OK?' Camilla asked Dan kindly. The locations manager had gone rather white, as if he wasn't quite sure what the film company had taken on. Muttering his excuses, he fled outside for a cigarette.

Two hours later, and the local ale and free-flowing champagne were beginning to have an effect. Jack had gone ballistic when he'd found yet another crew member chatting up Stacey in the corridor with one hand on her bottom, promising to make her a star. 'He's got bleedin' "security" written on the back of his jacket, what's he going to do, make you head doorwoman?' he hissed, bundling Stacey into the kitchen and relegating her to washing-up duty for the rest of the night. The door slammed and Stacey defiantly stuck two fingers up after her dad. As she wobbled round, she suddenly noticed Marco, the new junior chef, standing at the oven.

'*Bon soir, mademoiselle*,' he murmured.

Stacey swayed and looked at the young Frenchman. She hadn't realized before quite how *fit* he was. 'You and me are gonna get pished, hot stuff,' she told him, and went to dig out the cooking sherry.

In the bar, things had degenerated into chaos. The whole room was filled with inebriated people talking too loudly and repeating themselves. Outside the ladies' loo one of the make-up artists was snogging Brenda Briggs's uncouth nephew from Bedlington, who'd announced to anyone who'd listen he'd come to get 'some film fanny'. Jack had tried to pull them apart, but they were stuck together like a pair of encrusted limpets, so he'd given up and gone back behind the bar. In another corner, Lucinda Reinard was now sitting behind the drums trying to play 'Paradise City' by Guns N' Roses, while the entire band had retired to the bar to do shots of flaming sambucas.

At 1 a.m., Calypso decided she'd had enough. She had to get up early to see a client. Leaving a drunken Camilla telling tales of her travels to the enraptured Fox-Titts, she wove her way out through the swinging melee.

Chapter 12

'Errol Flynn! Get back here now!' Camilla vainly tugged on the lead, but the black Labrador was on the trail of something irresistible. Nose pressed to the grass, he dragged Camilla behind him over the green, before coming to an abrupt stop at the gate to St Bartholomew's. Camilla almost went flying over it after him; when she'd mentioned to her grandmother that she planned a nice relaxing day off, this wasn't what she'd envisaged doing. Clementine was at the opening of a nearby garden centre and had asked Camilla to take Errol Flynn out for his morning walk. He'd been banned from attending public events because of 'unruly behaviour' and after ten minutes in his company, Camilla could see why.

As the dog snuffled around, Camilla stared up at the church. So much of her family's history and life were to be found between its four walls. Her great-grandparents, grandparents, and her own parents, Johnnie and Tink, had been married here. Clementine had buried Bertie here, his gravestone standing stoically under the yew tree in the corner. Camilla and both of her sisters had been christened here, and, ever since they were little, had attended Sunday service with their grandmother. The church was the heart of the village, and as well as honouring past generations, the future of new ones started here.

I wonder if we'll have our children christened here? This brief, hopeful thought gave way to a more melancholy feeling, as Camilla took in the crumbling brickwork and sagging roof, the moss-covered walls. The church was one of the most historic in the parish, and was the pride of Churchminster, but in recent years it had fallen into serious disrepair. It had been made even worse by the floods: the churchyard wall had suffered heavy subsidence and was leaning alarmingly to the left. With some effort Camilla pulled Errol Flynn away from it. Granny Clem would never forgive her if she let her beloved dog get buried under several tonnes of Cotswold stone.

'Hello, darling, is that naughty dog giving you trouble again?' Camilla turned round to see Angie Fox-Titt walking across the green towards her.

'I'm on dog-walking duty! Granny Clem's gone to that new garden centre outside Stow-on-the-Wold. She wants to pick up some new ideas for the competition.'

'Oh gosh, I'd forgotten about that. I've been run off my feet at the shop.' Angie owned Angie's Antiques, a quaint little shop on the other side of the village green.

'Business good?' asked Camilla. The shop was

another property that had been flooded, along with the Fox-Titts' house. It had been a big blow for them.

'I thought it would take for ever to get back to normal again, but it's picking up. Only a small amount of stock was destroyed, and nothing too valuable, thank God, but it does knock the wind out of one's sails.'

Camilla smiled sympathetically. 'I was just looking at the church. Poor old thing looks a shadow of its former self.'

Angie followed Camilla's gaze. 'It breaks one's heart, it really does. You know, your grandmother is convinced we're going to win this competition and restore St Bartholomew's to its former glory.'

They exchanged looks.

'Granny Clem is normally right on most things,' said Camilla, a bit too cheerily.

Angie nodded enthusiastically. 'I'm sure you're right, darling.' Her eyes travelled up again to the church. 'I just wish we could do something *now*. I can't bear to watch beloved old St Barts fall down by the day.'

Camilla looked thoughtful. 'I've got it! Why don't we put on some sort of event in the village hall? We can sell tickets and have a raffle, get people donating.'

'Camilla, what a fantastic idea!' cried Angie. 'The next Garden Party is only two days away, let's put it to everyone.'

For once, Clementine was in agreement with her fellow committee members. As well as kick-starting their fundraising again, it would give them a very big tick in the 'best community spirit' box for Britain's Best Village.

'The thing now is to decide what we actually want to do,' she told everyone.

Joyce Bellows's hand shot up. 'How about a sponsored knit-athon?'

Calypso pulled a face. 'I can't knit!'

'You won't catch me with a pair of needles,' grumbled Freddie.

Joyce sank back in her seat, looking disappointed.

'Thank you, Joyce,' said Clementine. 'I just think it's a little too *specialized*. We need something the whole village can take part in.'

'What about a poker night?' someone suggested. Clementine quickly shot them down with a look.

'Hang on, I've got an idea!' bellowed Lucinda Reinard. 'Why don't we put on some kind of talent evening? They just did one at Hero's school and it was jolly good.'

'Ooh, like *Britain's Got Talent*!' Angie piped up. 'That's my favourite show.'

Calypso was quick to agree. 'We can call it *Churchminster's Got Talent*! Granny Clem can be Simon Cowell.'

Everyone hooted with laughter, except Clementine, who looked rather perplexed. 'Simon Callow? Wasn't he that chap from *Four Weddings and a Funeral*?'

'Simon *Cowell*,' Calypso explained patiently. 'He's the head judge and he is like, totally nasty and everyone loves it! You'll make a great Simon, Granny Clem, don't worry.'

'I'd rather be me, darling, if that's all right,' Clementine told her. 'But I do like the sound of a talent show.'

'So that's that, then,' grinned Angie. 'We're going to put on our very own *Churchminster's Got Talent*!'

It was decided that Calypso and Freddie would be judges alongside Clementine, and the event would take place in four weeks' time at the village hall. Tickets went on sale for £10, and, to the Garden Party's delight, they'd all sold out within three days.

'This is going to be a night to remember!' Angie declared. She had no idea just how true her words would become.

101

Chapter 13

For the next week, it seemed that every villager was busy planning their turn for *Churchminster's Got Talent*. Even Stacey Turner decided to take part, and went off on mysterious trips in Beryl's car. For most residents, their act was a closely guarded secret, although everyone developed a pretty good idea what Jack Turner might be doing when an escapee white rabbit ran through the bar one lunchtime.

The excitement about the talent show was quickly brought to a premature halt. The skies over Churchminster turned heavy and thunderous, and, when the heavens finally opened, the rain wouldn't stop. Fat globules splattered windows, the green disappeared under sheets of water, and huge pools collected in the potholed roads. First one day passed and then a second, as the village lay drenched and despondent under the onslaught.

Everyone started to worry. At the Maltings, Freddie got the sandbags out. His wife stayed up all the second night drinking copious cups of coffee and watching the water inch up the driveway. At the Jolly Boot, which had shut during the previous floods, resulting in a huge loss of takings, Jack moved what furniture he could upstairs and sat down at the bar to wait and see if the place would come under siege again. As the rain dripped through the roof at St Bartholomew's, the Reverend darted around haplessly moving different buckets. It was like everyone's worst nightmare happening again, and they were powerless to stop it.

On the third day the village woke to yet another deluge. It was Brenda's day to clean Fairoaks, but when she didn't turn up Clementine was concerned: Brenda might be the worst housekeeper in the history of the Cotswolds, but she was always reliable. Getting in her old Range Rover, Clementine set off for the newly renamed Hollyoaks Cottage to see if things were all right. As she travelled along the Bedlington Road, she saw the fields in the distance had turned into mini lakes. Beyond them was the reservoir which had burst last time, and caused most of the problems. Clementine's lips tightened as she slowed down to avoid another flooded pothole. Things weren't looking good.

At Hollyoaks Cottage she was alarmed to see water was only inches from the front door. The gaudy new house name looked out of place in such a dismal setting. Clementine stepped over the sandbags blocking the driveway and went round the back. Seeing Brenda through the kitchen window, she knocked on the door.

A few moments later it opened. Brenda's red-rimmed eyes stared uncomprehendingly at Clementine, then her hand flew to her mouth. 'Oh Mrs S-F! What must you think of me? With all this going on, I totally forgot!'

'My dear, it doesn't matter,' Clementine said, gently guiding her over to the kitchen table. 'I really came to see how you were, and if I could do anything.'

Brenda sank down and put her face in her hands. 'We've been up all night moving sandbags,' she said in-between sobs. 'Ted's had to go to work now, and I'm sat here just watching it get closer and closer . . . I've only just had the new carpets put down. We've called the fire brigade, and they're up to their eyeballs already. I can't go through it again, I can't!'

Clementine patted Brenda's back. 'There, there.' Clementine couldn't say it was going to be all right because she just didn't know if it would be. It was a horrible feeling.

Clementine sat with Brenda until Ted came home. She tried to make conversation with the normally chatty Brenda, but the frequent silences were dominated by the *patter patter* of rain against the kitchen window. It was relentless and unforgiving.

That night few people slept easily in Churchminster, fearful of what the coming hours and day would bring. From Fairoaks to the Maltings, from the rectory to Hollyoaks Cottage, the silent prayers were all the same.

Please, if there is a God, don't let it happen again.

*   *   *

At No. 5 The Green, Camilla stirred sleepily. Jed was out of bed and standing at the window. He pulled the curtain back, and at first she didn't understand the bright light flooding into the room.

She sat up, hair mussed. 'Has the rain stopped?'

Jed was dressed in his work overalls already. 'Come and take a look.'

Camilla got out of bed and went over to the window. It was as if a fairy godmother had waved her wand over the village. The green was still sodden, but the skies above it were clear and blue. A pale yellow sun was rising steadily over the drenched landscape, which now looked shiny and new.

'Thank God for that! I really thought we were going to get flooded again. The water was inches away from the back door last night.'

Jed put his strong arms round her, keeping her warm in the morning chill. In her cotton nightie, Camilla stayed pressed against him. 'Come back to bed,' she whispered.

He looked down at her regretfully. Camilla stared at the golden flecks around his pupils that made his eyes even more mesmerizing. 'I've got tons to do today.'

Camilla untwined herself from Jed and let him go to work.

'That was a close call!' Brenda pounced on Calypso as soon as she walked in the shop. She looked tired but relieved, her hair sticking up all over the place.

Calypso smiled sympathetically. 'I know. Granny

Clem told me you'd got the sandbags out. It's all over now though.'

'Until the next time,' Brenda muttered.

'Hey, come on,' Calypso reassured her. 'Everything will be OK.'

Brenda didn't look very convinced. 'I'm sure you're right! Anyway what can I get you, lovvie?'

Calypso dropped her voice. 'Er, I'm after some tampons.'

Brenda looked apologetic. 'We're all out! The delivery let me down this week.'

Calypso groaned inwardly. She needed them *now*, bloody erratic periods. She'd come on two days early, but had luckily found a Lil-let in the bottom of one of her handbags. 'Shit, I'm going to have to drive into Bedlington now, and I've got a meeting in half an hour.'

'Hold on!' Brenda announced. 'I might have a spare box out the back.' She disappeared behind the counter, while Calypso waited hopefully. After a minute or so, Brenda reappeared holding something. 'Here we go! Thought I had one left.'

Calypso looked at the battered, dated-looking box. They weren't tampons – they were huge, unwieldy looking sanitary pads. Even worse, they seemed to have some kind of belt attached to them, which a smiling model was wearing round her waist. 'I'm not wearing those! They look like something out of the seventies!' Calypso exclaimed.

Brenda looked at the box. 'You're right! The sell-by date was March 1978. I'm sure they'll be OK, though.'

'Jesus!' Calypso looked down at the offending item. She had no choice. Opening her purse, she counted the money out on to the counter. At least the price tag was only 27p.

'You young girls don't know how lucky you are!' Brenda called after her. 'In my day it was like having a brick between me legs!'

Reeling from the unpleasant image of Brenda's gusset, Calypso fled the shop. She had just crossed the village green when a sleek sports car pulled up beside her. She hesitated for a moment, and, thinking the driver might need directions, leant down to the passenger window.

A man sat in the driver's seat, wearing a pair of aviator sunglasses. Calypso was just thinking he looked familiar when he pulled them off and smiled. The periwinkle blue eyes were unmistakeable. 'Hello there,' said Rafe Wolfe.

Calypso couldn't keep the surprise off her face. What was Rafe Wolfe doing here? She regained her composure. 'Driver got a day off?' she asked acerbically.

Rafe Wolfe laughed. 'I prefer to drive myself.' He was wearing an open-necked blue shirt, a cashmere jumper chucked on the passenger seat.

All he needs now is a Labrador puppy, thought Calypso.

Rafe cocked his head, trying to read her expression. 'Sorry, am I missing something? Every time we meet you seem to be having a private joke at my expense.'

Calypso raised an eyebrow. 'I don't recall meeting you before.'

His eyes travelled down to the box in her hands. Calypso wanted the ground to swallow her up.

'They're for my sister,' she said quickly, holding the box behind her back. 'So how can I help you?'

Rafe smiled. 'Do you play tennis?'

'Gave it up when I discovered fags and boys. Why?'

'I was wondering if you'd like to play a game with me.'

Tennis! Calypso tried to keep a straight face. Was this guy for real? 'Thanks, but I don't make a habit of going round playing ball sports with strange men.'

Rafe held her gaze. 'Coffee, then.'

'Haven't you got a girlfriend?' Calypso asked, before immediately regretting it. He probably thought she was a groupie.

'Had,' he corrected her. A smile hovered on the corner of his mouth.

Calypso straightened up. 'Sorry, I only drink tea. If you're that desperate I'm sure there're plenty of other coffee lovers out there.'

A look of disappointment crossed Rafe's face, but he smiled. 'Shame. Well, if you ever fancy it . . .'

He reached across and gave Calypso a card. 'That's my personal mobile number.' With that, the passenger window slid up again and the car glided off.

'Can you believe it? Handing me his card like I was some kind of minion. He probably thinks all us "simple country folk". . .' Calypso put on a comedy burr. '". . . are gagging for a piece of him". And can you believe he asked me to play *tennis* with him? I mean, how random is that? Does he think we all live in an episode of *Brideshead Revisited*, or something?'

'He still asked you out, Calypso!' said Camilla.

They were sitting round the kitchen table with cups of tea and Calypso had just relayed her experience.

'Who's asked Calypso out?' said a voice in the doorway.

Camilla spun round. 'Jed! I didn't expect you back. Is everything all right?'

He came over and kissed the top of her head. 'I had an hour off for once. Thought I'd come back for lunch.'

'Calypso's just been asked out by Rafe Wolfe!' Camilla said. 'He drove past her in his sports car.'

Jed raised an amused eyebrow. 'Ay-up. We'll be rolling out the red carpet for you, next.'

Camilla giggled.

'Oh shut up,' said Calypso. 'He is *so* not my type.'

'What, good-looking, famous and millions in the bank?' Jed asked wrily.

'I'm not into all that shit,' Calypso retorted.

Jed opened the fridge and brought out a plate of ham. 'If you say so.'

Calypso rolled her eyes at him. 'You're *so* annoying.'

'That film lot got to Clanfield today. It's bedlam up there,' said Jed, as he set about making a sandwich. Camilla got up to help him.

'Did you see any of the actors?' she asked, getting the butter out. 'Sophia Highforth was at the welcome party, she looked jolly glamorous.'

Jed looked nonplussed. 'Don't know who she is. I think it's just the crew setting up.'

Calypso stood up and tossed aside the paper she'd

started reading. 'I'm going back to work, see you guys later.'

The door slammed shut behind her, making Camilla wince. She looked at Jed's sandwich. 'Do you want anything else with that?'

'You,' he replied, with a serious expression on his face.

Camilla raised a teasing eyebrow. 'Oh really?'

'Come here,' he said, and sweeping her up in his arms, carried Camilla up the narrow staircase to their bedroom. He put her down on the bed, peeled off her clothes and made gentle love to her, their bodies moving together with a comforting familiarity.

Afterwards, they lay entwined, Camilla in post-coital bliss. 'Hey,' she said softly. 'Shouldn't you be thinking about going back to work?'

He hesitated. 'I was just thinking.'

'Thinking about what?' Camilla propped herself up on one shoulder to look at him.

'Well, maybe we could set up a bank account for the future. I could start paying some of my wages in. You know, for our kids, so they'd have a good start in life. Better than I had, anyway.'

'I think that's a lovely idea,' she said, quite taken aback. 'I can get something set up, and . . .'

'No.' Jed stopped her, caressing her collarbone. 'I know your parents would help us out, and I appreciate their generosity. I just want to make sure it's me looking after our children, not your family. Does that make sense? Of course, it won't be anything grand . . .'

Camilla felt a lump in her throat. 'They won't need anything grand,' she whispered. 'Neither do I.'

Jed smiled his crooked smile, making her heart do a somersault. 'Let's have another practice before I go back to work.'

Chapter 14

Camilla was due at the travel agent's in a few hours, and as she emerged from the shower felt that all-too-familiar feeling of dread creeping into her stomach at the thought of another afternoon being treated like a general dogsbody. She sighed and hung her damp towel on the back of the door. *At least I can make a good cup of tea*, she thought self-deprecatingly.

The mid-morning sun streamed in through the window. Camilla's heart lifted: it was a beautiful day. She went to open the window and stepped back, wondering what to wear. She was still floating on air from her conversation with Jed about trying for a family. While her friends had been settling down and producing babies by the dozen, Camilla had never pressed Jed. She hadn't wanted to scare him off, and it seemed her tactics were paying off.

We're going to have a baby!

Camilla wondered if they should start thinking about converting the spare room into a nursery. It was a sweet little room that looked out on to the apples trees in the back garden. A perfect nurturing environment. Camilla smiled at herself, she was getting carried away. Still, it wouldn't do any harm to start planning . . .

Lost in happy thoughts, she absent-mindedly looked down at her bikini line. God, it was getting rather overgrown; she must book in for a wax at the beauty salon in Bedlington. Calypso had been urging her for months to get a Brazilian – 'Big muffs are *so* 1970s' – but Camilla didn't know if she could bear the pain.

Camilla noticed an ingrown hair. *Definitely* time to get a wax. Especially with the amount of action she was getting at the moment. It wasn't fair on poor Jed, although, to be honest, it never seemed to put him off. Camilla squeezed the offending hair, and to her great satisfaction it popped free. Camilla looked round for her tweezers, which were on the dressing-room table. She was in the process of pulling out the offending hair, when she suddenly got the feeling she wasn't alone.

Slowly, afraid of what she might find, Camilla raised her head and looked out of the window.

Twenty-six pairs of eyes looked back.

'Oh my God!' she screamed. Rushing over, she wrenched the curtains shut.

Outside, the driver of the double-decker bus taking extras to the film set re-started his stalled engine and drove off.

At Clanfield Hall, Frances gazed out of her own bed-room window at the melee below. She'd known that it was a big production, but she had had no idea just how many *people* there would be. Girls in black with clipboards, men in overalls lugging toolboxes, white vans lined up side by side, from which a startling array of things – from lighting equipment to a life-sized pair of stocks – were being carried out. Frances found it all rather fascinating, but was equally apprehensive about Ambrose's reaction when he returned from visiting his sister in Scotland – to find his estate taken over by men shouting into megaphones and gaggles of filthy fake peasants with pustules and brown teeth. Even more so when he had to get through the paparazzi who had clustered at the front gates, hoping to get an off-guard shot of one of the cast.

For a moment Frances questioned her judgement in letting the film crew in. She wondered if her longing for a change of routine had influenced her decision. Seraphina Inc. were taking over the little-used east wing of the house, and the shoot was scheduled to last three weeks. The Frasers' fee for filming was going straight to the village fund, which would add much needed cash to the kitty.

Frances was roused from her thoughts by her mobile ringing. It was probably Harriet, for whom Frances had left a voicemail earlier. She picked it up and was surprised that rather than her daughter's number, the word 'call' was flashing up on the screen.

Maybe she's calling from work, Frances thought. She pressed the answer button. 'Darling?'

There was a chuckle down the phone. 'That's a helluva of a greeting.'

'Devon! Is that you?' Frances sat down in the chair heavily. Her hands started shaking.

The familiar cockney voice. 'The one and only, princess. How yer doin'?'

'Fine, thank you,' she replied awkwardly. Instinctively Frances ran her hand over her chignon to compose herself.

There was a pause. 'What's wrong, Frannie?' Devon Cornwall asked. 'You don't sound very pleased to hear from me.'

'Oh I am! You just caught me off guard.' Frances couldn't keep the smile out of her voice. 'Oh, Devon, it really is marvellous to hear from you!'

Another throaty chuckle. 'That's more like it. You know, I'm sitting here on some rich git's yacht having a bit of chill time, and you came into my mind. So I said to myself: "Sod it, Devon, get on the old dog and bone and give the lady a tinkle."'

Frances laughed. 'Where *are* you?'

'Somewhere bloody hot in the middle of the Indian Ocean. Don't ask me where, I've done eight countries in as many days.'

'I assume the tour is going well, then?'

'Going a blinder, but I don't want to talk all about me, princess. Tell me what you've been up to, and all the Churchminster news.'

They chatted for several minutes and Frances filled him in on the Britain's Best Village competition and the film.

Devon sounded impressed. 'Blimey, it's all going on there. Makes me quite nostalgic for the place.'

There was another pause, in which Frances didn't quite know what to say.

'Anyway, I'd better shoot. I'm on stage later.'

Frances was dismayed at the disappointment she felt. 'Of course, I won't keep you. It was lovely to hear from you.'

'You too, princess. I miss that lovely Joanna Lumley voice of yours. Take good care of yourself.'

She could hear a motor being started in the background. Frances hesitated. 'Devon, was there any particular reason . . .'

'I called? No Frannie, I was just thinking about you. Wanted to say hi.' His voice changed. 'I do miss you, you know.'

Frances felt a lump in her throat and swallowed it down. 'Well, I better let you go! It sounds very busy there.'

He reverted back to his normal chipper self. 'It's always busy in Devon world. See ya, Frannie. It's been really good to catch up.'

'You too, Devon.'

Frances ended the call and sat motionless in the chair. Her hands wouldn't stop shaking. It was so silly the effect Devon still had on her, but she couldn't help it. Frances leaned back and looked up at the ceiling. She wasn't sure if she was pleased or frustrated he'd phoned. Had Devon really only called to say hello?

Her mobile rang again, startling her. This time it was her daughter, Harriet. 'Hello, darling.'

'Mummy, are you OK? You sound a bit out of breath.'

'I've just been rushing around,' Frances lied.

'Oh, all right then.' Her daughter sounded as cheery as ever. 'I just phoned to see how things are going with the film! It's awfully exciting.'

'Touch wood, quite smoothly,' Frances told her. At that moment there was a loud crash outside.

'Oh, heavens, I'll call you back!' she exclaimed and ran over to the open window. Mrs Bantry had come rushing out the front door at the same time. An empty props truck had reversed into the stone statue of a lurcher, toppling it over.

Frances watched as her housekeeper went over to the fallen statue. 'Mrs Bantry, please don't bother yourself . . .'

'Ma, don't you dare pick that up!' Jed had suddenly materialized in his overalls, a stern look on his face. He easily righted the stone dog, before putting a tender hand on his mum's shoulder. 'I've told you not to lift anything. You know your back's playing up,'

The driver stuck his head out the window, looking relieved. 'No harm done, then?'

Jed looked over at him. 'No, mate, but I'd watch your driving in future. And next time, don't get my ma here to pick up your mess.'

'Sorry, mate,' the driver muttered, looking contrite. He drove off at a more sensible pace, and Frances watched Jed kiss his mother on the cheek, before striding back to work. Her phone started ringing again.

'Hello? No darling, everything's OK. We just had a small commotion . . .'

Chapter 15

May arrived in the village, bringing with it longer, warmer evenings and renewed hope. Everyone who had entered *Churchminster's Got Talent* was still practising madly. At the Jolly Boot one lunchtime, the music coming from Stacey's bedroom was so loud that Jack went to tell her to turn it down. 'Stace!' He banged on the door. Brittle pop music blasted from within. Suddenly, there was a large 'thump' followed by a shout and muffled expletives. 'Stacey!' Jack was getting alarmed. 'Are you all right?' He tried the door, but it was locked.

A few moments later the music went off and a merciful quiet descended over the building. Jack could hear cross stomping across the room, and then the bedroom door opened. Even though it was gone midday, Stacey was still wearing her dressing gown and looked extremely displeased at being disturbed. 'You don't have to kick the door in!'

'Your bleeding music is deafening my punters!' Jack said crossly. 'Keep it down.'

Stacey pulled a sulky face. 'Whatever. Most of them are probably too deaf to hear it, anyway.'

Jack looked over his daughter's shoulder. Her bedroom looked more like a tart's boudoir than ever, with various leopard-print clothes lying scattered around, and a pink feather boa draped across the top of her wardrobe. A heavy, exotic scent hung in the air. 'What's going on in here, anyway? Why are you still in your dressing gown in the middle of the day?'

Stacey pulled the door shut to a crack and glared through it belligerently. 'Keep your beak out, Dad! This is, like, a *total* invasion of my privacy.'

Jack sighed and gave up. She was getting more like her mother every day. 'Just keep it down,' he warned. Stacey rolled her eyes dismissively. At the top of the stairway, he stopped and looked back. 'So you're busy, then?'

Stacey stuck her head out the door. 'Duh, like yeah!'

'Fine,' he said nonchalantly. 'I'll tell Rafe Wolfe you don't want to serve him, then. He's in the bar.'

Stacey's eyes lit up like Christmas lights. 'Oh my God, he's here? Wait, I'm going to get changed! Who's he with?'

'Oh, Mother Theresa, Princess Di,' Jack replied. 'I think Freddie Mercury's here, too.'

A look of confusion entered Stacey's face, until she realized her dad was winding her up. She narrowed kohl-rimmed eyes. 'Oh *grow* up! That is so immature.'

119

The bedroom door slammed shut. Chuckling, Jack went back down the stairs to serve his customers.

The next day the *Daily Mercy*, a gossipy national newspaper, printed a double-page spread about the Britain's Best Village competition. In it, they assessed each of the four finalists and their good and bad points, with a final score out of ten. Clementine was furious to see that Churchminster had only scored four, the lowest by far. She was particularly incensed to hear it described as a *'country village lacking in rural charm'* and see that they had been marked down by the *'unsightly hole in the churchyard wall'*. There was an inordinate amount of detail, and none of it was good. To add salt to the wound, Maplethorpe had come out top with nine and a half out of ten, with a quote from Veronica Stockard-Manning that: *'even perfection can be improved on'*. Clementine wondered crossly why the journalist hadn't approached her; the whole article was biased towards Maplethorpe. Clementine sat back in her study chair, convinced that that ghastly Stockard-Manning woman was behind it all. She knew just how devious she could be. As the old, painful memories came rushing back, her jaw tightened with resolve.

Churchminster was not a village to be underestimated. This was war.

The speed of the Garden Party organized at Fairoaks that night surprised even those who knew Clementine. One minute Calypso was knee-deep in paperwork in her office, the next she had been ordered by her grandmother to photocopy reams of new Garden Party literature. Camilla was commandeered to go and buy supplies of Pimms and strawberries, and hunt down fresh mint from the garden. It was here that Calypso found her shortly after six o'clock, sunlight still dancing down on the lawns.

'What *are* you doing?' Calypso asked, as she saw Camilla's bottom sticking out of a bush by the side of the path. Camilla reversed out and stood up, her face rather red. She had a bunch of green leaves in her hand.

'Getting mint for the Pimms,' she puffed. 'It's in a terribly awkward place. That bush nearly had my eye out!'

Calypso reached over and picked something out of her sister's hair. 'Greenfly. What's the mega-urgency about this meeting tonight? We've got one on Sunday, anyway.'

'I'm in the dark as much as you are,' said Camilla. 'But Granny Clem has definitely got a bee in her bonnet about something.'

There was an air of tension in the drawing room as they gathered sometime later. Even Errol Flynn was subdued, lying under the chaise longue with just his paws visible.

Clementine strode into the room, carrying a large pile of A4 papers. She dumped them on a table and held up the newspaper, which had been on the top. It was that day's *Daily Mercy*. 'Have you all seen this?' she announced.

'Bloody outrage!' said Freddie Fox-Titt indignantly,

and heads nodded around him in agreement.

'How did they get all that *stuff*?' someone else said.

'Maybe it's one of those reporters who've been hanging round trying to get on the film set,' offered Angie. 'They can't get much on the actors so they've decided to turn the spotlight on us instead!'

Clementine frowned. 'It could well be. From now on, we all need to be extra vigilant!' Her voice rose an octave. 'May I remind you that this is not just a competition, this is our livelihood! Our dignity and pride is at stake here, and *we* need to fight to keep it!'

Camilla and Calypso exchanged glances. Their grandmother was seriously het up.

'Serious times call for serious action,' continued Clementine. 'Therefore I would like you all to give up your weekend to help round the village.'

Calypso pulled a face. It was meant to be her first lie-in for weeks!

'We've got friends coming to stay,' protested Lucinda Reinard.

'Good, they can join in as well,' replied Clementine crisply. She started handing out the printed sheets. 'I have devised a list of duties for each of you. We start at 9 a.m. on Saturday and work through until 6 p.m., with no more than forty-five minutes for lunch.'

'There's a hell of a lot here, Clementine!' said Freddie in alarm, scanning down the two-page list. His wife put a hand on his sleeve.

'Leave it, Freds,' she murmured gently.

'I know I'm asking a lot, but the future of this village is at stake,' Clementine said. 'I expect nothing less than a hundred per cent from all of you from now on, with none of this silly film business getting in the way. Do I make myself clear?'

Heads nodded meekly.

'Good,' said Clementine. She continued: 'There is no way we are going to let Maplethorpe and that disgusting Stockard-Manning woman win. No way on earth!'

She turned and exited the room abruptly.

'Another glass of Pimms, anyone?' Freddie halfheartedly asked, but the atmosphere was rather flat.

'What on earth is wrong with Granny Clem?' Calypso muttered to her sister. 'I thought her head was going to start spinning round.'

'I don't know,' said Camilla. 'But whatever it is, I'm sure it's got something to do with that Veronica woman. I've never heard her talk about a person with such fury.'

Chapter 16

Saturday morning dawned, blue and glorious. At No. 5 The Green, Camilla knocked on her sister's bedroom door with a mug of tea. 'Calypso? Are you awake?'

There was a muffled noise. Camilla pushed the door open and went in. The room looked like a tumble dryer had exploded mid-cycle: clothes were scattered over the floor, skimpy bras hung off the radiator, and a Mount-Everest-sized pile of shoes was spilling out of the open wardrobe. In the middle of it all Calypso lay face down in bed, her legs sticking out from under the duvet.

After a few seconds she groaned and pushed herself up. As usual she'd slept naked. Her generous breasts, still somehow defying the laws of gravity, sat perkily on her chest. Mascara clotted around her eyes, while dirty blonde hair tangled down her back and shoulders.

Not for the first time Camilla marvelled at her sister's raw sexiness. Some people just had *it*.

Calypso squinted through one eye. Bright sunlight

was streaming through the carelessly pulled curtains. 'What time is it?'

'Quarter past eight.'

Camilla moved a pile of magazines off the over-crowded bedside table and put the mug down.

Calypso gingerly took a sip and then flopped back down on the pillows. 'I'm bloody knackered! I can't believe Granny Clem is making us do this.'

'What time did you get in last night?' Camilla asked, sitting down on the edge of the bed.

'After two. I was doing this Roman-themed evening in Cheltenham and the hostess was really uptight, made me stay until everyone had gone. I feel like never going out again.'

'How about I cook us all a nice dinner tonight?' Camilla suggested. 'We can eat in the garden.'

'That would be a-mazing. I won't be fit for anything else after this.'

Camilla stood up, smiling. 'I'm making us all break-fast, come down when you're ready.' She went to tackle the vast amount of bacon and eggs in the kitchen.

It was an unusually hot day, even for May, and by midday the temperature was in the eighties. Above the village green the blue skies soared endlessly, while punters sat in the Jolly Boot's beer garden drinking jugs of Pimms and making the most of the weather.

In the farthest corner by the church, Calypso put down the bin liner and wiped the sweat off her face. Christ, it was boiling! At least she'd get a good tan in this weather. Her clothes had been coming off at various intervals during the morning, and now she wore only the shortest of denim shorts and a brightly coloured bikini top. Her long hair was scraped back in a ponytail, her eyes protected by a huge pair of Chanel sunglasses. Several silver necklaces hung around her neck, while a bejewelled belly chain caressed her slim hips. Only Calypso could make litter-picking duty look like a fashion shoot.

'Calypso!' a voice called out. Wiping another bead of sweat off her forehead she turned round. Her grandmother was walking towards her, a hideous straw hat in one hand. 'Darling, wear this in case you get sunstroke.'

Clementine tried to put it on her head and Calypso blanched. It reeked of mothballs. 'I'm fine!' she protested. 'I put sun cream on.'

Her grandmother eyeballed her. 'What factor?'

'Thirty,' Calypso lied. 'Honestly, I don't need the hat. Go and give it to Camilla, you know how she suffers in the heat.'

Clementine looked across the green, where Camilla was peeling an old poster off one of the trees. 'Maybe you're right.' Her eyes suddenly travelled down to Calypso's bare midriff. They widened in alarm. 'Don't move, you've got some sort of monstrous insect on your stomach!'

Calypso froze: she hated any kind of creepy-crawly. Camilla had had to remove a spider from the shower for her only that morning. 'Shit, what is it? Get it off me!'

Clementine started flapping at Calypso's body with

126

the sunhat. 'Get off, you ghastly thing! It seems to be stuck there!'

Calypso steeled herself to look down. Her face relaxed. 'Chill your boots, it's only a tattoo!'

Clementine peered closely at the black scorpion just above Calypso's left hip. She looked up at her youngest granddaughter reproachfully. 'Oh, darling, how could you! It looks dreadfully common.'

Calypso sighed. 'It's no big deal, loads of people have got them.'

Clementine wasn't placated. 'Has your mother seen this? No doubt she'll have something to say.'

'Of course she has, I've had it for years! Granny Clem, I am an adult, you know,' Calypso pointed out. 'I can do what I want with my body.'

Clementine was completely unimpressed. Young people! 'Well, if you can stop mutilating your body for long enough I'll leave you to get on.' She shook her head. 'Whatever next, one of those dreadful genital piercings?'

Calypso smiled sweetly at her grandmother. 'Oh, for heavens sake! I don't want to hear any more,' huffed Clementine, and she went off in search of some decent conversation with Camilla.

Calypso had just filled her second bin bag when a car pulled up beside her. It was long and sleek with blacked-out windows. The driver's side window rolled down. Calypso pulled up her sunglasses and squinted into the gloom of the car, before realizing that, yet again, the driver was Rafe Wolfe.

'Hard at work?' he asked pleasantly. He had

company this time: a dazzling blonde woman sitting in the passenger seat, whom Calypso recognized as Sophia Highforth.

Sophia flashed a smile from under her huge Victoria Beckam-esque sunglasses.

'We're on our way to filming, there's a weekend shoot,' Rafe said. He was wearing an immaculate white shirt that showcased his tan.

'Oh, right,' replied Calypso, wondering if she was meant to be impressed. A trickle of sweat was falling between her breasts and down to her flat stomach. Rafe glanced at it momentarily, before looking up. 'Do you need any help?'

Calypso wasn't sure if she'd heard correctly. 'Help?' she repeated.

Rafe waved an arm over the green. 'With this. I hear Churchminster has got into the final of Britain's Best Village. It must be very exciting for you all.'

Calypso raised a sardonic eyebrow. 'Thanks, but I don't think picking up empty Coke cans and crisp packets comes under the remit of a world famous film star.'

He held her gaze. 'I mean it, I'd like to help.'

'Rafe.' Sophia pulled on his sleeve subtly. 'We're meant to be in make-up by now.'

Calypso shot Rafe a look. 'Yeah well, if you fancy giving up your Sunday to weed the graveyard . . .' *That'll call his bluff,* she thought satisfactorily.

Rafe grinned at her. 'I might take you up on that.'

'Oh, hello there!' It was Camilla, looking rather hot and flustered in an old Laura Ashley summer dress.

She had seen the car stop, and, guessing correctly who was inside, rushed over.

Rafe extended a tanned, smooth hand. 'How do you do? I'm Rafe Wolfe.'

Camilla shook it excitedly. 'I'm Camilla, Calypso's older sister.'

'I can see the family resemblance. Your parents must be delighted to have such stunning daughters.'

Camilla looked thrilled at the compliment, but Calypso rolled her eyes. *Talk about cheesy!*

'*Rafe.*' This time Sophia didn't bother to hide her impatience.

'What's this? A mothers meeting?' This time it was Jed, who'd been hard at work moving fallen stones from the churchyard wall. He was stripped to the waist, his body covered in a fine sheen of sweat. Even though Camilla's nose and shoulders had turned bright pink, Jed's pale skin had somehow remained untouched by the sun. He looked like one of the beautiful marble statues that adorned the grounds of Clanfield Hall.

Sophia suddenly seemed in no hurry to go. She leaned across Rafe and extended a manicured hand. 'Hello there, I'm Sophia Highforth.'

Her nails were expertly manicured and painted a pale pink. Camilla blushed and hid her own bitten ones behind her back.

Jed stepped forward and took her hand. 'Jed,' he said.

'I haven't seen you round here before,' Sophia smiled. She had huge soft blue eyes, like a baby's.

'I've been working a lot. Up at the Hall.'

One of Sophia's groomed eyebrows shot up. 'Clanfield Hall? What a coincidence, we're filming up there! You must come and have afternoon tea in my Winnebago.'

There was a slightly awkward pause. Rafe looked at his watch. 'We'd better get going.' He smiled at Calypso. 'Might see you tomorrow, then.'

'You might,' replied Calypso shortly.

'Don't forget to come and see me, Jed!' Sophia called. 'I need someone to show me round.'

Rafe revved the engine and the car roared off. Calypso's mobile started ringing and, digging it out of her back pocket, she wandered off to take the call, leaving Jed and Camilla alone.

Camilla shot Jed an amused glance. 'So, Sophia Highforth wants to have tea with you!'

'I don't think she'd be so keen if she saw me covered in pigs' muck, cleaning out the sties,' he smiled.

'Or fast asleep on the sofa, cupping your balls.'

He shot her a cheeky look. 'I only do it when you won't cup them for me.'

'Bloody cheek!' she retorted, laughing.

He kissed her on the lips. 'See you later. Maybe I'll even get lucky in the ball-cupping department.'

'Maybe, if you play your cards right.'

He strode off grinning, as Calypso finished her call. Camilla walked over to her. 'Do you think Rafe *will* turn up tomorrow?' she asked.

'Who cares?' said Calypso airily. She mimicked Sophia's gushing tones. 'You *must* come and have afternoon tea in my Winnebago!'

They both giggled.

'Tell you what, sis,' Calypso said. 'Jed's lucky to have someone like you. Most of my friends would go mental if a film star asked their boyfriend out. Mind you, most of them are highly strung nutcases.'

'I think it's quite a compliment, actually!' Camilla said.

Calypso raised an eyebrow. 'Have you never seen *Notting Hill*?' Her mobile started ringing again. 'Oh God, now what?' She turned and threw an affectionate look at Camilla over her shoulder. 'I was only teasing you about *Notting Hill*, you know!'

'Ha ha,' said Camilla, for some reason not finding it very funny.

Chapter 17

The next morning Calypso was back in the graveyard on her hands and knees. *It's like bloody* Groundhog Day, she thought grumpily. The protective gloves Clementine had given her were heavy and hot, adding to her discomfort. She was also nursing a hangover, as she and Camilla had sat up late in the garden drinking rather more rosé wine than was good for them. It was just as hot today, and Calypso's headache was showing no sign of abating.

'Ow, shit!' she yelped, as a stinging nettle brushed her leg. Red welts started to spring up immediately. Calypso looked in vain for a dock leaf, to calm the inflammation, and decided she was best off with aspirin and ice-cold Lucozade from the village shop.

Twenty minutes later, sitting in the shade of a tree in the graveyard, she was starting to revive. She stretched her legs out from under the tree, feeling the heat of the sun beat down on them.

Then she rolled a cigarette, lit it, and leant back

against the trunk. The smoke floated off lazily into the summer's day. She couldn't remember the last time she'd sat still for so long. Scene Events was going better than she had ever imagined, but there was a price to pay. She was feeling utterly exhausted, and a proper night's sleep was still a long way off in the future.

I need a holiday. Or some fun. Or something, Calypso thought, taking another drag. Her eyes were getting heavy and she let them close. She could really just go to sleep now . . .

'There's no point staying out of the sun if you're going to smoke those things,' a well-cultivated voice suddenly said from above.

Calypso blinked and looked up. To her utter astonishment, Rafe Wolfe was standing there. As usual he looked like he'd stepped out of a Ralph Lauren advert, in cargo shorts and a striped polo shirt that hugged his biceps. Expensive-looking loafers adorned his feet.

Calypso defiantly took another drag and blew it out towards him. 'No tennis today?'

Rafe grinned and squatted down beside her. She caught a waft of lemony aftershave. 'I've heard weed-killing is all the rage round here,' he said.

Up close, Rafe was as annoyingly perfect. His complexion was smooth, the contours of his jaw and nose straight and perfect. Straight from the stable of pin-up movie stars.

If you like that sort of thing, Calypso told herself. She preferred her men – and women – more dishevelled and dirty. She stubbed her cigarette out and flicked it

133

into the open bin bag lying a few feet away. 'So you think you're up to it? I warn you it's pretty physical activity.'

Rafe looked down at his strong arms, no doubt honed by hours in the gym with a personal trainer. 'I think I'm up to it.'

He offered her his arm and pulled her easily to her feet. For a moment he stood there, still holding her. Calypso felt his dry warm hand on her skin. She stepped away and threw him an empty bin bag. 'I'm assuming you know the difference between a flower and a weed.'

Rafe caught the bag with one hand. 'Hey, I'm a country boy. Born and bred.' He held his hands up at her sceptical expression. 'I'm serious! I was brought up in Cambridgeshire. In a place called Wincombe Hall. My family have been there for centuries.'

'Am I meant to be impressed?'

Rafe looked at Calypso evenly. 'No, I was just telling you about myself. Isn't that what people do when they meet each other?'

Calypso felt a stab of embarrassment and changed the subject. 'Better get on with it, then.'

She chucked him a pair of Granny Clem's old gardening gloves, which he took without a murmur.

'Right, where do you want me to start?'

Calypso looked at a particularly nasty patch of nettles she'd been putting off tackling. 'They need pulling up.'

'No probs.' Rafe strode over and immediately got to work. Calypso watched him tear weeds out of the ground for a few moments. She didn't know if she was impressed or annoyed that Rafe had put his money where his mouth was. It wasn't every day you saw a world-famous film star grappling with stinging nettles in your local graveyard.

For the rest of the morning she tried to thwart Rafe's attempts at being friendly, but he was so persistent that in the end, she gave up.

'Nosey, aren't you?' she remarked, only half-exasperated, when he asked her yet another question about herself. She'd spent the previous hour telling him about her family, her time in New York, and Scene Events.

They were sitting on the church wall having another break. Calypso was so hot she had tied her vest in a knot under her breasts to make an impromptu crop top. Despite a hard hour's work Rafe had hardly broken a sweat.

'I just like finding out about people. And as people go, you're pretty interesting.'

'Well, I suppose that makes a change, a celebrity who's not only interested in themselves.' Calypso cocked her head, sizing him up. 'What are you doing here?'

He looked confused. 'I just thought I'd come and help . . .'

'No, I mean what are you really *doing* here? Why is Rafe Wolfe, film star extraordinaire, giving up his precious Sunday to come down and get his hands dirty with the locals? I'm sure there's no end of glitzy events you could be at right now.'

For the first time Calypso saw a hint of something else beneath the perfect veneer.

'I just get a bit sick of it, you know? All the pomp and ceremony, people falling over themselves to suck up to you, when they've only ever got their own interests at heart.' Rafe ran a hand through his blond hair, giving her a sideways glance. 'It probably sounds like a line to you, but I got in this business to *act*, not be famous.'

'Well, you've certainly done a good job of the latter,' Calypso remarked drily.

'But that's not me,' he said, sounding frustrated. 'I hardly ever do press, only when it's contracted in a film, which you can't get out of. Aside from that, I can't control the paparazzi following me, or magazines putting me on their front cover.'

'It can't help, living in Hollywood,' Calypso said, but she was smiling.

'Point taken.' He smiled back. 'Unfortunately, it goes with the territory. LA is where the work is.' Rafe stood up, brushing a fallen blossom off his shorts. 'I want to hear more about *your* territory. Didn't you say half your ancestors are buried here? Must be a lot of family squabbling.'

'I wouldn't let my grandmother hear you talk like that,' laughed Calypso. She pointed out a tall, white headstone with an elegant inscription marked on it. 'That's my Great-uncle Edmund, Granny Clem's little brother. He died when he was quite young, though, I think he was quite sickly. Oh, and that's where Grandpa Bertie is. Hiya, Grampy!'

Rafe shot her an amused look.

136

'I always was his favourite,' Calypso confided. 'Come on, I'll show you my great-grandparents' grave if you like. It's quite something.'

She started towards an impressive white marble memorial on the other side of the graveyard. 'It's just over here,' she said, turning round.

'Watch out for that . . .' Rafe started to say, but it was too late.

'Oh shit!' Without looking where she was going, Calypso had tripped over a tree root and gone flying. She came down heavily on one ankle and winced. 'Fuck fuck fuckity fuck!'

'Lucky the vicar isn't here to hear that language,' said Rafe, kneeling down beside her.

'Good to see one of us has retained our sense of humour,' Calypso said, through clenched teeth. Her ankle was swelling by the second.

'You've strained it.' Rafe announced, after a careful inspection.

'No shit, Sherlock,' Calypso gasped.

Rafe helped her to her feet, his face full of concern. 'Can you walk on it?'

Calypso gingerly put one foot down and tried to put weight on it, but the pain was too much.

'We need to get you home so you can get an ice pack on it. Where do you live?'

'Just over the green, the thatched cottages,' Calypso said, her face creasing in pain. *Bugger, it hurt!* 'I don't know if I can make it over there.'

'Fine,' Rafe said purposefully. 'I'll carry you.'

'Are you mad?'

'I haven't been certified yet,' he said, and before she knew it Rafe Wolfe, world-famous movie star, had swept her up in his arms.

'What are you doing?' she gasped. 'Put me down!'

'You can't walk,' he said reasonably. 'Besides, you hardly weigh a thing.'

'Ha ha,' said Calypso. 'You probably say that to all the girls.' Grudgingly she put her arms round his neck.

Their faces were only inches apart. He grinned at her. 'That's better.'

Calypso didn't respond, suddenly aware how muscular his chest was under the thin shirt.

Rafe made his way through the church gate on to the green. Calypso pointed out No. 5. 'It's that one.'

'Very pretty,' Rafe said.

She got the feeling he wasn't talking about the cottage. Calypso was feeling more unnerved by the second. Rafe's hands felt like they were searing into her bare flesh. She was aware of his smell, his heartbeat, his rhythm as he walked. She wondered what he was thinking. They lapsed into silence, listening to the unspoken messages between their pressed bodies.

Camilla was washing her hands in the upstairs bathroom when she glanced outside. She did a double take, her eyes nearly popping out of her head. Coming across the green, like a conquering hero returning from battle, was Rafe Wolfe with Calypso in his *arms*!

Rafe gently deposited Calypso at the front gate. She hopped away from him, wanting to put a respectable distance between them. It had been the longest – and yet shortest – five minutes of her life.

'Thanks,' she said hastily.

'Will you be all right?' he asked.

Calypso turned round to see Camilla's head duck out of view behind the bathroom window. 'My sister's home. She's pretty good at all that first-aid stuff.'

'Just take it easy,' he told her.

Calypso put her hand on the gate. 'Well, I'll be seeing you.' She had started hobbling up to the front door when Rafe called out.

'Calypso! I was wondering if you'd like to go out with me some time?'

She turned to look at the handsome, charming man, who she'd written off as a narcissistic playboy with a girl in every port. 'I'll check my diary,' she said, and giving a brief smile turned to hobble up the garden path.

Chapter 18

It was the first day of filming at Clanfield Hall. An early riser herself, Frances had been woken at dawn by a flurry of activity outside. Ambrose – who'd got back from Scotland the previous night – had already left to go to the races, grumbling ominously that the film crew had better be gone by the time he got home.

After a solitary breakfast of a boiled egg and toast prepared by Cook, Frances left the vast echoing space of the dining hall and made her way towards the east wing. Dan, the locations manager, had offered to show her how everything worked, and Frances had to admit she was rather excited.

On her way she passed the drawing room. The door was open and Mrs Bantry the housekeeper was in there, cleaning the silver. She had been with the family for years and lived in a little cottage on the estate.

'Good morning, Mrs Bantry,' Frances called. The older woman looked up, her pale green eyes the only clue in her wrinkled face that she and Jed were related.

'Morning, ma'am.' Like her son, Mrs Bantry didn't fill the air with unnecessary chatter.

'I'm just on my way to the east wing to see how filming's going,' Frances said. 'It's the first day today.'

Mrs Bantry grimly polished a silver plate even harder. She seemed to share Ambrose's feelings about Clanfield Hall being invaded by these fast types from London.

'Well, I'll leave you to it,' Frances said.

Mrs Bantry nodded her head. 'Ma'am.'

Frances walked off, wondering if she was the only person round here who actually thought change was *good* for Clanfield.

At the entrance to the east wing Dan was waiting. He seemed unsure how to greet her, in the end settling for a bizarre half-curtsey.

'Your Ladyship,' he said.

'Frances, please.'

She looked over his shoulder.

'Good heavens!'

Her house had been completely transformed. Normally the east wing had an unlived-in, flat feel about it, but it had been brought back to life with a bang. Dozens of people were rushing around with clipboards, or chattering into walkie-talkies. Most of her own furniture had been replaced by props, although Frances could see that a few familiar things – including a very valuable seventeenth-century writing desk – had been kept. She was rather disconcerted to see a scruffy looking man eating a bacon sandwich off it, while he fiddled with some sort of cable.

It was also stiflingly hot. Blackout curtains hung across the windows, shutting out the natural light, while casually dressed men in shorts and T-shirts tested huge industrial-sized spotlights. A girl rushed in with a pot plant and placed it carefully on a table. Someone else staggered past under the weight of a china chamber pot and disappeared up the staircase with it. Bearded men wearing headphones stood behind the cameras, chatting idly.

'There's the director, Wes Prince,' Dan whispered. Frances saw a raddled blond man looking intently into what looked like a small television screen. He had a gold cross hanging in one ear and a pair of jeans that looked like they had been shredded by a pair of scissors. After a few moments he glanced up, and Dan took the opportunity to speak. He gestured at Frances.

'Wes, this is Lady Fraser. She owns Clanfield Hall.'

Wes Prince looked slightly irritated at the interruption, until he caught sight of Frances in her cream silk blouse and fitted skirt, her blonde hair in its usual stylish chignon.

'Delighted. Thank you for letting us film at your beautiful home.'

He had one of those annoying faux American accents that drove Frances mad. She shook his hand.

'Our pleasure.'

'I'm just showing Her Lady, er, Frances around,' Dan explained. 'We won't get in your way.'

Wes flashed his teeth at her. They'd cost him a fortune

142

at the hotshot dentist Sharon Stone used, and he was determined to show them off as much as possible.

'Wanna be an extra? Lots of owners love getting involved. We had the Earl of Blatchford being hung at the gallows in the background a few years back. Old chap loved it.'

'Wes!' There was a shout behind him.

Wes looked at Frances. 'Gotta get back. I hope you enjoy our little production here.'

'I'm sure I will,' she said and watched him saunter off self-importantly. What a funny little man!

'And over there,' Dan whispered, 'is the main attraction!'

Frances followed his gaze, where a dashing young man was sitting in a canvas chair, reading the *Daily Telegraph*. He was in period dress, cream breeches and a ruffled shirt, leather-riding boots showing off long legs. As if aware of her scrutiny, Rafe looked up and smiled, before going back to his newspaper.

'Look, both him and Sophia have their names on the backs of their chairs. Wes does, too,' Dan explained. Frances couldn't help but be impressed, it was just like one saw at the pictures! Sophia Highforth's chair was empty, conspicuous in her absence. 'Sophia's always late, she's got quite a reputation,' confided Dan. 'Thing is, she's such a talent everyone lets her get away with it.' Now he'd got over his awe of Frances, he had relaxed and was enjoying filling her in.

A friendly faced woman appeared in front of them. 'I don't believe we've been introduced. I'm Pam Viner, assistant director.'

'Pam is Wes's right-hand woman.' Dan explained. 'She's responsible for making sure everything runs smoothly on set.'

Pam smiled. Frances thought she had cheeks like rosy apples.

'I'm sure you've been told this a million times before, but you really do have a wonderful home. So much heritage!'

'Thank you,' replied Frances. 'It's a pleasure to have . . .'

She was interrupted by a commotion down the hallway. Sophia Highforth was hurrying towards them, looking radiant in a cherry-red gown with nipped-in bodice. A young girl was scurrying along behind, a pair of dainty costume shoes in her hand. As Sophia bustled past them, Frances noticed under her dress she was wearing a pair of those clumpy Ugg boots that seemed all the rage with girls these days.

'That's Katie, Sophia's dresser,' Dan said as Katie rushed past in Sophia's wake, various safety pins adorning her jumper.

'Pam! We need you!' yelled Wes Prince from across the room. She rolled her eyes good-naturedly.

'Uh-oh, the master is beckoning. Lovely to meet you, Lady Frances.'

Frances had been watching the proceedings for a few minutes when a fierce-looking man appeared beside her. Even though he was shorter than her, there was no mistaking the iron will in his face.

'No pictures, OK? You can have your shot with

144

Sophia afterwards like all the other competition winners, but don't go waving your camera in her face.'

'I beg your pardon?' Frances looked down at the man in astonishment. Dan, noticing her expression, rushed over.

'Gordon, this is Lady Fraser. She owns Clanfield Hall.'

'That's Mr Goldsmith to you, sunshine,' said Gordon, not taking his eyes off Frances. He stepped back, seemingly satisfied. 'Still no photos until afterwards, OK?'

'What a rude man,' Frances said, as Gordon sidled off, phone clamped to his ear.

Dan grimaced. 'You just had the pleasure of meeting Sophia's manager. Gordon Goldsmith, biggest pain in the world.'

'And I always thought it was the stars who had the egos,' Frances smiled. Dan shook his head and gave a mock groan.

'Oh piss flaps!'

Calypso watched as a fifty-pound note from her precious earnings fluttered across the road. She couldn't believe how much bad luck she was having: first her ankle and now this. Why couldn't her customers pay online and save her all these trips to the bank?

Another gust of wind threatened to lift her skirt up. Sighing, Calypso shut the metal money box the note had whipped out of and crossed the road. Limping slightly, she set it down on the verge next to her handbag. Then she looked into the ditch where the note had just disappeared. To her annoyance she saw it was bigger than a ditch, more a steep gully leading down to a stream. It was narrow, and surprisingly deep. Halfway down the tangled cow parsley and brambles, she could see the pinky colours of the note peeking back at her.

'Bollocks!' Calypso cursed again. She really hadn't got time for this. Gingerly she got down on her stomach and inched forward, her bottom sticking up in the air. The blood ran to her head, hair hanging into her face as she stretched her arm down into the murky depths of the gully. She had nearly got it . . .

Suddenly, gravity felt wrong. Calypso experienced a brief unreal moment in which her legs flew high in the air, before the rest of her body slid forward and down into the gully. She screamed and grabbed wildly at the undergrowth, before tumbling in a heap into two feet of murky water.

Luckily the weeds broke her fall, but that didn't stop her landing awkwardly on the other ankle.

'Fuck!' she moaned. She was wet from head to toe, her vintage dress covered in blobs of mud. To add insult to injury, the fifty-pound note was now floating soggily in the water in front of her. Calypso stuffed it in her bra, shuddering at the unpleasant wetness.

Now she just had to get out. This was so annoying! Calypso squinted up again; with both ankles throbbing the top suddenly seemed as high as Everest. Wincing she started to climb up using the undergrowth, but it came away in her hands. She tried scrabbling up the slimy walls, but slid back down again.

'Bugger!'

She was completely and utterly stuck. The narrow walls of the gully seemed to close in even more, suffocating her. Something unpleasant rustled past her ankle. Suddenly panicky, Calypso opened her mouth and shouted for help.

Nothing, except the odd bird sound and gust of wind. In the distance she could hear a car engine, getting closer and closer. She started shouting again.

'Can you hear me! I'm stuck!'

The car drove past, music blaring out of an open window. Calypso was getting seriously worried now. She was a few hundred yards away from the nearest house; what if she was stuck here all night and got hypothermia? She couldn't even ring for help. Talking of which, her mobile was in her handbag, along with three thousand pounds in cash. Suppose some unsavoury type drove past and nicked it?

'Help!' she screamed again.

An hour later, she was hoarse from shouting. At least a dozen cars had driven past, oblivious to her plight. Calypso leaned against the wall of the gully, trying to catch her breath.

Stay calm, she told herself.

'HELP!'

In complete desperation, she started tearing up clods of weeds and throwing them over the top of the gully. Surely someone would stop and wonder what was going on!

'Will someone come and help me?' she sobbed. She was cold, wet and thirsty, the scratches on her arms and legs stinging like mad. All of a sudden, like a mirage

147

shimmering across a desert, someone poked their head over the top of the gully.

'Christ! Are you all right?' Calypso looked up into the alarmed face of Rafe Wolfe. His eyes widened when he saw who it was. 'What are you *doing* down there?'

'Playing tiddlywinks,' she gasped. 'Now bloody well pull me out!'

'Hold on, I'll go and get some help.'

'No!' she cried. 'Don't leave me.'

Rafe reached down into the ditch, so the very tips of their fingers met. The touch instantly calmed her down. 'I'm not going far, I promise. I'll get you out of there.'

A few minutes later he was back. There were more voices now, and Calypso saw the concerned face of Brenda Briggs.

'Oh lawks!' exclaimed Brenda. 'What on earth are you doing down there?'

'Will everyone stop asking me that?' she retorted crossly. 'I'm not down here for fun.'

A rope was gradually lowered down into the gully.

'Tie this round your waist,' ordered Rafe's voice. Fingers trembling, she tied it round her as tightly as she could. 'Ready?' he said. 'One, two three!'

As if by magic, Calypso felt herself being slowly lifted up. The rope strained and chafed against her skin, and one Kurt Geiger sandal was left stuck in the mud, but she didn't care. She just wanted to get out of there. Then there was a superhuman pull at the other end of the rope and Calypso slithered out of the ditch and over the edge, where she lay face first on the grass, panting.

Rafe put the rope down and went over to her. He laid a concerned hand on her arm. 'Are you OK?'

'I've been better,' she said weakly.

Rafe averted his eyes discreetly.

Behind him Brenda made a coughing sound. 'Calypso, love, we can see your undies!'

With dawning horror, Calypso realized her dress had been dragged up round her waist, and her oldest, greyest G-string was now on show. Face puce, she pulled her skirt down.

'Can this get any worse?' she muttered to herself.

Suddenly two powerful motorbikes pulled up next to Rafe's sports car, and the riders jumped off. They pulled off their helmets and, producing cameras from their tail packs, started snapping wildly. 'Rafe, mate! Give us a shot. What's going on?'

'How the hell do they *know* about these things?' Rafe muttered.

'He just rushed in the shop and asked for a length of rope,' Brenda told the paparazzi in admiration. 'Pulled 'er out all by himself, just like in one of his films!'

'Wow! Rafe, can you give us a comment?'

One of them shoved his camera in Calypso's face. 'Are you his girlfriend?'

'No, I am not,' she shouted, aware her voice was rising hysterically. 'I fell in trying to get something.'

Another camera went off in her face.

'Look guys, I was just driving past and stopped

to help,' said Rafe. 'Could you stop taking pictures? I think this young lady has been through enough.' Helping Calypso to her feet, he picked up her bag and the money box.

'Where are you going?'

'Just get me home,' she muttered, limping towards the cottage. One paparazzo ran straight in front of her and started snapping away again. 'Get out of my sodding way!' Calypso said. She grabbed the man by his camera snap and swung him round, sending him flying. 'I don't how you bloody put up with this,' Calypso snapped at Rafe. There was no way she was breaking down in front of a camera. She just had to get away from everyone.

At the front door, she scrabbled for her keys, well aware the paparazzi were still snapping away, piranha-like, in the background.

Rafe put one placating hand on hers. 'It's fine, I'll have a word with them.' He shot her a humorous look. 'This is the second time in as many days I seem to have rescued you. If you want me to ask you out again, you really don't have to go to all this effort.'

The joke wasn't appreciated. The pain, shock and humiliation of the last few hours were finally too much for Calypso. She couldn't believe he'd pull that kind of line now! She located her keys and looked up, eyes blazing. 'What, do you think I did it on purpose? It might come as a complete surprise to you – but not every girl on the planet finds you irresistible!'

'I was only trying to—' Rafe began.

Calypso interrupted. 'I've got an idea about what you can do. Try climbing out of your own arsehole!'

Leaving the film star agape, a shaking Calypso hobbled inside and slammed the door in his face.

Chapter 19

To her huge relief, there were no incriminating pictures in the tabloids the next day. Calypso didn't know what Rafe had said to the paparazzi, but they'd obviously decided not to run the story. Probably had much bigger fish to fry.

Even though Calypso wanted to put the whole sorry episode out of her mind, Camilla was seriously impressed that Rafe had come to Calypso's rescue. 'It's awfully romantic, just like something out of a film!'

'No, it was wet, muddy, embarrassing and now *both* ankles are killing me. Can you stop going on about it?'

Camilla wasn't about to give up. 'But it's the second time he's rescued you!'

'Thanks for pointing it out,' Calypso replied through gritted teeth.

'*And* he's asked you out! Calypso, he's totally got the hots for you.'

'You mean he's totally got the hots for himself. He just wants to impress his own importance on some poor little yokel girl who's gonna think he's the bee's knees.' The thought of her own naked buttocks and grey thong, flashed through Calypso's mind. She cringed. She never wanted to think about them or Rafe Wolfe again! 'Enough already. What are you up to?' she asked, changing the subject. They were sitting in the study, where Camilla had been on the computer. Calypso looked at the screen, which was filled with lines of numbers. 'Bank stuff, how boring. I wish you'd do mine, might stop me falling in bloody great ditches.'

Camilla hesitated. 'Can you keep a secret?'

'Of course. What is it?'

'I'm setting up a bank account for our . . .' Camilla hesitated. 'For our baby.'

Calypso sat up bolt upright in her seat. 'What? Oh my God! Are you pregnant?'

'No, we're still trying. I've only just come off the Pill,' Camilla laughed, looking at the excitement in her sister's face.

'Well, it shouldn't take long with old super-sperm. I've heard you two shagging every night for the past two weeks!'

Camilla went red. 'Have you really?'

'Don't get embarrassed, sis. In fact, I'm rather jealous. I haven't had it for so long my fanny's become redundant. May as well start growing potted plants out of it and give myself to the local garden centre.'

'Don't be revolting!' Camilla scolded her, giggling. Her face grew more serious. 'Can you keep it to yourself? I don't want everyone asking every five minutes if I'm pregnant yet. You know what mummy was like with Caro, and because of my age it might take a bit longer.'

'You're hardly over the hill.'

'All the same, we can't be too complacent. Besides, I want it to be a lovely surprise for everyone.'

'Wow,' said Calypso in admiration. 'The Bantry enigma settling down and playing happy families. I can't believe it!'

'Neither can I,' admitted Camilla. Her life had never looked so perfect.

Sophia Highforth looked at the ceiling and sighed.

'Are you nearly finished? I've been on my feet for *hours*.'

So had her dresser Katie, who'd been trailing around after Sophia all day. Not that Katie would ever dare mention that.

'Just a few minutes more, Sophia,' she said through a mouthful of safety pins. 'I just need to take it in here.' Sophia was the one moaning about how the dress made her hips look big, anyway.

Sophia's BlackBerry started going. She walked over to pick it up, Katie shuffling along behind like some bent-over old lady. 'Bloody Gordon, that's the ninth time he's called today! *Why* doesn't he leave me alone?'

Katie wished he would, too; she'd had plenty of run-ins with Sophia's manager over the past few weeks. As if a bloke like him could tell her how to do her job properly!

Ignoring the call, Sophia looked out of the window

of her Winnebago. A strikingly handsome man was walking past. Sophia frowned, she was sure she'd seen him before. Hang on – it was that guy from the other day. Jed. Sophia murmured his name under her breath thoughtfully.

'Jed, Jed, Jed.'

'What's that?' Katie asked, trying to keep everything in place as Sophia suddenly walked over to the window. 'Sophia, if you can just keep still for a moment . . .'

The actress pointed out the window. 'He's rather a dish, isn't he?'

Katie followed her gaze. Jed was walking off in the distance. 'He's got a nice bum.'

Sophia let out a peal of laughter. Her face was an enchanting picture.

If only she was like this all the time, thought Katie. When Sophia bestowed you with one of her good moods, it was like having a personal ray of sunshine beam down on you.

'Hasn't he just? Oh, Katie, you are funny.'

'Are you going to get someone to introduce you, then?' Katie asked, eager to prolong the moment.

Sophia laughed again; the sound was like wind chimes tinkling in a summer breeze. 'Oh, darling, I'm hoping for much more than that.'

Katie wasn't surprised. She'd worked with Sophia before, and hadn't seen a man yet who'd resisted her charms.

She doubted this one would be any different.

Chapter 20

Calypso was in her office at Fairoaks, deep in a pile of invoices. No one had prepared her for the less glamorous side of her job.

Her grandmother's voice called up the stairs. 'Calypso! You've got a visitor.'

Calypso frowned. What now? She'd spent yesterday in back-to-back meetings, and wasn't scheduled to see anyone. Sighing, she stood up, wincing as one of the grazes on her leg caught the edge of the chair. 'Who is it?' she whispered from the top of the stairs. 'Can't you get rid of them?'

'Don't be so ridiculous, one should always keep one's appointments.' Clementine disappeared back down the hallway.

'Oh God!' huffed Calypso. She really hadn't got time for this. If it was that travelling salesman from Gloucester selling office stationary again, she knew where to shove his biros. She took a cursory look in the mirror, wiped a smudge of black from under her eyes, and went downstairs.

In the kitchen, Clementine was pouring hot water into the coffee pot. 'The drawing room,' she said. 'Run along, you've been ages.'

Calypso dragged herself down the long, sun-filled corridor. As she walked into the room, her mouth dropped open in surprise. It wasn't salesman Terry Locket, with his greasy hair, flasher's mac, and eternally hopeful expression. Sitting on one of Clementine's antique chairs, looking perfectly at home amongst the surroundings, was Rafe Wolfe. The terrace doors were open, beckoning in the beautifully sunny day.

'Hello, Calypso,' he said easily. 'How are you feeling?'

He looked freshly shaved and showered, a tang of lemon aftershave already filling the room.

Calypso had barely time to answer before Clementine bustled in with a tray. She put it down on the table. 'Don't just stand there gawking,' she told her. 'Offer Mr Wolfe a ginger thin.'

Calypso took the plate over. 'Biscuit?' she offered sarcastically.

Rafe leaned forward and took one. 'Thanks.' He looked round the room. 'You have a beautiful home, Mrs Standington-Fulthrope.'

'Thank you,' said Clementine. She went to pour the coffee.

Rafe leapt up. 'Here, let me.'

'If you insist,' she said, rather pleased. She did like a young man with nice manners.

Rafe started expertly pouring the dark brown liquid.

'This reminds me of visiting my own grandmother.' He handed a china cup on a saucer to Clementine. 'On a day like today we'd sit out on the balcony and try to identify all the different bird calls.'

'Rock 'n' roll,' Calypso murmured under her breath. They both looked at her.

Clementine raised an eyebrow. 'Mr Wolfe and I were talking about your latest exploits earlier.'

Calypso didn't want to dwell on that and swiftly changed the subject. 'What brings you here, Rafe? In fact *how* did you know I'd be here?'

'You mentioned you worked out of your grandmother's house,' he said casually. 'And, well, I thought I'd drop by and see if I could take you out for lunch.'

Calypso didn't know whether to be impressed or irritated by his confidence.

Clementine took a sip of her Fortnum & Mason's Akbar blend. 'Now then, Mr Wolfe,' she said briskly.

'Rafe, please.'

'Rafe, then. You must tell me all about the filming at Clanfield. I want to keep a close eye on the proceedings because I am so concerned about the effect the film crew will have when it moves down to the village . . .'

Calypso couldn't help but smile as her grandmother started grilling Rafe about whether everyone was behaving themselves, and expressing her concerns for the grass on the village green. From baker boy to baronet, Clementine treated everyone the same. It didn't faze her in the slightest that he was a world-famous film star, having coffee in her drawing room.

'. . . So of course I told the ghastly little man where to go,' she said. She had been telling them about her run-in with the paparazzo.

'There will be a few more of them, I'm afraid,' said Rafe apologetically. 'It's a regrettable by-product of the job. If it's any consolation I feel the same way about them that you do.'

'Hmmm,' said Clementine, but she didn't sound cross. Rafe had turned out to be a very polite young man and easy to talk to.

Calypso's stomach rumbled loudly.

Rafe smiled at Clementine, 'Would you like to join us for lunch? I've been hearing excellent things from the crew about the Jolly Boot.'

Clementine declined graciously. 'That really is very kind of you, but I have lots to get on with here.' She looked pointedly at Calypso. 'Darling?'

Calypso was rather miffed Rafe had just assumed she'd say yes to his invite. But the lunches there were bloody good . . .

'All right,' she said grudgingly. She looked at Rafe, perfectly turned out as always, and then back down at her crumpled T-shirt dress. 'I'm not changing, though, I can't be bothered.'

'Darling!' reprimanded Clementine, but Rafe looked amused.

'You look great as you are.'

Clementine rose from her seat. 'Well, Rafe, it was a pleasure to meet you.'

'The pleasure was all mine.'

A girlish flush appeared on Clementine's cheeks. It

wasn't every day one got complimented by a handsome chap fifty years one's junior.

'"The pleasure was all mine",' mocked Calypso, as they pulled up in his sports car outside the pub. 'What are you like?'

Rafe turned off the ignition. 'I meant it. All the women in your family are perfectly charming.'

'You haven't met my mother yet!' laughed Calypso, as she got out of the car. Tessa 'Tink' Standington-Fulthrope was a lively woman of fifty-two, who kept the family in uproar with her dirty jokes and stories.

Rafe gazed at her across the car roof. 'Maybe I will one day.'

The pub was half-full as they entered, but it didn't stop the excited whispers when they saw who Calypso was with. Jack Turner was on them like a flash. 'Calypso, nice to see you,' he said. He extended a hand to Rafe. 'Jack Turner, pleasure to meet you. My daughter Stacey's a big fan of yours. She's got the day off today; she'll be pulling her bleedin' hair when she finds out you've been in.'

Rafe laughed. 'Maybe I could sign something for her.'

Jack looked as pleased as Punch. 'If you wouldn't mind! Now, you folks go and make yourselves comfy and I'll be with you shortly.'

They found a table for two in the corner. 'Looks great,' said Rafe, glancing at the chalkboard menu on the wall. He was doing a good job of ignoring the stares in his direction.

'Pierre's the chef here,' Calypso said. 'Jack poached him from a five-star Michelin restaurant a few years ago. Ruffled quite a few feathers in the culinary world, but people come from miles round to eat here now.'

'I'm not surprised, it looks fantastic,' Rafe said. He looked at the board again. 'I'm going to have the oysters and steamed snapper.'

Calypso shot him a humorous look. 'Watching your waistline?'

Rafe pulled a face. 'You have no idea how tight those breeches I have to wear are. Your grandmother's ginger thins may have given me a muffin top.'

Calypso allowed herself a little smile. He was actually quite funny. 'Look, I think I owe you an apology. And a thank you. I'm sorry I was so rude to you after you helped me, I was in a bit of shock at the time.'

He grinned understandingly. 'It didn't help having the paparazzi turning up. Trust them to be driving past.'

Calypso was intrigued. 'What did you say to them?'

'Those particular two owed me a favour. They'd taken some other intrusive shots of me that I should really have complained about, but I let it go. I told them if they didn't run the pictures, we'd be even. They'd missed most of the action, anyway.'

Calypso shook her head. 'I don't know how you put up with all that.'

Rafe shrugged. 'I try not to.'

Jack came over with their drinks and set them down on the table. They toasted each other: gin and tonic for her, sparkling water for him.

'Anyway, tell me more about yourself,' Rafe said.

Calypso groaned. 'Not me again! Let's talk about you instead.'

Rafe took a sip of his water. 'There's nothing to tell really.'

'Oh, come on, you're hardly Barry from Bedlington are you?' Calypso paused, tasting her drink. 'What about your love life?'

'There was someone in LA,' he said. 'But it's over now.' He didn't volunteer anything else.

'Nasty break-up?' Calypso enquired. Rafe shrugged.

'As break-ups go it was OK. But I don't really like talking about it; it's not fair on Daphne. Water under the bridge and all that.' He changed the subject. 'How about you? Any significant relationships?'

Their starters arrived. Calypso waited until the waitress had left. 'There was someone,' she said, loading her toasted bread with pate. 'Sam. But it didn't really work out, we wanted different things.'

'Did he come from round here?' Rafe asked.

'She, actually.'

Rafe stopped, oyster halfway to his mouth. He looked startled. 'She?'

'Yeah,' said Calypso wrily. 'Does that offend you?'

Rafe recovered himself. 'Of course not. I was just, well, surprised. I thought you'd be with some cool rock-band type.'

Calypso laughed. 'Never judge a book by its cover.'

'So you're bisexual?' He seemed quite interested.

'I suppose if you had to define me, you could say

that,' she said. 'Sam's the only woman I've ever dated, though, and I've had plenty of boyfriends. I guess I'm just inquisitive. Like, it doesn't have to be about what sex you are, it's about how attractive you are as a person.'

'So would you date another woman?'

'Don't know,' she replied, finishing the last of the pate. 'Never say never and all that.' Her eyes studied him mischievously. 'How about you? Have you ever been with a man?'

'God, no!' Rafe exclaimed. 'I mean I've got nothing against it but . . .' He saw her expression and relaxed. 'Ah. You're pulling my leg.'

Calypso laughed. 'I don't think Stacey Turner would be able to cope if you swapped tits for testicles.'

After lunch, which Rafe insisted on paying for, he walked Calypso back to the cottage. He stopped at the gate. 'Here we are again, then.'

'Do you want to come in for a coffee?' she asked, suddenly not wanting the afternoon to end.

Rafe glanced at his watch. 'I need to get back. But I wouldn't mind a quick guided tour.'

He followed Calypso up the path. She unlocked the front door and pushed it open. The cottage was silent. 'My sister's at work today,' she explained. She briefly showed him the downstairs and the garden, which was now festooned with the summer flowers planted by Camilla. Leading Rafe back through to the hallway, Calypso paused by the staircase. She waved a hand upwards.

'It's just the bedrooms up there and stuff,' she

163

mumbled, suddenly feeling self-conscious. Why was she being like this?

Rafe glanced up the stairs before his eyes settled back on her. She noticed their blue looked darker today, fringed by golden lashes.

'I've really got to go,' he said softly.

Calypso tried to sound airy. 'No problem.'

Neither of them made a move towards the front door.

Rafe took a step towards her. 'I've had a really nice time today.'

Calypso felt her heart quicken. 'Me, too.'

The air had suddenly become heavy and expectant. Calypso was sure she could *hear* her heart drumming. As if in slow motion, Rafe leant down and pecked her softly on the lips. Calypso felt like it wasn't happening to her, like she was watching someone else feel the soft touch of a famous film star on their mouth.

'I'd like to do this again,' he said, pulling away.

'Me, too,' she said again. For some reason, she had lost the power of normal speech.

Rafe ran his hand down her arm. 'I'll be in touch.'

Trying to regain her composure, Calypso saw him out. Afterwards, she closed the front door and sat down heavily on the staircase. Her lips were still tingling. Calypso ran her fingers across her mouth. She was trying to quell the excitement building inside her.

'My God,' she exclaimed finally. 'I've just been kissed by Rafe Wolfe!'

PART TWO

PART TWO

Chapter 21

It was the day of the *Churchminster's Got Talent* competition and the three judges were having a dress rehearsal. Clementine was nonplussed by the high-waisted trousers and black wig Calypso had brought along for her, and despite Calypso's pleas, was refusing to wear them.

'Granny Clem, it'll be hysterical!' Calypso said, holding the trousers up against her grandmother. The third judge, Freddie Fox-Titt, stifled a chortle.

Clementine was not for the turning. 'I'm not going to make myself a laughing stock. Besides, I don't even know who this Simon Powell character is.'

'*Cowell*,' Calypso corrected. The three were sitting behind a desk on a raised platform. Beryl Turner had lent one of her shiny gold tablecloths to drape over it and Ted Briggs had done a marvellous job of rigging up three buzzers.

Clementine was looking at hers uncomprehendingly. 'How does it all work, again?'

'The act starts, and if you don't like it, you press your buzzer,' Calypso told her. 'Three buzzes, one from each of us, and they're out. If they go through to the next round, they have to perform again, and the audience vote on the eventual winner.'

Clementine grimaced. 'The buzzer idea seems awfully cruel.'

'That's showbiz, Granny Clem,' Calypso laughed.

'We won't be merciless,' Freddie said reassuringly. 'Everyone has been practising so hard I'm sure they'll be jolly good.'

'Anyway, the bad ones are the best ones!' Calypso said. She looked round the hall. 'It looks pretty cool in here.'

The Garden Party had done a fantastic job of making it look atmospheric. A proper stage had been built with wings either side, which each act would enter from. A huge *Churchminster's Got Talent* sign painted by Angie Fox-Titt and Camilla hung from the ceiling. Disco lights and a stereo had been placed at the side of the stage. The back of the village hall was crammed with seats: at least 150 people were expected to turn up. Posters advertising the event with the words 'Sold Out' were stuck all over the walls. A trestle table with the raffle prizes on for later had been put by the front door, so everyone could eye up the goodies when they came in.

Calypso turned to the other two. 'Let's have one more run-through . . .'

*   *   *

At No. 5 The Green, Camilla was getting ready. She checked her watch and frowned. Jed was late. She tried his mobile. It was picked up immediately.

'I'm outside, I'll be two secs.' A few moments later he appeared in the doorway, breathing slightly heavily. He went straight over to the wardrobe and started stripping off. 'Sorry I'm late. Brenda Briggs was having trouble with her boiler, and I went round to have a look at it after work. Took longer than expected.'

'My hero,' smiled Camilla, studying him. He'd lost weight. Already lean, Jed's beautiful face was looking even more concave, his muscular torso sinewy to the point of showing off every muscle. 'You need to take it easy, darling, you're not invincible, you know.'

He looked up and smiled affectionately. 'You don't have to worry about me.'

The front door slammed shut beneath them and footsteps thundered up the stairs. Moments later, Calypso burst in the room. Now naked, Jed deftly stepped back behind the wardrobe door.

'Calypso!' Camilla protested. 'You could at least have knocked.'

Her sister shot a cursory glance in the direction of the concealed Jed. 'Whoops, sorry.'

She opened an expensive-looking bag with 'Boutique Babylon' written across it in looped writing and held up a gold-sequinned minidress. 'What do you think?'

Camilla didn't recognize the funky-looking label, but the dress was dazzling. 'You're going to look a million dollars!'

Calypso grinned. 'Cost me an arm and a leg, but

sod it. I haven't bought anything new for ages.' She bounded out of the room.

Jed chuckled as he reappeared. 'Someone's in a good mood at the moment.'

'Hmmm,' said Camilla perceptively. 'I wonder if that has anything to do with a certain film star.'

Jed raised an eyebrow.

Camilla was bursting to tell him, despite Calypso swearing her to secrecy. Jed wouldn't say anything, anyway. 'They had a snog in the hallway the other day!'

'*Here?*'

'Yes! Can you believe it?'

Jed paused, taking the information in. 'Knowing your sister I can, actually,' he said. 'Maybe we'll be needing that red carpet after all.'

In her own bedroom Calypso hummed merrily as she rifled through her underwear drawer for a clean G-string. She *had* been feeling on top of the world the last few days. The sun was out, her business going from strength to strength. Yet deep down, Calypso knew the exact reason her mood was extra buoyant at the moment.

It had been nine days since Rafe had kissed her. He had sent her several texts since, perfectly pleasant ones, interested in what she had been up to. Calypso had taken a perverse pleasure in not replying to them immediately. Normally quite vocal about her love life, for some reason she hadn't told anyone about her feelings, not even her sister. She couldn't explain it, but in the few moments their lips had met, Calypso's heart had done a complete flip, and it hadn't quite settled since.

This is ridiculous, I'm acting like a giddy schoolgirl! she thought. Calypso did *not* do giddy schoolgirl. At first, she had told herself it was the sheer novelty of the situation. After all, it wasn't every day one had a snog with a famous film star in one's hallway. Then she felt cross with herself for being so predictable and falling prey to Rafe's evident charms. He wasn't even her *type*. Clean living and clean-cut, Rafe Wolfe was definitely not Calypso's idea of a good time.

And yet, despite all her attempts to write the situation off, there was one glaring obstacle in the way.

She absolutely fancied the pants off him.

By 7.55 p.m., the village hall was bursting at the seams. As she peered out from behind the wings, Clementine was delighted to see half the district had turned out. It was so good that one could count on everyone to rally round. As well as the residents of Churchminster, she recognized a few faces from the Bedlington Bridge Association and a fair few young people. To her surprise there were also some film crew (as Calypso had warned her), including Pam Viner, who smiled and waved from her seat in the audience. In spite of herself, Clementine felt rather flattered; she applauded any efforts to integrate with a new community.

The door to the side of the building suddenly flew open. Clementine could see contestants lining up in the narrow corridor. Jack and Beryl were at the front, he looking very jaunty in his magician's hat, and she dressed in a glittery bodice and long skirt. Behind them was an explosion of noise and colour as everyone practised their act for the last time and made sure their costumes were right.

'Granny Clem, it's eight o'clock,' whispered Calypso. She, Freddie and Clementine were standing together, waiting to go on. Calypso's hair was piled in a sexy updo and the new dress clung to her like a second skin. Beside her, Freddie was looking very jolly in a multicoloured waistcoat.

Ted Briggs, in a dusty dinner jacket and bow tie, pressed *play* on the antiquated stereo system. As the entrance music started the three judges stepped out. The crowd began whooping and clapping.

Clementine waited for the noise to die down. 'Good evening, and welcome to *Churchminster's Got Talent*. For those of you who don't know me, I'm Clementine Standington-Fulthrope. Judging beside me tonight are Freddie Fox-Titt, and my granddaughter Calypso.'

There were a few wolf whistles as Calypso stepped forward to take her bow.

'I'd like a performance with you, love!' a male voice shouted.

Clementine shot a disapproving look in the direction of the heckler. 'While we are all here to enjoy ourselves, I would like to remind everyone why we are putting this evening on in the first place: to raise money for St Bartholomew's and improve the village. As I am sure all of you are aware, Churchminster has beaten off stiff competition to land a place in the final of Britain's Best Village.'

More clapping and cheering.

Clementine permitted herself a smile. 'As head of the Garden Party – the committee that has been formed to get this village ready – I know what a huge task we have taken on. We can leave no stone unturned, no hedge untrimmed to make Churchminster look the best it possibly can. This however, takes a lot of time and money. So I'd like to thank everyone who has bought a ticket for tonight, as well as my fellow committee-members for all their efforts over the past few weeks.'

There was an ear-splitting shriek of static from one of the speakers. Everyone winced. With a final plea for people to buy raffle tickets, Clementine wished all the contestants good luck and sat down behind the judges' desk.

'Bloody good atmosphere,' Freddie whispered. He gave his buzzer a honk for good measure.

'Freddie! I haven't started yet,' Clementine scolded.

He gave her a boyish grin. 'Sorry, Clementine, just warming it up!'

Clementine looked at the first name on her list. 'I take great pleasure in introducing master magician, the Grand Supremo!'

The speakers crackled into life and a jet of smoke started to shoot across the stage, gradually turning into a dense cloud. As the judges coughed and spluttered, Jack Turner strode on, hand in hand with Beryl.

'Greetings!' he announced in a funny, Transylvanian-sounding accent. 'I am the Grand Supremo, master of all things magical, and this is my stunning assistant, Violetta.'

Brenda did a provocative little jiggle. Behind Angie, the Blackford-under-Bridge Women's Institute gasped collectively.

'A woman of that age shouldn't be showing off so much flesh!' said one.

'That corset doesn't give much support,' exclaimed another.

Angie Fox-Titt turned around and smiled sweetly at them, shutting them up.

On stage Jack had produced a white rabbit from his black silk cape. 'For my first trick, ladies and gentlemen, I give you the exploding rabbit! Three, two, one . . .'

For the next ten minutes, the Grand Supremo thoroughly entertained the audience with a variety of half-decent magic tricks, from Violetta being sawed in half to the Jolly Boot's pub cat Pebbles seemingly vanishing into thin air. None of the three judges pressed their buzzers until the end, and the Grand Supremo exited the stage to loud cheers.

Next on was a dog trainer from Bedlington whose 'break-dancing fox terrier' got an attack of stage fright and dived under the judges' table, only to be cajoled out when Angie found an old Hobnob in her handbag. Ted Briggs then stunned everyone when he got up and sang 'Nessun Dorma' in a beautiful tenor. There was hardly a dry eye in the house.

'He used to be in the operatic society,' a proud Brenda Briggs told Angie.

Ted was followed by a very good string quartet, and then a middle-aged stand-up in a tiara, who had them all in stitches with an endless supply of rude jokes about the royal family. Clementine resolutely pressed her buzzer when he made a particularly risqué one about Prince Philip and one of the Queen's corgis, but Calypso and Freddie let the comic stay on. Unfortunately things started to go downhill from then, when Lucinda Reinard's precocious daughter Hero came on to do the Riverdance. Unfortunately 15-year-old Hero, who seemed to be taking after her mother in the hips and bum department, tripped over a cable and had to be heaved offstage by a sweating Ted Briggs. It got even worse when Reverend Bellows and Joyce took to the stage dressed as Sonny and Cher to do a toe-curling rendition of 'I Got You Babe'. Clementine had only just recovered before she had to announce the next act, a thankfully rather good trumpet player from the other side of the Cotswolds.

An hour and a half later, nearly everyone had performed. Only Stacey Turner was left. Her mother and father had changed back into their normal clothes and were sitting with Angie in the audience, waiting expectantly. The booze from the bar had been flowing freely and things were getting more raucous, especially amongst the younger people at the back.

'Stacey has been so secretive about what she's doing, I'm dying to find out,' Brenda told Angie. 'Jack thinks it's going to be a ballet recital.'

The lights had been dimmed and sultry music was playing softly in the background.

Ted Briggs walked on to the stage carrying a large metal pole.

Jack frowned as he watched it being screwed it into place. 'What's all this, then?'

The music got louder and Clementine had to shout to be heard. 'Our last act of the evening is Stacey Turner.' She paused and shot a worried look in the direction of the Turners. 'Otherwise known as "Harem".'

The lights went off and the hall was plunged into darkness. The audience held their breath expectantly. There was a crash backstage and someone shouted 'Shit!' as they walked into something.

Thirty seconds passed. Everyone was starting to fidget when the stage lit up in a crescendo of light and music. In the middle stood Stacey Turner, wearing a tiny two-piece costume made from latex and diamanté. In her navel was a glittering jewel, and her eyes were heavily made-up and mysterious-looking. A feathered headdress and six-inch heels made up the rest.

A babble of male voices erupted, calling and cheering. Jack was out of his seat like a shot, but his wife pulled him down warningly.

'Jack! She's been practising like mad for this. You can't go up there.'

'She's practically bleeding naked!' he spluttered.

'Stacey's an adult now, you've got to trust her!' Beryl warned, but she did look a bit concerned when her daughter turned and shook her assets at the judging panel.

As the hypnotic music started to play, Stacey writhed and wiggled her nubile young body. The shouts from the back of the hall got even louder. Stacey smiled and flashed her eyes, enjoying the effect she was having. Throwing her head back, she arched her spine and started sliding up and down the pole.

Jaws dropped with a collective clang.

'She's got wonderful rhythm,' Angie remarked over-brightly, feeling she should say something. Two seats down Jack was stiff with shock and anger, a vein in his forehead pulsating.

Stacey sped faster and faster round the pole. The music reached fever pitch. As the final crescendo built, she turned her back on the crowd and pulled off her top. Throwing the garment to one side, she held her arms aloft, framed like a Middle Eastern nymph.

'Bleeding Nora!' Jack spluttered. But just when he thought it couldn't get any worse, Stacey whipped round to give a full frontal of the most famous D cups in Gloucestershire, their modesty barely protected by a pair of nipple tassels. Stacey gave one final, saucy jiggle before the lights went off.

It was too much for Jack. 'What the hell do you think you're doing?' he howled, leaping up.

A few moments later, the lights came back on again to reveal Stacey, this time covered up with a silk kimono. Jack's fury was drowned out by shouting and jeering from the back of the hall. Angie turned, frowning, it looked like a bad lot from Bedlington had turned up.

As Stacey went to take a bow, someone threw a beer glass and it shattered yards from her feet. She stumbled back, looking shocked. A shard had struck her face and blood was seeping down her cheek.

'Show us yer tits, you slag!' someone shouted.

Stacey put her hand up to feel the cut, looked at the blood on her hand and burst into tears. It was enough for her father. With the agility of someone half his age, Jack vaulted over his chair and ran towards the back of the hall.

'Christ alive, someone stop him!' wailed Beryl, running up onstage to comfort her daughter.

Jack squared up to the rowdy youths. 'Which one of you bastards threw that glass?'

'Fuck off, wanker!' one of them jeered. Making a disgusting noise in the back of his throat, he opened his mouth and spat at the landlord.

There was uproar: chairs were knocked over and drinks went flying. The raffle table collapsed like a soufflé. Fists going like pistons, Jack threw himself at the troublemakers. As punches were thrown and insults traded, the melee spilled out through the doors.

Calypso jumped down from the stage and pushed her way through the crowd. 'Call the police!' she screamed.

Outside it was utter bedlam. One of the youths was already sprawled out on the floor and Jack had another held tight in a headlock. A chunky man, who looked like one of the security staff from Seraphina Inc., was rolling his sleeves up and wading in. Jed was dragging an acne-ridden youth away, while the boy screeched blue murder.

'I know me rights, gerroff!'

Suddenly a car screeched up and a man jumped

out, the motor still running. The fearful shouts from onlookers turned into ones of astonishment as they recognized the blond good looks, and the muscular physique under the golfing outfit.

'It's Rafe Wolfe!' someone squealed.

Fearlessly the film star strode into the fracas and started pulling the attackers off. 'All right, that's enough!' he shouted. A fist went to hit him and he stopped it with his forearm. 'I said, "That's ENOUGH".' His voice was so commanding the two youths he was grappling with stopped punching and kicking.

One of them looked up at Rafe, who was easily twice his height and weight. His eyes goggled in sudden recognition. 'Fuck me!' he exclaimed, all traces of aggression quickly fading. His face lit up hopefully. 'Hello, mate! Can I have your autograph?'

A wailing sound heralded the arrival of the police. PC Paul Penny, of Bedlington police station, stepped out of the panda car and drew himself up to his full five feet two inches. 'What have we got here, then?'

Relatively new to the job, PC Penny still treated every day at work like an episode of *CHiPs*. His enthusiasm for filling his little black book with every incident that had happened within a twenty-mile radius of Bedlington knew no bounds.

'We should sue you lot,' spat one of the youths.

'From what I saw, these gentlemen were merely trying to placate you,' Rafe told them pleasantly. The yobs glowered but remained inert.

PC Penny looked disappointed. 'No one wants to press any charges?' He looked at Jack hopefully, but the landlord himself didn't want any trouble. It was bad for business.

'No complaint here, officer. It got a bit tasty inside, but it's all been sorted out now.'

With no imminent arrests on the cards, PC Penny tried to send the gang on their way with a strict warning. 'I know who you lot all are, any more trouble and I'll be down on you like a ton of bricks!'

'Ton of feathers more like,' mumbled one of them in a last show of defiance. They shuffled towards their car and drove off, exhaust pipe between their legs.

'Can we please all go back inside!' cried Clementine. 'We've still got a competition to judge!'

People started to file back in, including a curious PC Penny. He'd always had a thing for amdram.

Only Calypso and a few hangers-on were left outside, the latter anxious to get an autograph from their hero. After the pleased fans had gone back into the hall, Rafe walked over to Calypso.

'Tell me,' she said. 'Do you actually do any work or do you just drive around saving people?'

He laughed. 'I do have a habit of turning up at the right time. Or should it be the wrong time?' His eyes travelled over her outfit. 'I hope you don't mind me saying so, but you look beautiful.'

Calypso found herself blushing. 'Thanks,' she mumbled. 'Don't tell me you've come to take part in *Churchminster's Got Talent.*'

'Hell, no,' Rafe said. 'I imagine the standard is far too high. I was just passing through on my way home and saw the commotion.'

'Calypso!' Her grandmother stuck her head out of the door. 'We're waiting for you.'

'I've got to go,' Calypso apologized to Rafe.

Rafe grinned, 'I wouldn't want to keep you from your audience. But before you go, I was wondering if you'd like to have dinner with me?'

'When?' she blurted stupidly.

'Tuesday is my next evening off. I'll pick you up, we can eat back at mine.'

'Calypso!' This time Clementine's voice brokered no discussion.

Calypso laughed. 'I've *really* got to go!' She grinned at Rafe. 'Dinner would be cool.'

Chapter 22

It felt funny walking up the familiar drive to Twisty Gables, the house where Camilla had grown up. The Reinards had bought the rambling house on the Bedlington Road from Camilla's dad Johnnie some years ago, when he and Camilla's mother had moved to Bermuda. Camilla had had an idyllic childhood growing up at there. As she stood in front of it, remembering playing chase with her sisters through the corridors and concocting imaginary kingdoms in the gardens, Camilla felt a pang of nostalgia.

From outside, things hardly looked any different, except for a new door knocker and different-coloured curtains in the windows. Lucinda Reinard's mud-splattered Volvo estate was parked out the front, with the contents of what looked like an entire saddlery on the back seat.

Camilla rang the bell and a few moments later, a harassed-looking Lucinda opened the front door. Behind her Camilla could see a scene of domestic mayhem. Lucinda's youngest son Julien was lying on his stomach in the middle of the hallway playing on a PlayStation, while the family's golden retrievers chased around him. Trashy music blared from an upstairs room, and skateboards, school satchels and kicked-off trainers littered the floor.

Lucinda stuck her head up the stairs. 'Horatio! Turn that bloody racket down,' she shouted shrilly. She turned back to Camilla. 'Sorry about that, but if it's not bloody Horatio with his dreadful thrash metal it's his sister with her ballads. Hero wants to be the next Leona Lewis, you know.'

Camilla privately thought that if the poor girl's singing was as bad as her dancing, Hero didn't have much hope.

Lucinda readjusted her neck scarf. She looked rather red and bothered. 'I'm going through a load of Pony Club paperwork. Not great with a hangover, I can tell you. Nico and I got in last night and polished off another carafe of red wine. Bloody acid indigestion is playing havoc.'

Camilla smiled politely and held up a white envelope. 'Granny Clem asked me to bring over the raffle prize you forgot to claim last night. An hour's full body massage at the beauty clinic in Bedlington.'

Lucinda's horsy face lit up. 'I'd forgotten about that! God knows I bloody need it, I'm so stressed at the moment my shoulders are up around my ears. You are a dear for dropping it off. Won't you come in?'

A blood-curdling shriek went off upstairs.

Lucinda twisted her head like the girl out of *The Exorcist*. 'Hero! Horatio!'

'I'd better get back—' said Camilla.

'Nonsense!' Lucinda interrupted. 'You must come in, see what else we've done to the place.'

Camilla couldn't think of an excuse quickly enough. 'Thanks, I'd love to.'

As she stepped inside, the door to the downstairs loo opened and Lucinda's husband Nico came out. Camilla could see he had some sort of lurid pornographic magazine in his hand, which neither he nor Lucinda seemed embarrassed by. '*Bonjour* Camilla,' he murmured and floated off enigmatically.

Camilla followed Lucinda through to the kitchen. It certainly hadn't been this untidy when her family had lived there. A saddle was propped up next to the Aga, while a fat tabby cat sat on one of the work surfaces cleaning her paws.

'Bugger off, Pickles,' said Lucinda, shoving the disgruntled creature on to the ground. She turned to Camilla. 'Is fresh coffee all right? I've just brewed a pot.'

'Lovely.'

'Sit down and make yourself comfortable,' said Lucinda. 'I won't be a tick.'

Camilla moved a pile of washing from one of the chairs round the kitchen table and sat down. 'I see you've added on a conservatory,' she remarked, looking out the window.

Lucinda carried the cafetière over, kicking a dog's bowl out of the way. 'Yes, we had it done last summer.

My goodness, haven't you been round since then? I really should host some sort of drinks party, blasted Pony Club does rather take over one's social life, though.'

She sat down and poured Camilla's coffee into a mug with 'Give the bitch her caffeine' written on it. Through the French windows into the garden, Camilla could see a chicken coop, still standing empty since the last occupants had perished in the floods.

Lucinda followed her gaze and sighed. 'It's like the site of some ghastly battleground, isn't it? Nico and I have talked about it, but we've decided it's not a good idea to get more. You know, in case it happens again. The children were dreadfully upset by it, I had to go to Holland & Barrett's and get Julien some herbal antidepressants!'

Camilla watched as Lucinda moved towards the whisky decanter on the sideboard. 'Do you fancy a splash? I'm meant to be cutting down on the grog, but it does help along one's hangovers.'

'I'm OK, thanks.'

Lucinda added a healthy glug to her own coffee. 'Haven't got to drive the children anywhere later, for once. May as well make the most of it.' She took a sip and sighed happily. 'Top-notch bash last night, although Hero was rather upset she came second from last.'

In the end, Stacey Turner had won by a landslide. Even if people hadn't liked her act, they'd felt sorry for what had happened and voted for her anyway. The cut on her cheek had turned out to be superficial, and

Stacey had gone home very happy – even if her father had not. With the ticket sales, bar and raffle, they had raised £5,250. Stakes in the raffle had been significantly raised when Frances Fraser had donated a rare antique dinner set. It would go some way towards improving the church.

Lucinda took another sip of coffee. 'Have you ever tried anal beads?'

Camilla spluttered into her mug. 'I'm sorry?'

'I said, have you ever tried anal beads?' asked Lucinda. 'Nico and I are looking to spice up things in the bedroom. One of my friends recommended them.'

'I really wouldn't know,' Camilla said, her face bright pink.

'I must admit, I was rather surprised, too. I thought they were for the gays, but apparently half of Gloucestershire is using them!'

'Well, I don't know anyone . . .' Camilla replied weakly.

'No?' said Lucinda. 'Oh well. I just thought I'd ask. I know how the younger generation are into experimentation. Anyway, have I told you about Hero winning Best Turned Out at the Pony Club show last week? We had a moment in the morning, though, when we discovered that little horror Aristotle had been rolling in his own muck all night . . .'

For the next thirty minutes Lucinda droned on about the best way to clean poo stains off one's mount and the logistics of organizing the next year's Pony Club camp. Camilla didn't care, at least Lucinda wasn't talking about sexual paraphernalia. She finally managed to escape after an hour, pleading errands to run.

As she drove towards the village crossroads, she slowed for a horse and rider coming the other way. It was Frances Fraser, mother of her best friend Harriet. Camilla wound down the window.

'Morning, Frances.'

'Camilla!' Frances looked pleased to see her. 'I was going to call your grandmother later, actually, to see how last night went.'

'Your dinner set went down a storm!'

'Oh, anything I can do to help.' Ride and mount were both impeccably turned out, the family crest of the Fraser family embellishing the horse's saddlecloth.

'Hello, Dante,' Camilla said to the thoroughbred. She and Frances chatted about their mutual interest, Harriet, for a few minutes, until the horse starting pawing its hoofs on the road.

'Someone wants to get going!' said Camilla. A thought came into her head. 'Just before you go, I've got a bit of gossip. Lucinda was telling me there's all sorts of activity going on at Byron Heights.' Camilla didn't notice Frances's shoulders stiffening.

'Oh?' Frances said in a disinterested tone. 'Yes, there's been lots of traffic going back and forth. Do you think he's coming back? That would be too exciting!' Dante pawed the ground again. 'I should be getting back,' said Frances, and after inviting Camilla to afternoon tea at Clanfield, she set off.

*   *   *

187

Dante sensed his owner's sudden change in mood and started to bounce along, tail swishing high in the air.

'Dante!' Frances ordered, pulling back on the reins. Still, she couldn't restrain her rising hopes. According to his website, Devon was meant to be in Bangkok at the moment.

Urging the horse on, Frances trotted past Twisty Gables. As she rounded the curving bend, the Gothic spires of Byron Heights came into sight. Frances put a hand up to shield her eyes and looked: there *were* vehicles parked outside. She could see people carrying flowers, and what looked like bits of furniture, into the house. A white van was bumping along the long drive. As it passed Frances, the driver tipped his head and smiled at her. Frances didn't recognize him, but the flurry of activity could mean only one thing.

Devon was coming home.

Chapter 23

'Hello there!'

Jed stopped his wheelbarrow and turned round. Sophia waved from the top step of her Winnebago. He was even better looking than she'd remembered.

She turned on the dazzling smile that made men's hearts worldwide flutter. And stirred their loins. 'Jed, isn't it? We've met before, I'm Sophia Highforth.'

He walked over, giving her a wry smile. 'I know who you are. It's the talk of the estate.'

'And here's me trying to keep a low profile!' she laughed. She looked down at the wheelbarrow. 'What is it you *do* exactly? It seems very hands-on.'

'Estate manager, which means I'm pretty much in charge of keeping this place going.'

Sophia laughed again. 'I would have thought pushing wheelbarrows would be a bit beneath you.'

Jed grinned. 'We all muck in round here.'

Sophia sat down on the steps, arranging her skirts round her. They were on a lunch break and she was looking exquisite in a silk green dress that complemented her cream complexion. She fanned herself prettily. 'I've just been reading about my co-star's exploits in the paper.'

Somehow the *Daily Mail* had found out about Rafe breaking up the fight at the talent evening. There was a full-page article entitled: 'WONDER WOLFE – THE REAL-LIFE ACTION HERO!'

'Sounds like it's never dull round here,' she said playfully.

'Oh, we can be a bit lively.'

Sophia gave him a coquettish look. 'I was wondering would you have time to take me on a tour of the estate sometime? You obviously do such good work here.'

A squawking chicken ran past, a member of the crew in hot pursuit trying to round it up.

Jed studied her. 'Wouldn't have thought it was your bag.'

Sophia had already done her homework and got the low-down on Jed from one of the gardeners. She knew exactly which buttons to press. 'Oh, I love the countryside. I think all the nature conservation here is marvellous.'

Jed looked pleasantly surprised. 'OK, best to come find me in my office. It's over by . . .'

'Oh, I know exactly where your office is.'

He cocked his head, a half-smile playing on his lips. 'What's this, been checking up on me?'

Sophia grinned cheekily. 'Maybe.'

Jed laughed and picked up the wheelbarrow. 'I'll see you around, Sophia.'

'You can bet on that!' she called after him, smiling.

At Top Drawer Travels in Cheltenham, Camilla was having a very trying morning. Mr Fitzgerald had already sent her out on two cappuccino runs, and now he was about to swan off for yet another two-hour lunch at the swanky Japanese place round the corner.

Camilla thought she would try and catch him before he went. She got up from her desk and went over to his door, which was always shut unless he opened it to bellow an order. She knocked confidently.

'Enter!' Mr Fitzgerald brayed. Camilla opened the door and went in.

He looked up from his desk. 'I haven't asked for another coffee, have I?' Mr Fitzgerald had the puffy, florid face of a heavy red-wine drinker, and a penchant for loud pinstriped suits.

Camilla took the liberty of sitting down in the chair opposite. 'Er, no. Mr Fitzgerald, I was wondering if you'd had any thoughts about the South America package tour I suggested? I really think it would be a good—'

He interrupted. 'We're adding it to our winter brochure.'

Camilla was delighted. 'Really? That's fantastic!' *Maybe he is taking me seriously after all*, she thought.

Mr Fitzgerald threw the new brochure across the desk at her. 'Yah, I'd been looking to expand into South American for a while, it was just a matter of timing. I must say, I think it's one of my best ideas yet.'

'Um, your idea?' she asked delicately.

Mr Fitzgerald looked at her as if she'd just lifted her leg up and let an enormous wet fart rip. 'Yes, *my* idea. What's your point, missy?'

'It was actually my idea,' Camilla ventured. 'I came to you with the itinerary, remember, and lists of prices and contacts.'

He waved a podgy hand dismissively. 'A small detail. Listen, girlie, you'll learn quickly enough in this business that with the calibre of our customers, they want to know that Mr Jonty William Fitzgerald *himself* is looking after them personally. You can't just turn up and bat your eyelids, expecting a piece of the action! It takes years to get to my position. That's if you're even made of the right stuff in the first place.' His dismissive look made it clear he thought Camilla wasn't.

She looked down at her lap awkwardly. 'I just thought—'

'Thought what?' enquired Mr Fitzgerald in a sugary sweet voice. 'Before you say anything, might I remind you that Top Drawer Travels is an extremely prestigious firm, and there are plenty of people who would bite their hand off to be in your position.'

'Yes, Mr Fitzgerald,' Camilla replied miserably.

Mr Fitzgerald smiled and looked at his pocket watch again. 'I'm pleased we understand each other. Get out now, I've got a lunch appointment.' He stood up. 'Before I forget, my Dearly Beloved phoned. She's got some evening dress at the dry cleaners, be a good girlie and pick it up for me, will you?'

*   *   *

By 7 p.m., a nice glass of G and T by her side and an assurance from Jed that he was on his way home, Camilla was feeling better. She'd given herself a talking-to. She needed to hang on in there and get more experience. Besides, jobs at prestigious companies like Top Drawer Travels were few and far between at the moment.

It'll get better, she told herself, always the optimist.

There was a tap on the back door and when she turned to see who it was all thoughts about Mr Fitzgerald were temporarily forgotten. There, standing at her kitchen door, was Rafe Wolfe. He smiled at her through the window panel. Heart jumping, Camilla rushed over and opened the door. The blond film star was dressed in jeans and a fresh white shirt, enough buttons open to reveal a flash of brown chest.

'There was no answer at the front,' Rafe Wolfe said apologetically.

'Oh! Sorry, do come in. I've had the kitchen door closed, I didn't think we were expecting anyone. I was just about to start making dinner,' she added rather stupidly.

'Anything nice?' Rafe asked politely. Like Jed, he was so tall his head nearly touched the beams on the roof.

'Just a stew – er, there'd probably be enough for you . . .' Camilla trailed off uncertainly. Had Calypso told her Rafe was coming to dinner? Surely she wouldn't have forgotten a thing like that!

Rafe looked bemused. 'I think Calypso and I are going over to mine?'

Camilla nearly dropped the tea towel. 'Over to yours?' she asked weakly.

Rafe frowned. 'Hasn't Calypso told you?'

'Haven't I told her what?' Calypso appeared in the doorway, putting a dangly earring in one ear. She was wearing a short black skirt and a simple tank top, silver Grecian-type sandals on her feet.

Rafe's appreciative once-over didn't go unnoticed. 'I was just telling your sister about our date tonight,' he said.

At the word 'date' Camilla's eyes shot into her hair-line. 'You didn't tell me about this!'

'Didn't I?' said Calypso airily. 'Anyway, we must dash. See you later.' With that she propelled Rafe out of the kitchen, leaving a gobsmacked Camilla in their wake.

'So where do you live, exactly?' Calypso asked, as Rafe's sports car zoomed out of the village. The roof was down and her blonde hair blew round her face.

Rafe changed down into third to negotiate a hairpin bend. 'Hedgewater.'

Hedgewater was a little hamlet ten miles outside Churchminster, which consisted of little more than a row of houses and a decrepit pub.

Calypso looked puzzled. 'But there's nothing there.'

Rafe grinned. 'You'll see.'

Ten minutes later they were driving slowly down a little road Calypso had never known existed, on the way out of Hedgewater. Gravel crunched under the wheels as the most extraordinary building appeared in front of them. It was two storeys high and appeared to be made completely of glass, a huge balcony running the entire length of the second floor. As the car pulled up outside, neon fibreglass lanterns over the entrance lit up.

'Not your average Cotswolds cottage,' Rafe said. He got out of the car and went round to Calypso's side to open her door.

'It's wicked,' she said admiringly, giving him a hand to help her out.

Inside was even more spectacular. A palm tree was growing up through the concrete floor in the hallway, while each room had been designed like something from a James Bond film, with gold silk sheets, a casino and even a huge mural of Bond girl Ursula Andrews emerging from the sea in her iconic bikini. In one room there was even a high-tech gym, with running machines, bikes and an impressive set of weights.

'A bit too OTT for my tastes, but I'm hardly ever here,' said Rafe, leading Calypso into an ultra-modern kitchen. 'Seraphina Inc. have rented it for me for the duration of the picture. My co-star Sophia prefers the more genteel, sociable atmosphere of Cheltenham, but I like it here.' He pulled open a fridge, which was fully stocked with champagne, beers and bottles of spirits. 'What can I get you?'

'Vodka and Coke, please.'

Rafe pulled out a bottle of Louis Roederer Cristal instead. 'Why don't we have something a bit special? A film sponsor gave me this, and I've never had the occasion to drink it.'

Calypso raised an eyebrow. The stuff was at least a grand a bottle, but who was she to argue?

It was still warm enough to sit outside, so Rafe carried

an ice bucket and two flutes outside to the terrace. A large hot tub sat in one corner, near a barbecue. Calypso went and sat down on the huge swing seat in the other. It was big enough to stretch her legs out on. She nodded at the hot tub. 'Is that where you entertain all the groupies?'

Rafe looked up from pouring the champagne. 'Unfortunately not. The only chicks I've seen in this garden have been of the fluffy winged variety.' He handed Calypso a glass and sat down at the other end of the swing seat. He raised his glass. 'Cheers.'

They clinked glasses.

'God, that's good,' said Calypso as the ice-cold liquid went down her throat. She leant into the comfortable cushions. 'So how's work going? You know, I don't even know what the film's about.'

Rafe filled her in. 'I'll give you the basic version. It's set in the eighteenth century, and I play Theodore Wallingford, a dashing duke who gets quite a reputation for being a good-for-nothing ladies' man. Anyway, the only person he gives two hoots about is Evangeline, his beautiful second cousin. Theo has an epiphany one day and realizes she's the only woman for him, but she gives him the brush-off.'

'Ha, serves him right.'

Rafe smiled. 'Indeed. Anyway, to prove to her and his father, the Duke of Wallingford, that he *is* a good man, Theo joins the army and becomes a hero on the battlefield. He comes back a different person, Evangeline falls for him, and they get married. But then Theo is called back into service and gets killed the day

Evangeline finds out she is expecting their first child. She is devastated, but vows to keep alive his memory, and gives birth to a son who looks just like him. It's a bit of a tear-jerker.'

'Camilla will be weeping buckets, it's just her sort of thing.' Calypso finished her glass.

'So does life imitate art?' she asked idly. 'You playing a playboy and all that.'

Rafe cocked his head, sizing her up. 'I'm not sure I like the impression you've got of me.'

'Oh yeah, and what's that?' she said teasingly.

Rafe started to count off on his fingers. 'Arrogant, womanizing, selfish . . .'

'. . . having an ego the size of Hollywood,' Calypso added helpfully.

Rafe shot her a half-amused, half-exasperated look. 'You've been reading too many Frank Sinatra biographies.'

Calypso wasn't about to let him off yet. 'What about all these lovelies you're pictured with? I'm not knocking it, most guys I know would give their right arm to be in your position.'

'Most of that stuff's made up! I only have to be in the same vicinity as someone and suddenly I'm getting married to them. Come on, Calypso, you must know how it works.'

Calypso was suddenly aware of his arm, warm against her bare leg. Trying to ignore the sensation it was giving her, she threw her hands up in mock surrender. 'OK, point taken. I was only winding you up.'

'"Winding me up",' he muttered, smiling. He got up to refill her glass.

'So what are we having for dinner?' asked Calypso. 'I didn't see a chef anywhere.'

Rafe raised his eyebrows, as if to say: *I thought we'd got past this?*

'I thought I'd do a barbecue. I find the dining room a bit stuffy and formal.'

Calypso looked over at the high-tech contraption in the corner. 'Go for it, Delia.'

An hour later, Calypso topped up her glass for the umpteenth time. They were on their second bottle of champagne, which she seemed to have drunk most of. She was feeling more than a little light-headed. 'Are you sure I can't do anything to help?' She delicately stubbed out the roll-up she'd been smoking, and slid the ashtray under the seat.

Rafe looked up from the lifeless barbecue, frustrated. 'I can't understand why it won't work.'

Calypso went over to stand next to Rafe as he flipped through the instruction book. He smelt good: of health and vitality, clean living. She bet he'd never had a nicotine hit in his life. Her eyes skimmed the booklet. It looked overly complicated. 'Don't stress about it, let's just have a cold supper.'

Rafe shot her a sideways glance. 'Ciabatta rolls and Kettle Chips, not very glamorous, is it?'

She laughed. 'I'm so hungry I'll eat anything.'

*   *   *

After the impromptu picnic outside, Calypso leaned back in the seat and sighed contentedly. 'I'd never have thought crisp sandwiches would taste so good.'

Rafe was sitting on the other end of the swing seat, his feet resting on the little garden wall. The remnants of a packet of strawberries sat between them. 'Do you normally eat that much?' he asked.

'No, normally I have a lot more.' Calypso wriggled to get more comfortable. 'I'm a greedy pig. It's all right to say it.'

Rafe laughed. 'I like a woman with a good appetite. It makes a change from seeing someone push a lettuce leaf round her plate.'

'Actresses, eh?' said Calypso drily. 'Talking of which, what's it like working with Sophia Highforth?'

Rafe considered her question. 'She can come across as a bit of a diva but that's only because she's such a perfectionist. Bloody talented.'

'Ever mixed business with pleasure?'

'With Sophia? No, actually.' Rafe finished his drink and put it down on the floor. 'She's very beautiful, but not my type. Actresses can be pretty demanding.'

Calypso wasn't about to ask who was his type. They lapsed into silence, listening to the sounds of the nocturnal wildlife coming alive.

'Fantastic night,' he remarked eventually. They were looking up at the velvet-blue sky, pinpricks of light shimmering down.

'Mmmm,' said Calypso. His leg had fallen against hers and she was finding the sudden warmth rather distracting.

His rich voice came suddenly out of the darkness. 'You do know I like you, don't you?'

Calypso hesitated, digesting his words. 'I suppose so,' she admitted.

'And would it be arrogant to think that you like me, too?'

She laughed. 'Uh-oh, that ego's coming out again.'

'You're very good at deflecting things with that dry wit of yours, aren't you?'

'One of us has got to have a sense of humour,' she joked, but the intensity building up between them was getting hard to ignore.

Suddenly he swung his legs down, puncturing the moment. Calypso's disappointment didn't last long. He put the strawberry packet on the floor and moved next to her.

'What I really want to do is kiss you. Properly, this time.' He leant down and took her face in his hands. She realized she was holding her breath. 'I haven't been able to stop thinking about you, Calypso.'

As his lips crushed down on to hers, she found herself responding with a surprising passion. His mouth was warm and sweet, his tongue probing but not invasive. Instinctively Calypso parted her legs, pulling him down on to her. She raked her hands up and down his broad back, feeling his erection growing by the second. She rubbed it and then took one of his hands and pushed it into her knickers. He groaned appreciatively.

'Christ, you're wet.' His fingers started caressing her clitoris, sending little shock waves of joy through her body.

Calypso wrapped her legs round him, her breathing becoming laboured. Rafe's hands were running over her bra now, pushing aside the lacy material to get at her breasts . . .

'I can't do this.' With some difficulty he extricated himself and sat up, breathing heavily.

'Are you *serious*?' Calypso panted incredulously. Surely he wasn't going to tell her he was secretly married after all!

Rafe touched her face. 'I want to prove to you it's not just about a one-night stand.'

'Don't worry about that!' she exclaimed. *Don't you know how long it is since I've had sex?* she thought.

Rafe pulled his shirt together. 'I mean it, Calypso; I want you to know I'm not some sort of bastard. You're very special to me.'

'Oh, for God's sake,' she said, but she couldn't keep the pleasure out of her voice.

He carefully pulled her top down, stroking her flat tummy. 'I'd better call you a cab. I'm over the limit, and if you stay here, I don't know if I can be trusted to keep my hands off you.' Kissing Calypso again, he led her back into the kitchen.

Chapter 24

Joyce Bellows finished her tea and sighed happily, like a wine connoisseur swilling the last sip of a Chateau Latour 1970. She got up from her armchair in the old-fashioned sitting room at the rectory and made her way through to the kitchen. Brian was away on a two-day conference in London – promising to bring back Joyce her favourite lilac creams from Harrods. 'A decadent choice,' she always said, 'but if you couldn't have one bit of naughtiness, what was life about?'

Today was her day at St Bartholomew's doing the flower arrangements. After the last Garden Party meeting, Clementine had praised Joyce's efforts, and the vicar's wife was determined to keep up the good work. That was what united people, after all. A strong faith and sense of community. She and Brian had moved around so much since they'd married that Joyce had never really felt she'd belonged anywhere. Until she'd come to Churchminster. She felt *good* living here.

Joyce gave herself a cursory look in the hallway

mirror, applied her only bit of make-up – an old beige lipstick bought from an Avon lady years ago – and opened the front door. Sunlight washed into the house, reflecting against her glasses. After a few grey days, Churchminster had woken to a perfect May morning.

She got her old bicycle out of the garage and, after a wobbly start, turned left out of the rectory and started along the lane. It was wonderfully quiet, no sound apart from the turning of her tinny wheels and the stop-start rattle of birdsong. Clouds dappled the faded blue sky, while splodges of white cow parsley lined the dewy green verges below. Joyce pedalled faster and felt the wind through her hair, a gust of joy within. At the village shop, Brenda Briggs was just opening up.

'Morning, Brenda!' Joyce called gaily, as she cycled past. 'Lovely morning for it!' *I always did wonder*, she thought, *lovely morning for what?* She gave a sudden cackle at the absurdity, leaving a bemused Brenda in her wake.

Slightly breathless, Joyce leant her bicycle on the wall outside the church and pushed open the creaky gate. The churchyard was as serene as ever, the shadow from St Bartholomew's a cool, comforting blanket. Joyce had been in many churches in her life, but something about St Bartholomew's always caught her heart. It was so stoic and proud, majestic even in its battle scars and whatever the ravages of time had thrown at it.

The ancient, heavy wooden door was already ajar. Joyce was surprised; it was very early for someone to be in here. In a rare show of force Reverend Bellows had insisted the doors be left unlocked, so parishioners could visit the church whenever they felt the need.

Tentatively, she pushed the door open and walked in. Accustomed to the sunlight, her eyes took a few seconds to adjust to the gloom inside. When they did, Joyce blinked once, twice and then again, as if not sure she could believe what she was seeing. Her hands clutched at her cardigan and, uttering the kind of words one would not expect from a vicar's wife in the house of God, Joyce Bellows ran out.

PC Penny rocked on his heels in what he thought was a superior manner and turned over another page of his notepad. 'You say the door was ajar when you got here, madam?'

'Yes,' said Joyce tearfully, 'but I just thought someone had left it open from evening prayers. Oh dear, what a dreadful thing to happen!' She burst into tears again.

Angie Fox-Titt put a comforting arm round her. 'There, there, darling, don't let yourself get in a state.'

'Bloody bad business though,' Freddie Fox-Titt said. The four of them surveyed the wrecked interior of the church. Flower displays had been pushed over, bibles ripped and shredded, pew cushions scattered. Worse, the vandals had sprayed the words SCUM in red paint along the back wall. Even PC Penny, who worshipped at the altar of *CSI: Miami*, felt a sense of utter sacrilege.

'At least they haven't smashed the windows,' Angie tried to console the others. 'And all the valuable things are locked up for special occasions.'

'That may be, Mrs Fox-Titt,' PC Penny said. 'But from now on, I suggest the church door is kept locked. You can't be too careful.'

Angie bit her lip, nodding unhappily. 'Do you think it's those gatecrashers from *Churchminster's Got Talent*?' Freddie asked. 'They were a pretty rum lot.'

'We will be following up all lines of inquiry, don't you worry about that.'

'It's just such awful timing,' Angie told PC Penny. 'With Britain's Best Village coming up, this is the last thing we need.' She sighed again, making her impressive chest heave. PC Penny averted his eyes hastily.

A scene of crime officer was called down to fingerprint the church, and didn't hold out much hope of success – 'Hundreds of people have been in here, it's like looking for a needle in a haystack' – but he did what he could, packed up his bag and left. That evening, when St Bartholomew's was declared a free zone again, the Garden Party went down to put it back together. Apart from the bibles, which would have to be replaced, it seemed no real damage had been done.

With a bit of elbow grease, Jack had got rid of the graffiti. He used a special concoction he bought over in a bucket. 'I've worked in enough inner-city pubs to know how to get rid of this stuff,' he said grimly.

Afterwards, Clementine, Calypso and Brenda walked back over the green towards their own houses. Everyone was tired and depressed at what had happened, but Brenda tried to lift the moment with her chatter. "Ere, I've got a bit of gossip for you. My Ted saw all sorts of vans outside Devon Cornwall's place when he went to work the other morning. Ted reckons he's moving back in!'

'Last I heard he was in Bangkok,' Calypso said. 'Playing to sell-out arenas. I can't imagine why he'd come back here.'

Brenda sighed, she was a huge fan of the rock star. 'Fingers and everything else crossed he does, my "Devon is a Dish" T-shirt could do with an airing.'

Three motorbikes in close convoy were driving rather too fast round the other side of the green. The riders were all in full leathers and blacked-out helmets.

'That'll be the paparazzi,' said Brenda knowledgeably. 'They were in the shop earlier asking if there was another way to get into Clanfield Hall. I said not unless they wanted to risk getting pellets in their bums from his nibs and his air gun!'

The three watched as the bikes zoomed out of sight towards the stately home. Clementine frowned; more photographers had appeared in the village recently. They'd clearly never heard of keeping to the speed limit.

'Of course, I didn't tell them he *had* been in,' said Brenda self-importantly.

Calypso spun round. 'Who?'

'Rafe, of course! He was all disguised up in a baseball cap and sunglasses, but I knew it was him from the moment he walked in. I bleedin' near wet me pants, all me bingo friends are green with jealousy.'

Calypso's stomach dropped unpleasantly. If Rafe had visited Churchminster, why hadn't he been to see her? Despite the high octane they'd left on, she hadn't heard from him since. Calypso didn't like the way she felt so put out.

'He didn't stay long, just to buy a box of chocolates and a newspaper,' Brenda said. She gasped theatrically. 'I wonder who the chocolates were for?'

Obviously not me, thought Calypso, hating how disappointed she felt.

At the crossroads Brenda left them and continued on to Hollyoaks Cottage. Calypso studied her grandmother. 'Are you all right, Granny Clem?' she said.

Clementine gave a weak smile. 'I'm fine, really, darling.' She looked back at the church. 'Why would someone want to do that? It just seems so *mindless*.'

Calypso shook her head. 'God knows, probably just some local thug's idea of a good time. But PC Penny says he'll step up the patrols in the village, and he's confident he'll find out who did it.'

Clementine had dealt with PC Penny before. He reminded her of a dreadful yapping Yorkshire terrier her friend Elizabeth Etherington had once owned. 'We'll see,' she said pessimistically. 'I really hope that we don't get any more reporters sniffing around, we can't afford any negative press in the papers.'

Calypso looked up at the darkening sky. 'Do you want me to walk you back to Fairoaks?' she asked.

'No, you go inside and have some supper. I'll be fine.'

After bidding her grandmother goodnight, Calypso started towards No. 5. A few moments later, the one person she hadn't been able to stop thinking about telephoned her.

'Hey there.'

The line was crackly, Clanfield Hall always did have crap reception.

'Hey, yourself,' she responded, trying to quench the sudden feeling of joy. 'I was beginning to think you'd dropped off a cliff.'

She could hear the smile in Rafe's voice. 'Why, have you been missing me?'

'You should be so lucky,' she retorted, but a tingle of happiness went through her body.

Rafe chuckled. 'Sorry I haven't been in touch. We've been doing fifteen-hour days and I haven't been good for anything when I've got home.'

Calypso didn't bring it up about Brenda seeing him in the shop; she didn't want to sound like a stalker. She wondered why he hadn't mentioned it, though – and who were the mystery chocolates for?

Rafe didn't notice she'd gone quiet. 'Anyway, to make the most of my absence, I'd like to take you out again.'

'Crisp sandwiches again?' she asked, but the sharp remark seemed to be lost on him. He'd obviously got used to her being a sarcastic cow by now.

'Are you free this Saturday?'

'I think so,' Calypso said, in spite of herself.

'Great! I'll pick you up at 9 a.m. Look, I've got to go, we're doing another evening shoot.'

'Wait!' she said. 'What do I wear? Where are we going?'

'It's a surprise. Wear something pretty. Oh, and bring your passport.'

'*Passport?*' she started to stay, but the line crackled again and went dead.

Chapter 25

The smell of pork filled the kitchen. Camilla inhaled blissfully; the joint from Daylesford Organic was an extravagance, but it was going to be delicious. She finished pouring the chocolate mousse mixture into glass ramekins and put them in the fridge to chill. Next, she set the kitchen table and filled a vase with flowers hand-picked from the garden. She and Jed always preferred the cosiness of eating in here to the dining room. Camilla had decided on her way to work that morning to surprise him with a special dinner, and had spent the afternoon shopping for all his favourite things. As she put the finishing touches to the dauphinoise potatoes she smiled, looking forward to the evening ahead. Jed had been rather preoccupied the last few days, and Camilla was sure it was to do with work. A nice dinner would take his mind off things.

*　　*　　*

At 9.15 p.m. Camilla tried Jed's mobile for the umpteenth time. Still off. She was getting really worried now. Where could he be? Surely if he was working this late he would have phoned to tell her.

It was gone 10 p.m. by the time Jed finally walked through the front door. Camilla came rushing out into the hallway. 'Where have you been?'

'Sorry, I got caught up at the Hall.'

Camilla thought of the dinner congealing in the kitchen. Irritation flared up. 'You could have phoned, darling!'

'Will you get off my back?'

Camilla looked surprised at his uncharacteristic sharpness.

Jed caught himself. 'Sorry babe; it's just been a long day. I should have called.'

'You're working too hard at the moment,' she told him, noticing the dark shadows under his eyes. She followed him through to the kitchen. Jed stopped dead at the sight of the table, all laid out. 'What's this?'

'I thought I'd cook us a nice dinner . . .' she trailed off.

Jed sighed. 'I've really fucked it up, haven't I?'

He looked so tired and rundown that despite the fact dinner was ruined, Camilla felt sorry for him. 'Look, I can make you something else. What do you fancy?'

'I'm not that hungry, don't worry.'

'Do you want me to run you a bath, then? We can get in together.'

A bath – or rather sex in the bath – was one of Jed's favourite things.

He shook his head, avoiding eye contact. 'I don't think I'm good for anything. I'll probably just hit the sack.'

'Jed!' she said, as he went to walk out.

'What?'

'You haven't even kissed me yet.'

He came over and dropped a perfunctory kiss on her cheek. 'Night.'

Camilla was left alone in the kitchen, wondering what on earth had just happened between them.

The hairy man looked up from the toilet seat, overalls round his ankles. He was reading a copy of the *Sun*.

'All right, love?'

'Oh, I say!' exclaimed Frances and shut the door quickly. A smell of nether regions curled out distastefully into the corridor. 'Could you please lock the door in future?' she called out irritably. 'You're not even meant to be in this part of the house, there's a perfectly good lavatory in the east wing.'

'Gary's blocked it up with a massive shit, dirty bugger,' the man called back cheerfully. 'Can you get me some more bog paper? You've run out.'

Frances tutted and went to tell Mrs Bantry. She'd already found two heavily tattooed men asleep in the library, their feet up on a Regency reading table that had been in the family for over two hundred years. Frances needed to have a word with Dan.

As she approached the east wing, Frances was aware of the utter quiet. For the past few weeks the house had been alive with noise and chatter from the film crew, but today everything was strangely silent, bar the intermittent sound of muffled voices upstairs.

At the foot of the sweeping staircase stood a group of the crew, some of whom Frances recognized. They greeted her with hushed voices.

'What's happening?' Frances asked.

One of them, a tiny girl with a chipmunk face, called Ellie, chirped up, 'It's a closed set today, Rafe and Sophia are filming a love scene, and she doesn't want anyone else up there. We've all been told to keep quiet.'

Frances had had enough of being told what to do in her own home. 'Do you know where Dan is? I need to speak to him.'

'He's upstairs, in one of the bedrooms,' Ellie said. 'But really, you can't go up there . . .'

'I can go anywhere I want in my own house, young lady,' Frances said imperiously as she started up the stairs.

At the top there was another girl, studiously checking her clipboard. When Frances enquired after Dan she pointed at the Blue Room, one of the bedrooms down the corridor.

'In there,' she mouthed. 'But keep your voice down!' Frances frowned, but walked on quietly. The love scene was obviously taking place in the palatial Red Room, as it had a sign saying 'Closed Set' on the door. Knocking on the Blue Room's door Frances went straight in, without waiting for an answer.

Dan was sitting on an uncomfortable-looking high-backed chair, working away on his BlackBerry. The cavernous room had been turned into a makeshift office, with computers and monitors everywhere. A coffee vending machine stood in one corner, while the four-poster bed had mounds of paper, bits of cable and abandoned headphones piled on top of the covers.

Dan jumped up, surprised to see her standing there. 'Hello, Lady Fraser!'

'Daniel, I have just found a strange man using my own personal lavatory,' she said. 'And yesterday I found two tattooed gentlemen eating fast food in the library. They even left their litter behind for Mrs Bantry to clean up. It really isn't good enough.'

The locations manager flushed. 'That'll be the sparks. I'm sorry, I'll make sure it doesn't happen again.'

'Sparks?'

'The electricians, they're the ones who set up those huge lights you've seen. Once their job's done they have a habit of roaming.'

'Well, make sure they don't roam again, please.'

Dan looked contrite. 'I will, Lady Fraser. I can't apologize enough.'

'Apology accepted,' she said, slightly mollified.

Dan put his BlackBerry down, offering another olive branch. 'Do you want to see a bit of filming? I'm sure I can sneak you in for a few minutes.'

'Isn't it a closed set?' Frances wasn't entirely sure it was appropriate for her to go and watch.

'Rafe and Sophia are behind screens, so you won't see them,' Dan assured her. 'It's quite fun to see the whole set-up, though.'

Frances's curiosity got the better of her. 'If you insist.'

Outside the Red Room Dan put his finger to his lips. 'We'll stand at the back for a minute.' Silently he pushed the door open and Frances followed him in.

It was easy to see why they'd picked this room: with its high vaulted ceiling, four-poster bed and deep red curtains and furnishings, it oozed sensuality and romance. Frances couldn't see the bed today, however, as the far end of the room had been blocked off with two large screens. Behind it, they could hear the distinctive tones of Wes Prince as he discussed camera angles.

A lone person, who Frances recognized as Sophia's dresser, stood on their side of the screen, holding a large fluffy dressing gown.

'It's only Wes and Pam, plus one cameraman and a sound guy,' Dan whispered. 'Love scenes are pretty intimate, so you can imagine why the actors don't want all the sparks and carpenters watching.'

'Pan in on Sophia's face, Keith, we want to catch the emotion,' Wes instructed someone. 'OK, start rolling!'

Dan put his finger to his lips, signalling for Frances to keep quiet. A young, female voice could be heard behind the screen: tender, passionate, euphoric in its emotion.

'Oh, Theodore, my world has been one of shadows and darkness since you left. I never thought I would feel whole again, but now here you are, in as much flesh and blood as I dare to imagine, because the whole thing feels like a dream. My darling! Tell me you've come back to me.'

A second voice, masculine yet tender in tone. 'Only

when I had lost what I had, did I really know what it meant. It's only ever been you, Evangeline.'

The intimate exchange brought an unexpected tug at Frances's heart. She suddenly remembered the raw power of being completely in love, where a simple touch or kiss could bring joy into one's heart, fill one's world with vibrant colours. Would she go through her whole life without ever having that again? Frances was aghast to find her eyes filling up.

Suddenly there was an angry shout from downstairs. 'Where's my bloody wife?'

Frances quickly blinked the tears away. Ambrose! She heard heavy footsteps up the staircase, but before she could rush out and try to placate him, he stomped in, closely followed by a tail-wagging Sailor.

'Frances! One of these bloody idiots has parked in front of the Range Rover, I can't get out.'

'Ambrose, let's discuss this *outside*,' she hissed.

Wes's satsuma-coloured face popped round the screen, incredulous. 'What's going on here?' He caught sight of Sailor and his eyes widened. 'Is that a fucking *dog*? Get this lunatic and his mutt out!'

Ambrose shot the director a filthy look. 'This lunatic and his mutt happen to own Clanfield Hall, so if you don't keep a civil tongue in your head, I'll have the whole damn lot of you thrown out!' His eyes swivelled to a bare portrait-sized space on the wall. 'And what the dickens have you done with Great-uncle Algie?'

'Wes?' Sophia's voice came from behind the screen. She didn't sound happy.

As Pam poked her face out, looking startled, Dan

turned to Frances beseechingly. 'I'll get someone to move the van if you can just get him out . . .'

But as Frances pulled on her husband's sleeve, the sheepdog shot past them yapping and disappeared behind the screen. There was a huge commotion and the sound of things being knocked over.

'Get down, you stupid animal!' Wes Prince shouted. 'Jesus, stop humping Sophia's leg!'

Amidst the screaming Frances closed her eyes and wished, just wished she was a million miles away.

Half an hour later, she was still seething. They were in Ambrose's study, facing each other like two combatants preparing for battle.

'What in heaven's name is wrong with you?' she cried. 'You can't just march in and disrupt everything. Dan says they're going to have to reshoot the whole scene at a huge expense of time and money. Sophia Highforth was so distressed, she's had to take the rest of the day off.'

Ambrose grunted. 'Shouldn't have blocked me in, then. I think you, along with everyone else Frances, seem to have forgotten this is our *home*.'

Frances sighed. 'You could have found a more civil way of asking them to move!'

His eyes narrowed. 'For Christ's sake, you're the one who invited this circus in.'

Something snapped inside her. 'Oh, so it's all my fault,' she shot back, voice shaking. 'Have you ever thought, Ambrose, just for *one single second*, that I might not be happy here, either?'

He looked at her, genuinely surprised. 'What are you on about? I've always given you everything you wanted, haven't I?'

Frances went to open her mouth and thought better of it. 'Forget it, Ambrose, just forget it.'

He looked at her quizzically. 'Come on, what is it?'

'I said, forget it!'

Ambrose paused and then shook his head, as if to say 'women'. 'What's for lunch, then? I told Cook I fancied one of those pheasants the gamekeeper got.'

Frances's fists had squeezed into tight balls by her sides. 'If you think I'm spending another moment in your company, Ambrose Fraser, you've got another think coming. I'm going for a walk, to get as far away from this sodding place as I can.'

Ambrose watched, open-mouthed, as his normally composed wife stormed out, slamming the door after her.

Chapter 26

On Saturday Calypso's alarm went off at 8 a.m., but she'd been awake for ages. A gentle breeze was coming in through the window, making the curtains billow out lazily. The weatherman had predicted a lovely day.

Calypso stretched out in bed and put her arm behind her head, thinking. Part of her still couldn't believe she was going on a proper date with Rafe Wolfe. It seemed so *surreal*, so silly. Her London friends would wet themselves laughing if they found out she was going out with Mr Cheesetastic.

Outside there was a creak on the landing.

'Is that you Camilla?' she called out.

The door opened and her sister came in, dressed in her nightie. 'I was just going to make myself a cup of tea. Do you want one?'

'Mmm, please.' Calypso smiled at her. 'Did I hear Jed go earlier?'

Camilla paused a fraction too long. 'Yes, he's had to go to work.'

Calypso knew her sister too well. 'Is everything OK?'

Camilla leaned against the door frame. 'Jed seems a bit offish with me,' she admitted. 'I'm worried he's having second thoughts about trying for a baby.'

'I'm sure he's not. What makes you think that?'

'Oh, I don't know,' Camilla sighed. 'What if he's not cut out for this domesticity? What if I've pressured him into doing something he doesn't want to?'

'Bull crap,' said Calypso. 'From what you've told me, he wants this as much as you do. Have you told him how you're feeling?'

'I have brought it up.'

'And?'

'He says it's not that, he's just tired from work.'

Calypso stretched her arms above her head and yawned. 'He probably is just tired, Bills, he's working like a dog at the moment.'

'I suppose so – he does want to start putting money aside for the baby.'

'There you go, then! I really wouldn't read too much into it.'

Her sister's assured tone cheered Camilla up. Calypso was right, she was putting two and two together and coming up with eight.

'I didn't expect you to be awake,' she said instead. 'You're not working today, are you?'

Calypso looked at her. 'Don't wet your pants, Bills, but I'm going out with Rafe Wolfe again. He's picking me up at nine.'

All thoughts about Jed temporarily forgotten,

Camilla's mouth stretched into an excited 'O'. 'Wow!'

'Please, don't make a big deal of it,' Calypso said grumpily. 'It's not like I'm spending the day boating with Dave Grohl.' She had long lusted after the Foo Fighters' front man.

'If you say so,' replied Camilla. Her eyes widened. 'Ooh, I wonder where he's taking you!'

Calypso threw a cushion at her and Camilla ducked, laughing.

'Piss off and make my tea!' Calypso said. 'And *don't* tell anyone about it, or the whole village will be in uproar!'

At 9 a.m. precisely there was a knock on the front door. Before Calypso could get there, her sister was opening it.

'Hello, Rafe!'

Rafe stood on the doorstep, casually sexy in a V-neck white T-shirt and petrol-blue slacks. He took off his Ray-Bans. 'Hello, Camilla.'

Her sister appeared behind her, in a waft of Agent Provocateur.

Rafe smiled at Calypso, taking in the striped minidress and knee-high gladiator sandals. 'You look nice.'

Camilla stepped aside. 'Well, I'll let you get on. Have fun!'

'Are you going to tell me where we're going?' Calypso asked, as they buckled up in his Porsche.

Rafe started the engine. 'All good things come to those who wait.'

Calypso sat back and wondered if her and Rafe's

idea of a good time would be similar. To her relief she hadn't seen any golf clubs on the back seat.

The weather report had been right. Under the pale-blue morning skies, a patchwork of delightful hues stretched as far as the eye could see. It looked like Mother Nature had thrown a quilt over the landscape: topsy-turvy green fields, daisy-yellow rape flowers rippling in the breeze. Calypso leaned back against the headrest and drank it all in. She'd been all over the world, but there really was nowhere as spectacular as home on a sunshine-filled day.

Rafe was obviously thinking the same. 'Beautiful isn't it?' he remarked as they sped past the apple-coloured hedgerows. 'That's the one thing I miss about living in LA, all this.'

'You wouldn't be saying that in the middle of winter, when it's all muddy and shit.'

'Ah, but then you have long walks muffled up and pub lunches in front of the fire.'

Calypso picked a stray thread off her dress. 'I'd still rather be hiking round the Hollywood Hills in seventy degrees. You'd die of exposure before you got to the front gate here in December.'

Rafe laughed. 'Maybe.' He glanced down at her long bare legs, crossed messily in the footwell. 'Do you wear that stuff all year round?'

Calypso raised an amused eyebrow. 'Stuff?'

'You know, micro skirts, skin-tight leather trousers . . .'

He had obviously remembered what she had worn at the Jolly Boot welcome party.

'Have you been perving after me?'

'No!'

To her greater amusement, Calypso was sure Rafe blushed.

'I think you have a very good dress sense, that's all,' he said. 'It's very individual.'

'Thanks.' Calypso didn't know what else to say. Though she had noticed how his white V-neck showed off a tantalizing flash of bare, broad chest.

After half an hour of negotiating the twisty roads, Rafe slowed down and indicated right down a little track.

Calypso read the signpost. 'Toplands Farm?' She shot him a look. 'Just because I live in the country doesn't mean I know how to drive a tractor.'

He chuckled. 'You'll see.'

It was an isolated spot high up, surrounded by acres of farming land. As they bumped along she could see a square house, surrounded by outbuildings. Calypso crinkled her brow. What was going on?

As they reached the top of the track, instead of turning right towards the main house, Rafe turned left and drove slowly round the back of a large shed. There was a huge field behind, flat and grassy, with what looked like a runway down the middle. A sporty red and white light aircraft stood at one end of it.

Calypso still didn't understand. 'We're going flying?' she asked. 'Where's the pilot?'

Rafe turned off the engine. 'You're looking at him.'

Calypso's mouth gaped. '*You're* flying it?'

'I got my private pilot's licence a few years ago. I fly

when I can,' he told her. He nodded at the plane. 'I normally keep her at a private airfield in Suffolk, but I had someone fly her over last night.'

Calypso admired the sleek contours of the aircraft. It was one cool machine. 'Nice.'

'Cirrus SR 22. Same one Angelina Jolie's got,' he told her.

'Got a job lot, did you?' Calypso shot back good-naturedly. *Camilla was going to give birth when she told her about this!*

'Can you tell me where we're going? Or will I be blindfolded for the journey?'

Rafe grinned. 'No point, you'd miss the best part. We're going to Le Touquet, a nice little resort on the Côte d'Opale. *Qu'est ce que tu pense?*'

'*Ça serait vachement bien!*'

He looked relieved. 'Great. I tend to fly to France mostly, as I don't get recognized as much over there. They don't hold much truck with famous faces, thank God.' Reaching across her, Rafe pulled open the glove compartment. 'Before we go, I've got a present for you.'

'What's this?' Calypso said, as he handed her a box of Milk Tray. 'They're for me?'

'Who else would they be for? I was going to come round to your office and surprise you until the damn paparazzi showed up. I've been quite good avoiding them, but I didn't think your grandmother would appreciate me turning up with a whole load of photographers in tow.'

So they were for her, after all. A beat of happiness

skipped across her heart. Calypso turned the battered box over in her hand. 'Wow, so this is what the girls get when they go out with Rafe Wolfe, eh?'

'Not my first choice, I have to admit. But your village shop is rather limited on the Belgian chocolate selection.'

Calypso squinted at the box. 'They've only been out of date six years, too.'

Rafe whipped his head round. 'You're joking?'

'Don't worry,' Calypso laughed. 'We're all used to Brenda's habit of hoarding by now.'

A short while later, they were ensconced in the tiny cockpit. Calypso pulled out her Ray-Ban aviators; thank God she'd gone for them and not the Chanel sunglasses.

Rafe handed her a pair of headphones, and as she put them on, he switched on the ignition and the propeller stuttered and roared into life.

'Ready?' he said into his mouthpiece.

Calypso gave the thumbs up.

Eyes fixed ahead, Rafe pushed in the throttle. The little plane started trundling down the runway, picking up speed as she went. Just as Calypso was convinced they were going to crash into the hedgerow at the other end, the plane's nose picked up and they soared off into the blueness beyond.

Calypso had been in private aircraft before, but never on a flawless day like this. The sky was endless, the countryside mapped out intricately beneath. It looked like a little toy kingdom. Rafe handed her a map, pointing out their route. They flew down to

Southampton and then along the south coast to Dover. As they approached the white cliffs of Dover, Rafe pointed out a sprawling train station on his left.

'That's the terminus to the Channel Tunnel.'

As they soared over the cliffs, the plane climbed up to five thousand feet. Even with the headphones, there wasn't much chance for conversation above the roar of the engine. Calypso was content to look out of the window at the cross-channel ferries and huge tankers below, mere dots in the expanse of ocean.

After ten minutes, the north-east coastline of France came into view. The plane got lower as they approached Le Touquet airport.

'I'm going to speak to air traffic control,' Rafe said. 'Le Touquet, this is Golf Romeo Romeo. Request descent.'

He landed smoothly on the tarmac runway and taxied the aircraft in. It was a small airport, with dozens of private airplanes lined up next to each other. Their passage through customs was quick; the immigration officer raised a casual eyebrow when he read the name on Rafe's passport, and wished them a good day.

The pair made their way out of the air terminal, into a sprawling wood of pine trees. They started to follow a winding path. After the assault on Calypso's eardrums it was blissfully quiet.

'All these houses were built around 1910 by an English developer,' Rafe explained, as they passed another luxury villa tucked away in the trees. 'Along with the Parisians, the cream of British society would come and rent them for the summer season. I think Noel Coward and his set were rather big fans.'

Half an hour later they were in the centre of the town, which sported beautiful turn-of-the-century buildings, immaculate flower lawns and a casino. Rafe steered Calypso towards a cobbled street lined with ice-cream shops, brasseries and expensive boutiques. Even though it was crowded with people enjoying the weekend sun, Rafe attracted few double takes. With his cap down low and wraparound sunglasses, it was hard to make out who he was. Calypso's long blonde hair and even longer legs were getting more attention from the waiters in restaurants.

'They're probably wondering what Kate Moss is doing with such a boring bloke,' Rafe said drily.

'Ha ha,' Calypso smiled back. He certainly was no Pete Doherty.

The end of the street branched out into a wide promenade. Beyond was a stunning beach, wide and sandy for miles in each direction. Families and couples alike played or sunbathed happily. The golden sand was clean and there wasn't a tattoo or Kiss Me Quick hat in sight.

'Beautiful isn't it? We'll go for a walk after lunch,' Rafe said. 'I've booked us into this little place round the corner.'

The tiny, bustling restaurant was down a side street. The number of locals in there was a good sign, and the place didn't disappoint. Afterwards, pleasantly full of wonderful flavours and food, the pair took a long meandering walk along the shoreline. Calypso found herself taking Rafe's arm as they chattered companionably about music and movies. For someone

226

she'd dismissed as a lightweight actor, Rafe was surprisingly knowledgeable and passionate about his craft. She learnt that he was frustrated at being typecast, and was looking to change agents.

'I haven't told anyone that, not even my manager,' he told her. Calypso felt another glow of pleasure.

Around 4 p.m., Rafe looked at his TAG Heuer watch.

'We'd better be off,' he said regretfully. Thirty minutes later, they were making their way back across the Channel, leaving behind Le Touquet – and one of the best days Calypso had had in ages.

They were ten minutes into the journey when Calypso had an idea. All that French champagne had made her feel rather horny. She shot Rafe a sly look, he was just studying the map on his lap. She slid her hand under the map and placed it on his groin.

He looked down.

'Is there anything to say it's illegal to have oral sex three thousand feet up in the air?' she asked saucily.

Rafe looked over his sunglasses, eyes wide. 'No, but I'm not sure it's a good idea. Oh Christ.' He shut his eyes momentarily as Calypso started rubbing his cock. To her satisfaction, she felt him grow hard almost immediately. It was *big*.

Instinctively Rafe glanced out the window, making Calypso laugh. 'It's not as if anyone's going to see us up here!'

'I was just checking, oh Jesus!'

He stopped short as Calypso leant over and un-zipped his trousers, coaxing his cock out of his Ralph

Lauren pants. It bounced out like a rubber truncheon. Calypso had to get her mouth round it.

'Mmmm,' he moaned, as she slid her tongue up and down his shaft, sucking enthusiastically on his bell-end. He tasted of good, healthy skin, mixed in with the faint tang of washing powder. Calypso loved it. She started licking and sucking harder, her long blonde hair flopping in his lap. Trying to stare resolutely forward, Rafe moved one hand from the control panels on to her head.

'I'm going to come . . .'

Calypso stepped up her pace, filling her whole mouth with his shaft. God, it was a nice cock!

'Aah, aah,' he moaned. 'Oh, CHRIST.' As he ejaculated into Calypso's mouth the plane nose-dived forward and it took all Rafe's efforts to regain control of it. 'Calypso, that was incredible!'

She winked, savouring the taste of his cum. 'I like to provide an in-flight service.'

Rafe exhaled, still panting. 'I'd love to know what you give your first-class passengers.' He tucked himself back in. 'I seem to have lost my train of thought. Where were we?' He consulted the map. Surprise flittered across his face. 'We've come across one county too many!'

'Hope they didn't get too wet,' quipped Calypso, looking out the window. She couldn't believe she'd just sucked Rafe Wolfe off!

'What are you smiling at?' he asked, face intrigued.

She shot him a playful look. 'Oh, this and that.' She sat back, basking in the glow of what had just happened. As the sun seeped in, she began to feel her eyes getting heavy. *Don't drop off*, she told herself, as the drone of the engine became a soothing background noise. *Don't drop off* . . . Calypso opened her eyes with a start. They were on the ground. Dry-mouthed, she looked around. The seat beside her was empty. She peered groggily out the window; they were back at Toplands Farm.

Rafe poked his head inside the cockpit, making her jump. 'How's Sleeping Beauty?'

'I can't believe I did that!' Calypso said, hastily wiping a bit of dried saliva off the front of her dress where she'd dribbled in her sleep. At least she hoped it was saliva.

'The blow job, or sleeping through the landing?' Rafe grinned. He leaned across and unsnapped her seat belt, before pecking her softly on the lips. 'I have to say, that was a first for me. The former, I mean.'

'Me too,' lied Calypso. Flying always made her randy, maybe it was something to do with the altitude. Rafe helped her out of the cockpit and down on to the ground. Her legs were feeling a bit shaky.

'I've got a few checks to do, do you want to wait in the car?' he said. 'I won't be a minute.'

Ten minutes later they were bumping back down the track.

'Did you enjoy your little sojourn in France?' Rafe asked.

'It was bloody brilliant! Thank you for asking me.'

Rafe briefly touched her thigh with his left hand. The gesture made her stomach flip over.

They carried on driving in silence for a few moments. Calypso looked out the window, a thousand questions running through her mind. Was he going to make a move on her now and step it up a gear?

'You've gone quiet,' he said.

She smiled. 'Just thinking.'

'About what?'

Calypso threw him a languid glance. 'Oh, you know . . .'

There was another silence, in which the atmosphere abruptly changed. Calypso wound down her window; she was finding it hard to breathe.

Suddenly Rafe pulled off down a track, tyres screeching.

'Jesus!' Calypso screamed. The Porsche came to a sudden stop a hundred metres or so down the track. It was narrow and overgrown, surrounded by woods. Vehicles probably hadn't been down there for years.

'Have you gone mental?' Calypso turned to Rafe, but he'd pulled his seat belt off, and his blue eyes were heavy-lidded with lust.

'Calypso,' he said, taking her face in his hands. 'I hope you don't think I'm being forward, but I'd really like to finish what you started.'

'Hallelujah!' she said as his mouth crushed her lips, warm tongue seeking hers out. He pushed her already short skirt up even more, stroking the inside of her thighs. Calypso pulled up his shirt, and was rewarded with a flawless, muscled torso, the only bit of hair a fine line of blonde snaking down to his groin. This was the torso that millions of cinema-goers worldwide had lusted after. She could certainly see why.

The cramped conditions of the car were making it difficult for them to get at each other. Rafe suddenly sprang out, ran round to her side and hauled her out. He lifted her up, pressing her against the side of the car, his hands gripping her bum. Calypso wrapped her long legs round his back and they starting grinding together.

'I need to see you properly,' Rafe said. He carried Calypso round to the bonnet and laid her down on it. Then he pulled the straps of her minidress down, exposing her breasts. Nipples rock-hard, Calypso arched her back, wanting more. 'Your breasts are incredible,' he said huskily, running his hands over them. He pushed her legs open and moved his hand up, slipping it inside her G-string. Calypso moaned loudly. Aside from her bullet vibrator, it had been so long since she'd been touched there. It felt good. No, it felt *brilliant*.

Rafe was unbuttoning his trousers now, playing with his hard penis as he looked at her. 'I *really* am going to have to fuck you now.' He produced a condom from his back pocket and slid it on, before plunging inside her. Calypso wrapped her legs around his hips, pulling him in even deeper.

'Let's do it against a tree,' she gasped. Rafe picked her up and they staggered over to a large oak. Calypso could feel the bark scratching her back, but she didn't care. She felt *alive*, nothing else mattered. This was so fucking amazing . . .

Half a mile away in another wood, a poacher stopped, puzzled by the piercing cry. It didn't sound like anything he'd heard before, but then again it was probably just two badgers fighting. Vicious little buggers, they were. The poacher shook his head and went back to the dubious task in hand.

Chapter 27

The next day was the Garden Party's fortnightly meeting. Clementine wasted no time in getting down to business.

'Now then, after completing my weekly round of the village, I am delighted to see everyone's efforts are paying off. Having spent all of last Tuesday tackling Babs Sax's front garden, the village green has never looked so good. Even if I do say so myself.'

Babs Sax was an artist who lived in a house next to the village shop. Unfortunately she was more bothered about tone and texture than the ten-foot-high weeds. Clementine had taken advantage of Babs being away on a six-month painting retreat and had attacked the weeds with gusto. She knew the silly woman had her head in the clouds most of the time, and wouldn't even notice when she got back, anyway.

'Where is Babs, anyway?' Calypso whispered to her sister.

'India, I think.'

'Calypso!' her grandmother said crossly. 'You two haven't stopped gassing since you got here.'

'Sorry, Granny Clem,' Calypso apologized, but it didn't wipe the huge smile off her face. She had been buzzing, literally buzzing, since yesterday. She'd sworn Camilla to secrecy about her romance with Rafe, but it hadn't stopped her sister excitedly pressing her for more details. Calypso had stopped short of telling Camilla about the frenzied pumping she'd received on the bonnet of Rafe's sports car, but one look at Calypso after she'd arrived home last night and Camilla had known.

Daydreaming about Rafe's cock, Calypso suddenly realized her grandmother was saying something.

'Does anyone know where Freddie and Angie are?' Clementine frowned. 'They didn't tell me they weren't coming.'

Everyone shook their heads. A few minutes later the Fox-Titts rushed in through the back of the hall, looking rather flustered.

'Sorry we're late,' Angie called. She looked rather subdued. 'We've had a bit of an emergency at the Maltings.'

'My dear, what's happened?' asked Clementine.

Freddie sat down heavily in a spare seat. 'Bloody perimeter wall finally gave way. Squashed all of Angie's flowerbeds and took down an apple tree. Looks like a bloody disaster.'

The Cotswolds wall surrounding their property was nearly as old as the hills themselves. It had been submerged by the floods and ever since had looked decidedly wobbly. The Fox-Titts were already wrangling with their insurance company to repair the huge holes left by the floods in the driveway up to their house.

'The patch-up job hasn't worked, we're going to have to get the whole wall redone,' sighed Angie. 'God knows how many thou that's going to cost. If we get flooded again, we're buggered.'

The rest of the committee made sympathetic noises.

Angie smiled gratefully. 'Thanks, everyone, but I don't want to give the bloody thing another thought until we get home. Have we missed much?'

Clementine briefed them quickly on what had been said so far.

'All sounds tip-top,' said Freddie.

'Did anyone see that piece about Britain's Best Village on the news the other night?' asked Beryl Turner. 'Looks like we're up against pretty stiff competition.'

'The other villages are probably saying the same about us,' Clementine said rather frostily. She was annoyed that Veronica Stockard-Manning had been interviewed, and given the chance to gush about how marvellous Maplethorpe was. The revolting woman didn't need any more encouragement.

After Clementine had given everyone their new lists of duties, the meeting came to an end. As Joyce Bellows fussed around, making everyone tea, Calypso watched her idly. She wondered how old Joyce was; she was one of those women who looked like they'd been born middle-aged. Joyce was wearing a dowdy floral dress, and no cardigan for once. To her surprise Calypso could see she had quite a pair of knockers on her. She had a sudden comic vision of Reverend Bellows's beardy face burrowed between them.

'What are you smiling about?' Camilla asked, returning with two cups of tea. 'Or should that be *who*?'

'Oh, bugger off,' Calypso said playfully. 'I was just thinking, how old do you think Joyce is?'

'I think Granny Clem said she's in her late thirties.'

Calypso spluttered into her tea. 'What? She looks about sixty!'

Camilla smiled. 'Don't be mean.'

'I'm not, I'm just being truthful.' Calypso looked at Joyce's dull hair, scraped back off her face with an old-fashioned Alice band. 'Maybe I should offer to give her a makeover.'

This time Camilla laughed. 'Joyce would have a blue fit if you tried to put her in a miniskirt!'

'I wouldn't go that far.' Calypso was still studying Joyce. 'She's actually got quite a good figure under all that frumpiness. Someone needs to tell her to stop dressing like she's escaped from a geriatric ward.'

'Don't you dare,' said Camilla.

The next day Frances was on her way home from a charity luncheon. It had been an extremely boring affair, and she'd become depressed with the constant talk about what Lady So-and-so was up to, and did she know they'd had to sell a Rembrandt to pay for the school fees?

Even though it was out of her way, Frances decided to drive past Byron Heights. Devon was creeping more and more into her thoughts, but since Camilla had mentioned seeing activity outside his house, it had all gone quiet. Frances had quelled her curiosity so far, but now she had a sudden burning need to satisfy it. At the Bedlington crossroads she carried on straight for Churchminster, instead of going the quickest way round the back to Clanfield Hall.

As the turrets of Byron Heights loomed up in the distance, Frances's heart did a little flutter. It was the scene of so many happy memories for her: for the first time she hadn't been Lady Fraser, wife and mother, and had just been *herself*. Those fun-filled summer evenings with Devon, enjoying each other's company, seemed a lifetime ago.

Frances pulled up outside the entrance, which was flanked by two scary looking eagles. She realized she was holding her breath. But as she peered down the long driveway to the house, there were no vehicles outside, no signs of life. The windows stared blankly back at her, mirroring her own feelings of emptiness.

Frances sighed and started the car again. There was no one there. Lucinda Reinard must have got it wrong. Devon hadn't come back. Heart now heavy, she drove off.

Chapter 28

Camilla was in the deli deliberating over the stuffed vine leaves or the chilli chicken when she became aware someone had stopped close by. She looked up to see a young woman with a baby in a pushchair smiling at her. The woman had bleached blonde hair and a pretty, beauty-queen face.

'Camilla, isn't it?' She had a strong local accent.

'Er, yes.' Camilla said, wondering wildly where she'd seen her before. The girl noticed Camilla's quizzical expression and laughed.

'Don't worry. I'm not some nutter. Me and Charlie were just in the queue behind you and I couldn't help noticing. I'm Sarah Jackson. I live in Bedlington. I used to go out with your fella Jed a long time ago. I'd heard on the grapevine he'd fallen in love with one of the Standington-Fulthropes. Y'know, we always used to call you the posh girls from Churchminster.'

It was said in such a friendly way that Camilla couldn't help smiling.

'Oh right, were you and Jed together for long?'

Sarah laughed.

'God, no. And when I say together, it was hardly that. Jed had an eye for the ladies, like any typical red-blooded male.'

She smiled conspiratorially at Camilla. 'And now here he is, all settled down.'

Camilla smiled back rather stupidly. She looked down at the chubby-cheeked little boy in the push-chair.

'He's adorable, how old?'

'Eight months,' Sarah replied proudly. 'Me and Phil, he's my other half, we always wanted kids.'

She sighed. 'Hope you don't mind me saying, but I did use to dream about having kids with Jed. Talk about good genes! We were only kids ourselves then, but you have those silly conversations, don't you?'

'What did Jed say?' asked Camilla, feeling a bit sick.

Sarah frowned.

'Well, that he didn't want them of course. Said he never wanted to be tied down like that.'

She looked sympathetic.

'It must be hard you know, in your mid-thirties and wanting to start a family.'

'Oh, don't worry about me!' said Camilla, trying to sound bright. 'Anyway, I must dash, Sarah, I'm on my lunch break.'

Sarah stepped aside.

'Of course, nice talking to you.'

'Nice talking to you too,' lied Camilla.

'And good luck!' Sarah shouted after her. Camilla

smiled falsely and made for the door, her lunch forgotten. Once outside on the street, she stopped and gulped in the fresh air, trying to quell the nausea. Was fate, in the form of one of Jed's exes, trying to tell her something?

'There was some woman in 'ere earlier asking after you,' said Brenda. She gave Clementine her change back and pushed the loaf of bread towards her. 'Right bossy cow she was, wanting to know all about this and that and where to get hold of you. I told her if she wanted answers to her questions, she'd be better off going to the tourist office.' Brenda chuckled. 'She didn't take it too kindly, looked like the kind of woman who's used to getting 'er own way.'

Clementine groaned. 'It sounds like Nancy Drake-Simmons. She's been trying to get me to join this dreadful "Still Sexy Over Seventy" group she's set up. Apparently they went nightclubbing in Oxford last week!'

'If she comes in again, you don't want me to tell 'er you've gone lap dancing?'

'Anything but that, thank you, Brenda,' Clementine said crisply, picking up the loaf. 'I'll see you tomorrow as normal?' On Wednesday mornings Brenda came to clean Fairoaks.

'See you then Mrs S-F,' she replied. As Clementine left the shop Brenda went back to reading her copy of *Take a Break* under the counter.

Clementine decided to pop over to No. 5 and see Camilla. Her middle granddaughter had seemed rather quiet of late; Calypso had mentioned Jed was working all the hours God sent, and that she thought Camilla was feeling a bit lonely. Clementine decided a bracing walk with her and Errol Flynn would do Camilla the world of good. The old woman was a big advocate of the restorative effects of fresh air and exercise.

But before she could put her hand on the front gate, a voice stopped her.

'Hello, Clementine.'

Startled, she turned round to be confronted by the sight of Veronica Stockard-Manning. She had put on even more weight in the years since Clementine had last seen her: her once-beautiful face was now lost in rolls of fat, her substantial bulk hidden under a voluminous scarf and waxed jacket. She was wearing the same strong sickly perfume she'd always worn, though.

'What are you doing here?' Clementine asked bluntly, more out of shock than anything.

Veronica smiled, cheeks creasing up like Play-Doh, and gestured to a gaggle of ladies standing further down the road outside the Jolly Boot. A minibus was parked up outside. 'We've been on a WI trip to Hidcote Manor Gardens, and seeing as it's almost on our way back, I suggested popping into Churchminster.'

'Hidcote is a forty-minute drive away . . .'

Veronica flicked a dismissive hand. 'Details, my dear, details. We went to your public house for lunch, although I have to say it wasn't really to my taste. Some

241

of the others enjoyed it, although Mary Saundersfoot thought she found a hair in her salmon en croute.'

'I doubt that very much, Pierre is a Michelin-starred chef,' Clementine said, hating herself for rising to Veronica's jibe.

Veronica gave a non-committal smile. 'How are you, old friend? It seems like yesterday I was here in Churchminster. You and I, playing in the gardens at Fairoaks. I did love that house.'

Clementine's stomach clenched. She couldn't believe the sheer brazenness of the woman, talking as though nothing had ever happened. 'What are you doing here?' she asked again, although she had no doubts about Veronica's motives. She had come to spy on the village and see what they were doing.

'How *are* preparations for Britain's Best Village going?' Veronica enquired solicitously, ignoring Clementine's questions. 'It doesn't look like you've done much, but then I suppose you were facing an uphill battle from the start.' She waved a fat hand towards a rather sorry looking St Bartholomew's. 'Surely you're not going to leave the church in that state, are you?'

Clementine finally lost her temper, something she hadn't done for many years. 'Just get out of here, you vile human being!'

Veronica was quick to bite back, decades of bad blood boiling over. 'I wouldn't take that tone with me. There's no law to stop me wandering around your pathetic little village. And it is pathetic, you know, just like all you Standington-Fulthropes. That's half the reason I—'

Clementine's voice dropped, each word dangerously enunciated. 'Don't you *dare* say a word more!'

'Granny Clem, is everything all right?' Camilla had come out.

'Perfectly, Camilla.' Her grandmother's voice was brittle with anger.

'Camilla!' Veronica gushed. 'I've heard about you. I'm an old chum of your grandmother's.'

'You are no friend of mine, Veronica, and I'll thank you if you'll leave this village right now.'

Veronica tried to look shocked. 'Darling! There's no need to be like that, but I can see you're under dreadful pressure with the competition. It affects some of us more than others. Goodbye, then.' She shot a falsely sympathetic look at Clementine and waddled off back towards the minibus.

'Was that the woman you've talked about? The one from Maplethorpe?' Camilla asked.

'Unfortunately, yes.' Her grandmother's face had gone white.

'I say, are you OK, Granny Clem? Why don't you like her?'

Clementine didn't reply for a moment. 'It was something that happened a long, long time ago, darling,' she said eventually.

Camilla sensed that whatever it had been, it was still a massive deal for her grandmother. 'Are you going to come in?' she asked.

Clementine hesitated. 'Do you mind if I don't? I've suddenly got the most dreadful headache coming on, I think I should go home and lie down.'

Camilla was worried about Clementine. She'd never seen her look so angst-ridden. 'OK, I'll give you a call later instead.' She watched her grandmother walk wearily across the green, looking as if all the life had been kicked out of her.

Chapter 29

The hamper was almost as big as the delivery boy. Joyfully, Calypso signed for it and thanked him. Before she'd even shut the door properly she was ripping open the card's envelope to see who the gift was from.

'Thought I'd better make up for the box of Milk Tray. Can't wait to see you, Rx.'

Calypso opened the basket and gasped. Inside there must have been a thousand pounds' worth of beauty products and make-up. Laura Mercier eyeshadow, Crème de la Mer face cream and Jo Malone bath oils were just a few of the names packed in there. Rafe certainly knew his stuff. She was dabbing perfume on her wrist from a huge bottle of cologne when her grandmother came through.

'My goodness,' she said, looking in the hamper. 'Has Christmas come early?'

Calypso smiled coyly. 'It's from Rafe.'

Clementine looked mildly surprised. 'As in the actor

chap that came round to see you? The one from the film?'

'Don't tell anyone, Granny Clem, I don't want a big thing made of it.'

Calypso was still reeling from her encounter with the paparazzi. The last thing she needed was word getting out, and them following her around.

Clementine bent down and picked up an exotically shaped perfume bottle. 'Mr Wolfe certainly seems rather taken with you.' She looked enquiringly at her granddaughter. 'Are you an item? I do believe that's the expression you young people use these days.'

'Whoa, hold your horses. I don't know about that yet.'

Calypso couldn't help the grin. 'But I do like him.'

'I don't think I've ever seen you so smitten before,' Clementine laughed.

'Ha ha,' said Calypso, but she didn't protest. 'I'm going to take this up to my office and try it all out.'

Once she got upstairs she flopped down in her chair, thinking. *Was* she smitten? She knew she'd never fallen for someone this hard and this fast before. Her mind flickered back to last night, when Rafe had fucked her over every machine in his gym before bringing her to orgasm against the mirror. Calypso had never had such a good workout. She and Rafe had turned out to be sexual dynamite, and for someone who looked so clean-cut, he was dirty as hell in bed.

Calypso sighed happily, reliving the noisy climax they'd both reached last night. God, she was getting turned on just thinking about it . . .

The phone rang, startling her out of carnal thoughts. She snatched it up. 'Hello, Semen Events. I mean, Scene!' She listened to the exclamations on the end of the line. 'You're looking for someone to do your daughter's sixteenth? No, madam, I can *assure* you it's not that kind of company . . .'

Angie had slept badly the night before, and the last thing she needed was Joyce Bellows knocking on her back door and waving. She got up from the kitchen table where she'd been unsuccessfully trying to finish off Freddie's *Daily Telegraph* crossword, and let Joyce in. Avon and Barksdale, the Fox-Titts' two energetic brown border collies, swarmed round her, tails wagging furiously.

'Good doggies!' exclaimed Joyce nervously. They only had a goldfish called Judas at the rectory. As Angie shooed the dogs outside Joyce rummaged around in her satchel and brought out a parish newsletter. She handed it to Angie.

'Just doing the rounds. Brian's written a splendid one this month, he's even included my "Forgiveness Flapjacks" recipe!'

'How splendid,' Angie replied, sounding a lot brighter than she felt. 'Won't you come in for refreshment?'

'Ooh, yes please,' said Joyce. She was wearing at least two cardigans and an ageing high-necked shirt and skirt. Her glasses hung on a chain round her neck. Angie thought it looked like Joyce had fallen into an OAP's dressing-up box wearing a suit of Velcro. The poor woman really had no idea.

'What can I get you?'

'A cup of tea would be super.'

Angie suddenly thought of the lovely Chablis Freddie had got, sitting temptingly in the fridge. 'Why don't we have a glass of wine instead? We can go and sit in the orangery.'

Joyce blushed, as if Angie had just asked her if she wanted a go on her crack pipe instead. 'Oh, I shouldn't.'

'One won't hurt. It's a jolly nice vintage.'

The vicar's wife hesitated. 'Just a teeny tiny one then.'

Heading over to the huge American-style fridge, Angie got the bottle out and poured them both a healthy glass. She settled the bottle and glasses on a tray and motioned for Joyce to follow her through to the orangery.

'It is lovely in here,' Joyce said, blinking up at the light, spacious room.

'Isn't it?' agreed Angie. 'Even on a dull day, sitting in here lifts one's spirits. It's my favourite place in the house.'

They settled themselves on two chairs.

'Bottoms up!' Angie said.

Joyce took a sip and started spluttering as it went down the wrong way.

'Are you all right?' Angie asked in concern.

Face purple, Joyce coughed into her handkerchief. 'Fine, thank you!'

Angie settled herself back and waited until Joyce had started breathing normally again. 'Do you feel like you've settled properly into Churchminster? I know how these things take time; it must have been awfully disrupting, moving from parish to parish.'

'Oh, it was!' Joyce said. 'But we can't pick and choose where God wants us to go.' She took another sip of wine, eyes watering. 'I hope we stay here, though, Brian has such plans for the village.'

'He really is doing a marvellous job,' Angie told her.

Joyce looked thrilled, as if the compliment had been paid directly to her. 'Oh, I'm so pleased you think so. Poor Brian does have a crisis of confidence sometimes, but I always tell him how wonderful he is. We have a "Buck Up Brian" night round the kitchen table at the rectory!'

Angie laughed. Despite the endless layers of beige, Joyce really was a sweet woman. It was obvious she was devoted to her husband.

An hour later, they'd just had a surprisingly lively conversation about everything from politics to pop music. Angie had laughed out loud when Joyce admitted she owned every Britney Spears album that had ever been made.

'I wouldn't have thought it was your type of music!'

Joyce shot her a wry look. 'Did you think I'd be more into organ recitals? I suppose I should, being a vicar's wife, but I do find it relaxing at the end of a day to kick off my shoes and dance round the living room to "Baby One More Time".'

Angie raised her eyebrows in amusement. She wondered what the vicar thought of Joyce's nightly shenanigans. She looked at the bottle of Chablis,

249

standing on a side table. To her surprise they'd nearly finished it. 'Can I get you something else?' she asked.

Joyce looked at her wristwatch. 'Goodness, look at the time! Thank you, Angie, but I'll say no. I've still got all these newsletters to deliver.'

As Angie stood up, she wobbled, suddenly feeling rather light-headed. Joyce caught her arm. 'Are you all right?'

Angie laughed. 'Wine just went to my head! It doesn't help I haven't had lunch yet.'

'I can always pop home and bring round some of my home-made soup,' Joyce offered.

'That is nice of you, but don't worry, Joyce. I've got some smoked salmon and salad to use up. I'll be fine.'

Joyce looked relieved. 'That's all right, then. I know Brian would want me to take care of his parishioners!'

Angie waved goodbye and watched the vicar's wife cycle off in a perfectly straight line.

Good Lord, she thought, chuckling. *I've just been out-drunk by Joyce Bellows!*

Chapter 30

'Sorry, Cam, I'm just really tired.'

Jed stopped kissing her and rolled back on his pillow.

'Hey, don't worry,' she said, trying not to feel too rejected. They hadn't had sex for over a week now, even though she kept trying to initiate it. Normally Jed would have just jumped on her.

He sighed, running his hands over his face.

'What's wrong?' she asked gently. He'd barely said two words to her all week. Sometimes it felt as though he was hardly aware she was there, and was lost in secret thoughts instead.

He stared up at the low-beamed ceiling.

'Is there a problem?' she ventured, feeling sick at the thought of what he might reply.

He glanced at her. 'What do you mean?'

She hesitated. 'With me trying to get pregnant, you know, I thought maybe you might be having second thoughts . . .' Camilla stopped. He almost looked angry. *Have I touched a raw nerve?* she thought.

'Jed?'

'What?'

'Have you changed your mind about us having a baby?'

'No!'

Not entirely convinced, Camilla pushed on. 'Is it work, then? You've been working harder than ever recently, it's enough to get to anyone.'

There was a short pause. Jed nodded his head. 'You're right, it is work. I should probably take it easier.'

Camilla's hands moved down under the duvet towards his groin. 'I can always make you feel better . . .'

Jed's hands stopped hers, pulling them up on to his chest. 'Not tonight, eh?' He tried for a smile. 'Night, babe.'

'Night,' said Camilla, as he switched off his bedside light. She lay staring into the darkness. Despite his assurances, something suddenly felt very wrong between them.

'Don't stop! Don't stop! Aah! Aah! That's amazing!'

A few miles away in the hamlet of Hedgewater, Calypso flopped back on the pillows, gasping. It had been one of her most intense orgasms yet.

Rafe looked up from between her legs.

'Was that all right?'

'It was more than all right!'

Calypso ran her hand through her hair, trying to catch her breath. Her legs were so wobbly that if she stood up now, she'd fall over.

Rafe moved up and kissed her left nipple. 'I aim to please.'

Calypso sighed happily. 'You certainly do that.'

He pulled her on to his warm, broad chest and she nestled in, listening to the sound of his heartbeat. It was a few moments before she spoke again.

'Rafe?'

'Uh huh?'

Calypso lifted herself up to look at him. 'What's going on with us?'

He stroked her hair. 'What do you mean?'

Calypso ran her fingers over his lips softly. 'I mean, I know it's a difficult situation with stuff, but I was just wondering how you feel about . . .'

She trailed off. Rafe looked into her eyes, his own resembling sea-blue pools that she could have lost herself in.

'Calypso, ever since I first laid eyes on you in the pub I've wanted you. Even if you did give me the runaround.'

She grinned. 'You weren't my type.'

He returned the grin. 'That's what I like about you. The fact that you're not impressed by any of this stuff – me. In this industry you have to be careful who you get close to.'

'Are we close, then?'

Rafe traced the outline of her cheek tenderly. 'We're more than close. I think you're amazing, Calypso. I want to be with you.'

A warm feeling spread through her body, and she started kissing him again.

Chapter 31

Clementine was feeling rather anxious. It was the start of June, and tomorrow was the day the film crew were starting to shoot on the village green. For the last twenty-four hours, prop and lighting trucks had been trundling in, causing havoc and traffic jams in the narrow lanes. The actual green seemed to have disappeared under a sea of scaffolding and people. As she edged past in her Volvo, Clementine was alarmed to see the grass was already getting churned up. She had to do something about it. Putting her foot down and scaring a man carrying a brace of dead pheasants out of the way, she headed back to Fairoaks. She knew she had put that business card somewhere.

Ten minutes later, she was dialling the number. The phone rang and rang. Clementine was just on the verge of hanging up when it was answered. The voice sounded out of breath.

'Hello?'

'Pam? It's Clementine Standington-Fulthrope.'

There was a short pause. 'Oh, hello there!'

'I hope I haven't disturbed you.'

'Not at all. I'm just in Bedlington, actually, picking up a few bits and pieces. Just got back to the car. How can I help?'

'Pam, I'm rather concerned about all the activity on the green. I've just driven past and there's no plastic sheeting or anything down. The grass is getting dreadfully churned up.'

Pam made a sympathetic noise. 'Someone's probably forgotten to tell someone else to do it. Don't worry, I'll get on to it straight away.'

'I would be tremendously grateful,' Clementine said. Feeling reassured, she put the phone down. Pam sounded like a woman who would get things done.

When the occupants of Churchminster drew back their bedroom curtains the next morning, they couldn't believe their eyes. Overnight, the square patch of village green had been completely transformed into an eighteenth-century market. The centrepiece was a very realistic fountain, around which stood wooden stalls selling their wares. There was even a life-sized pair of stocks for some unfortunate miscreant, and a pen filled with real pigs dozing happily on a straw bed.

To protect the film set and cause minimum disruption, the police had closed all the roads in and out of Churchminster for the day. This hadn't stopped gaggles of onlookers from cloistering around the film cordons, hoping to catch a glimpse of Rafe Wolfe or get Sophia Highforth's autograph. The paparazzi had turned up in their droves as well, and the hard-looking security men – who made the Mitchell brothers look like the Chuckle brothers – were patrolling the perimeters, keeping a close eye on things.

True to her word, Pam had got the grass crisis sorted out and Clementine had been pleased to see plastic mesh down on the busiest thoroughfares. It was a pity others weren't so conscientious: Clementine had already had to tell a group of giggling schoolgirls to pick up their empty bottles of Coke and discarded chewing-gum wrappers as they took pictures on their camera-phones, screaming every time they saw a blond-haired man.

Camilla had the morning off, so she'd come out to stand by her garden gate and watch. It certainly was something. A gaggle of local schoolchildren dressed as ragamuffins were herded past, while a gang of extras filled in the time by playing impromptu football with a stray pumpkin. All around was noise and shouting and movement, as everyone rushed around chaotically, each with a different job to do.

'Camilla!' It was Angie Fox-Titt, in a peasant woman's dress and floppy servant's cap. She appeared to be wearing a false set of stained brown teeth

'Nice outfit!' laughed Camilla. The Fox-Titts had both signed up to be extras.

'You should see Freddie, he looks like a relic from the Black Death!'

A woman with a loudspeaker started calling for all the extras.

Angie waved, 'Might see you later! I'm going to need a glass of something after this!'

Suddenly, there was excited screaming from the on-lookers and Camilla could see Sophia Highforth had appeared, dazzling in a full-length crimson gown. Compared to the scruffily dressed people around her, Sophia's blonde hair and soft complexion were more luminous than ever. Camilla noticed the suited man from the Jolly Boot party was with her, while a young woman walked alongside Sophia, anxiously pulling out her long skirts to make sure they sat properly.

The screams intensified as she came over to sign a few autographs. Camilla couldn't help but stare enviously at the gracious way Sophia worked the crowd. Her fans were putty in her perfectly manicured hands,

'Sophia!'

'We love you, Sophia!'

For a few minutes she chatted and laughed along with them, happily posing for pictures. It was easy to see her star quality. Sophia just radiated an aura.

The suited man tapped his watch with his fingers, looking agitated. Sophia registered the gesture.

'I've really got to get back now, but it was so lovely to see you all,' she said to the assembled crowd.

'Don't go!' someone shouted. Sophia bestowed another sunbeam smile in his direction and floated off, acknowledging the shouts and calls in her wake. As she passed Camilla, Sophia caught Camilla's gaze and after a pause flashed a vague smile.

Camilla dropped her eyes, embarrassed to have been caught staring. When she looked up, Sophia was saying something to her female companion. The companion glanced in Camilla's direction before the two walked off, the suited man scurrying in their wake.

Cheeks burning, Camilla looked away. Had Sophia been talking about *her*? A nasty paranoid suspicion started in her stomach. Jed hadn't mentioned it, but had he seen Sophia again? The Hall was a pretty easy place to bump into someone, and Sophia had made no secret of her appreciation of Camilla's boyfriend. The memory of Sophia leaning out of her car and giving Jed an eyeful of her cleavage shot through Camilla's mind. The film set had suddenly lost all its appeal. Turning on her heel, she retreated back up the garden path.

At the centre of all the action, Wes Prince scowled into the little screen monitor that allowed him to see every angle of filming. No one could get it bloody right today, and they'd already had to shoot this crowd scene five times. That was the trouble with extras: most of them were a bunch of bloody weirdos who wouldn't know how to take direction if it came up and bit them on the arse.

'All right, let's try again,' he shouted. 'Action!'

Cameras rolling, the three cameramen panned out to show the crowd, each getting a different angle. So far, so good. As instructed by Wes, the trio started to move back in, showing the stalls and customers going about their business.

They'd just done a nice montage of crowd shots – Wes had told them not to linger on anyone in particular – when one camera suddenly homed in on a young woman. She was enormously well-endowed, her assets spilling out of her low-cut bodice. Wes frowned; surely people hadn't worn dangly earrings and glitter on their eyes in the eighteenth century?

'All right, move it back,' he muttered, but the camera zoomed in even closer, giving Wes an eyeful of juicy cleavage. It could have been his imagination, but he was sure the young girl gave her boobs a jiggle. Wes looked up from the monitor and signalled frantically to Evelyn Vesper, who was standing behind the camera in question. 'Too much tit! Oh, for Chrissakes! CUT!'

As Wes stalked over to yell at Evelyn Vesper that they weren't filming a bloody smut movie, Stacey Turner hoisted her breasts up even higher. She was going to get in this film if it bloody killed her.

It had been a long day and dusk was falling by the time they started to pack up. Clementine had decided to come down with Errol Flynn to make sure the green was left as it had been found. From the amount of activity going on earlier, she was convinced a huge mess was going to be left behind.

She was pleasantly surprised to see the village green was nearly back to normal. All the stalls had been dismantled, the pigs taken back to the local farmer, and the grass had thankfully escaped unscathed. Despite her earlier reservations Clementine was impressed; they obviously ran a tight ship. She watched as the last of the props were loaded into a huge white lorry parked by the side of the green. It was a simple job for the truck to reverse back along the road, but for some reason, the back wheels were heading towards the green. Clementine hurried over waving her arms.

'Stop! You're going to go on the grass!' But under the noise of the engine her shouts went unheeded. Clementine watched in dismay as the vehicle reversed on to the green, leaving two huge tyre tracks in its wake. It was going to take months to grow back!

'Why didn't you look where you were going, man!' she cried at the cab driver. He wound down his window.

'Sorry, love, I was only following that woman's directions.'

He pointed his arm and Clementine saw Pam Viner, with both hands over her mouth.

She looked distraught. 'Oh good heavens, I'm so sorry!' She rushed over.

'I said reverse to your right!' she cried at the driver.

'You said left!'

'No, I didn't!'

Pam turned to Clementine, face stricken. 'Mrs Standington-Fulthrope, I don't know what to say.'

Clementine didn't, either. A sinking feeling washed over her. 'It was just an unfortunate accident, please don't upset yourself.'

'If I can do anything . . .' Pam trailed off. There wasn't anything anyone could do.

Clementine shot a death stare at the driver. 'Honestly my dear, don't blame yourself. There was an obvious *breakdown* in communication.'

''Ere, are you talking about me?' exclaimed the driver. 'She told me left, God's honest.'

'I suggest you get your vehicle out of here before you do any more damage,' Clementine said icily. After placating Pam one more time, she made her excuses and left. She couldn't bear to look at the damage for one moment longer.

Sometimes it felt like invisible forces were conspiring against them.

Chapter 32

Camilla had been asleep when Jed had finally got in, and he was already gone by the time her alarm went off the next morning. A pair of dirty socks on the floor by the door was the only indication he had ever been there. Camilla felt a stab in her stomach that he hadn't at least woken her to say goodbye.

Is that all we are now? Ships that pass in the night?

She lay staring at the Cath Kidston rosebud wallpaper. Something imperceptible had shifted between her and Jed. From having complete faith in herself and their relationship, Camilla now felt as if she were on shifting sand, no longer able to be sure of anything. Having the boss from hell didn't help either; she felt she was going from one bad atmosphere to another each day.

Why had Sophia's companion looked at her in that way? Camilla was convinced that she wasn't being paranoid. A nasty little thought that had been rustling at the back of her mind flared up. Was *Sophia* the reason

Jed had been so funny recently? Camilla realized with growing panic that she didn't really have a clue what Jed got up to at work. He could be off with Sophia at this very moment!

Stop this, she told herself. She was getting carried away. Camilla sighed, she was sick of this: thinking and dramatizing everything in her head. It was exhausting. She had to stop worrying about whether or not her boyfriend had the hots for a gorgeous film star. Camilla shook her head wrily, even she could see the irony in that sentence. But apart from Jed being a bit distant, where was the real, hard evidence? He'd told her the reason for that: he was tired and a bit stressed from work. Their conversation about Sophia flashed back into her head, after she'd been flirty with him on the green. Jed had made a joke about how Sophia wouldn't fancy him if she saw him mucking out the pig sties and Camilla had joined in.

'Or fast asleep on the sofa, cupping your balls!'

'I only do it when you won't cup them for me.'

Camilla couldn't help but smile at the memory. *That* was what their relationship was about: affection, closeness, sexuality. It was as if a little light had been switched back on, making her feel a hundred times better. She and Jed were rock solid. He wouldn't have his head turned by someone like Sophia Highforth, no matter how stunning. She was going to go up to the Hall and tell him how she'd been feeling, and they'd both have a good laugh about it. Full of resolve, Camilla swung her feet on to the bare wooden floorboards. She'd take him some lunch, start building the relationship back up again.

A few hours later she was driving along the sweeping drive to Clanfield Hall, two rounds of doorstep sandwiches and a large piece of fruitcake in a basket beside her. It was Jed's favourite. She'd got a bottle of home-made lemonade out of the pantry and put it in there as well. With lunches like this and a home-cooked dinner every night, she'd have Jed back up to speed soon.

As she drove up she saw Jed's van, parked outside the little trailer he was using as a makeshift office. Camilla parked up behind it and got out, clutching the basket. There was a small patch of daisies growing in the grass outside and Camilla plucked two and put them behind her ears.

'Jed,' she called out. 'Flower-girl delivery for your lunch . . . oh!'

Jed and Sophia Highforth looked round, surprised expressions on their faces. He was sitting in his chair behind the desk, and even though there was a chair on the other side, Sophia was perched on the desk in front of him. There was an air of intimacy in the room that Camilla really didn't like.

'Hey, you!' said Jed, springing up. 'I didn't expect to see you here.'

Camilla tried to smile. She noticed Sophia looking at the flowers tucked behind her ears, and pulled them out, feeling stupid.

Jed gestured to Sophia, who was looking even more ravishing than normal in her costume, her hair piled up sexily and a low-cut dress making the most of her creamy white décolletage.

'Er. This is Sophia. Sophia you remember meeting Camilla, don't you?'

Sophia smiled, showing little white teeth. 'Hello Camilla.'

The use of her name made a nasty little stab in Camilla's stomach.

'Hello!' Camilla said over-brightly. There was an awkward silence. Camilla didn't know what to do. 'Well, don't let me keep you.' Putting the basket down on Jed's desk she walked out. Camilla felt sick to her stomach. What was Sophia doing in Jed's office? *Isn't that perfectly obvious?* a nagging little voice said in her head. She hadn't gone ten yards before he'd caught up with her.

'Camilla! Are you OK?'

She turned to look at him. 'I don't know. Are you?'

He flushed. 'Is this about Sophia being in my office?'

Camilla tried to keep her voice neutral. 'It was a bit of a shock, if I'm perfectly honest.'

'She just dropped in, I could hardly shut the door in her face.'

'Does she often drop by, then?'

Jed hesitated, uncomfortable at the tone of her voice. 'A few times. She wanted me to show her round the estate so . . .'

The shock hit Camilla like a punch in the stomach. 'You've been on *walks* with her? No wonder you've been so "busy" at work!'

265

Jed took a step towards her, surprised. 'Whoa, calm down it was only once!'

Camilla bit her lip. She was sure Sophia was listening at the office door. 'I'm going now.'

'Camilla . . .' But she was already halfway back to the car.

'I'm sorry.'

His apology didn't sound heartfelt. They were in the kitchen, washing-up in silence. Camilla had put together a half-hearted supper of cold meats and salad, neither of them having an appetite for much.

She carried on drying the plate in her hands, not knowing what to say.

Jed turned to her. 'Did you hear me? I'm sorry.'

Camilla remained silent. Jed threw the dishcloth down in exasperation. 'Why am I being made to feel like the bad guy, anyway? I haven't done anything wrong. I can't keep myself under lock and key when I'm away from you!'

Camilla's irritation flared up. 'That's not what this is about,' she replied hotly, 'I've never stopped you being your own person, Jed. It was just a shock, coming in and finding you together like that.'

'Like what? We were just having a chat, for Christ's sake.'

Camilla threw her hands up in exasperation, 'Sophia fancies you, Jed! And don't tell me you don't know it.'

Jed sighed. 'I can see how it might have looked. But it didn't mean anything, OK?'

Camilla looked at him evenly. '*Do* you fancy her?'

An almost imperceptible expression crossed his face. 'No! He was defensive, almost angry.

Have I hit a raw nerve? Camilla wondered.

There was a long silence. Jed sighed again. 'Why are we fighting like this?' He caught Camilla's wrist and pulled her into him. 'I'll avoid Sophia from now on if that makes you happy.'

'You can't do that, it's silly,' she sighed. 'I'm not trying to be difficult . . .'

'The estate's big enough,' he interrupted. 'OK? Please can we make up? I really don't need this at the moment.'

Numbly, Camilla let herself be embraced by him. Jed was hiding something from her and she knew it.

Chapter 33

Frances had arranged to have lunch with her daughter at Claridges, but Harriet had apologetically cancelled at the last moment because of a work commitment. Frances was disappointed, but understood. Harriet had a career now, and was awfully proud of what she was doing. A career was something that had never been an option for Frances: she had been married off young and expected to provide an heir for Ambrose. Even though she had failed in that, Frances had thrown herself into what was expected of an aristocratic wife.

I wonder where I'd be now if I'd had a career? she wondered. Would she be happy, satisfied with her life?

A sudden bleep made her jump. It took several moments for Frances to realize it was her mobile phone. No one really sent her text messages apart from Harriet.

The text had been sent from a number she didn't

recognize, but Frances's heart skipped a beat when she realized who it was from.

'*Hey, princess, how ya doing? D xx.*'

Devon! Just as she was thinking what to reply, her mobile started ringing. Startled, she put it to her ear. 'Hello?'

'Hello, darlin.'

'Devon! Is that you?'

A chuckle. 'The one and only. Are you going to let me in or what?'

Frances didn't understand. 'Let you in where?'

'Your front door, you doughnut! I've been standing here for ages.'

The phone cut off. Frances stared at the screen, disbelievingly. Devon was outside? He couldn't be! She rushed over to the front window and sure enough, saw the little MG Devon used as a runaround when he was in Churchminster parked on the gravel outside.

She ran over to her handbag and pulled out her silver compact mirror to apply a fresh coat of lipstick. Thank God she'd had her hair done that morning at the hairdresser. Smoothing her chignon down, Frances shoved a dirty teacup and saucer behind the curtains and hurried out down the long hallway. One of Ambrose's ancestors, in full armour astride a rearing horse, seemed to look down on her frowningly. As Frances got to the huge wooden door she paused to regain her composure, took a deep breath and pulled it open.

At first she didn't recognize the strange man standing on the doorstep. The tall, lean physique looked familiar, but the man was wearing an odd combination of a stripy top, baggy black trousers and a floppy hat on his head. A bushy beard covered the lower part of his face, and his eyes were hidden behind dark round sunglasses.

The man pulled the glasses down his nose and winked at her. The piercing blue eyes were unmistakable. They were ringed by more crows' feet than she'd remembered, but that didn't stop Frances's heart doing a full somersault.

'Hello, princess,' said Devon Cornwall. 'What do you think to the outfit? I call it my "French painter" look.'

'Devon! What on earth are you doing here?' Frances exclaimed, but she couldn't keep the smile off her face.

Devon grinned back. 'Come to see you! Are you going to let me in, or what? I'm bloody dying of heat under this get-up.'

Frances quickly checked to make sure Mrs Bantry or Hawkins the butler hadn't heard the front door open and come to investigate.

'Of course, how rude of me. Do come in.'

As she shut the door behind him, Frances could smell the woody scent of his aftershave. Even though they were being careful to maintain a polite distance, just being in Devon's presence was having a disturbing effect on her.

She led him back down the hallway into her study, where the pair settled opposite each other in rather formal hardback chairs. With a sigh of relief Devon removed his hat, glasses and beard, flinging them on the table. Now Frances could see again the long, lean face properly. It was still on the right side of craggy, and with an obnoxious tan, hair curling round the back of his neck and a small gold crucifix in one ear, she thought he looked more like a raffish pirate than ever.

'Can I ring for anything?' she asked. 'Tea, coffee? Or else I've got sherry in the decanter.'

Devon shook his head. 'No thanks, Frannie, I'm on a bit of a detox at the moment.' After spending two decades battling drink and drugs, Devon had turned his life round and was now the epitome of clean living.

He settled himself back on the chair, one long leg thrown over the other and looked approvingly at Frances's Chanel shift dress, pearls at her ears and neck.

'Looking as good as ever, babe.'

Frances accepted the compliment with a gracious nod. She hesitated. 'How did you know Ambrose was out?'

Devon grinned. 'Thought I'd take a bit of a punt and see if his old Range Rover was here. If he'd caught me out I was gonna plead ignorance and pretend I'd got lost on my way to some art convention. Can't say my French is up to much, though.' He pulled a funny face.

Frances laughed. 'Oh, Devon, it is good to see you!'

And then the ice was broken and it was like they'd never been apart. Devon entertained her with tales of his touring, while Frances filled him on the latest with the film crew and what had been happening down the village. Devon did like a good gossip.

She was just telling him about how well Harriet was doing when she noticed Devon studying her intently. Frances raised a hand self-consciously.

'Is there something on my face?'

'It's not that, you look different.' Devon reached over and touched her cheek. 'There's a sadness to you Frannie, that wasn't there before.'

'I don't know what you mean,' she said, rather defensively.

Devon's gaze was unfaltering. 'What's up, princess?'

Frances stared back, before her eyes dropped to her lap. She could feel her bottom lip starting to wobble. 'I know how lucky I am to have my life. I really do. It's just that I feel something is . . .'

'. . . missing,' Devon finished softly. *Missing.* That was exactly the word she had used before. In a heartbeat Devon had understood everything.

Frances sighed unhappily. 'Still, what can one do about it now? One must accept one's lot in life. It's too late to change anything.'

Devon took her hand and it comforted her. 'It's never too late to change things. Look at me.'

After two decades in the pop wilderness, Devon had had a career comeback and was bigger than ever.

There was an expectant pause, in which Devon gripped her hand harder. The next thing he said knocked her for six. 'I'm selling Byron Heights.'

'Oh!' Frances sank back heavily in her chair. She felt as if she'd been punched in the stomach.

Devon tried to smile. 'Not much sense having a huge place like that when I'm hardly ever here any more.

Least that's what my financial advisors keep telling me. They're on to me to buy some poncy condo in Hawaii, most of my work will be that side of the world over the next coupla years.' He looked at her. 'What do you think, Frannie?'

Frances still felt like she'd been punched in the gut. 'I think you should do whatever feels right,' she said eventually.

If Devon was disappointed by her non-committal answer, he didn't show it. 'After all, there's not much left here for me, is there? The meaning was explicit. 'Is there, Frannie?' he repeated.

Frances looked at him sadly. 'Oh, Devon.'

Somewhere in the depths of the house, a grand-father clock struck.

Frances looked at the dainty watch on her wrist regretfully. 'Ambrose will be home soon.'

Devon jumped up. 'I should be off, anyway.'

'You're staying at Byron Heights?'

'Nah, all me stuff's been cleared out of there. I'm staying at an old mate's pad near Stow-on-the-Wold.' He looked hopeful. 'Say you'll come and visit me? We'll have the place to ourselves.'

Frances knew she shouldn't. 'I'm sure we can arrange something,' she heard herself saying.

Smiling, she watched Devon put his disguise back on, and walked him out; this time there was a companionable silence between them.

At the front door, Devon paused and leaned in softly to kiss Frances on the cheek. 'I can't tell you how good it's been to see you, princess. I'll be in touch.'

As Frances closed the door behind him, she leaned on it, her mind a turmoil of confusion and emotions. She had a sudden desperate urge to talk to someone, but realized the only person she could bare her soul to was Devon.

Chapter 34

The village's luck was about to get even worse. Early one morning, Brian and Joyce Bellows awoke to find the vandals had struck again. By the time Angie Fox-Titt had walked down there, after the phone call from Joyce, it was even worse than she had imagined. Lurid graffiti covered the entire length of the rectory wall, making it an utter eyesore for anyone who drove past. Someone had also sprayed 'WANK' on the 'Welcome To Churchminster, Drive Carefully' sign, and smashed up the old-fashioned red phone box.

A marked police car was already parked there. With a solemn look on his face, PC Penny was standing by it, slowly writing down everything Joyce and Reverend Bellows had to say.

Joyce looked tired and upset. 'Isn't it dreadful?' she said, as Angie walked up. 'And such offensive words!' Joyce shuddered, as if she couldn't bear to think such profanities existed.

'Did you see the culprits?' Angie asked. The Bellows both shook their heads.

'I was just telling the officer that Joyce and I are tucked up by half past nine with our Ovaltine,' the Reverend said. He looked momentarily brighter. 'PC Penny has found a clue, though, a size 13 Nike trainer in the hedgerow.'

'I'll take it off for processing,' PC Penny declared. 'It's a significant clue: the blighter's fingerprints will be all over it.'

'What if the trainer was there already?' Angie pointed out quite reasonably.

PC Penny's face dropped. 'I hadn't thought of that.'

By the time PC Penny had bagged up the trainer, informing them it would probably take ages to get anything back because of staff shortages, the three of them felt quite despondent.

'The whole place seems to be falling down her around our ears,' Joyce said miserably. Brian put a placating hand on her shoulder.

'There, there, God will punish them in his own way. Come back inside and watch GMTV, your favourite bit is on in a minute.'

Angie bade them goodbye and glumly started for the Jolly Boot to tell Jack his graffiti-removal services would be needed yet again.

Compared to the Bellows and the Fox-Titts, Calypso was positively buoyant. These past few weeks with Rafe had been like a wonderful dream. From someone who was normally a social butterfly, Calypso had turned into a hermit: all she wanted to do was have Rafe to herself. Every spare second they'd been holed up at his: cooking, making love, watching DVDs, talking. Each day Calypso found a new depth to him, something else they had in common. Even when Rafe was on night shoots she was happy to spend time at his place, thinking of what to cook him when he got back or sexual positions she could tease him into later. So far they seemed to have added several new ones to the *Kama Sutra*.

That evening, it was late by the time Rafe got back. The sun had set on the pale blue horizon, and salmon-pink and mauve clouds were smeared across the sky. Sitting in the garden with a G and T, one of Rafe's jumpers keeping her warm, Calypso had been gazing up, thinking how breathtaking it looked. There seemed to be touches of romance in everything at the moment, like she was seeing the world for the first time through a new set of eyes.

Rafe came out on to the patio, doing that easy smile that made her stomach flip. 'Don't get up.' He walked over to the swing seat to kiss Calypso and then flopped down beside her. 'Phew.'

'Long day?' she asked sympathetically, sitting up to rub his broad shoulders.

Rafe closed his eyes. 'Mmm, that's good.'

His mobile, which he'd chucked on the patio table, started ringing, the screen glowing in the darkness. He groaned. 'I've only just got home!'

'Don't answer it,' Calypso told him.

'I've got to,' he said regretfully, getting up. 'It's probably work.' He picked up the phone and looked at it. 'Yup, it's my manager. Do you mind if I speak to him?'

'Course not,' Calypso said, as he wandered back into the kitchen to take the call. She smiled to herself, Calypso loved the way he called it 'work' as if he was working in an office or shelf-stacking in Sainsbury's. It was so cute.

A few minutes later, Rafe came out. His shoulders looked rather tense.

'Everything OK?' Calypso asked, as he sat down again. Rafe had been getting a lot more work calls recently: if it wasn't Wes Prince or one of the crew ringing about *A Regency Playboy*, it was his management team, chasing him about a new film project or an endorsement.

He nodded. 'He wanted to run something past me.'

'They should give you the bloody night off!'

Rafe smiled and leant over to kiss her. 'You should meet Sophia's manager, Gordon. He makes mine look positively lax. Are you hungry?'

'Starving, obviously.'

'I could throw a few things together from the fridge.'

Calypso considered it. 'Why don't we go to the Wheatsheaf instead? They're probably still serving.' The Wheatsheaf was a little pub a mile down the road that did quite good food. She saw Rafe hesitate. 'What?'

'Nothing.' He smiled. 'I just like it when it's the two of us, that's all.'

'We still have to eat,' she laughed. 'They do amazing pints of prawns, you know. And I bet they'll be cool about you being a hot shot film star.'

As if on cue, Rafe's stomach rumbled. He looked at her and grinned. 'You've won me over. Let's go.'

Fifteen minutes later they were sitting in an enclave in the pub's dining room. True to Calypso's word, Rafe had attracted little more than a cursory look from the locals standing at the bar when they had walked in.

The middle-aged waitress came over and did a good job of pretending not to recognize him, too. 'What can I get you both?' she asked.

'I'll have a G and T please,' Calypso said.

'I'll have the same,' said Rafe. 'What the hell.' Normally he didn't drink through the week.

'Ice and lemon?'

'Lime if you've got it. Thanks.'

The waitress left.

'Special occasion?' smiled Calypso,

'Everything's a special occasion with you.'

Calypso rolled her eyes, loving every moment.

Fifteen minutes later, two pints of succulent prawns were brought out. The pair started to work their way through them.

'So what are your plans when filming has finished?' Calypso asked casually, pulling the head off a prawn. It was already the middle of June and Rafe only had a few weeks left on the shoot. She hoped her voice hadn't betrayed how much she'd been thinking about it.

'I'm going to take a holiday!'

'Oh right. Anywhere in particular?' she asked.

He paused and looked at her. 'Why, anywhere you fancy?'

Calypso flushed, was she that obvious? 'I wasn't assuming . . .'

'I didn't say you were,' he smiled. 'My parents have a nice place on the French Riviera, I was thinking of taking a trip out there anyway.' He popped a prawn in his mouth. 'Maybe you'd like to come with me?'

'I'd love to!'

They ate in contented silence for a few moments, before Rafe started telling her about his day. Apparently Sophia had been difficult, and throwing histrionics.

'That's why I'm so late, we had to redo one scene until she was happy with it.'

Calypso didn't ask if it was a love scene. She knew it was part of his job, but they never talked about it. Even though she'd told herself she was cool with it, the idea of Rafe running his hands over another woman's body made Calypso feel alarmingly sick. 'That's a bit annoying,' she said, instead.

'You get used to it. At least it shows Sophia cares about what she's doing, I suppose. She's a total perfectionist.'

'Camilla thinks Sophia has a crush on Jed,' Calypso remarked. Her sister had told her they'd had a ding-dong about Sophia being in his office. Even though Calypso thought her sister was getting her knickers in a twist about nothing, she'd promised to do a bit of fishing.

To her surprise Rafe looked serious. 'That's not good.'

Calypso put her prawn down. 'What do you mean?'

Rafe shrugged again. 'Sophia has got a bit of a reputation. I believe she's had quite a few affairs with people on set before.' He seemed unwilling to pursue the subject.

'Is there something you're not telling me?' Calypso asked.

Rafe looked across at her, eyes honest. 'No, I've just heard a few rumours.'

'Jed wouldn't do anything like that, he loves my sister,' Calypso said hotly.

Rafe put a placating hand over hers. 'Hey, I don't want to upset you. You're probably right.'

He released her hand and they continued eating. Calypso suddenly realized she'd been spending so much time at Rafe's, she hadn't seen her sister properly for ages. She suddenly felt a bit guilty.

'Are you still thinking about it?' Rafe asked. 'I don't want to set a cat amongst the pigeons, I'm sure it's nothing.'

Calypso looked up from her plate to see Rafe looking at her in adorable concern. It was physically impossible to have a long face around him. The waitress came to clear their starters. As she walked off, Rafe's phone beeped. He looked surprised. 'Sorry, I didn't think we'd have reception here.' He looked at the text message and pulled a face.

Calypso smiled. 'Don't tell me, work.'

He nodded apologetically. 'Sorry, I just need to reply quickly. I won't be a sec.'

'Sure.'

Calypso watched as his eyes darted back and forth under his long eyelashes, concentrating. She did appreciate him warning her about Sophia, even though it was clear he felt uncomfortable talking about it. A swell of emotion swept up inside her, Rafe was so gorgeous, so honourable and principled . . .

Suddenly, Calypso had to tell him how she felt. 'Rafe.'

He looked up from his phone. 'Uh huh?'

'I think I love . . .'

But instead of looking at her, Rafe's gaze travelled over her head instead. Instantly his face darkened. 'There's a photographer over there taking pictures!'

Calypso whirled round to see a greasy little man standing in the doorway of the dining room, furtively taking photos.

'That's not bloody on,' Rafe said and jumped up from his seat. Calypso followed him.

The quick-thinking landlord had already cornered the man in the corridor.

'This man was taking pictures of us eating dinner,' Rafe told the landlord angrily. 'It's a total invasion of privacy.'

'It's a free country,' whined the paparazzo. It had been total chance he'd popped in here for last orders and found the golden goose sharing a fishy starter with a stunning blonde.

'Not when it's under my roof, mate,' the landlord

said. 'This is private property.' He held out a hand. 'Give me your film.'

'Ow!' protested the paparazzo, taking the film out of the back of his camera. He begrudgingly handed it over. 'That's a whole day's work there, ruined! I should bill you!'

'And I should call the police to tell them you're harassing my customers,' warned the landlord darkly. 'Now, scoot.' Muttering insults, the man slid out of the pub.

The landlord looked at Rafe. 'You're working on that film, aren't you? I recognized you when you came in, didn't want to say anything. You must get it all the time.'

'You have no idea,' said Rafe gratefully. 'Thank you.' He looked at the loops of film, in the landlord's hand.

'Can I take it anyway? You can never be too sure these days.'

The landlord deposited the trailing mess in Rafe's hand. 'Do what you want with it, mate. Sorry about the interruption, I'll leave you folks to continue your dinner in peace.'

They sat back down. Rafe looked at Calypso. 'Sorry, what were you about to say?'

The moment had been lost, but Calypso didn't mind. 'Don't worry about it,' she smiled. 'I've got plenty of time to tell you.'

Chapter 35

Camilla pressed the buttons for Jed's number. It rang a few times before a male voice picked it up.

'Hello, Jed's mobile.'

'Oh, who's that?' Camilla asked in surprise.

'It's Pete.' Pete was one of Jed's team, a short chunky capable man who was always smiling. Camilla liked him.

'Hi, Pete, it's Camilla. Is Jed around?'

'No, I think he's got an appointment. Must've forgotten his phone.'

Camilla frowned. Jed hadn't told her about any appointment. 'Do you know where he's gone?'

'Haven't a clue, sorry.'

Camilla suddenly felt rather silly; as if she didn't have a clue what her boyfriend was up to. Thanking Pete she put the phone down. Where was he? An idea struck her and she scrabbled round for the card he'd given her, finding it in the inside of her wallet. The phone was picked up after two rings.

'Dan speaking.'

'Dan, hello, it's Camilla Standington-Fulthrope here.'

Seraphina Inc.'s location manager seemed surprised to hear from her. 'Hi, Camilla, is everything all right?'

'Oh yes, it's nothing urgent,' she said. 'Um, I know it's a strange request but do you know if Rafe and Sophia are filming today? My grandmother wants to know for something.' Camilla blushed at the lie; at least Dan couldn't see her over the telephone.

'No, they've both got the afternoon off. Can I help with anything?'

'No, no, that's all I needed to know. Thanks, Dan.' Before he could ask any more questions, Camilla said goodbye and put the phone down. Paranoia and worry coursed through her. Was Jed off with Sophia? Or was she just going completely mad?

As the tears sprang from nowhere she rushed for the downstairs loo.

Frances sat in the driver's seat, wondering what on earth she was doing. In front of her was a huge mock-Tudor house that looked like a bad-taste relic from the eighties. It had looked rather nice from a distance, but the closer she got the more it was like driving into an architectural nightmare. Gargoyles were dotted everywhere, sneering down on her unwelcomingly. As she peered up through the windscreen Frances saw that one of them was giving her the middle finger. She frowned; as she'd driven in she'd passed a letter box that was suspiciously close in shape to a woman's vagina.

As she sat there summoning up courage, the front door opened. Devon waved at her, looking more rakish than ever. He had at least four strands of beads round his neck and his white linen trousers were rolled up to show bare brown legs and feet.

'All right, Frannie!' He came over and opened the door. They kissed rather awkwardly on both cheeks, noses almost banging in the middle. Devon looked back at the monstrosity.

'What do you think to my digs?'

'I don't quite know what to say, Devon,' Frances replied. At least she was being truthful.

He studied her for a second and laughed. 'Minging, isn't it? I don't think Snorkel has been back here for twenty years. He lives on a two hundred foot yacht in the Caribbean these days. Likes the free life, does old Snorkel.'

Frances got out of the car. 'What does Mr, er, Snorkel do?'

'Big time record-producer in the seventies. Been living off it ever since.'

'I assume with a nickname like Snorkel, he's a keen fisherman?'

'Er . . .' Snorkel had actually got the moniker from the amount of muff-diving he'd done over the years, not that Devon would ever dream of telling Frances that. 'Something like that. Come in, I thought we'd have lunch al fresco on the terrace.'

Inside, the house was even more garish: six-foot statues of naked women with huge boobs, a velvet couch in the shape of a red-lipsticked mouth. Frances went up to study a collection of charcoal illustrations on the wall only to discover they were in fact more vaginas.

'Snorkel is a big collector of erotic art,' said Devon, hurriedly steering her away.

He led her through the rest of the house – bypassing the room dedicated to vibrators through the ages – and out on to a sweeping terrace. A table with a white table-cloth had been laid out, a bottle each of Dom Perignon and San Pellegrino chilling in an ice bucket. A vase of what looked like flowers that had been hand-picked from the garden stood in the middle. And, with their backs to the house, they could take in the stunning un-interrupted views of the Cotswolds.

'Oh, Devon, how lovely!' Frances said. 'You've gone to all this trouble for me.'

He grinned. 'You're worth it. Come and sit down, I'll get us an aperitif.'

They sat there savouring the views, Frances with a glass of champagne and Devon with his sparkling water.

'Is Nigel not back with you?' she asked. Nigel was Devon's extremely efficient PA.

'He's gone to Europe for a few weeks, some dusty sightseeing tour. He sends his love, though.'

Frances had a sudden pang of longing for the dis-creet, loyal Nigel who had cooked them wonderful meals when she'd gone over to see Devon at Byron Heights.

'Are you hungry?' Devon asked. 'I've got some lovely smoked salmon in the fridge.'

Actually Frances's stomach was full of butterflies, but she smiled politely. 'Sounds wonderful.'

As Devon busied himself in the kitchen Frances took a sip of the ice-cold champagne, looking out over the lawns. When Devon had texted her, asking if she'd come for lunch, Frances had agonized over it for hours. But in the end, she had always known she'd go. *This was so wrong, yet it seemed so right*, she thought, *so comfortable and domesticated*. She couldn't remember the last time she and Ambrose had shared a glass of something on Clanfield's terrace: he always preferred a glass of whiskey in his stuffy study at 6 p.m. Frances hated whisky.

A few minutes later he returned with the smoked salmon on a silver platter. It was dressed simply with cracked black pepper, lemon wedges and cucumber strips.

'This is delicious,' Frances said, delicately helping herself. Devon held up his glass.

'Cheers, princess.' He forked up some smoked salmon. 'So how's life been treating you since I saw ya?'

'Fine, I suppose.'

Devon raised an eyebrow. 'Just fine?'

'All right then, wonderful, sparkling, fantastic,' she said wrily. 'As you so perceptively put it last time, I think you know how I feel at the moment.'

Devon put his fork down and looked at her. 'What are you going to do?'

'I don't know,' she admitted.

'Are you going to leave him?'

There was a long silence. 'I don't know that either.'

'Run away with me,' Devon urged, but he was only half-joking.

She smiled. 'Is that why you've really come back, to come and sweep me off my feet like Prince Charming?'

He conceded with a grin. 'I'd give you a fantastic life, Frannie, think of all the things we could do together, all the places we could go!'

She laughed. 'Are you suggesting I become one of your groupies?'

Devon reached across and took her hand. 'I'd like you to be a lot more than that, Frannie.'

Frances found she couldn't speak.

Suddenly Devon leaned across the table. 'I've been wanting to do this since I saw you,' he said softly and kissed her gently on the lips.

Frances found herself melting helplessly into the moment. How many times had she had thought about this happening since he had left? She pulled away, heart hammering in her chest. 'Devon, I . . .'

He stroked her face. 'Sorry, princess, I came on a bit strong. I just couldn't help myself, you look so beautiful and elegant and fresh sitting there.'

'No, I wanted you to,' she said. 'I just . . .' She trailed off again. 'I should go,' she said abruptly.

Devon put a placating hand on her arm. 'Don't. Let's just sit here and have a nice lunch, eh? It's such a beautiful day and I've got raspberry syllabub for afters. I'll stop being a silly old fool and declaring my undying love for you.' He grinned at her, blue eyes twinkling.

'Well, if you have got syllabub . . .' she laughed, relieved he'd lightened the moment.

'I'll go and get the next course,' Devon told her. He paused in the doorway for a moment, face serious. 'I'm not putting pressure on you, but just think about what I've said. Promise me.'

'I promise, Devon.'

'How was work?' Camilla tried to keep her voice casual.

Jed barely glanced up from across the kitchen table, where he was reading the *Bedlington Bugle*.

'Fine, thanks.'

She took a sip of tea. It was lukewarm. 'Go out anywhere?'

Jed looked up this time. 'No, I was on the estate as normal.'

Camilla put her mug down. 'Only I rang you earlier, and Pete answered your phone, and said you'd gone off on an appointment somewhere.'

Jed's face flushed. 'Have you been checking up on me?'

'No, Jed, that's just what Pete told me!'

'Oh right, yeah, sorry, I did go out, actually. Had to pick up some new stock.' He gave her a sheepish grin. 'You know what it's like, one day runs into another.'

He picked up the paper and disappeared behind it. Unseeingly, Camilla stared down into her tea.

Chapter 36

Angie and Lucinda Reinard were sitting in Lucinda's Volvo estate in a little lay-by a mile outside Churchminster. They were on fly-tipping duty. Fly-tipping was the scourge of the Cotswolds: beautiful parts of the countryside ruined by people dumping old mattresses, rubbish and anything else they couldn't be bothered to take to the tip.

Fly-tipping had become Lucinda's particular bugbear, after she'd found an old washing machine dumped in one of the ponies' paddocks. Angie glanced across at her fellow Garden Party committee-member. With her daughter Hero's old hockey stick clutched firmly in her hands, Lucinda looked like she was about to go into battle.

'Do you think the hockey stick's a bit much?' Angie asked tactfully. It had been Lucinda's idea to sit here and do a stake-out – this particular lay-by was a notorious dumping spot – but so far no one had driven past apart from a farmer in his tractor and a fleet of lycra-clad cyclists.

Lucinda's grip tightened on the stick. 'They've got it coming to them. I've some Mace in my handbag, too, if anyone tries any funny business.'

'Isn't Mace illegal in this country?' Angie asked in alarm.

Lucinda muttered darkly about doing what was needed to protect one's village.

Twenty minutes later even she had to concede that they could sit there all day and not see one fly-tipper. Angie suggested driving round all the other dumping areas instead, to make sure they were clean and tidy. At least they wouldn't get arrested for doing that.

But at another spot on the far side of the village, they were dismayed to see scattered bags of rubbish and old clothes that had been carelessly chucked in the hedgerow. One of the carrier bags had split, tatty old magazines spilling out.

'Bloody people! Have they not heard of recycling?' cried Lucinda. 'If I could get my hands on them now . . .'

'Hang on!' Angie cried. 'There's a car parked down that track. Do you think it's up to something?'

Lucinda squinted into the distance and saw a dark vehicle parked in the shade of a small wood. She reached over into the back seat for the hockey stick. They could catch the buggers in the act!

'Maybe we should call the police,' Angie said anxiously. 'They might turn nasty!'

'We'll be all right,' Lucinda said. 'You stand behind me.'

Silently, they approached the car. The driver's window was open and someone had chucked an empty Lucozade bottle and cigarette packet out on the ground. As they reached the car, they saw that it too was empty. Lucinda tutted and reached in the car window, then looked about, frowning.

'Maybe they've gone into the wood!' They inched forward, eyes darting back and forth. Angie wished Freddie were with her.

All of a sudden, Lucinda stopped dead in her tracks, making Angie bump into her. 'Look!' She pointed her arm towards a little enclave of trees. Angie followed it with her eyes. In amongst the gloom, she could see a flash of white. Then a loud moan was emitted.

'Someone's having sex!' announced Lucinda. She didn't care if they were in the middle of copulation; she was going to tell them exactly what she thought of them chucking their rubbish out of the car windows.

'Lucinda!' whispered Angie urgently. 'We can't just barge in on them!' But Lucinda was already tramping towards the trees, hockey stick swinging purposefully. There was nothing for Angie to do but follow her. As they got closer, they could see it was a young couple, both completely naked, except the boy on top still had his baseball cap on, perched high on his head. He was going hammer and tongs rogering the life out of the girl underneath. Angie winced in memory, young men could be so *relentless*. She didn't have her first orgasm until she was twenty-three.

Intent on their rutting, the couple didn't realize they weren't alone until Lucinda was nearly on top of them.

'What's going on here?' she said.

Startled, the couple looked up. The girl, a pretty young thing with long blonde hair, screamed, but the youth, a gangly creature with a Celtic tattoo round one of his stringy biceps, curled his lip.

'What are you, some kind of pervs? Fuck off!'

'I will do no such thing, you little oik,' Lucinda retorted crisply, 'until you come and clear up the mess you've left outside your car. You can't treat the countryside as your own personal rubbish dump, you know!'

Angie noticed the girl turning her head away, shielding her face.

'Celia!' Lucinda suddenly cried. 'Celia Blakely-Norton, is that you?'

'Oh Christ, District Commissioner, don't tell Mummy!' the young blonde cried.

Lucinda shook her head and looked at Angie. 'Celia's one of our stars in pony club. Has a wonderful mount called Teddy.'

Angie thought Celia was being quite wonderfully mounted by this young chap as it was.

'Don't tell Mummy, she'll kill me!' Celia implored again.

Lucinda sighed. 'Well, as you're not underage I suppose it's none of my business. I must say though, Celia, I thought you would have more class than to go cavorting round the countryside with undesirables.'

'Oo you calling undesirable?' said the youth. Lucinda recognized him at the same time Angie did.

'You're one of that lot from Bedlington, who turned up and tried to ruin our *Churchminster's Got Talent* evening!'

The youth sniffed, seemingly unperturbed his skinny white buttocks were out on display for all to see. 'So what if I am? Place needed livening up anyway.'

'I'll give you livening up!' cried Lucinda, prodding his bony bum with the hockey stick.

'Ow, get off!'

'I'm giving you thirty seconds to get dressed, and then you'll meet us back at the car.' Lucinda dangled a pair of car keys in the air. 'And I've got these, so don't try any funny business.'

The youth's face darkened. 'It's my old dear's car. Give 'em back!'

'Driving round in mummy's car?' enquired Lucinda. 'Not so full of it now, are we?' A minute later she and Angie watched as the youth picked up his litter, muttering under his breath. 'And don't you dare let me catch you around here again!' Lucinda said.

The youth got back in this car. Once behind the safety of the locked door, he seemed to rediscover his confidence. 'You Churchminster lot are a bunch of tools! Someone ought to teach you a lesson.'

'And I'll teach you a lesson if you don't sod off!' shouted Lucinda. The youth revved his engine and roared off, flicking the bird, while Celia Blakely-Norton looked back apologetically out of the rear-view window.

'Honestly,' Lucinda said, watching the Ford Mondeo disappear in a cloud of dust. 'What on earth does Celia find attractive in someone like that? She comes from a jolly good family. Her parents would have a blue fit.'

'Oh, you know what it's like when one is young. Lure of the bad boy and all that,' said Angie. 'You were awfully brave then, Lucinda!'

Lucinda snorted. 'When you've had two hundred rowdy kids at Pony Club camp to deal with, a mouthy hoodlum from Bedlington is nothing!'

Drama over, they got bin liners and plastic bags out of the boot and set to work clearing up the rest of the rubbish.

'How can some people live with themselves?' Lucinda said crossly a few minutes later, holding up a doll with no head and what looked like a rusty hamster cage.

Angie didn't reply, she had her head stuck under the hedge trying to pull a length of old carpet out. She had just managed to stuff it in her bag when Lucinda gave an exclamation. 'I say! Look at these!' She held up a collection of tatty old magazines. 'It's someone's porn collection.' She started flicking through them. '*Soapy Tit Wank*, *Dirty Angels*, *Filthy Farm Girls*.' Lucinda gave a dismissive sniff. 'It's very tame, I've seen a lot harder.' She brandished one at Angie, in which an excited-looking man was chasing a nubile young girl round a bedroom. She was wearing a big smile, a tiny pair of panties and not much else.

'They don't look recent,' said Angie, taking in the 1980s perms and tacky furnishings.

'Someone's wife has obviously found this little stash

and told him to get rid of it,' said Lucinda. 'How frightfully cul-de-sac and *suburban*.'

She started stuffing the magazines into the bin bag, and both of them were blissfully unaware that if they'd just turned over the page, they would have had the shock of their lives.

Katie knocked on the door of Sophia's Winnebago. There was no answer, even though she could hear Sophia speaking to someone inside.

A fat splodge of rain fell, threatening to stain the delicate silk gown bundled up in Katie's arms. She knocked again, harder. She was going out for drinks with some of the girls from make-up later, and had no desire to be stuck for ages with Sophia doing this dress fitting.

Eventually the door opened and Sophia stood there, wrapped in a fluffy white bathrobe. 'You interrupted my phone call!' she scolded, but her tone was playful, not cross.

Katie followed her back into the van. A script stood on the kitchen table, waiting to be read.

'Yes, I was just on the phone to someone,' Sophia repeated.

'Anyone important?' Katie dutifully asked. It was obvious Sophia wanted her to ask.

Sophia looked mock shocked. 'You can't ask me that!'

'OK.' Katie didn't give a shit anyway. She thought longingly of that first vodka and lime in the pub later.

'But since you asked, it was someone very special.'

297

'A bloke?'

'A gentleman, yes.' Sophia looked coquettish. 'But it's going to cause awful ructions when it gets out, so I'd rather you didn't say anything.'

Katie went to open her mouth, but Sophia went on. 'A girl's got to follow her heart, after all. Have you ever had such chemistry with someone that you just have to be with them, no matter the repercussions?

'No,' said Katie. 'I can't say that I have.'

Sophia looked off dreamily. 'This man is amazing. He's going to change my life!'

Katie thought fleetingly of the black-haired estate manager Sophia was always banging on about. It was a bit of a comedown for Sophia, who normally dated the rich and titled, but Katie didn't blame her. Jack, or whatever he was called, was bloody gorgeous. *It is him*, she thought. *I'd bet my life it is.*

Chapter 37

As the weather had held out all weekend, Clementine decided to hold that week's Garden Party meeting in her garden at Fairoaks. Calypso and Camilla came over early to help put out chairs on the veranda, while Clementine busied herself making jugs of Pimms in the kitchen. She decided not to make the mixture too strong: with the heat the alcohol would go to everyone's heads, and she needed them to have their wits about them. She had also made trays of canapés to keep hunger at bay, as Jack Turner was lugging over his barbecue to cook them all dinner afterwards.

Calypso came bouncing in and went to the fridge to help herself to orange juice. 'Smoked salmon blinis, my favourite.'

'Get your hands off, those are for later,' Clementine said, as Calypso stuffed one in her mouth.

She swallowed loudly. 'They're bloody good, Granny Clem.' She threw her arms round her grandmother, planting a fishy kiss on her wrinkled cheek. 'Isn't it a lovely day? I do love you.'

Clementine couldn't help but smile at her granddaughter's exuberance. This Rafe Wolfe chap seemed to be doing wonders, and for once Clementine thoroughly approved of Calypso's choice of boyfriend. She thought briefly of Calypso's ex-girlfriend, who had turned up at a rectory sherry evening with a T-shirt with 'Helmet Hater' emblazoned across it, and shuddered. 'Where's your sister?' she asked, trying to disentangle herself from Calypso's perfumed grip.

'Gone for a walk. I did ask if she wanted me to come but she said she wanted to be by herself. She says she'll be back for the meeting.'

Clementine was concerned. 'Camilla hasn't seemed herself lately. Is everything all right?'

Calypso hesitated, Rafe's words ringing in her ears. 'I think her and Jed are having a few problems.'

Clementine thought very highly of Jed. 'Oh dear, I do hope it's nothing serious.'

'Mmmm,' said Calypso non-committally. 'I'm sure they'll work it out.'

Calypso had agonized over whether to tell Camilla what Rafe had said about Sophia. She had finally decided not to, it was only hearsay and she didn't want to make Camilla any more miserable. But Jed was behaving strangely and Calypso had her doubts. Especially with his history, she knew he'd been a bit of a shagger before he'd started going out with Camilla. She would have had a word with him herself, except he was barely at home and seemed to be avoiding her when he was. *Jed mate, don't fuck it up*, she thought. *Why were some men such cheating arseholes?*

By 6 p.m. everyone had arrived and was enjoying drinks on the terrace. Clementine clinked her glass, signalling the meeting was about to start. She waited until people had sat down and made themselves comfortable.

'Welcome to the seventh Garden Party committee meeting. As I'm sure you'll agree, the last two months have flown by and we have achieved a great deal, but there is still even more to be done. We only have four weeks left until the judges come round and change the fate of Churchminster. For ever!'

Slightly alarmed, everyone glanced at each other. It had all come round so quickly. Four weeks was nothing!

Clementine looked down at her list of copious notes.

'As you know, we have had to use up some of the money meant for the Church that we raised at *Churchminster's Got Talent* to not only reseed the village green from where the film truck reversed over it . . .' At this her mouth set in a grim line as she thought to herself: *I told you the film was a ridiculous idea.* '. . . but more worryingly, we have had to repair the spiteful acts of vandalism this village has suffered recently.'

Despite Clementine's hopes that they could have started restoring St Bartholomew's, they'd ended up having to call out industrial cleaners to get rid of the graffiti on the rectory wall because the paint was impervious to Jack Turner's special brew. Only days later, the new flower tubs had been kicked over on the village green and ruined. PC Penny was proving as much help as a chocolate teapot, and short of sitting up playing vigilante all night, they didn't know what else to do.

'Bloody disgrace,' shouted Brenda Briggs. 'If the police didn't spend so much time giving out speeding tickets to anyone who goes above 15 mph through Bedlington town centre, they'd have this lot by now!'

'Angie and I had a run-in with some yobbo from Bedlington the other day,' boomed Lucinda. 'I bet it was him!'

'Unless we install CCTV cameras on the village green, I don't know how we're going to prove it,' said Freddie gloomily.

'CCTV cameras are not going to help us become Britain's Best Village,' said Clementine.

Joyce Bellows cleared her throat. 'Has anyone seen the Maplethorpe website?'

Angie made a frantic chopping motion, but it was too late.

'Website? What website?' Clementine said.

'Er, they've got their own website,' said Angie.

Clementine was a bit behind the times. 'And what's on it? Why has no one told me?'

Several people exchanged looks. No one had wanted to tell Clementine because they knew it would only get her hot and bothered. But now it was too late.

'It's just like a parish newsletter, really,' said Angie.

'Only they seem to spend an awful lot of time criticizing Churchminster. It's nothing to get upset about, I'm sure it's sour grapes.'

Clementine looked shocked. 'Criticizing us about what?'

'Oh, just saying how we're a failing village, that we're not really pulling our weight,' Angie said. 'They've done it to the two other villages as well,' she added hurriedly, seeing the anger building in Clementine's face.

Clementine shot a look at Calypso, who normally helped her out with the Internet. 'Why didn't you inform me about this?'

'I didn't know!' protested Calypso. 'I'm up to my eyeballs with work, do you think I've got time to go searching for random websites?'

'I want to see it for myself,' Clementine said. 'Come along!'

She marched off to her study, followed by everyone. They all crammed in as Angie turned on the computer and brought the website up. It was a well-designed thing, with a picture of Maplethorpe's pristine village green on the home page. A banner saying, 'Winners, Britain's Best Village!' had been designed to hang above it.

'It's here,' said Angie, clicking on to an icon saying 'Veronica's BBV Blog'.

'What on earth is a blog?' asked Clementine.

'It's like an online diary, that anyone can read,' explained Calypso.

Clementine shuddered at the thought of anything

303

so self-indulgent and vulgar. But then again, Veronica had always been a terrific show-off. She started reading.

> *Churchminster is a rather woe-begotten little place and one does wonder if the judges only felt sorry for it to put it through to the final. It certainly isn't up to the usual standard of the competition, as well as the hideous ivy choking the rectory, which should be one of the most important houses in a village, I hear the village shop repeatedly sells items past their sell-by dates! Rather a case for health and safety to investigate, don't you think?*

'Bloody cheek, that tuna I had in was only six months out of date,' said Brenda.

Joyce cast a worried look at her husband. 'I told you we needed someone in to trim it back,' she murmured.

Clementine's brow darkened as she leant over Angie's shoulder to scroll back through previous entries. Everyone stood in silence, until she stood up again, grim-faced.

'They seem to know an awful lot about us and what we're up to. For instance, how could Veronica Stockard-Manning know about us painting the recycling bins?' Clementine fixed them with a beady eye. 'In my mind it is perfectly clear that we have had an undercover journalist or spy amongst our midst.'

'Well, it's not me!' Brenda Biggs exclaimed. Clementine rolled her eyes.

'I don't mean *us*. As you said before, one of those

ghastly reporters that always seems to be hanging round the place, asking all sorts of questions. I had another run-in with one outside the village shop yesterday; she only put her tape recorder away when I threatened her with my walking stick.'

'Steady on, Granny Clem!' Calypso laughed. Her grandmother was lethal with that thing.

Lucinda wasn't about to give the spy theory up. 'Why couldn't it be one of us?' she boomed. 'This Britain's Best Village is serious stuff. Someone could be getting paid a handsome backhander. God knows, people need the money.' She eyed Beryl Turner suspiciously. 'You were wearing a very nice sequinned jacket the other day. It must have cost a fortune.'

'I got it from TK Maxx!' Beryl said indignantly. 'What are you implying?'

Clementine interjected. 'Now then, now then. I'm sure it's not one of us.' She couldn't stop the thought. *Could it be one of us? Lucinda's right about people taking the competition seriously.* She dismissed the idea quickly. It was far too silly. 'I want you all to keep an eye out for any suspicious-looking characters and report back to me. Now then, let's get on with the agenda . . .'

By the time they'd finished it was past nine o'clock. The shadows were lengthening on the terrace, bringing a much-needed coolness to the heat of the day. Smoke from the barbecue, which Jack had already started, was wafting over and Clementine could see several people glancing over at it. She was rather hungry herself, by now.

'Right, everyone, I think that's it,' she called. 'Thank

you for being patient. If you've got any questions about your list, please do come and ask me.'

The meeting broke up, and for a moment Clementine stood observing her fellow villagers, chatting and laughing as they helped set up the barbecue. Everyone had bought along something, whether it was Lucinda's new potato salad recipe or Ted Briggs's home-made potent cider that he'd been brewing in his potting shed. Clementine felt a pang in her heart; Churchminster was such a close-knit community and they all looked out for each other. She couldn't bear it if it disappeared. Brenda Briggs had already said she'd sell up and move away if they got flooded again, and so had her next-door neighbour, Pearl Potts. Could the Jolly Boot and Angie's Antiques withstand more months of being shut if they got deluged again? These were people's livelihoods. It seemed one thing after another was threatening their little idyll, so warm, so helpful, such a rich tapestry of British life. Clementine couldn't even bring herself to think about what would happen if St Bartholomew's was closed down. *Churchminster would cease to exist*, she thought, stricken. *And I would, too, along with it.*

Over by the buffet table, Lucinda was getting stuck into her fourth glass of Pimms. Unbeknown to the hostess, Lucinda had emptied another bottle of Pimms mixture into the jug. Mrs S-F was a dear, but she did stint on the booze sometimes.

'Another top-up, darling?' she asked Angie Fox-Titt.

'Please,' said Angie, holding her glass up.

Joyce Bellows bustled over, holding a tray of cucumber sandwiches. She put them down on the table.

'Fancy a drinkie, Joyce?' Lucinda boomed. Her voice got even louder when she'd had a few.

'No, thank you, Lucinda. I never drink on the day of our Lord.' Joyce poured herself a glass of Clementine's home-made ginger beer instead. 'Are you enjoying your Garden Party duties?' she asked eagerly. 'I'm simply thrilled with the progress of the hyacinths in the churchyard, they look wonderful!'

'Wonderful!' echoed Lucinda. A mischievous glint entered her eye.

'Actually, Angie and I found a load of porn magazines when we were on fly-tipping duty.'

'Oh!' squeaked Joyce, going bright pink.

Angie shot Lucinda a half-warning look. *Don't wind her up!*

Luckily, at that point Lucinda's mobile went off. She scrabbled round in her huge handbag.

'It's from the house. What have the children done now? Hello! Yes, Hero, what is it?' Her face dropped. 'Oh bloody hell! One of the ponies has escaped!' She looked round frantically for her husband, who was deep in conversation with Calypso. 'Nico! That little sod Pippin has got out again, apparently he's galloping up the Bedlington Road! You'll have to drive, I'm feeling squiffy.'

Lucinda dragged her reluctant husband away, tripping over a stone badger and almost going head over heels on her way out. A minute later they heard the screech of Volvo estate car tyres as the Reinards took off in hot pursuit of the four-legged escapee.

'I wouldn't want to be Pippin when Bedlington Pony Club's District Commissioner gets her hands on him!' laughed Angie.

Chapter 38

'Feel my balls . . . that's it . . . bloody hell!'

Calypso's blow job was just reaching its finale. As she paused to take breath (deep throat always did take it out of her) Rafe blissfully ejaculated, white spurts shooting skywards like an atomic explosion.

'Oww, shit!' she yelped.

He looked up in alarm, chest still heaving. 'What?'

Calypso winced. 'You just shot in my eye!'

'You're kidding me.' Rafe sat up to take a better look. Calypso was kneeling between his legs, her right eye half-shut and beginning to turn red. Rafe let out a snort of laughter. 'Sorry. It's just quite funny.'

'That's easy for you to say. It's stinging like fuck!' Calypso tried to open it without much success.

'I've got some eye drops in the bathroom, hold on,' Rafe said and leapt out of bed. Moments later he was back. Calypso turned her face up and waited for them to be administered. Rafe started putting the drops in with the utmost care. Calypso winced again.

'Urgh . . .'

'Hold still for a second more . . . there you go.'

Calypso flopped back on the bed. 'Still bloody hurts.'

Rafe chuckled. 'It'll get better, although I'm not sure if the manufacturers intended them to be used for this. Just keep putting the drops in.'

'Eye eye, Captain,' she grumbled.

Rafe looked down at her, sprawled naked with one hand over her eye. He started laughing again. 'You might be the most beautiful girl I've ever met, but you're also the most accident-prone. What are we going to do with you?'

'Get me an eyepatch next time I give you oral sex?'

Rafe grinned. 'I think I can do better than that.'

Leaning over to the bedside table, he opened a drawer and bought something out. Through her one good eye Calypso could see it was a small box. She sat up, the pain in her eye temporarily forgotten. Was it a ring? Her stomach did a somersault. He was going to propose!

Rafe came to sit by her and slowly opened the box. Instead of a silver band, however, a stunning pair of diamond studs glittered back. Calypso's stomach did another funny whirly thing and finally settled.

Rafe looked at the plastic anchors dangling from her ears. 'I know they're probably a bit safer than anything you'd choose, but I still thought they'd look good on you.'

'Oh my God!' she gasped. The pang of disappointment she'd felt when she'd seen they weren't an engagement ring had quickly been replaced by excitement. They must have cost a bomb!

Rafe watched as she took her own earrings out and put the diamond studs in.

'What do you think?' she asked, suddenly a bit self-conscious.

He looked at her, face full of meaning. 'They look stunning, but you're stunning anyway.'

'I adore them! Thank you so much,' she breathed. She leaned in and started kissing him in the way that drove him wild. It didn't take long before his breathing became more laboured, coming in short, moaning breaths.

'And now,' Rafe murmured. 'If the patient feels up to it, I'd really like to fuck you in them.'

'Told you I was a diamond shag,' Calypso sighed happily.

Despite his best efforts to remain incognito while he was back, someone had spotted Devon going into an organic deli in Stow-on-the-Wold and tipped off the local press. The next day Frances happened to see Cook's copy of the *Bedlington Bugle* lying on the kitchen table, when she went in to make herself a pot of Earl Grey.

'THE RETURN OF DISHY DEVON' proclaimed the front page, together with a photograph of Devon on stage, and a picture of the deli he'd bought his vegetarian red bean pâté in. The shop-girl was breathlessly reported as saying he looked as good as ever and she was convinced he was staying somewhere near by, as he had left his bicycle propped up outside. The report went on to say how he was rumoured to be selling Byron Heights to a private owner.

Frances read it with a sinking feeling of dismay. If the press were on to Devon, it would make it very difficult to see him again. *That's if I wanted to*, she quickly told herself.

Her mobile was ringing as she walked back into her study. Frances carefully deposited the tea tray on a nest of tables and picked it up.

'Princess, it's me.'

'Oh, hello!' Frances lowered her voice, just in case a member of staff was walking past outside. 'Have you seen the papers?'

Devon groaned. 'Tell me about it! It was on local radio this morning as well. I can't believe people are making such a fuss!'

'You are Gloucestershire's most famous rock star,' Frances pointed out. 'People are terribly excited to know you're back.'

'As long as you're excited I'm back,' he told her. 'I need to get out of here, all this genitalia is making my eyes hurt. Can I come over and see you?'

'I don't know if it's entirely appropriate.'

'Let's go for a walk then, get some fresh air.'

Frances felt anxious. She was nearly as well-known in the Cotswolds as he was. 'What if people see us together?' She sighed. 'If only one could take an invisible potion or something! It would be so nice to go out and not have to worry.'

Devon paused, thinking. 'I've got an idea! I'll be over

312

in an hour to pick you up. The code word is . . .' He searched round for a word. 'Red apples.'

'What on earth are you on about?' she exclaimed, but he'd already hung up.

At first Frances thought she'd misheard Hawkins.

'Could you repeat that?'

'I said, there's a large panda on the doorstep to see you, your Ladyship,' the butler said sonorously, as if he were announcing the arrival of the Prince of Wales.

Frances stared at him from behind her desk. Had her normally sane butler gone completely mad? 'Hawkins, please explain yourself. I haven't got time for tomfoolery.'

He said with exemplary patience, 'There is a woman on the doorstep in what seems to be some kind of panda costume. She declined from giving me her name, but insisted on seeing you. She said you'd know what it was about, your Ladyship.'

'Oh, for heaven's sake!' Frances got up. If this was another one of those cold-calling marketing firms, she'd give them what for. She'd already encountered a full salsa group jiggling on the doorstep last summer, trying to sell her some sort of new alcopop.

But as she got to the front door, Frances was confronted by the astonishing sight of a six-foot panda. It stuck a huge paw up in greeting.

'Hello, my dear!' a falsetto voice said from somewhere within. 'Are you ready?'

Frances looked uncertainly from the bear to Hawkins, who had followed her down the hallway, and back

313

to the panda again. She recognized that voice. But it couldn't be . . .

'I've packed us a splendid picnic for afterwards,' trilled the voice. 'Some lovely red apples.'

Frances's jaw slackened. Devon! She looked quickly at Hawkins to see if he'd caught on, but as usual, the butler's face was calm and inscrutable.

'Hawkins, this is er . . .' she said, desperately hoping Devon would save her.

'I'm Geraldine Moffat-Lowley, one of Frances's old friends! We're going on the animal rights protest today in Chipping Campden.'

At this announcement, Hawkins's right eyebrow rose a millimetre.

The panda turned round. 'I'll wait for you in the car, my dear! Don't be long.'

In silence, Frances and Hawkins watched the creature shuffle towards a clapped-out old three-wheeler van painted in lurid rainbow colours.

'Geraldine's rather eccentric,' Frances said desperately.

Hawkins nodded solemnly. 'She seemed like a very nice lady, your Ladyship.'

'I'd better shoot off, then,' Frances said. 'Don't worry about afternoon tea, Hawkins, I'm not sure when I'll be back.'

Hawkins bowed. 'As you wish. Enjoy the march.' As he closed the huge door behind her, a smile twitched on the butler's face. He'd wondered how long it would be before his mistress met up with Devon Cornwall again.

'Devon! What on earth is going on?' Frances exclaimed as they bumped back down the drive. She looked up at a pair of furry pink boobs hanging from the rear-view mirror.

'Where on earth did you get this thing?'

'It's Snorkel's, found it rusting in one of his garages along with a Rolls-Royce Silver Shadow and a 1956 vintage Harley.'

'Is it roadworthy?' she asked anxiously, as the engine spluttered alarmingly.

'Probably not, the tax disc ran out in October 1978!'

'Oh dear,' said Frances faintly. She still hadn't asked the most obvious question, why had Devon turned up in a giant panda costume? She soon found out.

'Snork used to put on these mental fancy-dress parties! Found a whole room full of stuff like this.'

'You still haven't explained *why*, though.'

The panda, or rather Devon, turned to look at her. It was rather disconcerting. 'We wanna meet up without being hassled, don't we? It was just by chance I heard about the animal protest on the news this morning.'

'Oh, for heavens sake, I'm not going on any such thing! Especially with you dressed like that. What on earth would people think?'

Devon chuckled. 'They're not going to think anything, because they won't know it's you, princess. Your beaver costume's in the back!'

Frances could feel a trickle of sweat rolling down her back. Even though she had taken her cashmere cardigan off, it was still stifling hot inside the costume. Through the tiny eyeholes she could hardly see where she was going. As they passed a shop window, she caught sight of herself. A brown furry rodent, complete with outsized front teeth, looked back. The beaver even had a little bow tie round its neck and was wearing a badge saying 'Beaver Fan' pinned to the front.

'This is utterly absurd!' she exclaimed aloud, crossly. She couldn't believe Devon had talked her into this!

He turned to her. 'What's that, Frannie? Having fun?'

'I most certainly am not!' she said, but her objections were drowned out by the protesters' shouts.

'Down with animal cruelty! Stop this inhuman abuse!'

There had been a meagre turnout for the protest, but they were more than making up for it with their chanting and vigour. Besides Devon and Frances, there were two pigs, one elephant, four monkeys, three dogs, and a rather incongruous woman dressed as a tree – who had mistakenly thought it was an environmental march, but had decided to stay on anyway.

'Nice weather,' Devon remarked cheerfully, as if it was perfectly normal to stroll down the road dressed as a giant bear.

Frances ignored him. They'd both been given flags by the procession's leader, but she had refused to wave hers, holding it limply in her paw as though it wasn't there. Devon however, was getting into the spirit of things. As they traipsed down the charmingly quaint High Street, he started running up to people, shaking his flag. 'Gerbils have rights, too!' he yelled at a group of bemused shoppers.

'Bunch of nutters,' one of them muttered.

Frances knew what they meant. She was going to kill Devon! Out of the corner of her eye she suddenly saw one of her society friends, watching the procession with evident distaste. 'That's Adelaide Horsworth!' she whispered frantically at Devon.

He looked over at where she was pointing. 'She a mate?'

'More of an acquaintance, she's a bit po-faced really. What are you *doing*?'

Frances watched in horror as Devon ran over to Lady Horsworth, picked her up and swung her round. 'Woo hoooo!'

Lady Horsworth was thunderstruck. She hadn't been touched so intimately since conceiving her third daughter, Eleonora, on the first day of the 1974 Cheltenham races.

'What on earth are you doing?' she said, voice shrill. 'I command you to put me down!'

But the more she struggled, the more Devon twirled her round. Noticing the kerfuffle, one of the pigs and the elephant ran over and, to whoops and shouts from onlookers, hoisted Lady Horsworth up on to their shoulders. Huge handbag dangling, she looked round wildly for someone to get her down, but the crowd laughed and cheered instead.

In spite of herself, Frances started to giggle. Lady Horsworth looked so funny! In all the time Frances had known her, she'd never known Adelaide Horsworth to

317

have a hair out of place, nor a smile on her stony face. Yet here she was, like some undignified Glastonbury reveller, being swept down Chipping Campden High Street. Gloucestershire society would be talking about this for months!

By the time Lady Horsworth finally managed to attract the attention of a dozy looking policeman, she was apoplectic with rage and shock. 'I want these hoodlums arrested!' she shouted, as the bobbie helped her down.

'For what?' the pig asked innocently. 'You asked us to pick you up. Didn't she, Tom?'

The elephant nodded his trunk enthusiastically.

The policeman shrugged. 'It's your word against theirs, ma'am.'

'This an outrage!' Lady Horsworth thundered and stormed off.

Frances and Devon witnessed the whole thing.

'I can't believe you did that!' she gasped. 'Oh Devon, did you see her face!'

He laughed. 'Thought she needed cheering up a bit.'

Music started up from someone's stereo and a party atmosphere took over. People started dancing, and not just the animal protesters. As she marched along, waving her flag properly, Frances felt a huge sense of liberation. She'd never done anything like this in her life: abandoned her social code and not cared what people thought. It felt *wonderful*. She linked arms with Devon, one arm aloft.

'A beagle's for life, not just for Christmas!' she shouted.

Afterwards, bonded by a new-found camaraderie, the group retired to a nearby pub, still wearing their costumes. Frances couldn't remember the last time she'd been in a public house – had she ever patronized one? – but she loved the chatty, sociable atmosphere and cosy furnishings. Devon bought her a half of cider, and with some difficulty she sucked it through a straw. The appley liquid felt wonderful going down her dry throat.

Devon clinked her glass with his. 'Cheers, Frannie.' He leaned back against the bar. 'Aah, this is good. Can't remember the last time I was in the boozer without people asking for me autograph.'

He sighed theatrically. 'Or telling me my music was complete horseshit.'

Frances giggled. She sucked the last of her cider up noisily.

'That's my girl.' Devon put a furry arm around her furry shoulders. Frances nestled in beside him, basking in a glow of pleasure and contentment. Despite the incongruity of the situation, she felt happy, excited, normal. With a sudden rush of insight, she realized she felt like *herself*.

She realized Devon was looking at her. Very slowly he leaned forward and rubbed plastic noses with her. She could hear the 'tap tap' as they rubbed one way, and then the next. All around them there was noise and laughter, but the two of them were lost in a private moment. For a reason she found hard to justify, Frances found the moment unspeakably erotic.

'You wanna get out of here, princess?' Devon's voice was even more gravelly than normal.

She felt a jab of excitement in her stomach. 'Yes, please.'

Without finishing their drinks, they left.

By the time they'd got back to Devon's house, the erotic undertone had been replaced by a more humorous mood. On their way back to the car Devon had tripped over his massive panda feet and gone flying into a greengrocer's display, scattering cucumbers and oranges everywhere. After trying unsuccessfully to pick them up with their huge paws, they'd run off giggling, as the furious grocer had come out and shaken his fist at them. Now Frances was having trouble getting her huge beaver's bottom out of the car seat.

'Devon, I'm stuck!' she cried, helpless with laughter. He tried to pull her out, guffawing.

'Shit, Frannie, you are as well!'

With one final effort, he yanked her out and she fell straight on top of him. Anyone driving up and seeing a giant beaver seemingly wrestling with a six-foot panda would have taken one look and called for the men in white coats.

'Oh, Devon, this is ridiculous!' Frances's stomach was hurting from laughing so much. With some difficulty they managed to get up, wiping the tears from their eyes.

'I've done some mad things on tour in my time, but this takes the biscuit.' Devon unlocked the front door and they went in, Frances almost shutting it on her tail as she closed it behind her.

In the hallway Devon pulled his panda's head off. Underneath his face was red and hot. 'I must have lost about two stone in sweat! Here, I'll help you.'

He grasped hold of Frances beaver's head and pulled it off. It was a wonderful relief, but Frances felt wet hair stuck to her forehead and became very self-conscious. She must look dreadful.

Devon guessed what she was thinking. 'You look sexy, princess,' he said, and meant it. 'It's good to see you a bit messed up for once.'

Frances didn't agree. Her back was wet with perspiration and the crotch of her pants felt disagreeably damp. She couldn't go back to Clanfield like this.

'Would you mind if I had a shower?' She flushed as she said it. She would never have dreamt of being so forward and inappropriate normally, but she really did feel unpleasant.

Devon didn't bat an eyelid. 'Course you can. Here, you can use my en suite. It's a bit over-the-top, be warned.'

He wasn't joking. Beyond the massive bedroom with its satin revolving bed and overhead mirror was a bathroom that looked like it had been stolen straight from the Luxor Hotel in Las Vegas. A gaudy gold bath big enough for six stood in the centre of the floor, while a tacky mural of nubile Egyptian goddesses was painted on the ceiling above.

'Power shower's good, though,' Devon offered, as he

gave her a black-and-gold Playboy bath-towel. 'I'll be downstairs,' he told her and left her to it.

Ten minutes later she was drying herself with the towel in the bedroom when the door opened.

'Oh!' said Frances, clutching the towel closer to her.

'Shit, sorry, princess! I thought you were in the bathroom still.'

She raised an elegant eyebrow.

'I did, honest! I came to knock on the door and ask if you wanted a drink or anything. I'm making us a bit of grub.'

'An Earl Grey would be lovely, thank you,' she replied, trying to compose herself.

Frances was suddenly aware of the amount of flesh she was showing, and felt aroused and oddly vulnerable at the same time.

Devon's eyes wandered to her white, delicate shoulders, barely ravaged by the passing of time. 'I'll go and make that brew for you,' he muttered distractedly, but it was clear by the urgent look in his eyes that his mind was on something else.

They stood and gazed at each other across the bed. Suddenly, before she knew it. Devon was upon her, taking her in his arms. 'Fuck, Frannie, I've missed you!'

'I've missed you, too,' she tried to gasp, but then his mouth was on hers, his tongue in her mouth: exploring, revisiting, hungry for her. She could feel the bristle of his stubble against her skin; smell the mixture of sweat and aftershave. Frances flung her arms round Devon's neck, feeling the familiar leanness of his body. The

322

towel had fallen to the ground, but she didn't care, as Devon's hand ran over her smooth back and small buttocks, down the back of her thighs.

Very carefully, as if he were handling priceless china, Devon laid her down on the bed. His shirt was open now, revealing an impressively toned chest for a fifty-something, with remnants of a six-pack, and a few dark hairs peppering his yoga-toned pectorals.

Frances stared up at him longingly, opening her legs without even really realizing what she was doing. Devon looked at her triangle of pubic hair, and the pink contours of her clitoris. His erection, already hard, swelled to bursting against the flimsy fabric of his trousers.

The thought of Ambrose shot into her mind, but somehow she squeezed it out again. 'Come here,' she said, voice shaking. Devon needed no encouragement as he lay down on top of her, skin on skin, caressing the dusky pink of her nipples. Frances's manicured fingers were pulling underneath, at his zip. Devon moved on to his side to make it easier for her. She sighed with satisfaction as her hand found his cock and closed round it. 'Devon, darling,' she whispered. 'I must have you inside me.'

Frances's cut-class tones had always given him a boner. Another rush of blood surged through his erection. Devon kicked off his pants and nudged her knees even wider apart with his own. She wrapped her thoroughbred legs around him, waiting for him to enter her.

'Fuck-a-duck, Princess, you're incredible!' Devon

closed his eyes and pushed inwards. He'd been thinking about this moment for so long.

Frances gasped slightly with pain as Devon entered her, but then he was inside, filling her up, making her body tingle from top to toe. They started rocking back and forwards. Devon's hands slid round her bottom, and she arched her hips up, wanting him in her even deeper. Over his shoulder, Frances looked up at the mirror and saw his long, lean body covering hers, backside pert, back muscled from years of yoga. Her own face was looking back, flushed and free. Frances wrapped her legs round him even tighter. 'Fuck me!' she said.

He needed no encouragement and eventually they both came, and collapsed on each other in sweaty contentment.

'I love you, princess,' he murmured into her ear. Frances' eyes welled up with emotion.

'Oh, Devon . . .'

All of a sudden there was an ear-splitting shriek, causing them to jump apart like scalded cats. Devon looked round in confusion and panic, before his face dropped.

'It's the fire alarm!' he shouted. 'I'd forgotten I'd left the bacon on!'

He jumped off her and ran out. Frances grabbed the towel off the bed and followed in hot pursuit down the stairs. The kitchen was filled with smoke, the blackened remains of the bacon Devon had been going to add to the Caesar salad now smouldering in the sink.

The alarm was deafening.

'How do you turn it off?' cried Frances, as Devon poured cold water on the grill pan, making steam sizzle and hiss.

'Haven't got a Scooby!' he shouted. In the distance there was the wail of a fire engine. Devon went pale. 'Shit, it's the boys in red! Snork mentioned something about being wired up to the local fire station.'

Frances was horror-struck. She couldn't be found here, practically naked! 'I've got to get away before anyone sees me!'

'But how?'

Frances's mind whirred into action. It was a desperate measure, but this was a desperate situation. 'Never mind,' she shouted. 'I'll be in touch!' With a quick lingering kiss on his lips, she turned and ran out.

Chief Fire Officer Norman Stanton stared grimly through the windscreen. He knew the property they were headed for belonged to some rich old bloke, but the fact he lived abroad most of the time made it very suspicious indeed. Chief Stanton smoothed down his dour moustache, assessing the situation. Unless an arsonist had torched the joint to get a thrill, it was probably some little toe-rags who'd broken in to have a party, and one of their funny fags had set fire to the curtains.

Just as he rounded a bend in the narrow track, the most unbelievable sight confronted Chief Stanton. A psychedelic three-wheeler van, being driven by what appeared to be a giant beaver, screeched to a halt in front of them. The beaver stuck its head out of the window and pointed back in the direction it'd just come from.

'That way, gentlemen!'

And with that, the decrepit old van nudged past the gawping fire officers and hurtled off down the track like a rally car.

Chief Stanton turned to his fellow firefighter. 'Did I really just see that?' The stunned look on his colleague's face told him he had, indeed.

Chief Stanton shook his head. They were a bunch of fruit loops round here! The firefighters pressed forward, unaware they were about to discover the whereabouts of Devon Cornwall.

PART THREE

Chapter 39

Clementine was at Clanfield Hall, having promised to take a cure for leaf mould up to one of the gardeners. Jed had mentioned to her they'd been having problems with the tomato plants, but when she drove up the driveway, she was surprised to see him standing on one of the lawns engrossed in conversation with that actress Sophia Highforth. She was in costume and Jed was carrying his toolkit in one hand, probably on his way to mend something, but there was a closeness about them that gave Clementine a nasty feeling. As she pulled up Sophia brushed something off Jed's face and smiled at him.

'Hello, Jed,' she called through the window, wanting to put a stop to this exchange as soon as possible. Jed turned and when he saw it was Clementine, jumped apart from Sophia like a scalded cat.

'Mrs S-F, hi there.'

Clementine shot him a quizzical look.

'I'm just dropping off the fungicide for the leaf mould, as I said I would.'

Jed looked blank for a moment, and then recognition dawned.

'Oh yeah, of course.'

He said something in an undertone to Sophia. Giving him a meaningful look, she squeezed his arm and walked off.

'Is everything all right?' Clementine asked pointedly, as Jed reached the car. He flushed.

'Er yeah.'

Clementine bit her tongue and handed the bottle through the open window. Jed seemed relieved at the diversion.

'Thanks for this. It's going to be a godsend.'

He was having trouble meeting her eyes. There was an awkward silence, one Clementine had no intention of filling.

'I guess I should get back to work,' Jed said eventually.

'Yes, I think you should,' she said meaningfully. Flushing, he mumbled a goodbye and walked off quickly. Clementine drove back down the drive, casting concerned little glances in the rear-view mirror. If Jed wasn't a man with a guilty conscience, he was doing a jolly good job of acting like one.

'What are you up to, young fellow?' she said aloud, frowning.

Calypso bounded up the stairs to her office. Despite having a pinky eye and being asked continually by her grandmother if she wanted some conjunctivitis cream, she was in a really good mood. For once, Rafe had two days off, and she was looking forward to spending some quality time with him. Maybe they could go out and do something: impressive as Rafe's place was, Calypso was starting to go stir-crazy, staying in the whole time. Now she'd got over the incident with the paparazzi, she felt ready to step out and show the world they were a couple. She was Rafe Wolfe's girlfriend, goddammit! Calypso knew there would be media interest, but she was savvy enough to deal with it. She could take anything that was thrown at her as long as she had him.

Later, she was just finishing off a few things when her mobile rang. It was the man himself.

'Hello, sexy.'

Calypso leaned back in her chair, smiling. 'I was just thinking about you. What time are you back later?'

He paused. 'There's a bit of a problem. I've just had some bad family news.'

She sat up straight. 'Oh no. No one's died have they?'

'Thankfully no. Well, not yet anyway. It's my grandmother, she'd been ill for some time and my mother has just called to say she's taken a turn for the worse. I've got to go to Norfolk tonight.'

Disappointment seeped through Calypso, but she understood. She knew how she'd feel if it was Granny Clem.

Rafe sounded gutted. 'I'm sorry, I was really looking forward to spending some proper time with you.'

'Me too, but family is important, Rafe. You must go and see her.'

'You're quite a gal, you know?'

'Oh, stop it with the cheesy compliments,' she smiled.

He gave a soft chuckle. 'I'll call you later when I've got there.'

'OK, I miss you.'

'I miss you, too, Calypso.'

Camilla was in the guest bedroom at No. 5, putting away some spare bed sheets in the cupboard. As she put the last one up, she heard the top set of the stairs creak and a low voice speaking. It was Jed. She couldn't hear what he was saying as he went into their bedroom and shut the door.

Without really thinking what she was doing, Camilla crept out of the room and down the corridor. Heart beating furiously, she put her ear to the wood. Whoever Jed was on the phone to, he was just finishing the call.

'I can't put it off any longer.' There was a pause. 'Yep, you too. Bye.'

Suddenly the bedroom door was pulled open. Camilla jumped back as if she'd been scalded. She fished wildly for an excuse. 'I was just getting some towels . . .'

Jed looked angry. 'Were you listening at the door?'

'No! I was just getting some fresh towels from the airing cupboard. I didn't hear anything, if that's what you're getting at . . .'

A weird look came over Jed's face. For a moment Camilla thought he was about to tell her something, but then it was gone.

'I'm going to put the kettle on,' he asked. 'Do you want something?'

'No, I'm fine,' she said shortly, before turning away so Jed couldn't see the dull flush working its way up her neck. She was sure he'd been on the phone to a woman. In fact, one particular woman.

Camilla was watching, or rather staring, at the television when Jed came down the stairs later. He was carrying an overnight bag.

'I'm going to spend the night at Ma's,' he said. 'I've got a really early start tomorrow and I don't want to disturb you when I get up.'

He'd had early starts before and it had never been a problem, Camilla thought. Anger, born out of weeks of anxiety, flared up. 'Do you think I'm stupid?' she said.

'What do you mean?'

She stood up, facing him. 'Were you just on the phone to Sophia Highforth?'

Jed flushed, but didn't deny it.

Shock and anger coursed through Camilla. 'What the hell are you doing calling each other?'

'Sophia called *me*. She must have got my number off one of the lads at the Hall.'

'I'm supposed to believe that? Are you going off somewhere with her?'

His jaw tightened. 'Don't be ridiculous.'

'Well, what am I supposed to think?' she cried.

'You're certainly acting like a man with something to hide. Phone calls, secret meetings, and you haven't even touched me for weeks. I don't understand, Jed.'

He looked at her, face suddenly blank. 'I haven't got time for this, Camilla.'

'That's right, walk off and leave just like you did with all the others!' As soon as Camilla said this, she regretted it. Wordlessly Jed turned round and walked out.

Hearing the front door slam from upstairs, Calypso came down. 'Whoa, what's going on?' she asked. She stopped dead at the sight of her sister's pale, tear-stained face.

'It's Jed. I've just asked him again if he's having an affair with Sophia Highforth. He said no, but I don't believe him.' Camilla took a deep shuddering breath. 'I can't go on like this, Calypso. *We* can't go on like this.'

Calypso set her jaw. 'Right, I'm having it out with him.'

'Calypso, wait! You'll only make things worse!'

But the front door had slammed for the second time that night.

As Calypso ran down the garden path she could see Jed still sitting his van, engine running. 'Jed, wait!' She ran round to his window and rapped loudly. Surprised, he looked up. Calypso noticed his face was as white as Camilla's. She didn't beat around the bush. 'Jed, what the hell is going on? Are you having it off with Sophia Highforth or what?'

His knuckles tightened round the steering wheel. 'Not you as well.'

'Well?' she demanded.

Jed looked pained. 'Calypso, please don't get involved. You don't know what you're talking about.'

As he went to drive off, Calypso put one hand on the window frame. 'I swear to God Jed, if you're cheating on her I'll rip your balls off!'

Jed looked up, his face drained of blood. 'Fuck you.' He screeched off in a cloud of dust, leaving Calypso open-mouthed.

Chapter 40

A few days later, on a scorching June afternoon, the film crew packed up and left Clanfield Hall. Frances watched as a line of white trucks snaked down the drive and on to their next location. Even though she had been looking forward to getting things back to normal, Frances felt a slight regret as the last tail light disappeared through the front gates. The film crew had bought an energy and life to Clanfield Hall, made the place sit up and take notice after centuries. Would they go back to the stifling inertia she had been suffering from before? Frances couldn't bear the thought.

Cook and Mrs Bantry hadn't known what to say when the old van had screeched up at the back of the house, and they'd been even more nonplussed when they realized the giant beaver driving it was Lady Fraser. She'd tried to make an excuse, but they'd been so dumbstruck that Frances had given up. Luckily Ambrose hadn't seen her, and by 6 p.m. she had been back in her study sipping Earl Grey as if the whole thing had been a dream. In fact, the more she thought about it, the more it seemed as if it hadn't happened. Aside from when she'd given birth to Harriet, Frances couldn't remember the last time she'd been so happy. The last time she'd had proper *fun*. Frances had expected to feel guilt about the sex, the way she had before, but to her surprise she didn't. If anything, she felt revitalized.

'Frances!' Ambrose strode into her study without knocking. 'Have you seen the bloody mess that film lot have left behind?'

'They're going to clean everything up. Don't get worked up, Ambrose,' she said, sitting back down behind her desk to finish her correspondence.

'It's not bloody good enough,' he complained. 'The east wing is upside down and I still can't find Great-uncle Algie. Some bloody buffoon hasn't put him back in the Red Room.'

Frances looked up sharply. Her husband stood before her, red-faced with indignation, eyes bulging furiously. 'Oh, who gives a shit about Great-uncle bloody Algie!' she said.

The next day Clementine opened her bedroom curtains to be confronted by the most alarming sight. Against her better judgement, she had allowed the last few scenes to be filmed in the back fields of Fairoaks. At least, she had thought, she would be able to keep an eye on them and Dan the locations manager had told her they would only be there a week.

She'd been told they were filming some sort of

wedding scene, but Clementine still hadn't been prepared for the huge gazebo that had somehow been erected overnight. It was almost as big as Fairoaks. Clementine had to admit it was rather striking, but it was still disconcerting to wake up and discover a structure as big as the Taj Mahal just outside one's garden.

She was putting on her pearls when Errol Flynn started barking. Someone had to be at the door. Clementine slid her feet into her brogues and hurried downstairs. To her surprise, Pam Viner was there, waving a package. Clementine went over to let her in, Errol wagging his tail behind her furiously. 'Good morning, Pam, do come in.'

'I hope I haven't disturbed you,' Pam said, cheeks rosier than ever. 'I just thought I'd come with a peace offering, seeing as we're rather taking over the place.' She handed Clementine the package. 'Catering do a mean fruitcake, I thought you might like to try some.'

'That really is very thoughtful.' Clementine put the cake on the kitchen table, well out of reach of Errol Flynn's quivering nose. Fruitcake was his favourite.

'I was just about to put the kettle on. Would you like something?'

Pam smiled gratefully. 'A cup of coffee would be heavenly. Unfortunately catering's coffee doesn't match up to its fruitcake.'

Clementine gestured for her to take a seat. 'Yes, I must admit I was alarmed when I woke up and saw the set today,' she said. 'It's a lot bigger than one thought it would be!'

338

Pam laughed. 'It always feels like that, especially when it's practically in your backyard. They won't leave a trace, I promise.'

Clementine handed her a steaming cup of coffee.

'Just what I needed. Lovely.' Pam said. She took a sip. 'How are things going with Britain's Best Village? I still feel awful about the truck reversing on to the green, you know.'

'Oh, don't be silly,' Clementine said. 'It was just an awful accident.' She sighed. 'Things could be going better, to be perfectly frank, and now we keep getting these awful acts of vandalism round the place.'

Pam made a sympathetic noise. 'Aren't some people awful? I read in the local paper police are following up leads.'

'Yes, they think it's that lot of hoodlums from Bedlington,' Clementine said. 'Although I'm not holding out much hope – the Bedlington police force aren't the sharpest tools in the box.'

For a while they chatted about the competition and what plans the Garden Club had, before a mobile phone started ringing. Pam apologized for the interruption and answered it. 'Wes? Yes, I'll be there in a minute.' She ended the call and looked regretful. 'Time's up for me, I'm afraid, back into the eye of the storm! Clementine, thank you for the coffee.'

'And thank you for the fruitcake,' Clementine told her, walking Pam over to the back door. Behind them, and with surprising agility for a dog his age, Errol Flynn jumped up at the table and quickly exited the kitchen with half the fruitcake in his mouth, to devour in the drawing room.

Down on the film set, Wes Prince's day hadn't started well. He'd stubbed his toe getting dressed at the crack of dawn that morning, and now one of his cameramen had called in sick, just as they were getting to a pivotal scene. It was all Wes needed.

A full English breakfast in the catering truck, snappily called 'Lights, Camera, Snacktion' was just getting his spirits up when the door flew open and Gordon Goldsmith, Sophia's manager, stormed in. Wes groaned inwardly. The guy was a pain in the butt on set and was getting worse every day. He swallowed a tomato as Gordon came bustling towards him.

'Wes, a word please.' Gordon had seated himself opposite Wes before Wes had even had a chance to reply. Gordon's thinning brown hair was slicked back, his keen brown eyes channelled straight on to Wes's.

'Graham, isn't it?' Wes said pleasantly, knowing it would get the manager's back up. The little shit strutted round like he was more important than the talent.

Gordon narrowed ferret-like eyes. 'Gordon. Wes, I'd like to speak to you frankly. Sophia's Winnebago is far too cold. She's been complaining of a sore throat, and if she loses her voice, that's the last thing *you* guys need. I'd like her moved to a new one, I was never happy with the one you gave her anyway, it's far too small.'

Wes speared a grilled tomato into his mouth. ''Fraid

340

that's not my bag. You need to speak to the assistant director. Or maybe one of the runners can help.'

Gordon didn't look appeased. 'And what's this about you cutting Sophia's lines? I'm not happy about that at all.'

Wes was beginning to lose patience. He didn't have time for a five-foot-nothing telling him how to run his own film. 'The scene was too long and needed cutting. Sophia should know it's routine.' *And so should you, you stumpy-legged imbecile*, he thought.

'Sophia didn't bring it up, *I* am. I've got to look after my client's interests.'

Wes gave a strained smile. 'Then we share the same goal. Now, if you don't mind?' He looked pointedly at the rest of his breakfast. 'I can't work on an empty stomach.'

He watched the little man bustle out to go and terrorize someone else. Did Sophia have any idea what a tosspot he was?

Chapter 41

'Jed, you have to say something to her.'

Sophia reached out and took his hand. They were in her Winnebago, facing each other over untouched cups of tea on the coffee table.

Jed's jaw clenched momentarily.

'I know. I just don't want to break her heart.' His dark eyes met Sophia's blue ones.

'It'll devastate her.'

Sophia squeezed his hand again, savouring the warmth of his touch.

'Jed, you know it's the right thing to do.'

His jaw clenched again.

'I hate the thought of letting her down.'

Sophia smiled tenderly.

'Darling, sometimes the right choices in life are always the most difficult ones. You and I both know that.'

Eventually Jed nodded.

'You're right Soph, you always have been. I just need a bit more time. Do you understand?'

Sophia gritted her teeth and smiled falsely.

July came to Churchminster in a flurry of azure skies and soaring temperatures. Beryl Turner was on official watering duty, which involved going round every house in the village to make sure the hanging baskets were all they possibly could be. Everywhere people's hard work was paying off, and from the luxuriant and glossy flowerbeds on the village green to the graffiti-free walls, the village looked happy, healthy and as neat as a pin.

As she took Errol Flynn for a walk that evening round the village, Clementine felt a huge sense of pride in what had been achieved. There was little trace of the devastation that had been wreaked on them last year. It wasn't just outward appearances, either: peoples' lives were getting back to normal, too. Beryl and Jack Turner had smiles back on their faces as the pub went from strength to strength. Brenda Briggs was throwing herself into the community more than ever, setting up all manner of groups she urged everyone to join. Even if Clementine didn't fancy learning how to burlesque dance in the village hall on Tuesday evenings, she was thrilled that Brenda was back to her sociable, interfering self. A subtle harmony had been restored, and it could be sensed in the way Angie's shoulders had stopped hunching in unconscious worry and the strength of Lucinda Reinard's gusty hellos when she screeched over in the Volvo estate to have a natter. Last summer Clementine had despaired of things ever being the same again, but Churchminster had almost regained its rhythm.

Almost. Clementine stared at the green, drinking it in. It all looked so lovely, but what was the point, really, when they lived in constant fear of being flooded again? Clementine wanted to reach a moment in her life where she could turn on the weather forecast and not have her heart sink every time rain was predicted. It was no way for anyone to live their life. They just had, had, had to win the Britain's Best Village competition!

The next morning, Clementine was woken early by the telephone ringing. It was Beryl Turner. Her tone was serious.

'Sorry to call so early, but you'd better get down here. Something awful's happened.'

Clementine surveyed the mess with disbelief. The vandals had done a really good job this time. The new flowerbeds, which Beryl and Clementine had spent so long nurturing, had been ripped apart. Pink fuchsias and blue begonias lay there like deflated balloons, while the earth had been kicked about viciously, leaving crater-like holes. Every one of Beryl's hanging baskets, her pride and joy, had been pulled down and now lay like a line of collapsed puddings in the road outside the pub.

Beryl was in tears. 'Bastards! If I get my hands on them!'

Jack put his arm round his wife, squeezing her protectively. Clementine could see the anger and upset in his tense jaw.

Stacey Turner came out of the pub. She was bleary eyed and dressed in a silky black dressing gown. Face solemn, she handed her mother a steaming mug of tea. 'Drink this, Mum, it'll make you feel better. I've put three sugars in, it's what you do when someone's in shock.'

Beryl took the mug. 'Thanks, Stace.'

Silently, all four took in the ruined green. Stacey eventually verbalized what they were all thinking. 'It looks like shit.'

'Stacey,' said her mother, shooting a look at Clementine.

'Are you gonna call the police?' Stacey asked.

Clementine didn't see the point. What could the police do? Vandalized flowerbeds were hardly going to be high on their crime-prevention agenda.

'I bet it's that lot from Bedlington,' muttered Jack darkly. 'I've got a good mind to go across there . . .'

Beryl stopped him. 'Leave it, Jack, the last thing we need is to have you banged-up for assault.'

'No, we don't need that at all,' Clementine said hurriedly.

'So what are we gonna do?' Stacey asked.

Clementine gave a small smile at her use of the word 'we'. There was nothing like times of trouble to pull people together. 'Start again, my dear,' she said wearily. 'That's what we do here. I suppose I'd better get down to the garden centre.'

Word spread quickly, and by mid-morning they had a good turnout. People had taken time off work, or juggled child-care arrangements to make sure they could come down and help in whatever way they could. To Clementine's surprise, even Frances Fraser turned up, looking slightly out-of-place amongst the muddy-kneed volunteers, in an immaculate white shirt and razor-pressed trousers, a gold clip holding her neck scarf in place.

'Mrs Bantry told me at breakfast what happened,' she told Clementine. 'I had to come down and see what I could do to help.'

'It really is very good of you, Frances,' said Clementine.

'It's the least I can do. Now, where would you like me to start?'

Clementine looked at the dead plants and flowers lying strewn about. 'They all need picking up, the bin bags are over there.'

She thought Frances might turn her nose up, but she nodded enthusiastically.

'Righty-ho, I'll get started.' And with the offer of a pair of smelly old gardening gloves from Brenda Briggs, Frances got on with it.

A few hours later all the new flowers had been planted and Jack had re-fixed the hanging baskets to their hooks, from which they'd been ripped down earlier.

They all retired into the pub for much-needed refreshment.

'That looks a lot better!' declared Angie, but

Clementine knew she was only being kind. Where they'd once had flourishing flowerbeds, there were still large patches of brown earth. It would take months for everything to grow properly, and they only had three weeks.

She took a gloomy sip of her tonic water and contemplated the dire state of affairs. It was like two steps forward, six blasted steps back.

Unfortunately, it was about to get a lot, lot worse.

The judging day for Britain's Best Village loomed ever closer. Clementine had gone into full organization mode and stepped up the Garden Party meetings to every evening, where the committee would report back on what they had been doing. She had a checklist as long as her arm and slowly but surely everyone had been working their way through it.

On the Monday before however, Clementine was concerned to see Joyce Bellows absent from the meeting. Reverend Bellows did nothing to ease her state of mind when Clementine asked after Joyce.

'Is she ill?'

Reverend Bellows squirmed, telling untruths weren't in his repertoire.

'Not exactly.'

Clementine frowned. 'Then what?'

Reverend Bellows flushed under his beard. 'I'm not sure, to be completely honest with you. Joyce has been acting awfully strange all day, and when I went to get her to come along tonight, she'd locked herself in our bedroom and told me to go away.'

347

'That doesn't sound like Joyce,' said Clementine.

'I know. I'm quite worried about her.' The Reverend looked pained. 'I hope it isn't something I've done, I did use a curse word in front of her the other day.'

Clementine wondered if it was unkind to think that if Joyce was having some kind of breakdown, she couldn't have picked a worst time to do it.

The next morning the residents of Churchminster woke up to the most shocking revelations. Clementine had just returned from taking Errol Flynn for his morning work, when Brenda Briggs turned up at the back door. She was red-faced and gasping for breath, a rolled-up newspaper in her hands.

'My dear woman, are you all right?' Clementine asked.

'Just run from the shop,' Brenda puffed. 'I 'ad to show you. Have you see the *Daily Mercy*?' The newspaper was Brenda's favourite read.

'Certainly not! I don't read that rag.'

Brenda brandished the paper at her. At first Clementine stared uncomprehendingly at the headline across the tabloid's front page.

'VICAR'S WIFE IN PORN SHAME!' shrieked the headline.

'Why are you showing me this?' Clementine asked tartly. 'I'm really not interested in any of the tawdry tales this paper is obsessed with printing.'

Brenda jabbed her finger at the photograph accompanying the headline. 'Just *look*.'

Clementine did, and then her eyes almost popped

348

out of her head. The picture was slightly fuzzy, the permed hairstyle on the naked young woman out of date, but there was no mistaking who it was. 'Good grief, it's Joyce Bellows!' she gasped.

'I couldn't bloody believe my eyes when I saw it, but it is her! Listen.' Brenda started reading aloud excitedly.

As one of the finalists for Britain's Best Village, the sleepy Cotswolds village of Churchminster has been working hard to ensure they grab the coveted trophy. But any chance of getting their hands on the £750,000 prize money has come under threat as we sensationally reveal that 38-year-old Joyce Bellows, wife of the village's resident vicar Brian Bellows, hides a shameful past as a porn star! Joyce, who used to work under the name Jade Ferrari, appeared in a number of low-rent men's magazines in the 1980s.

Brenda opened the paper and her eyes goggled.

'Blimey, you should see what she's doing in 'ere with a banana!'

Clementine put her head in her hands and groaned. This was all they needed.

By the time she'd got round to the rectory, Angie was already there at the kitchen table, her arm round a hysterically sobbing Joyce. Joyce's thick-rimmed glasses were lying upended on the table like a dead insect.

'I've only just persuaded her to come out of the downstairs loo,' Angie said quietly over Joyce's head. 'Apparently she's been in there, hysterical all morning.

The Reverend called me, he didn't know what to do.'
A white-faced Reverend Bellows sat perfectly still on
a chair in the corner, gazing into space. Clementine
guessed his wife hadn't told him about her racy past.

'I can never show my face again!' wailed Joyce, her
eyes so puffy they were almost shut.

Clementine pulled out a chair and sat opposite. 'Oh,
Joyce,' she said, not quite sure what else to say.

'It's not as though you killed someone, darling,'
Angie said kindly. 'I'm sure lots of people have done
much worse things.'

'That's not what they'll think,' gulped Joyce. 'I'm the
vicar's wife! I've worked so hard to get where I am, and
now I've ruined it all.' Her voice rose an octave. 'Poor
Brian, what will people say?' Joyce flung her head into
her arms and started sobbing afresh.

Angie and Clementine looked at each other.

'So it is true?' Clementine asked eventually.

Joyce looked up, cheeks wet. 'Yes, but not in the
horrible way they've made out. Oh, I've been so
stupid!'

Punctuated by sobs, it all came out. How Joyce, then
living in Southampton, had been persuaded to pose
for raunchy pictures by an ex-boyfriend who'd been an
amateur photographer. How she had been facing evic-
tion from her bedsit for not paying the rent, and when
he'd told her she could start making good money, Joyce
had gone along with it.

'I didn't do it for long,' she sobbed, 'and it was
never really hardcore stuff.' She looked at them both
beseechingly. 'I needed the money! I was going to be

thrown out on the street again and I couldn't go back to that.'

'You were homeless?' Angie gasped.

Joyce nodded dolefully. 'For six months. I'd never got on with my mother and when I turned sixteen she threw me out.'

'Oh, Joyce!' Angie said.

'She wasn't a nice woman, my mother. Last thing I heard she was running an illegal betting ring out of a flat in Portsmouth. We haven't spoken for years.'

Clementine was appalled. 'My dear, what about your father? Couldn't he have helped?'

Joyce flushed shamefully. 'I don't know who he is. My mum refused to tell me, told me he was scum she had no intention of wasting her breath on.'

'You told me you were an orphan! You said your father was a m-m-missionary who'd died in Africa.' Reverend Bellows had wrenched his eyes away from the kitchen wall and was staring at his wife.

Joyce's top lip trembled. 'I know I shouldn't have lied to you, Brian, but I was so ashamed of my past! I knew from the moment I met you what a kind and lovely man you were and that I wanted to be with you, but would you have felt the same if you knew what I had come from?'

He said nothing. Tears filled Joyce's eyes. She looked back at Angie and Clementine. 'Brian saved me! When I walked past his church that day, I had no intention of going in. I'd never been religious; all my mum believed in was where her next drink and cigarette were coming from. But something made me go in, and there was

Brian, putting out the hymn books for evening service.' She gave a weak little smile at the memory. 'Suddenly it all fell into place and I knew I wanted to make a better person of myself. And I have Brian!' She looked pleadingly over at him. 'I'm so happy with you and our life with the Church. It's all I ever wanted.'

He remained silent.

Joyce sprang up and went over to him, sinking to her knees. 'Please Brian,' she sobbed. 'Don't make me go, I can't live without you.'

Very slowly, he looked down at her. A solitary tear rolled down his cheek and disappeared into his beard. 'J-Joyce Geraldine Shanice Bellows, I'm proud to call you my wife. You've made *me* a better person since we've met. You've taught me that you can be a servant of God and still laugh at the lighter things in life. Every morning when I wake up and look forward to the day ahead, it's b-b-because you're in it.'

Angie felt *her* eyes brim momentarily, she had had no idea the Reverend could be so romantic!

'Oh, Brian!' Joyce collapsed into fresh sobs, but this time ones of happiness.

Brian leant down and stroked her dowdy, fuzzy hair. 'I understand why you did what you did. And I don't care what people might think. G-God will judge you in his own way, Joyce, and I've an inkling he'll feel the same as me.'

Angie and Clementine made their excuses and left the Bellows to it. Outside, they stood at the rectory gate and looked at each other.

'Can you believe it!' exclaimed Angie.

'No, my dear, I cannot,' replied Clementine. 'But who knows what each of us hold in our pasts?'

Angie laughed. 'Rest assured I haven't got any skeletons in my closet, unless you count the time I flashed my boobs at Henley one year. It was the eighties, wild times.'

Clementine smiled. 'How on earth did the *Daily Mercy* find out, though? It seems so bizarre.'

'Ah, I think I know that one.' Angie said. 'Joyce told me that a private investigator had been sniffing around, said if she didn't go to the newspapers herself, he'd sell the story. Aren't some people perfectly horrible?'

'So that was why Joyce hadn't come to the Garden Party meeting,' Clementine said. 'The poor woman must have been in turmoil.'

'Who on earth would put a private investigator on to Joyce?' Angie asked. 'Unless it was her mother, it sounds like there's no love lost there. But what would she gain from it?'

Clementine had a sudden sinking feeling in her stomach. 'I know exactly who would do such a thing. Veronica Stockard-Manning. She'd do anything to try and smear us in the run-up to judging day.'

'The woman from Maplethorpe?' gasped Angie. 'Surely not.'

'*That woman* will stop at nothing to get what she wants, and will happily wreck people's lives in the process,' said Clementine hollowly. 'I've had first-hand experience.'

Was it Angie's imagination or did a tear glimmer in the corner of Clementine's eye? 'Well, I'd better get home,' she said. 'Or Freddie will start to think Joyce has killed herself or something.'

'Poor Joyce,' said Clementine, briskness restored. 'The gossips round here are going to have a field day.'

Fifteen minutes later Clementine was back at Fairoaks, sitting by the bureau in the hallway. She pulled one of the drawers open and got her old address book out, slowly starting to flick through the pages as if she was putting off reaching the number. Once upon a time, she had known it off by heart. She reached the page, and grim-faced, picked up the phone and dialled it.

It was picked up after a few rings. 'The Stockard-Manning residence.'

Clementine gripped the receiver. 'It's Clementine.'

'Oh, hello, dear!' exclaimed Veronica. 'What a surprise to hear from you, I didn't know you still had my number. Everything coming along well for Britain's Best Village?'

Clementine gritted her teeth. 'Why did you put a private investigator on to Joyce Bellows?'

Veronica's tone was neutral. 'I'm sure I don't know what you mean.'

'I'm sure you do. Why?'

Veronica tittered and Clementine could imagine her fat body rippling maliciously. 'If you want scandal, always start with the vicar's wife! Everyone knows that.'

'You dreadful creature! What has Joyce ever done to you?'

Veronica's tone was suddenly deadly. 'She lives in

Churchminster, that's enough. And before you start scurrying around trying to prove it, don't bother. I've covered my tracks.'

'You've done this sort of thing before!' gasped Clementine.

'As you of all people should know, one will do anything to keep one's village at the top. I've worked hard over the years to make Maplethorpe the best, and I have no intention of some scrubby little Cotswolds town usurping me.'

'You are a disgusting human being,' Clementine told her.

Veronica laughed nastily. 'You Standington-Fulthropes! You think you're better than everyone else, don't you? Why, that's precisely the reason I—'

Clementine stopped her, voice shaking with anger. 'Stay away from us, stay away from our village. If you ever step foot in Churchminster again, I'll personally set my dog on you. Do you understand?'

'Perfectly, dear,' sang Veronica Stockard-Manning.

Chapter 42

Despite Joyce's fears about what they'd think, most people were very supportive. The leggy Danish wife of the vicar in Bedlington even rang up to say she thought it was a *good* thing.

'It sexes up the church, darlink,' she said, in her clipped tones. 'I'm sick of people thinking vicars' wives are old and boring. It shows prostitutes can be decent people, too.'

'I wasn't a prostitute!' Joyce exclaimed in alarm.

'Whatever, darlink.'

Calypso was similarly unfazed. 'I always thought Joyce Bellows was a bit of a dark horse,' she declared to her grandmother.

'What on earth do you mean?' Clementine asked. 'Joyce Bellows was the last person I'd ever have suspected of hiding a secret.'

Calypso wrinkled up her nose dismissively. 'She was always too much of a cliché, you know? All that beige and home-baking. It was like she'd picked up a *How to*

Dress Like a Vicar's Wife handbook and studied it to the letter.'

She cast a mischievous glance at her grandmother, in her tweed skirt and twinset. 'People might look at you, after this, and suspect you were a part-time pole dancer!'

'Oh, for heaven's sake,' Clementine retorted. Sometimes her granddaughter was too much.

But although she and the rest of the Garden Party were rallying around the Bellows, Clementine was secretly worried about the effect it would have on Churchminster's competition chances. Especially when she read a profile piece in the *Daily Telegraph* about the head judge, Marjorie Majors, who sounded like a cross between Mary Whitehouse and Ann Widdecombe. Clementine couldn't imagine that Mrs Majors hadn't heard about the scandal, and she assumed she wouldn't be impressed, and would think it lowered the tone of the competition. Clementine made a mental note to keep Joyce out of the way on judging day. She wouldn't put it past Joyce to fling herself prostrate at the judges' feet, begging forgiveness.

Aside from Angie, Clementine hadn't told anyone Veronica Stockard-Manning was behind the story. The Bellows wanted to put it behind them – even though Joyce was in fact enjoying a surge in popularity – and Clementine didn't want to distract anyone from the task they had in hand. But it had made her realize, once again, that underneath her waxed jacket, Veronica was a very dangerous woman.

Chapter 43

'Are you going to go and talk to him, then?'

Calypso eyed her sister over the marmalade. It was the next morning, and she'd made breakfast for them both, but Camilla hadn't been able to eat a thing.

'I don't know, darling,' said Camilla wearily. She'd cried so many tears in the night she didn't think she had any left to give. Now she just felt hollow, listless.

'Come on, you can't just give up!' urged Calypso. 'If there is something going on with him and Slutty Sophia, then you bloody well need to know!'

'I keep asking him, he keeps saying no. What else am I supposed to do – put a private detective on to him?'

'No, you need to get yourself up there and sort it out once and for all. Do you want me to come with you?'

'That's very sweet, but don't worry,' said Camilla hastily. She knew how protective her younger sister could be.

Calypso looked at the clock on the wall. 'Aren't you going to work?'

Camilla rubbed her hands over her face. 'I've called in sick. I barely slept a wink. Mr Fitzgerald wasn't too happy, but I don't care.'

Calypso smiled, reassuring her sister. 'Why don't I go and run you a bath? You can have a nice soak and then go up there to see him.' She repeated herself. 'You need to sort this out, Camilla.'

'I know,' Camilla sighed. 'I know.'

By ten thirty Camilla was driving the familiar route to Clanfield Hall, feeling more sick and nervous than she had in her entire life. It was so weird: the one person in the world she was meant to be the closest to, was the one she was the most awkward around, right now. Jed had become like a stranger to her, and in a few minutes she was about to find out what kind of man he really was. Had he been brazen enough to conduct an affair with Sophia right under her nose? All the warning signs were there, it was a classic textbook affair. Camilla gulped down another wave of nausea.

She'd expected to find Jed in his office, or off on the estate somewhere, but as she turned left into Clanfield Hall, another vehicle coming from the opposite direction was turning in as well. As Camilla and Jed's eyes met through the windscreens, both their mouths dropped open; Camilla's in astonishment, Jed's in what looked like blind panic. He was driving Mrs Bantry's neat little Peugeot and was wearing, she noted with even greater surprise, a suit and collar. She hadn't even known he owned one!

Jed gestured to her to pull in at Gate Cottage and she

did so, his car following closely behind. Even before she had cut the engine, he was at her window. He was freshly shaved, his black hair tamed by gel.

'Camilla, I haven't been honest with you. But it's all right now, I can explain.'

She jumped down from her vehicle. Wild possibilities whirled through her mind. The nice suit, the spruced-up appearance: had he been off in some five-star hotel with Sophia? Instinctively, she looked for another car following, but there was none. She faced him, trying to contain the anger and shock.

'Have you just spent the night with Sophia?'

Jed looked pained. 'Camilla, please don't start this again. I've told you. Of course there's nothing going on with her.'

Her voice was shaking now. 'So you keep telling me, Jed. But I can tell you, from where I'm standing it doesn't look that way at all. You're hiding something from me and I know it. Just *tell me.*'

He dropped his eyes, face paler than ever. 'I've made a right cock-up of this.'

'That's one way of putting it!'

Jed stepped forward and gripped Camilla's hands so tightly it hurt. She gasped in surprise. 'I see what you must have thought; I understand that now. But I was so wrapped up in it, I thought it was the best thing not to tell you. I thought I could handle it by myself, shield you from it.'

'Jed, what on earth are you talking about?'

He dropped her hands abruptly, stepped away. 'I found a lump, Camilla.'

His statement was so shocking, so unexpected, that it completely blindsided her.

'A lump?' she stuttered.

A vein throbbed in his forehead, indicting high stress. 'In my right testicle. I found it weeks ago, when I was having a shower one morning.'

The realization of what he was saying started to dawn on Camilla. 'Oh, Jed, no,' she whispered. 'Why didn't you say anything?'

His jaw clenched. 'Because I didn't want to admit it to myself! I was scared of going to the doctor's, scared of what I might find, so like a stupid idiot I buried my head in the sand. I thought if I didn't think about it, it didn't exist.' He gave a humourless laugh. 'Unfortunately it doesn't work like that.'

Camilla's mind was racing. Jed's weight loss, him complaining of being tired when normally he was as strong as an ox. It was too dreadful to contemplate.

His voice was toneless and void of emotion. 'I couldn't ignore it, no matter how hard I tried to, so eventually I went to the doctor. He took one look and said it didn't look good, not with my family history.'

Camilla felt sick, Both Jed's grandfather and his aunt had died of cancer. She couldn't believe this was happening, not to her Jed! He was so strong, so healthy. It seemed like a horrible joke.

'It all happened so quickly. The doctor did blood tests and then I was referred to the hospital for urgent X-rays. I've had to take quite a bit of time off work.'

So that was what Jed's mysterious appointment had been about.

'But you and Sophia . . .'

Jed sighed again.

'I haven't been having an affair with her, Cam. Sophia came into my office one morning when I wasn't there and found a letter from the hospital on my desk. She was waiting for me when I got back. At first I was furious she'd been going through my things, but she said she'd only picked it up because she recognized the consultant's name on the top of the letter.'

Jed paused.

'It turned out she'd had a cousin who had been through exactly the same thing. Sophia said she knew how I felt. I didn't want anyone knowing but she said she wouldn't say anything.'

Camilla felt a burn of jealousy that Sophia had been there for Jed and not her. He sensed it from her face.

'I didn't go looking for sympathy from her,' he said quickly. 'Sophia was the one popping in to see me, leaving me little notes. To be honest it made me feel a bit awkward, but I only thought she was being nice. She called me last night to wish me luck at the hospital, but I swear we've never spoken on the phone before that.'

Relief started to seep through Camilla. She knew he was telling the truth.

'Jed, I can't believe you've gone through all this by yourself!'

Her voice cracked.

'Why didn't you just *tell* me?'

362

He ran a hand over his face.

'Cam, I've handled this whole thing so badly. I was so wrapped up in myself; I never stopped to consider how you would see it. The stupid thing is I thought I was protecting you, by not telling you the truth. And my ma.'

This time it was Jed's voice that went.

'I'm all she's got.'

Tears spilled out of Camilla's eyes. 'Oh, Jed,' she sobbed. The lack of interest in sex, his cagey behaviour. It all fell into place now. All along she'd been thinking he'd been losing interest, or having an affair with Sophia Highforth. What a waste of precious time and energy.

Jed swallowed. 'That's where I've been today, seeing the urology specialist at the hospital. Today was D-Day, Camilla. To find out whether the lump was cancerous or not.'

She could hardly bear to hear his answer.

Jed stared at her, eyes channelling on to hers, searching, haunted. 'It's benign.'

For a moment Camilla didn't understand. 'Benign?'

'Yes, benign. As in non-malignant.' Jed's face relaxed into a smile. 'I haven't got cancer.'

Her knees literally buckled in relief. Camilla flung her arms around him. 'Oh, thank God!' she wept. 'Thank God!'

Jed held her tightly, and together they stood for a minute, just taking the news in. Finally he released her.

'I couldn't believe it myself when the specialist

told me,' he said in a shaky voice, 'I still can't, really. I had literally convinced myself that that was it. I was going to die and there was nothing I could do about it.' He shook his head as if in wonderment. 'He had to repeat the results about five times. Apparently it's a harmless cyst. After all that, a bloody cyst! It's causing no harm being there, so they're going to leave it. I've got to keep checking myself regularly from now on for any changes, but that's about it.'

'I need to sit down,' Camilla said weakly. The last five minutes had been the most terrifying and happy of her life. She sank down beside the car, Jed crouching in front of her. 'I thought you were having an affair with Sophia!' she told him. Camilla shook her head, exasperated. 'You had me acting like a nutcase! I really thought something was going on, Jed.'

He held her to him. 'I'm sorry. I handled it so badly, but it was the only way I *could* handle it. Please believe me.'

Camilla nestled into him. 'None of it matters now. All I care about is that you're going to be all right. Jed, I love you so much . . .'

Calypso was shocked. 'He thought he had cancer? Bills, that's terrible!'

'I know. But instead of saying anything, Jed kept it to himself. I can't bear to think how he must have felt.'

'That sounds like Jed, I suppose, soldiering on by himself.' Calypso winced. 'So my parting shot about ripping his balls off if he messed you about probably wasn't the best thing to say.'

'You weren't to know,' Camilla said kindly.

'All the same, I'd like to say sorry. Is he upstairs?'

'Yes, I've sent him to bed for the day. Poor man is exhausted.'

Calypso climbed the stairs and knocked on their bedroom door. Jed answered immediately.

'Come in.'

She pushed the door open. Jed was sitting up in bed, surrounded by magazines and books. A jug of water with fresh lemon slices in it was sitting on the bedside drawer.

'This all looks very pleasant,' she remarked.

Jed smiled. 'Camilla seems to think I need some rest.'

'I think Camilla is probably right,' Calypso said. She sat down on the bed and shook her head, smiling. 'You're a dick. Why didn't you say something?'

'I've had just about as many conversations about dicks and balls as I can handle, if that's OK.'

'Shit, sorry.' Calypso paused. 'Look, you had your reasons for doing what you did, and I do understand that. I just wanted to say, you know, sorry for accusing you of shagging Sophia Highforth.'

He gave a nod. 'Apology accepted. I didn't exactly inspire confidence in you.'

'Well, that's water under the bridge now.' Calypso leaned across and kissed him on the cheek. 'I'm really pleased you're OK, Jed.'

'Get away with you,' he smiled as she got up and made for the door.

'See you later?'

'Not if I see you first . . .' he teased.

As she left the room Jed's smile faded abruptly. Face darkening, he turned to stare out of the window.

Chapter 44

An announcement had caused much commotion in the film industry. Sophia Highforth was parting ways with her manager Gordon Goldsmith and employing the services of his brother Stevie instead. The Goldsmith brothers' rivalry was well known and the story made the entertainment pages of several of the dailies. It was one of these newspapers that Katie the dresser found Sophia reading, when she entered her Winnebago early one morning.

'Katie, hello!' Sophia gushed over the top of it. 'I'm just reading about myself in yet another newspaper. Can you believe everyone is making such a big fuss about it?'

From the smug look on her face, Sophia could indeed believe the hype.

'How did Gordon take it?' Katie asked.

'Went completely ballistic, as you can imagine. Threatened breach of contract and all that, but I'm confident my lawyers can come to some arrangement.

Stevie just understands me, you know? He is going to take me to even greater places in my career!'

That's who she was on the phone to that time, Katie thought.

'So when you told me you had a special chemistry with someone, you didn't mean that hot estate manager?' she asked innocently.

Sophia's face fell, then she regained her composure. 'Oh *him*. He was madly in love with me, of course, but I found it rather off-putting. I had to let him down gently.'

Katie stifled a smile. It had become patently obvious to anyone but Sophia that the bloke wasn't interested. 'He must have been devastated,' she remarked cheerfully.

Sophia flushed. 'Well, of course he was.' She shot Katie a look. 'You ask far too many questions. Anyway, is that my dress? You've taken far too long to finish it, as usual. I thought I'd have to do my scene naked.'

Bearing in mind Sophia had flung the gown at Katie at midnight, ordering alterations, Katie thought she'd done a pretty good job.

'Come on, then,' Sophia said irritably. 'I haven't got much time.'

Enough time to read about yourself in the newspapers, thought Katie as she hoiked Sophia back into the dress.

Calypso fingered the Eurostar tickets happily. What better way to start their holiday on the French Riviera than a three-day stop in Paris, the most romantic city in the world? Rafe was going to be over the moon when she gave them to him. Calypso had gone ahead and taken the liberty of booking it all anyway, Rafe kept saying how much he needed a holiday.

With her contacts, Calypso had managed to get them into one of the most exclusive hotels in Paris. Rafe's name would have been enough anyway, but she wanted to show him she was just as capable of calling the shots. They'd got the penthouse suite, and Calypso imagined lazy days wandering the streets and passion-filled nights screwing each other's brains out. It was going to be perfect.

Calypso looked at her watch. It was 5 p.m. 'Sod it,' she said aloud, 'I'm going to go down there now and surprise him.' Rafe had always asked her to stay away from the set because he didn't want to start the gossipy crew chattering but Calypso figured it was so near the end of filming it didn't matter. They'd be coming 'out' as a couple soon, anyway.

'Just popping out, Granny Clem!' she yelled. Five minutes later she was approaching the film set, where they seemed to be doing some sort of fight scene with two of the supporting cast members. Rafe was nowhere to be seen. A chunky security man stopped her and asked where she was going.

'I'm going to see Rafe Wolfe. I'm a friend of his.'

'You can't just walk in. You need permission.'

'How about you're filming on my grandmother's land?' Calypso said testily.

'You can verify that?'

'Not unless you want to go and ask her yourself. I warn you, though, she's quite moody round this time of day.'

The man's face relaxed. 'Sorry, love, we've got to be careful. Second Winnebago on the left.'

'Cheers,' said Calypso and walked off.

The Winnebago was quiet as she approached, curtains pulled across the windows. Maybe he was having a sleep. Calypso knocked softly on the door. 'Rafe?' She pushed it open slowly. The van was dark inside, the air rather stuffy, like walking into a person's bedroom first thing in the morning. 'Rafe?' she said again. She was standing in a little kitchen area, which led out to a bigger area on the right. Calypso turned, smiling, expecting to see Rafe fast asleep and looking cute on the sofa bed.

Instead she saw his head between the legs of a skinny brunette. One look at the woman panting in ecstasy and Calypso knew this was no dress rehearsal.

Chapter 45

The woman noticed her first.

'Oh my God!' she cried in an American accent, grabbing a cushion to cover herself. Rafe looked up, surprised. His tanned face went ashen.

Calypso was so shocked she couldn't speak for a few moments. 'What the fuck is going on?'

Rafe stood up and hastily did his trousers up. He was topless, his brown torso sweaty, blond hair tousled by having long talons run through it.

Calypso looked at the brunette, who had covered her modesty up in a silk robe, and then back to Rafe. His eyes dropped away. 'Rafe?' Calypso tried to make him look at her. 'I said what's going on? Who is *she*?'

The brunette swung her long legs and got up. Even though she was half-naked, Calypso could smell the money on her: from the expensively styled hair to the diamonds glinting at her ears and neck.

The brunette put a possessive hand on Rafe's

shoulder. 'I might ask the same question. Who is she, Rafe? Another one of your location conquests?'

He stared at the floor and the brunette laughed. It wasn't a nice sound.

'God, you're so predictable! I suppose he hasn't told you about me, I'm Daphne Winters. Rafe's fiancée.'

His *fiancée*!

Calypso's knees almost buckled underneath her. 'Rafe, what's she talking about?' She looked at him desperately, waiting for him to tell her it was all a horrible misunderstanding.

Daphne spoke instead. 'It hasn't been announced yet, but we're getting married next summer. Five hundred of our closest friends and family. It's going to be some party.'

Calypso fought back the tears, there was no way she was going to cry in front of them!

Daphne smiled patronizingly. 'There, there. At least you can pretend in your sad little world that you did mean something to Rafe.' Her eyes travelled over Calypso's denim miniskirt and vest, hair scraped back in a messy ponytail. 'He always does go for someone like you. I suppose when you've got steak at home, sometimes you fancy popping out for a hamburger.'

Calypso's fighting spirit flickered alive. 'With all that Botox I'm surprised Rafe can tell if you're dead or alive.'

Daphne's eyes widened in surprise. 'Rafe, she can't speak to me like that!' she snapped.

'Forget it, I'm out of here.' Calypso chucked the tickets on the table.

Rafe looked at the tickets, speaking for the first time. 'What are those?'

'Tickets, for a romantic break in Paris. Why don't you save them for your next *conquest*? Daphne here obviously has so little self-respect, I'm sure she won't mind.' Calypso turned and strode out of the Winnebago.

The brave front didn't last long. As soon as she was clear of the film set, the tears started coming thick and fast. She'd been so stupid! She should have seen the signs before, the phone calls from his supposed manager, the fact that Rafe had been so funny about them going out in public, Daphne's words came back to her:

'He always does go for someone like you.'

How many had there been? Calypso almost gagged. How many more, that he'd taken in with his humble manner and chivalrous act? He was a big fake and he'd conned her. From the sound of it, she wasn't the first one.

She started running, she had to get as far away as she could from Daphne and the man she thought she'd loved. The rug had been pulled from underneath her, her whole world re-written. There was only one person she wanted to see now. A few minutes later she ran into the kitchen at Fairoaks, mascara running and chest heaving.

'Oh, Granny Clem! I've just found Rafe with another woman!'

*   *   *

373

Once Calypso had stopped sobbing, she told her grandmother the whole sorry story. 'I should have listened to my instincts in the first place!'

Clementine smoothed her hair. 'You weren't to know, darling. He really did come across as a thoroughly decent chap.'

'I really loved him, you know. I thought we could build a life together.' Calypso burst into fresh floods of tears. 'How could I be so wrong about someone?'

Clementine's gaze darkened, as distant memories flooded her brain. 'We've all misjudged someone, darling. I know you feel dreadfully let down, but you must take strength from this and move on.'

Clementine held her granddaughter long into the evening. When Calypso asked if she could stay the night and share her bed, just as she had done when she was little, Clementine readily agreed. As Calypso finally dropped off to sleep, Clementine lay listening to the rhythm of her granddaughter's breathing. She herself had been taken in by Rafe. How could he treat her precious Calypso so appallingly?

The next morning a puffy-eyed Calypso was walking back to the cottage when a car pulled up. She didn't need to look and see who it was. The passenger-side window slid down.

'Calypso, can we talk?' asked Rafe.

She ignored him and carried on walking.

'Calypso!'

The car was beside her now, following. Rafe leaned over.

'At the very least, let me reimburse you for the Eurostar tickets.'

He tried to catch her eye. 'That was really nice of you by the way.'

'I don't want your money,' she said stonily.

Rafe pushed the door open.

'Get in Calypso. Please.'

She hesitated. *Might as well listen to what he's got to say for himself*, she told herself, as she climbed in.

They drove in silence until they reached a lay-by outside Churchminster. Rafe cut the engine.

'What did you want to tell me?' Calypso asked bluntly. He turned to face her, but Calypso resolutely kept her gaze ahead, afraid that if she did turn and look into those deep blue pools, she just might just forgive him for being a philandering, cheating arsehole. 'Actually let me ask you something first. Your dear grandmother on her deathbed, that was a load of bollocks wasn't it? You were meeting up with Daphne, weren't you?'

He looked away.

'That's really low.' Calypso was disgusted.

'It's not how you think,' he said.

She gave a derisive snort.

Rafe tried to touch her on the arm, but she pulled it away. 'Daphne is my fiancée, but I swear to you that when we first met, we were on a break.'

'And when did this "break" finish?' she asked, feigning big interest in a blackbird that had flown on to a branch in front of them.

'A few weeks after we met.'

'A few *weeks*?' Incredulous, Calypso turned to face

him. 'So basically, you've been pulling the wool over my eyes the whole time? For Christ's sake, Rafe!'

Despite what he'd done, Rafe still looked impossibly handsome. His full lips, the contours of his jaw, that she had traced with her fingers so many times . . . Calypso forced herself back against the car door, putting as much space between them as possible.

'You did mean something to me!' he urged. 'You still do. By the time Daphne and I got back together, I had fallen so badly for you I couldn't break it off.'

'So break it off with Daphne,' she said casually.

Rafe looked sheepish. 'It's more complicated than that. Daphne's dad is a big studio boss in LA; he's got great plans for my career.'

'Glad to see you've got your priorities sorted,' she said acidly. 'What's in it for Daphne? Why does she put up with your little indiscretions?'

Rafe gave a little grin. 'Come on, I'm not exactly a bad catch. Daphne's more of a social climber than her daddy, she wants to see us on every best-dressed list in town.'

Calypso looked at him, really *looked* at him properly for the first time, gazed beneath the film-star looks and charming veneer. She didn't like what she saw.

Rafe mistook her silence for something else. His hand edged on to her bare thigh. 'We had a great time, didn't we, Calypso? We can still go on having good times if you want to.' He gave her a meaningful look. 'The ball's in your court.'

She shot him an equally meaningful one back. 'Then take your fucking hand off and drive me home.'

Chapter 46

Two days later the film crew packed up and left the village, the only sign they'd ever been there a tatty luminous sign fluttering from a telegraph pole on the Bedlington Road. For Clementine, it was a huge relief. Even though it hadn't turned out as badly as she had expected and the location fee had come in very handy indeed, she was pleased they could finally get on with the task in hand.

Calypso had been left with a wealth of emotions. It was the first time she'd ever really been hurt, and boy, was it painful. Even though she had managed to keep up a front with Rafe, it didn't stop her spending hours sobbing while Camilla held her. The worst thing for Calypso was that she was grieving for a relationship that hadn't been real, for a man who hadn't existed. She was alternately furious with herself for falling for the nice-guy act, and with Rafe for pretending to be someone he wasn't. Most of all, though, there was heartache. A huge hole had been left in her life, a life that she had imagined ending happily ever after.

'Do you think I meant anything to him?' Calypso sobbed one night on the sofa in the cottage.

'Darling, I really do,' said Camilla. She'd seen the way Rafe had looked at her sister. Pity he'd neglected to mention there was a fiancée in the background. What a bastard! She'd never pay money to see a Rafe Wolfe film again.

Aside from Calypso's anguish Camilla was uncomfortably aware that things still weren't right with Jed. The euphoria and closeness they'd shared again on him getting the all-clear had been a fleeting experience. Several times she'd walked into the living room to find him staring into space and he seemed edgy with her, like he was back holding her at arm's length. They hadn't had sex since but Camilla didn't want to push it. She told herself that Jed was coming round from the shock of the whole thing, that it would take time to get back to normal after going through such a traumatic experience. These words were becoming harder to believe by the day however.

It was Thursday, the 17th of July. In twenty-four hours' time, the Britain's Best Village judges would descend on Churchminster, bringing their voting pads with them, along with the chance to change the lives of everyone for ever. The whole village was aware of the irony that it was almost a year to the day that the floods had rampaged through, ripping apart homes, businesses and people's livelihoods.

Churchminster would always carry the scars of that

dreadful summer, but over the past twelve months they had picked themselves up. In fact, standing on the green that warm summer's evening with the rest of the Garden Party, Clementine felt a huge sense of pride about what they'd all achieved. OK, so they had been blighted by the blasted vandals – who Bedlington police still hadn't caught yet – but there was no doubt the village was looking great. Front gardens were well-kept, with an array of flowers in each one. The village green looked pristine. The shop was doing a roaring trade, the Jolly Boot was filled with Pimms-drinking punters every lunchtime and evening. The notice board outside the village hall was festooned with flyers for mum and baby coffee mornings, charity bike rides, OAP bingo evenings and lunches, under-eighteen workshops, local gardens open to the public; all the elements that make for a happy, prosperous community.

This really, was what Britain's Best Village was about. It wasn't just appearance that mattered, but what was happening underneath. Did the village have a heart and soul? Did everyone look out for each other? It might not be the grandest place in the land, but Clementine took huge satisfaction in knowing that Churchminster was a place that people wanted to *live in*, not just drive through on a day out. It was this single factor that convinced her they could still win BBV.

Later, after they'd all had a celebration champers at the Jolly Boot, the members of the Garden Party retired to their respective houses, each hoping and waiting for the day ahead. The judges were due at 10 a.m., and would spend three hours walking through the village to assess how well all the categories had been met. As the residents of Churchminster climbed into bed that night, their minds whirred with possibilities, anxieties and excitement.

Could they, *would* they win it?

Clementine woke with a start. Something was wrong. She opened her eyes blearily and looked at her bedside clock. Ten past three in the morning. Then she realized why she could read it: instead of complete darkness, there was an orange glow creeping in through the windows, lighting up the room. Clementine frowned; that was strange. In the distance she could hear a strange crackle. It reminded her of the fat spluttering on a belly of pork when she took it out of the oven.

Suddenly she sat bolt upright, hand clutching her throat in fear. She knew that sound! Moving hurriedly, she got out of bed and went over to the window. The orange glow behind the curtains was even stronger, illuminating the rosebud pattern. Heart clenched with dread and in trepidation, Clementine yanked them back.

For a moment, she registered complete shock and disbelief at the sight before her. Then Clementine's face crumpled and she started wailing. 'No! No, it can't be! Oh, please Lord, no!'

St Bartholomew's was on fire. The building was a black silhouette against the thirty-foot flames that raged through it. As Clementine watched she heard a huge groan reverberate, as if the old church had finally given up in agony, and part of the roof caved in, disappearing in a crash of sparks.

Clementine gripped the windowsill, mesmerized by horror. It was like seeing one of her oldest, dearest friends dying a terrible death in front of her, and she could do nothing about it. She became aware of another, high-pitched noise, which, she suddenly realized, was herself screaming.

Suddenly in the distance, she heard another sound, which snapped her back into the present. Someone had called the fire brigade.

Within five minutes, Clementine was down on the green in her Wellington boots, her gardening over-coat pulled over her nightdress. Two fire engines were there, fruitlessly spraying water over St Bartholomew's, but the flames refused to relinquish their hold. Already the village green was dotted with people, their cars left parked haphazardly on the roadside as they rushed down to try and help.

Calypso was there, barefoot in a tiny pair of pyjama shorts and vest top. She started sobbing as soon as she saw her grandmother. 'Oh, Granny Clem!' she said, running into her arms, 'I can't bear to watch, it's just too awful.'

'Where's your sister?' Clementine asked anxiously, but Camilla appeared by her side, dressed in her nightie.

'I'm here, don't worry, but Jed's in there somewhere! He went in with Jack to try and save some things.'

Just then, two firefighters emerged from the smoke,

clutching a blackened-faced Jed between them. Camilla ran over in relief but Jed shook her off.

'I've got to go back!' he shouted. 'Jack's still in there!'

Stacey Turner, standing a few feet away with her arm round her mother, started screaming. 'What do you mean, my dad's still in there! He's gonna die! Someone get him, get him fucking out!'

She made a start for the church, but Beryl pulled her back, tears running down her face. 'No, Stacey!'

In the distance an ambulance siren could be heard. There was a large *whoosh* and another part of the roof collapsed. More people started screaming. One of the firemen moved towards the crowd, waving his arms.

'Get *back* everyone! This is dangerous!'

Suddenly, through the hiss and crackle, another fireman appeared, half-dragging something beside him. It was only when the exhausted man pulled the shape clear of the fire and laid it down on the wet grass, that everyone could see who it was.

It was the burned, blackened body of Jack Turner.

Stacey started screaming afresh and rushed over. 'Dad, dad, oh Daddy! Please, someone do something!'

Two firemen were there, one leaning down to his face to listen for Jack's breathing. He glanced at his colleague, face grim. 'We've lost him, start CPR.'

As the other fireman ripped open Jack's shirt and started to do resuscitation, Stacey Turner fell in a heap, almost animal-like in her hysteria. 'My daddy, my daddy, my daddy!'

Beryl tried to comfort her, crying hysterically and

white-faced in shock. They were all crying: Clementine, Camilla, Calypso, the Bellows, and Angie and Freddie Fox-Titt, with their arms around each other.

An ambulance pulled up and the crew jumped out to take over. One of the firemen looked up at them. 'I can't get his heart started!'

The ambulance crew took over, then, and the last sight everyone had of Jack Turner was of the doors closing on his lifeless body, a sobbing Stacey and Beryl by his side.

Chapter 47

They'd got the fire under control in the end, but not before it had swept through the entire church taking almost everything with it. In the end, all that was left standing were the four walls, windowless and roofless. As Clementine stood in the early morning light, debris floating down in front of her, she thought it looked like the carcass of a poor animal that had been ripped apart by vultures. A plume of smoke hung over the blackened wreck of St Bartholomew's, while a fine layer of ash had settled on the green and surrounding houses.

Freddie came over and squeezed her arm. 'How are you doing old bean?'

Wordlessly Clementine shook her head. 'Have you heard from the hospital?'

'Jack's in theatre now,' Freddie told her gently. Clementine's chin wobbled and she cast her eyes heavenward.

'Oh Freddie! How dreadful.'

Amongst the villagers still on the green, strange faces

were milling about. The local police had turned up, and the fire-investigation team were doing what they could before the building was cool enough to let them start their extensive work. It didn't bode well, one of them had already found a petrol can, which had been tossed over the graveyard wall. The residents rounded on PC Penny, desperate to express their despair.

'Who would do such a dreadful thing!' cried Angie angrily.

PC Penny looked overwhelmed. 'Madam, we will do all we can to find the culprits.'

'Don't you mean murders?' cried Calypso, 'Did you *see* Jack being carried out of there?'

Camilla put her hand on her sister's arm. 'Easy, sweet pea.'

'I bet it's the same bloody vandals who did all the damage last few times,' sniffed Calypso defiantly. 'The ones who kicked off at *Churchminster's Got Talent*. As far as I'm concerned they've got blood on their hands.'

'We will be following up all lines of enquiry,' stated PC Penny.

'I should go to Bedlington and find them myself,' muttered Jed.

'We don't need you in trouble as well,' Camilla told him.

'What do *you* think, Granny Clem?' asked Calypso. Her grandmother always knew what to do.

Clementine looked at her, eyes vacant.

'What do I think about what?'

'About who did it, if it was started deliberately? Do you think it was that lot from Bedlington.'

'Oh, who knows? It's pointless worrying about it now. We have a far greater tragedy on our hands.'

Everyone fell silent, thinking about Jack. Calypso gave another sob. The last few days had been an emotional roller coaster and now this. It was too much.

Eventually Freddie looked at his wristwatch.

'Christ, the judges will be here in a few hours!'

'Do you think we should try and put them off for a few hours?' Angie asked anxiously, 'We could try and clear up.' She trailed off. There was no point, Churchminster looked like a war zone. It would take weeks to get back to normal again.

Until that moment, Clementine had completely forgotten about the competition, which had so dominated her life the last few months. There was no way they would win now.

'I need to go to bed,' she said wearily.

'We'll walk you back,' Camilla said anxiously.

Clementine raised a hand. 'No darling, don't bother yourself.'

They all watched as her tall, hunched figure disappeared into the morning mist.

As well as poor Jack, it wasn't just the physical act of desecration that had so badly affected Clementine. It was all the memories that had been lost as well. She had married and put her darling Bertie to rest in that church, had her son christened there, seen the next generation of Standington-Fulthropes start there, along with many other families in the village. As she curled up in bed, exhausted yet unable to sleep,

Clementine reflected that a piece of her had gone, along with the church. And she would never, ever get it back again.

They lost Jack three times on the way to hospital. The surgeon who treated him said he was amazed anyone could come back to life with that amount of smoke in their lungs.

'My dad's a fighter,' Stacey told him proudly, as she and Beryl kept a bedside vigil in the intensive care unit. Jack, rigged up to breathing apparatus and unable to say anything, squeezed his daughter's hand. White bandages swathed his hands and forearms where he'd been burned.

'We thought we'd lost you, Dad,' Stacey said emotionally. The familiar feisty look returned to her face. 'Don't be such a *gaylord* and do anything so stupid again.'

'Hear, hear,' Beryl echoed weakly.

At ten o'clock precisely, the people carrier containing the three judges pulled up at the village green. Grim-faced they dismounted, taking in the scene of carnage. Marjorie Majors, a stout woman in her fifties with cropped grey hair, muttered something to the other two judges, who were male, and shook her head. As Clementine had taken to her bed, it was down to the Fox-Titts to welcome the judges and tell them a little bit about the village. As much as Angie gaily tried to tell them about their wonderful community spirit and picturesque beauty, the hulking blackened shell of St

Bartholomew's sat there in the background, like a great ugly albatross.

One of the male judges coughed. 'All this ash is getting in my throat. Could we get some refreshments at your public house?'

'I'm afraid it's shut,' said Angie apologetically. 'Jack Turner, our landlord, is in hospital. He went into the church last night, when it was on fire, to save some of the artefacts.'

Marjorie Majors shook her head again. Angie couldn't make out if it was a gesture of disapproval or regret. 'You have a lot of bad luck in this village, don't you? What with floods and now this.'

'Yes, but we are good at getting back on our feet again,' said Freddie hurriedly.

'Hmmm,' Marjorie Majors didn't sound convinced. Her eyes travelled over the freshly replanted flower-beds.

'You've left your planting a little late. Those violas should be flourishing by now.'

'Bloody vandals pulled up the lot before,' said Freddie. The three judges exchanged glances with each other.

'Yes, well, thank you, Mr Fox-Titt, I think you've told us all we need to know,' said Marjorie Majors. 'I think the only thing left now is for us to get started.'

For three excruciating hours, the judges walked every inch of the village, taking notes and leaving no flowerpot unturned. Brenda Briggs, watching through the net curtains at Hollyoaks Cottage, was convinced she lip-read Marjorie Majors saying something about 'being a total disaster'.

Knowing Brenda's dramatic imagination, most people tried to take that particular claim with a pinch of salt, but it didn't stop the sense of impending doom as the judges silently jotted down their thoughts, occasionally pointing something out to each other.

At one o'clock, after displaying disappointment they wouldn't be able to eat at the Jolly Boot and sample some of the wares – 'A good local pub is *essential* for a thriving village,' Marjorie Majors declared – the three judges climbed back in their people carrier and exited the village as silently as they had come in. It was exactly a week until the grand ceremony in London, when the eventual winners would be announced.

No one thought they had a hope in hell. They would have felt even worse if they'd heard the conversation as the judges' car left the outskirts of Churchminster.

'What a hellhole. I was glad to get out of there,' said one of them.

'Tell me about it,' said the other.

Chapter 48

The next day the *Bedlington Bugle* and the *Daily Mercy* ran stories about the fire, both suggesting it was foul play. The *Mercy* had a quote from the senior investigating officer at Bedlington police station, saying that if it *were* arson, 'they would do all they could to find the culprits'. It didn't make the residents of Churchminster feel any better. Clementine even talked of cancelling the coach they'd hired to take the Garden Party to London, but Angie managed to talk her out of it.

'Don't give up hope now, Clementine, there's still a chance we could win it.' Her words sounded hollow, even to Angie. The only good news was that Jack Turner continued to gain strength in hospital. His consultant had warned him he'd have to take things easy for a while, and Jack joked that his recovery was being hindered, rather than helped, by the rather unpalatable home-cooked meals Stacey kept bringing in for him. He reflected ruefully – as he nearly broke a tooth on yet another rock-hard dumpling

– that his daughter might take after her mother in feistiness, but definitely hadn't inherited her kitchen skills.

Twenty-four hours later, the villagers got the news they'd been dreading. The fire had been started deliberately in a potting shed beside the church. A full investigation was now underway, even though the police admitted they had little to go on. Meanwhile the skeleton of St Bartholomew's stood, barely able to support itself, as the insurance company started their own inquiry. Early conservative estimates put the cost of repair at two million pounds.

People dealt with the blow in different ways. At the Maltings, Angie and Freddie had pulled out of the wine cellar a hugely expensive burgundy they'd been saving for a special occasion, and commiserated with each other at dinner. Brenda Briggs started a 'Save Barts' collection, and came back from Bedlington market square one day with the grand total of fifteen pounds and twenty-seven pence, plus a randy war veteran's phone number. It wouldn't even buy a new pew cushion, but she felt so desperate she had to do something. It was a desperation echoed round the village. There was no way they'd win the competition now.

Camilla sidled up to Jed and put her arms round him. He tried to hide the flinch too late. Hurt, Camilla stepped back from the living-room window, where Jed had been staring out in the direction of St Bartholomew's. Instead, he tried for a smile.

'Hey, you startled me.'

Camilla remembered the times he used to pounce on her round the cottage, pulling her into the downstairs loo for a quickie. How long ago those carefree days seemed now.

He nodded out of the window.

'I was just looking at the church. What a bloody mess.'

She gave a small smile.

'Would a neck rub make things any better? You seem awfully tense.'

By the look on his face, one would have thought Camilla had produced an air rifle from her pocket and announced she was going to shoot him in the kneecap.

'I should get back to work,' he said hurriedly and left.

Afterwards Camilla wandered dejectedly from room to room. She'd worked so hard to make their own little nest here, from the photos adorning every wall to the hand-stitched patchwork cushion on the old rocking chair in the kitchen. Most recently, her thoughts had turned towards creating a home for their family. Camilla sighed, their conversations about trying for kids seemed almost unreal now. What if Jed had taken the lump in his testicle as some sort of sign he wasn't cut out to be a dad after all? Perhaps, rather than revelling in domestic bliss as she did, Jed was finding the whole thing suffocating. It was a horrible moment of realization.

He doesn't even want to be in the same room as me, she thought miserably. Where on earth could they go from here?

'Frannie? It's me. Can you come over? I need to talk to you.'

Frances paused. 'You must have a sixth sense, I was about to call. There's something I need to discuss with you as well, actually.'

Devon sounded pleased. 'Really? That's great! See you soon.'

'I'll be over in thirty minutes.'

Heart thumping, Frances put the receiver down. She had replayed the approaching moment so many times in her head, and what she would say to Ambrose, that her brain was starting to physically hurt. She had agonized over it at length, Frances knew what she was contemplating would cause huge ructions and leave people reeling. Her life would be changed irreversibly. Terrifying and exciting as the prospect was, the only way Frances would ever know if it was the right thing to do was to make the jump. She'd have to deal with the rest as it came at her.

Devon was already waiting on the doorstep as Frances pulled up. Even from twenty feet away she could see the anxiety etched on his face. He obviously had something big to say. Her stomach did a somersault.

'Princess!' He came over and opened her door. Frances unfolded her long legs and got out. Devon's heart did a thump, *God she was sexy!*

'Hello, Devon.' They kissed on both cheeks, before Devon moved in for a kiss on the lips. Closing her eyes, Frances savoured his soft dry lips against hers, the taste of his woody aftershave.

Devon drew back and smiled. 'Come on in.' Taking her by the hand, he led her in and through to one of the two garish living rooms. 'Can I get you a drink?'

'Water, thank you.'

'Still, sparkling?'

'Tap water is fine.' Frances tried to settle herself back on the uncomfortable settee, which was covered in glittery Union Jacks and guitars. Above the fireplace hung a huge painting of a topless cartoon woman, snakes writhing around her provocatively. Frances chose not to look where one snake's tail was going.

Devon returned after a few moments with two glasses of water. He slopped Frances's one as he put it down. 'Shit, sorry!'

'Don't worry,' Frances said. Devon seemed almost as nervous as she was. He sat down in a chair opposite her, took a sip of his water, put it down and picked it up again.

'Are you all right?' she asked.

Devon looked at her. 'Mouth's dry.' He took a big gulp of his water and put the glass down decisively. 'I'm leaving. I've got a buyer for Byron Heights and all me business in London's been taken care of.'

Frances felt like a leaden weight had suddenly appeared in her stomach. She had known Devon would have to leave soon, but it still was a shock to hear him say it. 'When?'

'Next week. Honolulu flight out of Heathrow.'

There was silence. Frances looked down at her hands, not sure what to say.

'Frannie, don't be sad.'

Something in Devon's voice made her look up.

He was smiling at her tentatively. 'I've booked two tickets.'

'Two tickets?' she asked, not understanding.

Devon broke into a big grin. 'Yeah, two tickets! I want you to come with me, you doughnut!' Bounding across the room, he took her hands in his. 'I know it's presumptuous, and I know what I'm asking you to give up. But I can give you a better life, princess! You want excitement and fun; we can tour the world with my music, go wherever we want, do whatever we want to do. The roadies will take a bit of getting used to, but they're good lads really.'

'Oh, Devon,' she said softly. He saw the hesitation in her eyes.

'It won't be rough and ready; I'll make sure we stay in the best places. You'll be Devon Cornwall's girlfriend, people will roll the red carpet out for us!'

She exhaled and looked down again.

Devon looked anxious. 'What's wrong? I know it's not a decision you're gonna take lightly, but I thought you'd be pleased. It's your ticket out of Churchminster!'

It was her who gripped his hands this time. 'Devon, I want to start by saying you are one of the most wonderful, special people I have ever met, and you will always hold a very dear place in my heart. Most of all, you've taught me how to have *fun* again.'

'Ay up, don't like the sound of this,' he joked, but the alarm was evident in his face.

'You're probably not going to believe this.' She took a deep breath. 'I'm going travelling.'

His mouth gaped open. 'You're having a giraffe?'

Frances gave a ghost of a smile. 'Sounds like complete madness, doesn't it? Lady Fraser donning her backpack and taking off. I've already asked Camilla Standington-Fulthrope to organize a tour for me. I'm going to Africa, to travel around and also do some charity work. Something that really fulfils me.'

Devon still couldn't quite take it in. 'Frances, you'll be lugging a big rucksack about, not being able to wash for days.' Devon's eyes widened in horror. 'I've heard they've got rats the size of cats over there! And what about the snakes?'

'And scorpions and Black Widows and angry lions,' she laughed. 'Yes, I know I've got all that to come.'

He stared at her, not comprehending. 'But with me you'd have five-star hotels and private jets! I could give you an amazing life, princess.'

'But Devon, don't you see? It will be *your* life.' Frances gripped his hands harder. 'All my life I've been dictated to by men and rules and conventions. I've spent thirty-five years being the wife of Sir Ambrose Fraser, and it's time for a change.' She laughed. 'I can't quite believe it's taken me to the age of fifty-four, but I'm ready. I want to travel the world, meet new people and have amazing experiences, not worry about where to place so-and-so at the table, and my bloody duty.'

'You wouldn't have any of the la-di-da stuff with me,' he offered. 'I still hold my knife like a pen and burp at the dinner table.'

She gave him a sad smile. 'You know what I mean.'

And, despite it all, he did. They'd been through

this before, when Frances had ended their affair in a fit of guilt about her family and her elevated position in society. Now she was doing something for herself – she needed to get out and taste life on her own terms, just as he had done. Devon only wished he'd met more members of the aristocracy that were as honourable and noble-hearted as his Frances.

His Frances. With a dreadful wrench, he realized she would never be that. 'Oh, Frannie, I'm gonna miss you,' he said, his voice hoarse with grief.

She put her arms round him, tears running down her cheeks. 'You'll always be my Devon.'

By the time Frances got back to Clanfield Hall, she had composed herself. She and Devon had had a heartfelt farewell, which, if she'd been weaker-willed, would have culminated in him carrying her upstairs into the bedroom. She still fancied and loved him in her own way, and that was the hardest part. But Frances knew she had to start putting her own needs first, and, romantic as it sounded, letting a rock star sweep her off into the sunset was not among them. They'd promised to keep in contact and Frances had no doubt that they would, but she knew the bond had been broken. For the first time in her life, she was about to embark on something entirely alone.

'Ambrose!' Frances didn't wait for an answer and went straight in. Her husband looked up from behind his desk. The *Racing Post* was spread open in front of him. He didn't look happy at being interrupted.

'Yes, Frances?'

'We need to talk,' she said firmly, sitting down opposite him.

'About what? Can't it wait until dinner?'

'This is *important*, Ambrose.'

He sighed heavily, leaning back in the chair. 'Well? I've said we'll donate to the church fund, haven't I?'

This time she came straight out with it. 'I'm going travelling. To Africa. For six months.'

Ambrose's mouth fell slack, before he let out a roar of laughter. 'Very good, Frances! I'd forgotten you could be quite so funny.'

She shot him a look. 'I mean it! I am sick to death of life on this bloody estate and I need a new challenge. I want to be me, Frances, not just a wife or daughter, or some silly Debrett's entry. Do you understand?'

Ambrose saw the determined glint in his wife's eye. 'You're serious, aren't you?'

'Absolutely.' Frances folded her arms. 'While I'm away I want you to go for anger management lessons, and when I get back, we are going for marriage counselling. That's if you want to save this marriage, Ambrose. I expect you'll have a lot to think about while I'm away.'

'Anger management!' he said, incredulously. '*Anger management?* I don't need some new fangled claptrap, of all the bloody stupid things . . .'

'Just listen to yourself!' she cried. 'You're off again, and you don't even realize it. Do you even think about what it's like for me, treading on eggshells day in and day out?'

He looked genuinely shocked. 'I'm not that bad, am I?'

'Yes, you are,' she replied quietly. 'And if you don't do something about your temper, Ambrose, there is a good chance I will leave you. It has become intolerable.'

Shamefaced, he stared down at the desk.

'Oh Frances.'

There was something in his voice that made her look at him. He sank back into the chair. 'I know I'm a bugger to live with.'

'At least that's something we agree on,' she said, but her voice had lost some of its anger.

Ambrose rubbed the bridge of his nose, something he only did when he was tired or upset. 'Life seems so much *harder* these days. I'm getting old, Frances. Clanfield is going on as always, stronger than ever. While I . . . I hate being old, Frances.'

'We all get old, Ambrose,' she said gently. He shook his head.

'You've still got your life ahead of you, you don't need an old man like me holding you back.' He grinned boyishly, a flash of the old Ambrose. 'Don't know how I bloody got you in the first place.'

Frances leaned forward and took his hand in hers across the desk. 'I had no idea you felt like that. You should have said something.'

'Ditto,' he said wrily.

She sighed. 'Oh heavens, what a pair we are!'

They looked at each other and burst into laughter. It was the first time in a long time and it felt wonderful.

'Are you going to go to the classes?' she asked eventually.

He rolled his eyes humorously. 'If it makes you happy.'

'No. I want *you* to be happy.' She gave him a look. 'Life is what you make of it, Ambrose, no matter what age you are.'

They fell silent for a moment.

'Africa, you say?' he said eventually.

'Malawi, Botswana and Namibia to be precise,' she said. 'Then on to Kenya to help build a new sanitation block for one of the poorest villages.'

He blew out heavily, considering. 'What will the likes of Lady Adelaide Horsworth say about you gallivanting around in some African country, elbow-deep in crap?'

'Quite frankly, I don't care,' said Frances.

Ambrose grinned, a cheeky glint in his eye that took thirty years off him. 'You know what, Frances, I don't give a damn, either. You go and show those bourgeois types what you're made of.'

'That's exactly what I intend to do,' said Frances. Walking round, she leant down and planted a soft kiss on her husband's lips, before sweeping gracefully to the door.

Ambrose watched her. 'You go get 'em Frances!'

She paused and winked. Ambrose guffawed.

When the door closed he settled back in his chair and a more serious look fell over his face. It had terrified him realizing just how close he'd come to losing her. From now on, Ambrose was going to try his damnedest not to.

Chapter 49

The Britain's Best Village ceremony was just three days away. Everyone was putting a brave face on and saying how much they were looking forward to it, but inside was a different matter. For Calypso, it was even worse. Her grandmother was still devastated by the desecration of the church; while Calypso was still struggling with Rafe's betrayal and the mess he'd left behind. To add to it all, the atmosphere in the cottage was getting worse by the minute. It hadn't escaped Calypso's notice that Jed was acting weirdly again. She didn't know what to say to her sister. While Camilla was as lovely and sweet as always and making sure Calypso was all right, she could see her older sister had her own problems. What a bloody mess!

The office was suffocating her today and Calypso decided she needed some fresh air to try and clear her head. She slipped out the garden gate at Fairoaks and started to make her way down the narrow lane to

The Meadows. She hadn't gone fifty yards before a car pulled up beside her.

'There you are. You're not an easy woman to track down.'

Calypso's stomach did a slow flip at the sound of the familiar voice. She turned to see Rafe in his sports car, smiling up at her. Under the baseball cap he was wearing she could see he was sporting a black eye. It looked swollen and painful, as if it had happened recently.

'Daphne hit you with one of her chicken fillets?' she asked acidly. Rafe looked a bit uncomfortable and ignored the question.

'Why haven't you responded to any of my texts or calls?'

She looked at him, mouth gaping at the audacity.

'Because you've got a fiancée, dumbass!'

Rafe looked pained, as if it was a minor detail. His bright blue eyes fixed on her searchingly.

'Calypso darling, please. I've driven all the way out from London to see you . . .'

He looked so gorgeous that Calypso felt that funny, butterfly feeling in her stomach again. Oh God, why was he so frigging sexy . . .

'Is everything all right?' As if in a mirage, Granny Clem appeared, Errol Flynn at her side. She ignored Rafe, but Errol Flynn growled at the film star, as if mirroring his mistress's silent thoughts.

'I saw you out of the window and was wondering if you'd like to accompany me on a walk,' she said firmly. She shot a look at Rafe.

'Just the two of us.'

Rafe gave Calypso another meaningful look.

'You know where to find me.' With that he sped off in a cloud of dust.

Calypso turned to her grandmother. 'Thanks for saving me.' Her lower lip wobbled. 'Oh Granny Clem!'

Clementine put her arm round her granddaughter. 'There, there my darling.'

The night before the ceremony Camilla was in the bedroom trying on outfits. Not that she was in the mood to go out and socialize she thought, as she held yet another dress against her. A movement at the door made her look up. Jed was standing watching her. 'Oh, hello! Aren't you meant to be at work?'

Jed didn't seem to hear her question. 'Camilla, we need to talk. Can you come down to the kitchen?'

An icy feeling started to creep up from the pit of her stomach. She dropped the dress on the bed, aware her hands were shaking. 'OK.'

Numbly she followed him downstairs into the kitchen. Jed stood on the other side of the table as if to put space between them. His face was paler than she'd ever seen it, making his green eyes appear almost iridescent.

'What is it you want to talk about?' she asked uncertainly.

Jed stared at the floor. When he looked up again his eyes were as hard. 'I think it's best if I move out for a bit.'

For a moment she stood still, not quite understanding

what he was saying. 'Move out?' she eventually repeated.

Jed wouldn't meet her eyes. 'I need some space, Cam, I'm not sure this is working.'

Camilla felt sick to her stomach. 'You mean us? Are you trying to finish it?'

Something like physical pain registered in Jed's eyes, but as quick as a flash it was gone again. 'I'm not saying that.'

'What *are* you saying then?'

'I just need to be by myself, all right? I feel like I can't breathe at the moment!' The words were almost shouted.

Camilla sank down on to the floor, as if her world had literally crumbled. 'Jed, what's happened to us? What's happened to you?'

He started to back towards the door. 'I'm staying at Ma's for a while. I'll come back and get some stuff tomorrow.'

She looked up, shocked. 'You're going? Just like this?'

'Don't make it any more difficult,' he muttered.

Camilla's pain turned into anger. 'Sorry if I want an explanation from my boyfriend on why he's suddenly decided to move out!'

'You want an explanation?' he shot back angrily.

'Yes!'

As Camilla's eyes filled with tears, Jed took a step towards her. He stopped as if he'd walked into an invisible wall. 'You deserve better than me, Cam.' He turned and walked out. 'That's my explanation.'

Left alone in the kitchen, Camilla put her head in her hands and started sobbing.

'Oh, darling, I really don't know what to say.'

Clementine felt dreadful that she could do nothing to ease her granddaughter's pain. They were sitting round the kitchen table at Fairoaks, drinking steaming cups of tea. When Camilla had appeared, face streaked with tears, at the door, Clementine had ushered her in. Through sobs Camilla had eventually told her what had happened. Clementine was shocked and upset. Camilla had told her about the cancer scare but Clementine had thought things had been better since then. Clementine had been relieved that her suspicions about Sophia Highforth had been put to rest.

'I thought that was the reason he'd been acting so strangely. But if anything, he's been even worse since. Oh, Granny Clem! He was so cold when he left. That thing about him not being good enough for me, what did it mean?' Errol Flynn stuck a comforting snout into her hand. He seemed to know something was up. Camilla stared into space, eyes stretched huge with misery.

'I think he's got cold feet about us, Granny Clem. I think he wants out of the relationship.'

Clementine squeezed her granddaughter's hand. 'Perhaps he doesn't know how to tell you,' she said gently. 'Maybe he simply isn't capable of having long-term relationships. He has always been a loner. It's a bitter pill to swallow, darling, but maybe that's what suits him.'

Camilla sniffed. 'Maybe the cancer scare has made Jed reassess things. About what he wants from life.' She made herself say the words. 'Maybe he's decided he doesn't want me.'

'He hasn't ended the relationship,' her grandmother pointed out. 'If he does want to make this work, it might be that in his own funny way Jed thinks it *will* make things better by moving out.'

Camilla looked at her. 'You don't really believe that, do you, Granny Clem?'

Clementine sighed. 'Oh darling, who knows the workings of young men's minds?' She paused. 'What are you going to do? You need to sort this out with him.'

'I don't know if I can handle another argument at the moment,' Camilla said wearily. *Maybe I'm just putting off the inevitable*, she thought. *Maybe I just don't want to hear him say the words 'it's over'.* 'You know, Granny Clem, we were going to start trying for a baby. Jed seemed so excited about it all.' Camilla's bottom lip wobbled. 'How can it have gone so wrong?'

Clementine squeezed her granddaughter's hand again. First Calypso and now Camilla. 'Oh, my darling. I just wish there was something I could do, to make you feel better.'

'Me too,' Camilla whispered through her tears. 'Me too.'

The next morning Camilla woke early. The first thing she did was check her phone. Jed hadn't texted in the night. The bed that they'd slept in, made love in and laughed in was now horribly empty. Calypso had offered to sleep next to her so Camilla wouldn't feel alone in the night, but she had turned down the offer. If this was the way it was going to be from now on, she might as well get used to it. Camilla felt numb, as if her once familiar, cosy surroundings were being viewed by a different person. She couldn't even remember what normal life felt like.

The front door bell had jangled a number of times before Camilla registered it. Had Calypso forgotten her keys again? Hair tousled with sleep, she made her way downstairs in her pyjamas. Everywhere seemed still, quiet and cold. But when she pulled the front door open, it wasn't her sister standing there but Mrs Bantry. The older woman looked awkward out of her natural habitat at Clanfield Hall.

'Nora, hello,' Camilla said wearily. Surely Jed hadn't sent his mother round to pick up his belongings? Then again, she could believe anything of him now.

Mrs Bantry's hands twisted round her handbag. 'May I come in?'

'Of course,' said Camilla. She showed her through to the living room. 'Please take a seat.'

As Mrs Bantry sat down, she looked at Camilla's pyjamas. 'Sorry, I've only just got up . . .' Camilla's voice faded away into the silence. Mrs Bantry's hands were twisting in her lap now.

'Camilla, I really don't want you to think I'm interfering, but I had to come over and say something.'

'I take it this is about Jed,' she said flatly.

'You've got to go and talk to him. He's in a dreadful state.'

'Mrs B, I don't know what Jed has told you, but he's the one who decided to move out,' said Camilla. Her voice was shaking but she was too tired to hide her emotions anymore. 'And you know what, maybe it *is* a good idea he's gone. I can't cope with his mood swings any more.'

Mrs Bantry looked pained. 'Just go and talk to him, you owe it to yourselves. There's something you don't know about Jed. He needs to tell you . . .'

Camilla frowned. 'Tell me about what?'

Mrs Bantry stood up, signalling the conversation was over. 'There, I've said too much now.' She looked at Camilla, the same arresting green eyes as her son's. 'Just go and talk to him. Please.'

And without really knowing why, Camilla agreed.

Chapter 50

'You look as bad as I feel.' She surveyed Jed from the front door step.

He smiled tiredly. 'I haven't slept a wink.'

'Me neither,' she admitted.

Jed gestured. 'Come in.'

She followed him down the narrow little corridor of Mrs Bantry's cottage to the bright and cosy front room.

'Can I get you something? Tea, coffee?' he asked.

Camilla shot him a quizzical smile. 'I don't drink coffee.'

'Shit, I know that.' Jed shook his head. 'I'm really nervous.'

She stared at him, trying to work out what could be going on. Compared to yesterday, their roles seemed to have been reversed. Trying to quell the sickness in her stomach, she sat down. 'Your mother said I had to see you.'

He sat down next to her, and then stood up again. 'This is really difficult.'

Every nerve and muscle in his body seemed to have clenched up. Despite all that had happened in the last twenty-four hours, she felt for him. Camilla stood up and put a placating hand on his arm. This time he didn't cast it off. 'Hey, it's OK.'

To her absolute horror, Jed's eyes filled up. She had never seen him shed so much as a tear in his life. 'No, it isn't,' he whispered.

Camilla stepped closer to him, so close she could smell his familiar scent, feel the warmth coming off his body. 'Jed, what on earth's wrong?'

He took a deep shuddering breath, trying to find the words. 'When I said I was moving out, it wasn't because I didn't want to be with you. It was because *you* wouldn't want to be with *me*.'

She shook her head. 'I don't understand.'

He said it so quietly she had to ask him to repeat it. He looked at her, face anguished. 'I'm infertile, Camilla.'

Camilla felt the blood rushing through her ears. She couldn't take it in. 'When did you find out?' she whispered.

'The doctor has been running tests ever since I found the lump. You know, just in case.' Jed shook his head. 'The result came back two days ago. Zero sperm count. Zilch.' He spat the words out. 'If you want the correct medical term, it's called "azoospermia". Apparently it's caused by "certain hormone disorders". The doc said it's very rare, affects two per cent of men.' Jed gave a mirthless laugh. 'Guess it was my lucky day.'

'Oh my God, Jed,' Camilla whispered.

He looked down at her, mouth twisted. 'So that's

it, I'm fucking useless, redundant. You don't want to waste any more time on me. What kind of man can't even father his own children?' The tears were falling freely now, rivulets running down his face. Camilla's heart literally broke in two at the disintegration of a man she still loved. Jed took a deep shuddering breath. 'It's all I ever wanted, you know, to have a family of my own to look after. I was going to make such a bloody good dad, Cam, I wanted to prove to myself and to him . . .' He stopped abruptly. 'You know what my earliest memory of my old man is?'

Camilla shook her head wordlessly.

'Shutting me in the cellar while another one of his "friends" came round. I can still remember the utter dark, the cold brick wall against my back, the scrapings of the rats. And all the time my ma was at work, working her fingers to the bone to keep that bastard in beer.'

'Oh Jed,' Camilla whispered. His jaw was so tight it was like granite. 'Did you tell your mum?' she ventured.

He shook his head. 'I didn't want to add to her burden, she was having a shit enough time as it was. The only good thing Dad ever did for her was leaving us.' A vein throbbed in his forehead. 'Even though he went when I was so young, he left his legacy. You learn to toughen up quick with that kind of start in life, put up defences. And I thought that was it, that was how things were going to be, until I met you. You made me realize I could let someone in, let them love me the way I loved them. And I thought if I could do that with you, then what could I do for our children . . .' He trailed off, shoulders heaving. 'I had so much to give.'

Camilla threw her arms round him, holding him so tightly her arms ached. 'You've *still* got so much to give! I don't care if you can't have children! I love you, Jed, and that's all that matters.'

'Cam, you want a family and I can't give you that.' His voice cracked. 'Don't compromise your life because of me.'

She pulled back, looking into his stricken face. She was crying now, too. 'Didn't you hear me? *I love you*, Jed Bantry! I love you whether we have children together or not. Do you understand me?'

A slight flicker of hope came alive in his eyes. 'You don't have to say that,' he muttered.

Camilla took his chin in her hands and made him look at her. 'I mean it! Just because we can't have kids together doesn't mean we can't have our own family! There's always adoption.'

He looked stunned. 'I thought you'd want your own kids, carry on the family line.'

'What's more important is that *we* carry on together,' she told him.

He stared at her, shaking his head in wonderment. 'I don't deserve you, after all I've put you through.'

'You're lucky I'm a forgiving person,' she smiled, wiping away his tears.

Jed pulled her into his arms, lifting her feet off the ground. As she melted in his strong embrace, it felt like she'd come home.

Chapter 51

In the days that followed they talked and talked, something they hadn't done properly for months. In a funny way, the news that Jed was infertile had hit him harder than it had Camilla. It was such an affront to his masculinity; strong, handsome, invincible Jed. In the hours that followed, no matter how much she told him it didn't make him less of a man, she knew he didn't believe her. All she could do was let time pass and hope it would heal him.

Of course, the stark fact that she could never bear his children was starting to sink in for her now as well, and it left her with a feeling of regret and despair. But she knew that even in her darkest moments, her love for Jed would override everything. Together they'd get through it and even though it was much too raw to discuss at the moment, Camilla knew they could still have a family of their own one day.

'How's Calypso doing?' Jed asked, finally changing the subject. 'I feel bad that I haven't really been there for her.' Mrs Bantry hadn't returned from work yet and they were snuggled up together on her small sofa.

'Coping,' sighed Camilla. 'Rafe turned up again yesterday, can you believe it? Calypso said he had a black eye, too, so at least his fiancée must have cracked him one.'

Jed looked at her. 'It wasn't his fiancée who hit him, Camilla.'

She sat up. 'What do you mean?'

'He came round to the cottage looking for Calypso. He made some arrogant comment about talking her round and I told him to back off. It all got a bit heavy, well for him anyway.' He looked solemn. 'I'm not proud of it.'

'Well, I'm proud of you, sticking up for Calypso's honour like that.' As she snuggled into his chest again, Camilla reflected how they'd had the good and bad guys mixed up all along.

Chapter 52

Friday 1st August came and with it, the prize-giving ceremony for Britain's Best Village. The special coach which had been laid on for the Garden Party was leaving Churchminster at midday sharp.

But before they left, there was something Camilla needed to do. She drove over to Top Drawer Travels and handed her notice in.

'What the hell are you talking about girlie?' said an astonished Mr Fitzgerald. He'd become a little too reliant on Camilla's organization skills and contacts to take the news in a positive way.

'I'm leaving, Mr Fitzgerald,' Camilla said with more confidence than she'd felt in months. 'I feel that perhaps I've reached the end of the line here, so I'm leaving to start up by myself.'

Behind his desk, Mr Fitzgerald's eyes boggled. 'What?'

'I'm starting up my own travel company.' Camilla couldn't help a little smile. 'I do hope we can remain on good terms as we'll be competitors from now on.'

'You're mad, girlie!' he spluttered. 'As if you're ever going to be able to compete with Top Drawer Travels.'

'I look forward to the challenge,' smiled Camilla.

He looked up at her, furious that someone was actually taking issue with his sense of authority, and leaving him to do all the work. 'Just go. Don't bother working your notice, I don't want you in here stealing all my ideas.'

'Goodbye Mr Fitzgerald,' Camilla said pleasantly. 'I'd like to say it was a pleasure, but unfortunately it wasn't.'

Within an hour, Camilla Standington-Fulthrope had her first client, and she was smiling as she boarded the coach.

At Jack's insistence, Beryl and Stacey were also on board, along with the Bellows, the Fox-Titts, Brenda Briggs, Lucinda Reinard, and of course, the three Standington-Fulthrope women. As they trundled London-bound in the slow lane of the M4, the atmosphere was still subdued, even though the prospect of a five-star hotel and glamorous ceremony awaited them later. People stared out of the window deep in thought, or whispered amongst themselves. Even the most optimistic in the group thought there was no way they could win the competition now. Too much had gone against them, no matter how hard they'd tried. Storm clouds gathered black in the skies above, a seemingly ominous foreshadowing of what was to come.

But by the time they'd got to the outskirts of London,

the mood had picked up a bit. Freddie had produced a bottle of champagne from somewhere, which was being passed around in plastic cups. 'Cheers everyone!' he said jovially.

Muted 'cheers' echoed back.

Freddie frowned. 'Come on, chaps! Whatever happens today, we're all in it together! And I for one am immensely proud of what we've achieved.'

In the aisle seat next to Calypso, Clementine felt the first stirrings of more vigour than she'd felt in a week. 'Well said, Freddie!' she called back.

Calypso nudged her. 'Say something, Granny Clem,' she whispered. 'You're like our leader, taking the troops into action.'

Clementine stood up, holding on to the back of the seat so she didn't fall over. The bus driver's over-taking was rather erratic. 'Freddie's right,' she said. 'We should all be very proud of all our efforts over the last few months. I set the bar high and every one of you surpassed what I expected.' She took a deep breath. 'We may not win Britain's Best Village . . .'

At this Brenda Briggs looked pained, but Clementine pressed on.

'But we will walk into that ceremony with our heads held high! Tomorrow is another day and we will live to fight it.' Clementine held her plastic cup aloft. 'To Churchminster!'

'To Churchminster!' everyone responded bravely. They all settled back in their seats, spirits temporarily renewed. Even if tonight was a lost cause, they might as well try to enjoy it.

*   *   *

At ten past six that evening, most of the Garden Party were down in the foyer of the hotel, dressed to the nines. Freddie looked very dapper in a dinner jacket and bow tie, while all the women were done up in pretty evening dresses, clutching purses and pashminas.

At a quarter past six Clementine, in a vintage Jaeger two-piece and gloves, looked at her wristwatch again. The Bellows and Calypso still hadn't appeared.

'Trust your sister to be late. Where are they?' she murmured crossly to Camilla. 'Our taxis are outside, we're meant to be there in fifteen minutes!'

'Do you want me to go and find out?' Camilla asked, but just then the Bellows appeared at the top of the staircase, followed by Calypso. As everyone looked up gasps echoed round the foyer.

Joyce Bellows looked stunning. Her hair had been cut into a shiny bob and coloured a deep chocolate brown. The thick-rimmed glasses had gone and her eyebrows had been plucked, showing off a beautiful face that looked twenty years younger. Smokey make-up accentuated her eyes, while a strapless black dress showed off youthful shoulders and an impressive décolleté. To finish the look, sparkly gems glittered at her wrists and ears, adding an air of sophisticated glamour.

Brian led his wife down the stairs, looking immensely proud.

'Sorry we're late,' Joyce said as they got to the bottom, 'I've been at the hotel's hairdressers.'

'Joyce, you look fabulous!' Angie exclaimed.

The vicar's wife shot a grateful look at Calypso. 'I've got Calypso to thank for that, she picked out my dress and high heels, and even did my make-up.'

Calypso winked. 'My pleasure, Joyce, I do love a good makeover!'

'You look very nice, dear,' Clementine told Joyce, mollified by the obvious joy on the other woman's face. It was like she was suddenly a different person.

As they all filed out, the doorman tipped his hat at Clementine. 'Good luck!'

Somehow she found a smile. 'Thank you.'

We don't need luck, she thought as she climbed in the waiting car. *We need a miracle.*

The ceremony was being held at the plush Grosvenor House Hotel, which was just off Park Lane. The line of Churchminster taxis pulled up at the start of a cordoned-off red carpet, from behind which a gaggle of photographers jostled and pushed to get the best picture.

Inside, the main foyer was packed with people in black tie being plied with champagne by passing waiters. Camilla had already spotted one well-known TV presenter and a glamorous socialite holding court amongst a circle of ruddy-faced men. It was so exciting!

With her endless legs and backless dress, Calypso was attracting enough attention herself. Through the sea of broad-shouldered outdoorsy types, she could see an extremely attractive man, standing by a stout grey-haired woman. Compared to the stuffed shirts

419

around him the man was a breath of fresh air, with his funky fitted black jacket and skinny trousers, a narrow black tie tied casually at his neck. As she looked again Calypso took in the sexy dark eyes and hair, the three-day stubble.

'Who's that fittie over there?' she whispered to her grandmother.

Clementine looked perplexed. 'Are you talking about a sportsperson?'

She followed Calypso's gaze and found herself looking directly at the head judge, Marjorie Majors. Their eyes met for a moment, then Marjorie looked away indifferently. Clementine felt her stomach drop. She turned and saw one of her old friends, Beatrice Field-Webber. A catch up with Bea would be a good distraction.

But before she could take a step, a familiar sickly perfume enveloped her. Clementine turned to see Veronica in full-on crimson chiffon, her mouth a ghastly slash of red. Another woman was with her, in a muted navy-blue dress, her face make-up free. She looked very familiar . . . As recognition dawned, Clementine's mouth dropped open.

'Hello, Mrs Standington-Fulthrope,' said Pam Viner.

Veronica burst out laughing at the expression on Clementine's face. 'Dear girl, you look like you've seen a ghost!'

Clementine eventually found the power of speech. 'What are you doing here, Pam?'

Veronica spoke for her instead. 'Why, she's here for the same reason I am.'

Clementine's eyes swivelled back to Pam. 'You're from Maplethorpe?' she gasped. 'Why on earth didn't you say anything?'

Pam smiled pleasantly, as if they were just having a conversation about the weather. 'Oh, that would never have done, I can't imagine you would have been quite so obliging. Still, rather good luck we ended up filming in Churchminster, don't you think?'

Clementine's mind was whirring furiously. All the information about Churchminster Veronica had on her website, the unflattering articles in the press . . . 'You've been feeding things back about us!' she said hotly. '*You're* the mole!'

'Mole, spy, call it what you will,' said Pam. 'I must say, you made it very easy for me.'

No wonder she had been so friendly, always offering to help out. Clementine cursed herself for her lapse in judgement. But Pam Viner had just seemed so *nice*. Another thought occurred, making her feel sick. 'That day on the village green, when the lorry reversed on to the grass. You told the driver to do that, didn't you?'

Pam's eyes twinkled. It chilled Clementine's blood. *The smiling assassin*, she thought.

Calypso spoke for the first time. 'Granny Clem, who *are* these people?'

Her dismissive look didn't go unnoticed by Veronica. 'I see the undesirable gene has been passed down in the family,' Veronica said pointedly.

'Excuse *me*,' Calypso started to say, but Clementine stopped her.

'Don't you dare bring my granddaughter into this!'

421

'Why not? It's clear all you Standington-Fulthropes are from bad stock. No wonder I had to give Edmund the heave-ho.' She paused, savouring the moment. 'I did try with him, you know, but he was a lost cause. Poor creature, no wonder he came to such an *unfortunate* end.'

Calypso was confused. 'Great-uncle Edmund? The one who died of tuberculosis or something when he was young?'

For a moment, Veronica actually looked shamefaced. Calypso looked at her grandmother. She had turned sheet-white, her liver-spotted hands shaking.

'Granny Clem?' she repeated. Clementine had never spoken much about her younger brother. The only photo Calypso had ever seen of him was a faded picture of an earnest-looking boy, holding a butterfly net in the garden of Fairoaks. He was an enigma; even their father Johnnie had known little about him.

When Clementine spoke again, her voice trembled. 'God knows why, Veronica, but that boy loved you! And then you threw him out like a discarded piece of rubbish when something better came along.'

'How dare you!' exclaimed Veronica. 'Your family were the ones who had me blacklisted from society, I was a pariah for years.'

'You blacklisted yourself, for what you did to Edmund!'

Pam and Calypso exchanged glances, briefly united by not knowing what was going on. Hearing the raised voices, a few people standing nearby had stopped talking to each other and were leaning in, trying to listen.

'I trusted you, Veronica! I trusted you with him.' Clementine's voice was strangulated with emotion. She stared directly into the other woman's eyes. 'You've got blood on your hands, Veronica Stockard-Manning! You might just as well have signed that poor boy's death warrant.'

Trembling, Clementine turned and walked away through the crowd.

'How dare she?' Veronica started to bluster. She looked at the onlookers, her fat face reddening with embarrassment. 'It wasn't like that, really!'

The onlookers glanced away, disbelief and disgust registering on their faces. Grabbing Camilla, Calypso took off with her after their grandmother, but not before she'd emptied her glass of champagne over Veronica's head – just for good measure.

They found Clementine locked in one of the powder rooms, and after a few minutes of pleading, she finally let them in. Both girls were shocked to see their strong, upright grandmother so dishevelled and shaking.

'Oh, girls, I'm sorry you had to see that,' she wept, putting her arms round them both.

'Are you all right?' asked Camilla, close to tears herself. 'What was that awful woman saying about Great-uncle Edmund?'

Calypso was more direct. 'Granny Clem, what on earth do you mean, she killed him?'

Clementine sank down on one of the stools.

'I shouldn't have said that here, with all those people

around.' She sighed and the girls could hear the grief in her voice. 'Even after nearly fifty years it's as raw as the day it happened.'

'What?' Camilla asked in a small voice.

'It's hard to believe now, but once upon a time Veronica Stockard-Manning and I were the best of friends.'

'What?' exclaimed Calypso. 'But she's a foul old cow! How could you have been?'

Clementine smiled regretfully. 'When Veronica was a young girl, she was a lot of fun. And really quite a beauty. All the chaps I knew pined after her, and quite a few of the girls, too.'

'Were you at school together?' Camilla asked.

Clementine nodded. 'We shared a dormitory, our beds were next to each other. Even though Veronica was a year younger than I was, we got on tremendously. She seemed to enjoy my company, and well, I liked being best friends with the most popular girl in the school. I was always rather tall and awkward-looking, you see, and it did wonders for my own social standing. You know how shallow young girls are.'

Clementine blew her nose gracefully with a tissue, before continuing. 'We were inseparable as teenagers, and one summer holiday Veronica came to stay with us at Fairoaks. We had a wonderful time, tramping through the Meadows in our long skirts, taking out the pony Father had bought me. But even then, I could sense something had changed with her. Veronica was very aware of her own charms, even from a young age,

424

and when Edmund laid eyes on her for the first time – well, the poor boy had no chance. He'd always been a fragile child. Mother nearly lost him at birth and he never really recovered. But Edmund had a kind of innocent beauty about him, something Veronica obviously found attractive. And he was head over heels with her. I asked Veronica, and then pleaded with her to stay away from Edmund, I could see she would break his heart eventually. But the more I begged her, the more intent she became on snaring him. It almost became like a game for her, Veronica always did have a habit of getting what she wanted.'

Clementine smiled bitterly. 'We fell out and grew apart after that, but Veronica and Edmund continued courting. They really did seem very content together. I'd never seen Edmund so enraptured or happy before. He came out of his shell for the first time, and was living life to the full. I started to think that maybe I was wrong. Maybe Veronica really did love him. After all, my parents were perfectly happy, and it was widely expected that Edmund would propose to Veronica on her eighteenth birthday, having turned eighteen himself a few months earlier.'

Her bottom lip trembled. 'He was so happy when he came to show me the engagement ring. He'd hunted high and low for something, and had spent practically half his inheritance on the right one when he'd found it. I remember him telling me, "Don't worry, Clemmie, you'll find someone to love just as I have, one day. Then you'll know the rest of your life didn't matter before you met them".'

She shook her head. 'Poor, naïve Edmund. I even got swept along with it: I telephoned Veronica the night before he was going to propose and tried to make amends. She was pleasantly sweet, assured me she had no intention of hurting my little brother. And, more fool me, I believed it.'

Camilla and Calypso were transfixed. This was a whole side to their grandmother they had never known about.

Clementine paused, reliving painful memories before carrying on. 'Edmund travelled to Yorkshire to ask for Veronica's hand in marriage and Veronica, who'd already humiliated him by making him get down on one knee and propose in front of her maid, scorned him for being so deluded in thinking anyone like him could ever have someone like her, and told him she had no intention of ever marrying him. She said, and I remember the exact words my brother told me, that she "wanted a real man and not a little boy". I believe she mocked the ring for not being good enough, before sending Edmund away to the sound of her maid giggling.'

'That's awful!' gasped Camilla.

Clementine's jaw clenched. 'It turned out Veronica had a bet going with her new circle of friends – horrid, flirty vacuous types – to see who could get as many marriage proposals as possible. Edmund was the first of quite a few, I believe. Eventually Veronica went on to marry a ghastly army colonel who was years older than her. He was a bluff, bigoted chap who spent most of his time carousing in his London members' club – nothing like Edmund. I believed Franklin Stockard-Manning died at the end of the seventies.'

Clementine's voice was empty, remembering. 'There wasn't much hope for poor Eddie after that, I'm afraid. He was completely broken-hearted, and felt that he was a laughing stock. As far as he was concerned, he'd laid himself bare to someone and they'd ripped him apart. Edmund lost all faith in the human race, and started drinking. My parents tried to get him help, but nothing worked. He wouldn't even listen to me. He left home when he was twenty, and spent the rest of his inheritance money drinking his way round every seedy establishment in London. Poor Mummy and Daddy were heartbroken.'

Camilla could hardly bear to hear what happened next.

'Edmund was found, the day after his twenty-second birthday, in a grotty little bedsit in Paris. He'd choked to death on his own vomit. He had no worldly possessions, except the clothes he was wearing and a picture of Veronica on the bedside table. Because, despite all that had happened, he still loved her.' The tears glistened in Clementine's eyes again. 'Veronica turned up to the funeral, swathed in fashionable black and playing the hysterical widow. Mummy and Daddy had her marched out, said it wasn't fair to Eddie's memory.' Clementine laughed bitterly. 'As if she hadn't done enough already! Friends rallied round, but our family never was the same. The day we buried him in St Bartholomew's, a little piece of each of us died as well.'

'But why would Veronica do that?' Camilla cried. 'It's so cruel.'

Clementine gave a weary smile. 'Because she could. I don't think she meant for poor Edmund to kill himself, but Veronica must have known the power she held over him. You know, in all the years since, I have waited for an apology, even an acknowledgement of what happened, but nothing has ever come. Veronica has grown from a spiteful young girl into a malevolent old woman.' She looked at them. 'Melodramatic as it sounded, you can see why I accused her of having blood on her hands. I honestly believe that if he hadn't met Veronica, Edmund would be alive today.' Clementine's lip trembled. 'I blame myself. You see, darlings, if I hadn't bought her home that summer none of this would have happened.'

She broke down in fresh sobs again. Now that they knew about the bad feeling between Clementine and Veronica, Calypso and Camilla realized what enormous significance winning Britain's Best Village had for Clementine. All they could do now was put their arms around her and try to console her – the way she had them many times before.

Chapter 53

By the time they'd all made themselves presentable again, most people were sitting down at their tables. The three of them descended the grand staircase into the main ballroom, Camilla and Calypso walking protectively either side of their grandmother. Physically and emotionally, the family had closed ranks. Even kind-natured Camilla had been left shocked and angry by the actions of Veronica Stockard-Manning, and didn't trust herself to keep quiet if she saw the vile woman again.

'Is everything all right?' Angie asked, as the three women sat down.

'Everything's fine,' Clementine assured her. Angie noted her red-rimmed eyes but didn't say anything.

Calypso reached for the white wine in a bucket on the table. 'Christ, I could do with a large glass of this,' she declared.

'Me, too,' said Camilla.

'And I as well,' echoed Clementine, who normally

never drank anything other than a daily glass of champagne – or a sherry on special occasions.

Calypso sloshed wine in each of their glasses and toasted the table. 'Cheers, everyone!'

She took a deep slug and sat back in her chair, letting the liquid wash over her with its calming presence.

Someone else came over to their table to offer condolences. The plight of Churchminster had made the national press, and everyone had been tremendously nice about it – everyone apart from the Maplethorpe villagers, of course, who sat at their table throwing supercilious looks at everyone else.

The blonde newcomer leant down beside Clementine. 'Carole Newbury, from Beasley village,' she said.

'Oh, hello!' Clementine said. Beasley was one of the other finalists, a charming little place on the Norfolk-Suffolk border.

Carole Newbury had the weathered nose and cheeks of someone who spends a great deal of time outdoors. 'I actually grew up in the Cotswolds,' she said. 'Not far from Churchminster, and it's still a very special place to me. I just wanted to say, on behalf of the Beasley committee, how sorry we were to hear about the dreadful business of your church burning down. We all know the importance the church plays in a village, so you must be feeling it, dreadfully. If there's anything we can do to help, please don't hesitate to ask.'

'Why, Carole, thank you.' Clementine was genuinely touched. A woman called Flora Birch from the other finalist village, a pretty place in Aberdeenshire called Little Haven, had already approached Clementine to offer her stoic Scottish condolences. 'It's so nice to know that we've all entered the competition with the right spirit.'

'All except Maplethorpe,' muttered Carole Newbury, throwing a dark look in the direction of their table. 'You know there's been a huge hoo-ha about them making it to the final again. People weren't happy when they won last year, and there's been talk of cheating and of some of the judges being buttered up. Thank God for Marjorie Majors, she'll tell it how it is.'

'We hope so,' said Clementine.

'Well, I'd better get back,' said Carole Newbury. She smiled round the table at them all. 'Good luck!'

'You, too!' they all called back.

Before the results were announced, they had a four-course dinner that seemed to go on as long as the contest had. There was a mounting frisson of excitement in the room, and people were desperate to know if their months of hard work had paid off. Bottle after bottle of wine was brought out, as nervous finalists tried to settle their nerves.

For Calypso, who had spent the last few months staying in at Rafe's, a night out was long overdue. As was a healthy amount of wine. *At least there's no one to tell me what to do any more*, she thought defiantly.

At nine o' clock, two hours after it had started, dinner was finally over. Waiting staff came out for the final time to collect the empty coffee cups, and everyone turned expectantly towards a big stage at the front of the room.

Suddenly the lights dimmed and music started up.

The stage flashed up with colour again and Marjorie Majors strode out, followed by her two male counterparts. She was clutching a large gold-plated trowel, which would be presented to the eventual winner. The audience started clapping enthusiastically. Marjorie climbed up in front of a lectern to the left of the stage and waited until the applause had died down.

'Welcome to this year's Britain's Best Village competition, in association with Greenacres Garden Centres! This is the tenth year the competition has been running, in which we have seen some worthy winners – and not forgetting their worthy contenders – from all over the nation. This year, the standard has been exceptional and I would like to say a huge well done to Maplethorpe in Yorkshire, Churchminster in the Cotswolds, Beasley in Norfolk and Little Haven in Aberdeenshire. All four villages were shortlisted from a list of thousands not only for their pride in making their village look wonderful, but for their strong sense of community spirit. Whoever is the lucky winner tonight, I would like to salute them all for their tremendous achievement.'

The whole room rose, to applaud the four tables of competitors.

Marjorie Majors looked down at her speech before continuing. 'Of course, there can only be one winner, one village who will scoop the *three-quarters of a million pounds* prize.' She emphasized each word dramatically. Clementine felt a shiver down her spine, and it wasn't a nice one. They so desperately needed that money! The thought of Maplethorpe scooping it, just to add another ostentatious fountain to their village green or something, made her feel quite ill.

'And now,' declared Marjorie, 'the only thing that is left for me to do is to introduce our very important guest this evening, who will be handing out the prize.' She paused for dramatic effect. 'Ladies and gentlemen, the one and only Alan Titchmarsh!'

As the celebrity gardener and TV presenter came out on to the stage, the middle-aged ladies in the audience went wild.

'Love you, Alan!' shouted one of them. Another elegant woman in her late sixties put her fingers in her mouth and wolf whistled loudly, much to the delight of the people sitting on her table.

'Ooh, he has got a certain something!' Angie whispered to Camilla. Camilla giggled, noticing even her grandmother had gone a bit pink around the cheek area.

Alan said a few words about how pleased he was to be there, and then stepped back to let Marjorie start the proceedings. A complete hush settled over the room of nearly one thousand people. On the Churchminster table, everyone held their breath, gripping each other's hands.

Please, by some stroke of good fortune, let us win! prayed Clementine. On her left, Calypso had shut her eyes tightly and was praying for the first time in her life. Angie Fox-Titt had her head buried in Freddie's arm, while Lucinda Reinard and Brenda Briggs held on to each other tightly. It seemed like an age before Marjorie Majors put on her pince-nez and slowly unfurled the scroll with the winning village on it.

'In fourth place,' she said. There was a long pause. Marjorie looked round at the crowd solemnly.

'Oh, get on with it!' hissed Stacey Turner, 'who does she think she is, Ant and Dec on *X Factor*?'

'In fourth place,' Marjorie repeated, 'Is the village of . . .'

Everyone looked at each other, on absolute tenterhooks.

'Churchminster!'

It was a few seconds before reality hit home. They hadn't won. The money they so badly needed was not theirs.

Freddie ran his hands over his face. 'Oh shit,' he said unhappily.

On the other side of the table, Brenda Briggs had collapsed in tears. 'We're going to have to move!' she sobbed. 'I can't live there if the cottage isn't safe, I can't!'

'We'll have to find the money to floodproof our houses some other way, darling,' Angie told her, but it was clear from the devastated look on her face that she hadn't a clue where.

All Clementine could think of was St Bartholomew's, standing broken and bent on the village green. Images started swirling through her mind: Edmund's funeral, her mother's devastated face, the new joy of her son Johnnie's christening . . . The pictures started to move away from her. Try as she could, Clementine couldn't hold on to them, recall the faces. Everything was lost for ever now.

Through the blur, she was aware of a strange noise, like a roar building. Someone was tugging on her arm. Dazed, Clementine turned to look at Calypso.

'Granny Clem, look!' she cried. 'They're giving us a standing ovation!'

And so they were. With the exception of Maplethorpe, every single person in the room was up on their feet applauding wildly. The members of the Garden Party looked around stunned, not quite able to take it in. As the clapping finally died down, Marjorie Majors spoke again.

'I feel I must say a word about Churchminster, which holds a place dear in my heart.' At this, she shot a loaded look at the other two judges. 'Even though, they came fourth, I think that this little village in the Cotswolds has worked tirelessly, and it is only bad luck and a tragic circumstance that has prevented them from having a good chance at winning. I understand that the police are working hard to find the culprits who burnt down St Bartholomew's and I hope that those who did such a terrible thing are soon brought to justice. On behalf of the judging panel, I would also like to send our best wishes to Jack Turner, landlord of the Jolly Boot, who is recovering in hospital for his heroic efforts.'

'That was nice of her,' Camilla said to the others. Her grandmother nodded vaguely but her eyes had glazed over again as if she wasn't really there. Stacey Turner was crying now, and being consoled by her strained-looking mother. Marjorie's words had brought back to both of them how nearly Jack had died.

435

Marjorie looked down at the scroll, her face more businesslike.

'Anyway, let's get back to the task in hand. Third place goes to – and it really was very close – Little Haven!'

More applause, as the occupants of Little Haven table commiserated each other with rueful grins and hugs.

'So it's only Beasley or Maplethorpe!' whispered Calypso. 'Shit, Beasley have got to win.' She cast a worried glance at Clementine, who was sitting perfectly still in her chair, eyes closed. *It's too much for her*, Calypso thought. First the shock of her run-in with Veronica, and now not winning; her grandmother was getting too old to cope with all this. She had aged ten years in the last week.

The atmosphere in the room was electric. In a few moments, the winner of Britain's Best Village would be announced to nationwide acclaim.

'Maplethorpe can't win it two years running!' Calypso said in an undertone to Camilla. Her voice was uncertain. 'Can they?'

They were about to find out. As Marjorie Majors waffled on about the standard being the highest yet, and what an honour it was to judge, the Beasley table shuffled on their seats restlessly. Christ, she was drawing it out! Finally, she looked out over the sea of people and took a breath.

'And the winner of this year's Britain's Best Village is . . .'

Someone whooped and cheered at the back of the room.

'And the winner is . . .'

There was a loud crash at the back of the room as one of the waiters dropped a tray of glasses.

'Maplethorpe!'

Chapter 54

So that was that. Her worst nightmare had come true. Clementine slumped in her chair, utterly defeated. Across the room the Maplethorpe table erupted gracelessly, as the Beasley table looked deflated. They had been so close. One of the Maplethorpe table, a florid-faced man with a huge handlebar moustache, stood up and faced the Beasley group. He was obviously drunk. 'Ha, trounced! We were always going to win, you're playing with the big boys now!'

Sounds of disgust sounded round the room. Veronica made a big show of pulling the man back on to his seat, but by the gleeful look on her face it was clear she felt the same.

Camilla looked anxiously at her grandmother. Her face had gone as white as a sheet.

'It's not bloody on!' exploded Angie Fox-Titt, who Clementine had confided in about Veronica Stockard-Manning's underhand tactics.

Freddie put his hand over hers. 'Take it easy, darling.'

Up on stage, Marjorie Majors frowned at the unseemly spectacle going on at the Maplethorpe table. The man who had stood up was now loudly demanding 'some more bloody champers'.

Marjorie shot him a death look and spoke into the microphone. 'I'd just like to say how close the competition was this year, and how Maplethorpe only *just* edged through to claim victory. Beasley village have been wonderful contenders, and I would like to take this opportunity to congratulate them on getting this far. There's always next year, chaps!'

Heartfelt applause rang out. Camilla wished they could have won, Carole Newbury had seemed like a lovely woman.

To a cacophony of female cheers, Alan Titchmarsh stepped forward to present the trophy and cheque to Maplethorpe. Even Marjorie Majors looked like she was swooning a bit, giggling coquettishly whenever Alan said something to her.

'If Maplethorpe would like to come up on stage,' she called. 'Ladies and gentlemen, I give you this year's winner, Maplethorpe village in Yorkshire!'

The party made their way up and scattered applause sounded, followed by a few boos. It appeared Maplethorpe's unpopularity was widespread. It didn't seem to affect Veronica, though, as she swept past the Churchminster table shooting a triumphant look at Clementine. It took all of Camilla's efforts to persuade her sister to not jump up and empty another glass over Veronica's head.

As they all filed on stage smugly, Veronica in the lead, Alan Titchmarsh was waiting, the gold trowel ready in his hand. But just as he stepped forward to present the trophy to them, the doors at the back of the room burst open.

Everyone turned to look, including the people on stage. Veronica looked furious. How dare someone spoil her big moment!

Clementine had to look twice; she couldn't believe what she was seeing. Sure enough, the uniformed figure of Bedlington's PC Penny was marching towards the stage, gripping the arm of a protesting youth.

'That's that little oik who was rogering Celia Blakely-Norton!' Lucinda exclaimed to Angie as he was frogmarched by. 'What in dickens are they doing here?'

They stared at each other, at a complete loss.

'What on earth is going on?' Marjorie Majors exclaimed angrily. 'You can't just storm in here!'

'If you don't mind madam,' PC Penny said. 'I've just picked up this young fellow on a public decency charge and he had rather an interesting story to tell.'

'That's her!' shouted the youth pointing directly at Pam Viner. Pam took a step back in shock.

'Are you sure?' demanded PC Penny. He seemed to be rather enjoying the drama of it all.

The youth nodded. 'I'd swear me mum's life on it. She's the woman who paid me to vandalize Churchminster and start a fire in the church!'

Gasps sounded round the room.

'*What?*' choked Clementine.

'I didn't mean for the whole thing to go up!' cried the youth, all swagger gone now. 'It was just meant to be the potting shed at the back of the church, but it got out of control. I couldn't stop it!'

'It was 'er!' the youth protested. 'Gave me a hundred quid each time, extra fifty for hush money.'

'I don't know what you mean,' Pam started to bluster. 'I've never seen this hoodlum before in my life.'

'All the same, madam, I'd like you to accompany me back to Bedlington police station,' PC Penny said. 'This is a very serious matter that needs investigating immediately.'

All pretence at good cheer went out the window. 'She made me do it!' Pam shouted, pointing at Veronica. 'She said if I didn't, she'd hound me out of Maplethorpe!'

Veronica's pudgy hand flew to her mouth. 'Why would you *say* such an awful thing?' Another police officer had turned up, slightly breathless and she turned imploringly to him. 'I can assure you I have no idea what Pamela is going on about. I'm afraid she's always had a vivid imagination.'

'If I'm going down, I'm taking you with me,' shouted Pam. 'I've even kept recordings of our phone conversations, just in case you did something like this to me, Veronica!'

'Shut up, you stupid bitch!' hissed Veronica, but the game was up.

The other police officer stepped forward sternly. 'Ladies, if you'd like to follow me.'

'I'm an old age pensioner, you can't do this to me!' Veronica shrieked, but it was no use.

To a chorus of boos from the audience, they were led off.

On the Churchminster table, mouths were wide open.

'I knew there was something fishy going on!' cried Lucinda Reinard. 'That bloody Viner woman always seemed to be creeping around!'

Clementine was speechless. Of all the low-down, despicable . . .

'Order, order!' shouted Marjorie Majors from the stage. She looked at the rest of the Maplethorpe party, left rather shamefacedly on stage. 'Please leave. You're a disgrace to the competition and I shall personally make sure you're all banned from entering again for life!'

They trooped off to catcalls and heckling.

Looking rather flustered, Marjorie Majors called the other two judges over and they went into a huddle. After lots of head-shaking and a few nods, Marjorie called for calm again.

'Ladies and gentlemen!'

The babble continued.

'Ladies and gentlemen,' she tried again. '*Please!*'

Gradually the noise died down.

Marjorie took to the lectern again. 'May I be the first to apologize for such a dreadful incident, and, rest assured, along with the police we will be carrying out our own thorough investigation. Maplethorpe may have tried to blacken the reputation of Britain's Best Village, but I will not stand by and let that happen!'

'Hear, hear!' cheered someone.

Marjorie continued. 'Never before has this happened in the history of the competition, but I have no choice but to disqualify Maplethorpe. Therefore, the winner of this competition and of the three-quarters of a million pounds prize money is Beasley!'

The room erupted again, including the Church-minster table. Bleak as their future might now be, they were delighted Beasley had snatched victory from Maplethorpe. But the Beasley table sat talking intently for a moment, heads bowed together.

'Come on!' bellowed a delighted Marjorie. 'Don't tell me you've all got stage fright!' The table stood up smiling, and made their way in a procession towards the stage.

'Bravo!' cried Clementine as they passed by.

All three judges joined in the applause as the Beasley committee filed on stage. Alan Titchmarsh stepped forward beaming, and presented Carole Newbury with the gold trowel trophy and cheque. She held it aloft, and they all hugged and congratulated each other. It was a heart-warming moment.

As the cheering died down, Carole Newbury turned to Marjorie Majors to ask something. The head judge's eyes goggled in shock, before she recovered and smiled, nodding heartily. Everyone watched in surprise as Carole Newbury handed the trophy to one of her friends and made her way over to the podium. This had never been the protocol before.

'Good evening, everyone,' she said confidently into the microphone. 'May I first take the opportunity to say how delighted we are that Beasley has scooped the top prize. It really is a dream come true.'

More whoops and cheers.

'Lend us a fiver!' someone shouted. Laughter rippled round the room. Carole Newbury smiled along with it.

'Actually, there is a reason why I'm up here now. As I said, winning this competition is the greatest accolade a village could have, and the three-quarters of a million pounds cheque really is the greatest gift we could wish to receive. But after consulting with the rest of the Beasley committee, we have decided that there is another village more deserving of the money. That is why we would like to donate half the cheque to the village of Churchminster.'

She waggled the cheque in the air, as the news started to sink in on the Churchminster table.

'Oh my God!' squealed Camilla. 'Granny Clem!'

Clementine sat there, frantically doing the sums. It might not build them a flood defence but it would pay for the most vulnerable properties to be floodproofed, not to mention all the other things Churchminster needed done – although not rebuilding the church, of course. It was a glimmer of hope amongst the blackness.

'I won't have to move after all! Oh my Lord, my giddy aunt!' cried Brenda, bursting into tears of relief.

A tearfully happy Angie put her arm round her. Her shop would be safe now, too. 'How wonderful!'

On stage, Carole Newbury was smiling and beckoning to Clementine. 'Come on up!' she mouthed. As if in a dream, Clementine stood. Someone put their hand on her arm and guided her towards the stage, amidst thunderous applause that seemed a thousand miles away.

As the Churchminster Garden Party walked on, the villagers of Beasley patted them on the back and shook their hands. Clementine made her way straight to Carole Newbury. The spotlights and overhead lights were blinding.

'Oh, my dear!' she said, voice trembling. 'What a truly generous gift, but I can't accept. It's your money!'

Carole Newbury gave a reassuring wink. 'I won't hear of it. I may live in Norfolk now, but I'm Cotswolds born and bred. It's in my blood. I couldn't stand by and do nothing.'

Truly touched by her kindness, Clementine threw her arms round their fairy godmother. 'Thank you, Carole! Oh, thank you.'

Marjorie bustled over. 'I'd like to say something if that's all right with you both.' She smiled and climbed back on the lectern. 'Excuse me, everyone!' she cried. 'A few more moments of your time.'

The crowd grew silent.

Marjorie looked at the people on the stage and back out again to the audience. 'Well!' Her voice wobbled slightly. 'What a turn up for the books!'

'Lend us a fiver, Churchminster!' the same voice shouted as before. Everyone laughed.

Marjorie smiled indulgently. 'As I've already said, it is a honour to judge Britain's Best Village but I have never been so proud as I am today! Beasley has shown the true neighbourly spirit of a village: not only limited

445

to the people who live within its borders. And after the disgusting behaviour displayed by Maplethorpe this wonderful act of altruism is to be commended more than ever. Well done, Beasley, you are worthy winners indeed!' Marjorie's eyes took on a fervent look. 'Which brings me to the warriors in Churchminster. In an age where Britain is in the doldrums and this country is going to the dogs, this little village has showed us that, even against the odds, the British fighting spirit is alive and well! No matter where one lives, or what problems one has faced, we should all be proud of what we've got and help one another!'

Several people in the audience rolled their eyes, but Marjorie hadn't finished yet.

'Churchminster has what I call the "F Factor". It has nothing to do with that blasphemous man Gordon Ramsay, but stands for "Feel-good Factor"! The "F Factor" should make us all feel proud of being British, and enable us to look forward to a safer, happier future. Churchminster, you're an inspiration to the nation! Here's to you and to spreading the "F Factor"!'

'To Churchminster!' the audience roared, roused to its feet. 'To the "F Factor"!'

Chapter 55

The rest of the night passed in a happy blur. They were bought so much champagne that Lucinda Reinard had to be stretchered upstairs to her room by a passing ambulance the doormen flagged down. Luckily they weren't out on a call, and were happy to oblige.

Down on the dance floor, Calypso was shaking her stuff to the disco when a man came up to her. It was the guy she'd been eyeing up earlier. Up close he was even better: his eyes fringed by enviably long eyelashes, and with touches of grey in the black hair around his sideburns. Rather than being ageing, it gave him a distinguished sexuality.

He stuck his hand out to Calypso. 'Hi there, I'm Isaac Majors.' He had a confident, yet laid-back edge that was very attractive.

'Majors as in Marjorie Majors, head judge of Britain's Best Village?'

Isaac grinned, revealing sexily crooked teeth. 'She's my grandmother.'

Calypso took in his funky get-up. 'Yeah, I was thinking you were a little out of place here.'

He looked her up and down. By now she was barefoot, her ponytail pulled out so a wild mane tumbled down her back. 'I could say the same about you.'

'Point taken,' she laughed. 'So what *are* you doing here? Offering Granny moral support?'

Isaac grinned again. 'Something like that. I've been coming here since it started. It's a good night. It may not sound very cool, but Gran and I share a love of gardening. Helps me wind down when I come off the road.'

'Off the road?'

'Yeah, I'm in a band. The Rattlesnakes. Don't know if you've heard of them?'

Calypso had. 'My friends went to see you last month at the Brixton Academy – said you were amazing!'

Isaac laughed, a deep husky sound. 'Your mates are very kind. You'll have to come and see us some time.'

She smiled. 'I'd like that.'

Isaac appraised her. 'You look like the kind of girl who knows how to have fun. Shall we hit the bar?'

Calypso shot back an equally mischievous look. 'That's if you can keep up with me.'

Clementine was standing on the other side of the dance floor with Freddie and Angie. They were talking about Frances.

'Good on her, for going off travelling like that,' said Freddie. 'Although I can still hardly believe it.'

'Quite a few people have changed in Churchminster

448

recently,' remarked Angie, as Joyce Bellows shimmied past, performing some kind of erotic dance for Reverend Bellows. He watched, open-mouthed, as she slid up to him, removed his bow tie and started pulling it seductively round her bare shoulders.

'Go, Joyce!' Angie cheered.

'Good lord,' Clementine said faintly. 'What have we unleashed?'

'She's just happy.' Angie laughed. 'As we all are. We've got a lot to celebrate.'

Clementine stared at Joyce for a moment, before shoving her glass in Freddie's hand. 'Hold on Joyce, I'm coming to join you!' she called out.

The next day the majority of the Garden Party woke up, hungover but happy. Camilla was slightly alarmed when she turned over and saw Calypso's bed hadn't been slept in, but minutes later her sister stumbled through the door, with what looked like a stubble rash all over her chin.

'You dirty stop-out!' Camilla laughed.

Calypso collapsed on the bed. 'Don't. I think I'm seriously in love. We spent the whole night snogging each other's faces off in some all-night bar in Soho. Isaac's just dropped me off in a taxi.'

'Ooh, so are you going to see him again?'

Calypso propped herself up on one elbow and looked at her sister.

'Yeah, I think so.' A haunted look flashed through her eyes, but she plastered a smile on. 'Fuck that cheesy actor boy, I'm out there again!'

'Good girl,' said Camilla, smiling. She knew it would take time for Calypso to get Rafe fully out of her system, but her little sister would get there in the end.

In her suite next door, Clementine switched the news on to find Gordon Brown on GMTV, talking about the 'F Factor' and 'Feel-good Britain'. He was saying, *'The "F-Factor" should be a byword for this nation and we should all use Churchminster as a role model.'*

Through her astonishment, Clementine raised a cynical eyebrow. That bloody Brown man would jump on the bandwagon for anything! She heard something being slid under the door. It was a newspaper. Still watching the television, Clementine got out of bed to pick it up. Her heart sank when she saw they'd given her the *Daily Mercy* instead of the *Telegraph*, but not for long. There was a big picture of Churchminster looking beautiful on the front page, accompanied by the headline: 'THE FACE OF FEEL-GOOD BRITAIN!'

Clementine read on, breathless. It was all there, how they'd encountered seemingly random acts of vandalism and then had the tragedy of St Bartholomew's, only to find out their rivals Maplethorpe village had been behind it all along. After praising Churchminster and urging everyone to adopt the 'F Factor', the article finished by saying that two women, and a youth, were now in police custody, being questioned in connection with arson and criminal damage. Clementine lay back on her pillow, thinking. She knew that as a devout churchgoer, she should really rise above such thoughts, but she was pleased that that woman had got her bloody comeuppance. Her thoughts drifted, to young blurred faces and halcyon days playing in the Meadows.

'Oh, Eddie,' she sighed. 'I do miss you terribly. Even after all these years.'

At least her darling brother was in a place now where no one else could hurt him.

Much like the night before, the morning, passed in a whirlwind. Practically every national newspaper had picked up on the story, and it was reported that Marjorie Majors had been approached by a representative of David Cameron's to ask if she would like a career in the Tory party. It wasn't just press-canny party leaders that had sussed this was a momentous occasion; cabbies, lawyers and hairdressers alike were all talking about Churchminster and the outcome of Britain's Best Village. It had provided a subtle but powerful shift in the nation's consciousness, after a period of doom and gloom; people believed things *could* get better again. The 'F Factor' was picking up speed in every household from Dundee to Dunstable.

Churchminster even had a police escort on the way home, passing drivers tooting their horns and giving the coach the thumbs up. *Sky News* even covered the event in a helicopter, giving a second-by-second account. *'Oh look, the coach is pulling out to overtake! Oh no, it's decided not to. Doesn't the M4 look nice today?'*

By the time they'd passed through Bedlington, where residents and shoppers had lined the streets waving – 'Is the Queen here?' one little boy asked his mum – the Garden Party were quite overcome. As the coach pulled on to the green, the rest of the village had gathered excitedly.

For the first time Clementine could bear to look at St Bartholomew's since the fire. *We'll get you back on fighting form, old chum*, she thought.

They climbed off the coach to a chorus of cheers. Ted Briggs was the first to run forward and give wife Brenda a bear hug.

'Oh Bren, I've been crying all night!' he sobbed happily.

Brenda ruffled his receding hairline fondly. 'You soppy bugger.'

A smiling Jed was there to meet Camilla, and even Sir Ambrose and Lady Fraser had turned out, and were standing on the edge of the proceedings watching. Frances looked more casual for once, in a plain white shirt and three-quarter length trousers, her hair pulled back in a neat ponytail. Glancing over, Angie Fox-Titt thought she looked wonderfully pretty.

Frances caught her gaze. 'Congratulations!' she called. 'What wonderful news. We're over the moon, aren't we, Ambrose?'

Her husband attempted a smile. It reminded Angie of a rusty drawbridge being pulled up. 'Yes, dear.'

Through the melee of people hugging and congratulating came a frail figure, propped up by a walking stick.

'Dad!' screamed Stacey and rushed over. He winced as she threw her arms round him.

'Careful, Stace! I'm a bit tender still.'

'You're more than that, Jack Turner!' declared Beryl.

'You're meant to be in hospital, what are you doing here?'

'Discharged meself.'

'Oh, Jack!' started Beryl, but he held up a bandaged hand.

'Don't go fussing, I'm fine. Besides, you think I'd miss this homecoming?'

They all gathered round him.

'My dear fellow, how *are* you?' asked Clementine.

He grinned, the old Jack back. 'I'll be a damn sight better once I've got a tot of Johnnie Walker's inside me. Come on, everyone, drinks on the 'ouse!'

The celebrations continued long into the evening.

Chapter 56

Calypso and Clementine were walking through the Meadows, Errol Flynn bustling nose-first through the undergrowth in front of them. It had been a week since the ceremony. It was a perfect summer's day: scorching blue skies, a lazy stillness in the air. A dragonfly darted in towards them, before zigzagging off through the green pasture.

'Isn't it just heavenly?' said Clementine contentedly.

Calypso nodded in agreement. 'It was worth it, wasn't it?'

'What, darling?'

'All the hard work we put in, even if we didn't win. I really think it's helped save Churchminster,' Calypso said.

'I think you're right. I've no regrets.'

Calypso shot her grandmother an amused sideways glance. 'What, even letting the film crew in?'

'They weren't as bad as I thought,' Clementine concluded, 'and the location fee has come in handy.

Though that's not to say I'd do it again,' she added hastily.

'That's a shame, I hear Seraphina Inc. want to film a crack-crazed lesbian zombie film here next.'

Calypso laughed at the look of horror on Clementine's face. 'I was just pulling your leg, Granny Clem!'

'Hmph.'

Calypso pulled the stem off a long piece of grass as she walked past it. 'Who are those flowers in the kitchen from, by the way? They're gorgeous.'

'Oh, just a well-wisher.'

'A bloody generous well-wisher! I wish someone would send me flowers like that.'

They walked on in silence for a few moments, before Clementine spoke again. 'Actually, darling, there was something I wanted to talk to you about. Camilla and I didn't know whether to or not, but I think it's best if you find out from us.'

Calypso stopped and looked at her. 'What do you mean? Is it something I'm not going to like?'

Clementine sighed, 'Let's go back, and I'll show you.'

Ten minutes later, they were in the cosy sitting room at Fairoaks, the one Clementine used herself when she wasn't entertaining. The comfy sofa and calming colours were doing nothing to quell Calypso's growing discomfort.

'What is it?' she demanded. Her voice was emotional. 'No one's died, have they?'

'Heavens, no!' Clementine said hurriedly. She reached into her large handbag and pulled out a magazine. 'Camilla came over and gave this to me last night. She'd kept it out of your way and wasn't sure what to do with it.'

Clementine handed it to Calypso. Calypso stared at it for a moment; it was one of those celebrity American trash mags that Camilla subscribed to.

'IT'S OVER!' screamed the headline on the front cover. Calypso felt sick as she recognized the people in the photo underneath. It was a paparazzi shot of Rafe and Daphne at a red-carpet do, looking impossibly glamorous. There was a big split down the middle of the picture. Calypso's stomach did an involuntary somersault.

And then in smaller print underneath: *'How Hollywood's golden couple hit the rocks! Full story inside!'*

Wordlessly Calypso flipped to the page and started reading. It was juicy stuff. Rafe had been sensationally dumped by his socialite fiancée Daphne Winters, after she allegedly found him in bed with their pretty young housemaid. Although Rafe and Daphne's spokespeople both issued a 'No comment', the fact that Daphne's daddy, the big studio boss, had dropped Rafe from his latest film had sent the rumours flying.

> *'Rafe also had this fling with a mystery woman a while ago, and it got pretty heavy,' said a source close to the star. 'Daphne had been pretty pissed about this other woman, that as soon as she realized he'd been unfaithful again, she called time on their engagement.'*

So Daphne wasn't as invincible as she had made out, after all. Calypso looked up, eyes hurting. 'First me and then the housemaid, eh? How classy, I feel really good now.'

'Darling, I know it hurts but this must only prove you really are better off without him.'

Calypso gave a short laugh. 'So why do I miss him so much?'

'You loved him, Calypso,' Clementine said gently. 'That feeling isn't going to go away overnight.'

'Well, I wish it bloody would!' Calypso smiled sadly. 'I'll tell you what, Granny Clem, I'm off men for life after this.' Her iPhone starting ringing on the table where she'd chucked it. Calypso reached across to answer it. Her face lit up. 'Actually, hold that thought.' She skipped out of the room saying: 'Hey, Isaac! How's it going? I was just thinking about you, actually . . .'

Clementine smiled as her granddaughter's chatter faded down the corridor. Getting up, she walked over to the bureau and unlocked the drawer. The card from the flowers lay there, just as she had left it.

'Hey sexy. Have you forgiven me yet? I'm coming back over to the UK for a bit and I'd love to meet up. Call me. I still think about you. Rafe X'

Clementine had met enough leopards in her life to know they never changed their spots. Without a second thought, she dropped the card in the bin, with the rest of the rubbish.

THE END

Acknowledgements

First and foremost, thank you to the two lovely women in my life who make this all happen, my editor Sarah Turner at Transworld and my agent Amanda Preston. Also a huge thanks to Emma Messenger, who gets more 'ideal' with every Churchminster story, Jo Hoare for her amazing tractor driving and the Grandpa Hoare shooting-stick stories, Kate Towns and Josh Yudkin for all their expertise on film sets, and Tim Barrett-Jolly for his wine knowledge. (With a name like that he should be in one of my books.) Much appreciation to Michelle Beynon and the staff of Cardiff hospital, to Gill Linley, the First Lady of the Cotswolds and to Christian Lang for his French translations, Oh, and I have to make an apology to *heat* magazine's Kay Ribiero for implying in the last book that the lift sex scene idea was anything to do with her. Kay, your name has been cleared! All my lovely friends and readers, you're brilliant, every last one of you. Finally, thank you to JT for putting up with my 'creative' moods, and the Carnegie clan, the best bonkers family I could wish for.

Country Pursuits

JO CARNEGIE

The gorgeous women of Churchminster know exactly
what they want – a constant flow of champagne and the
love of a good man. But faced with the likes of beer-
guzzling farmer Angus, foul-tempered Sir Fraser and
conceited banker Sebastian, their attentions are drawn to
more *attractive* possibilities . . .

Meanwhile, when a part of their beloved village comes
under threat from a villainous property developer,
the villagers are united by a different kind of passion.
Can they raise enough money to save Churchminster?
Will Mick Jagger turn up to the charity ball?
Will good (sex) overcome bad?

**Introducing a glamorous and unforgettable cast,
Country Pursuits is Jo Carnegie's raunchy, rip-roaring,
gloriously romantic début.**

'Pacy, racy and enormous fun!'
TASMINA PERRY

'Carnegie gives Jilly Cooper a run for her money…A racy read
that'll have you snorting with laughter'
Glamour

9780552157063

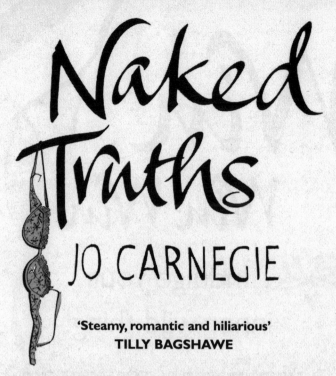

Naked Truths

JO CARNEGIE

'Steamy, romantic and hiliarious'
TILLY BAGSHAWE

Newly-weds Caro and Benedict have swapped country life in
Churchminster for an exclusive London mews. It's blissful…
until Benedict's sister arrives, bringing with her a dangerous secret

Fashionable **socialite Saffron** lives next door. She always thought
the countryside was boring, but when she's invited to Churchminster
she is shocked to learn just how *dirty* rural life can get.

Saffron's boss, **workaholic editor Catherine Connor**, is fighting
to save her ailing magazine. But her scandalous past threatens
to destroy everything, especially when rugged builder
John Milton strides into her life.

'Perfect for the plane or beach, I couldn't put it down!'
LORRAINE KELLY

9780552157339

Win
Win Win

Indulge your
inner wild thing!

To celebrate publication of Jo Carnegie's fabulous, raunchy
new romp we are offering one lucky reader £250 to spend
on gorgeous underwear from the shop of their choice.

For your chance to win visit
www.churchminster.co.uk/wildthing
and tell us where you'd like to spend the cash!